TALES OF YAMATO

Tales of Yamato

A Tenth-Century Poem-Tale

Translated by Mildred M. Tahara

Foreword by Donald Keene

Published with the support of
The Maurice J. Sullivan & Family Fund
in The University of Hawaii Foundation

THE UNIVERSITY PRESS OF HAWAII
Honolulu

In memory of
Charles S. Tahara
and Theodore T. Tahara

Manufactured in the United States of America

The following episodes were previously published in slightly different form in *Monumenta Nipponica:* Episodes 46, 64, 124, appended sections I and II in vol. 26(1–2):17–48; episodes 4, 11, 40, 99, 125, 126, 128, 147, 148, 149, 150, 151, 155, 156, 168 in vol. 27(1): 1–37.

Library of Congress Cataloging in Publication Data
Main entry under title:

Tales of Yamato.

Translation of Yamato monogatari.
A revision of the translator's thesis, Columbia University, 1969.
Bibliography: p.
Includes indexes.
I. Tahara, Mildred M 1941–
PL787.Y3E5 1980 895.6'1108 79-28535
ISBN 0-8248-0617-4

Contents

Foreword

Yamato monogatari belongs to a small but not unimportant group of works which the Japanese call *uta monogatari,* or poem-tales. The simplest form of a poem-tale is a bare explanation of the circumstances leading up to the composition of a particular poem. Such information, which might be provided in the body of a poem written in a European language or in Chinese, was not easy to fit into the thirty-one syllables that make up the most characteristic Japanese verse form, the *waka.* In order for so short a poem to be effective, it must rely on the poet's ability to evoke in the fewest words possible the most significant aspects of the experience that has inspired his poem. Because of the brevity, it is usually necessary to omit even personal pronouns: thus, to take an extreme case, the typical Western declaration "I love you" would be conveyed without either "I" or "you." This could be achieved with a noun such as "longing" or "thoughts," leaving the reader to conjecture that the longing or thoughts are directed by the poet to his beloved, rather than to, say, an uncle who happens to be traveling. But sometimes it is not obvious who the speaker is, or whether his tears (usually referred to as "dew," or, more indirectly, by mention of a sleeve soaked with his tears) have been occasioned by some temporary setback or by irreparable grief. Sometimes it is indicated that a poem was composed to an assigned topic; such information, though casting some doubts on the poet's sincerity, can unlock the ambiguities of expression. Often too, allusions to another poem of less ambiguous content will suggest the cause of the poet's tears. But even such clues are sometimes insufficient.

The Japanese have never shunned ambiguity. The language

lends itself most easily to expressions of greater or lesser degrees of probability, rather than to straightforward declaration. Indeed, particles are often appended to sentences in order to soften an overly explicit statement. Even in modern novels a heroine is rarely described as being either twenty-three or twenty-four; normally, she is "about twenty-three or twenty-four," the distinction being maintained between a work of art, which should have suggestive ambiguity, and a birth certificate.

But at times the Japanese have felt in need of more information than a waka generally provides. This was particularly true when a poet's works were collected after his death. It was natural to wonder who the woman was to whom he addressed an ardent waka or, for that matter, the identity of the unfortunate woman he mocked with a reference to fading charms. Sometimes people survived who remembered the incidents that inspired poems, and they provided prefatory notes to help clarify the background. The notes might give no more than the bare circumstances of composition. Such notes are useful, but add little to one's literary pleasure. On other occasions, however, the background of the poems so intrigued the commentator that he allowed his gifts as a storyteller greater scope, and the result is often a charming little story built around one or more waka. *Yamato monogatari* has both the brief and the extended "explanations" of poetry; the latter, of course, are of greater interest.

In addition to stories arising from waka composed at the court, the main body of the episodes in *Yamato monogatari,* others are closer to legends or are even out-and-out fiction. For that matter, the stories about amorous courtiers are apt to have fictional elements, if only because nobody except the lovers themselves was likely to be present when a man and woman exchanged farewell poems the morning after, and the commentator probably had to guess what took place. In general, the greater the freedom with which the unknown authors supplied backgrounds to the poems, the more effective their contributions are as literature.

The stories in *Yamato monogatari* are appealing especially because of the glimpses they give into life at the Japanese court at a period of unusual brilliance. Even the stories that are set elsewhere share the elegance of the writings associated with the court. No doubt this was why people of later ages, when elegance had largely disappeared, turned back to *Yamato monogatari* with nostalgia, and borrowed materials freely. Perhaps the most famous borrowing from *Yamato monogatari* is the Nō play *Ashikari* (The Reed-Cutter), written about five hundred years afterwards.

About the same time that the poem-tale was first being composed, in the middle of the tenth century, another variety of fiction was also being written in Japan. This variety was closer than the poem-tale to the romances and adventure stories of Greece or Rome or China. The most celebrated surviving work of this genre is *The Tale of the Bamboo Cutter,* the story of a tiny girl who is found in a stalk of bamboo and who (after she achieves a rapid growth) is pursued by various suitors, to each of whom she sets a task he must perform before he can win her love. In the end, all five suitors fail, and even the emperor himself is refused by the stony-hearted girl. She takes leave of the bamboo cutter and returns to her old home on the moon, to the desolation of all. Such a story, charming though it is, could never have been developed into a novel, either as the term is now used or as it might be used of *The Tale of Genji,* the greatest work of Japanese literature. It is hard to sustain the attention of readers beyond the compass of a fairy tale when one writes of beings who can transform their appearances or who possess other supernatural powers. The poem-tale, by comparison, is realistic. It deals largely, it is true, with people of exalted social status, but their joys and griefs are those of human beings, and when confronted with a crisis they cannot choose the easy way out of transforming themselves into dragons or songbirds. The realism of the poem-tale also sets it apart from the typical adventure story, with its successive episodes involving pirates, crocodiles, burning houses, collapsing bridges, and so on. The Japanese court romance, as it developed during the century after *Yamato monogatari,* would describe people whose lives are rarely troubled by external disasters, but who suffer nevertheless because they cannot find happiness with other human beings, particularly those they love. The most affecting novels of the eleventh and twelfth centuries have extremely few incidents but retain the attention of readers by the portrayal of emotions with a sensitivity that has no counterpart in the fiction written elsewhere in the world for some centuries.

In one other respect *Yamato monogatari* and the other poem-tales influenced later Japanese writing. *The Tale of Genji* and other novels of the period are full of poetry composed by the characters. Brief conversations often take the form of an exchange of poems, and every tryst was followed by poems alluding to the night before. The inclusion of such poetry presumably reflects what actually happened at the court, but it reflects even more the influence of the poem-tales. The courtiers were not all capable of composing acceptable verses on the spur of the moment, but the poem-tales do not dwell on their inadequacy; rather, they suggest in a manner that may be more romantic than realistic, that in this society people's thoughts were as easily expressed in poetry as in prose. The cult of beauty, which marked the Japanese court in the tenth century, extended not only to personal adornment but to the expression of thoughts that in other societies were usually no more than dull prose.

Yamato monogatari is appealing especially because of its evocation of a world that is given to the creation of beauty. Perhaps it is not entirely true to the world that actually existed, but the reader is bound to be attracted by a world that seems at once immediate and so beautifully remote.

DONALD KEENE

Preface

This translation of *Tales of Yamato* is based on the 1957 *Nihon koten bungaku taikei* (NKBT) edition of the Maeda (Tameie) text, which was annotated by Abe Toshiko and Imai Gen'e. Also consulted were the annotations in *Yamato monogatari shōkai* by Takeda Yūkichi and Mizuno Komao. Although the Nijō text used by Takeda and Mizuno differs from the Tameie text, the annotations are detailed and most informative. In the notes to the translation, I have indicated the instances when a textual variation was great.

Tales of Yamato has never before been translated in its entirety into English. Brief passages, however, have been translated into various Western languages and may be found in the following works: Aston's *A History of Japanese Literature* (pp. 89–91), Revon's *Anthologie de la littérature japonaise dès origines au XXe siècle* (pp. 173–175), Florenz's *Geschichte der japanischen Litteratur* (pp. 173–176), Gundert's *Die Japanische Literatur* (pp. 49–50). There is also an excerpt translated by Chamberlain entitled "The Maiden of Unahi" (TASJ, VI, i, 103–117), and one by Donald Keene in his study "Bashō's Journey to Sarashina" (*Landscapes and Portraits,* pp. 109–130). Excerpts of my translation have been published in *Monumenta Nipponica* 26 (1–2):17–48 and 27 (1):1–37.

There are 173 episodes in *Tales of Yamato.* In the modern printed editions of this poem-tale that I used for my translation, two long sections based on various episodes of *Tales of Heichū* are included. They are designated simply by roman numerals I and II. I have included them with this translation. Appended section I is a part of the Tameie text, which has been widely circulated since the Tokugawa period (1600–1868); appended section II is included between episodes 172 and 173 of the Mikanagi and Suzuka texts, which date from the Muromachi period (1336–1573). A fuller discussion of the extant texts of *Tales of Yamato* is provided in the Appendix.

There are 295 waka in the 173 episodes and 39 in the appended sections. An attempt has been made to give a five-line translation of the waka, but in a number of instances when this was not feasible the poem was translated in either four or six lines. When a poem in *Tales of Yamato* appears in another work, I have provided the *Kokka taikan* (KT) or *Zoku kokka taikan* (ZKT) number of the poem in the notes. When not included in the above volumes, I have given the page number of a printed text of the work in which the poem appears.

The court titles of historical personages are translated in accordance with Robert K. Reischauer's *Early Japanese History*. Often a historical figure is referred to in different episodes by different official titles. Although this may be somewhat confusing to the reader, I have in most cases translated the title as it is given in the text, supplying footnotes in order to identify the person.

Annotators sometimes disagree in identifying the historical figure mentioned only by his official title. For example, the Minister of the Left in episode 171 is identified by Abe Toshiko as Fujiwara no Saneyori; however, in *Yamato monogatari shōkai* he is identified as Fujiwara no Tadahira. In such cases, I have identified the official according to Abe Toshiko's annotation, for her work is the result of more recent research.

This book is a revised version of the doctoral dissertation submitted to the East Asian Languages and Cultures Department of Columbia University in 1969. I wish to thank Miss Umeyo Hirano who first assisted me in reading the original text of *Yamato monogatari* in the summer of 1965. The late Professor Ivan Morris read and commented on an earlier draft of my translation, and Professors H. Paul Varley and Burton Watson, who served as members of the dissertation committee, offered some very helpful suggestions. I am most indebted to Professor Donald Keene who first suggested this work as a dissertation topic and who, giving unstintingly of his time, read through several drafts of the dissertation.

Introduction

The Heian period (784–1185) began when the capital was moved to Nagaoka, thirty miles to the north of Nara, which had been the capital of Japan since 710. However, as the result of a series of calamities, the partially built city at Nagaoka was abandoned, and the capital was moved a decade later, this time to Heiankyō, the Capital of Peace and Tranquillity, later known as Kyoto. The plan of the city was modeled on Ch'ang-an, the capital of T'ang China, and for the first hundred years of the Heian period, the prestige of Chinese institutions and culture was extremely strong.

Several decades after the move to Heiankyō the Japanese government severed official ties with China. Then in 894, they sought to re-establish relationships by appointing Sugawara no Michizane (845–903), a great but ill-fated statesman, as ambassador to China. Michizane did not wish to go and petitioned the throne advocating the cessation of embassies to China for various reasons, but his chief motive may have been personal: his desire to remain in the capital in order to ensure a position of power in the central government. At the time the great families were constantly jockeying for power, centering their plots and counterplots around the throne and imperial succession, and Michizane was reluctant to leave the scene.[1] The petition was granted and official relations were broken for centuries.

Historically, a more important reason why the court broke relations with China was that the once glorious, seemingly all-powerful T'ang dynasty was by now in its death throes. The empire was beset by serious internal disturbances, including large-scale popular uprisings. Officials of the Japanese court probably felt that contact with the Chinese was not worth the risks of the extremely hazardous sea journey. At any rate, a new phase of Japanese cultural development began with the renunciation of relations with China, for the Japanese became increasingly conscious of their own rich culture. In the early part of the ninth century, virtually all literary composition was in Chinese. But by the end of the tenth century the best poetry and prose was in pure Japanese, and this was true of the great period of Japanese literature.

The period when Fujiwara no Michinaga (966–1027) served as the regent and leader of the Fujiwara family marks the height of glory of the Fujiwara as well as that of the Heian period.[2] The two outstanding woman writers in the history of Japanese literature—Sei Shōnagon (c. 968–1025), the author of *The Pillow Book (Makura no sōshi),*[3] and Murasaki Shikibu (c. 978–c. 1016), the author of *The Tale of Genji (Genji monogatari)*[4]—served respectively the niece and daughter of this powerful statesman, both empresses. Michinaga's age thus coincided with the supreme flowering of classical Japanese prose.

At the beginning of the Heian period, Japanese poetry was almost completely obscured by poetry written in Chinese.[5] Indeed, Japanese poetry was at its nadir during the first half of the ninth century, but between 850 and 890 we find that the *waka,* the thirty-one syllable verse form, was being revived by a group of poets known as the Six Poetic Geniuses.[6] At the same time, we find the development of waka in such court activities as poetry contests, the composition of poetry for silk screens, the compilation of private poetry collections, and the compilation of imperial anthologies.

During the early tenth century, the waka was beginning to enjoy a place of considerable importance, though skill in the composition of Chinese poetry continued to be considered more important in official circles. In the meantime, there was a gradual development of Japanese prose, aided by the invention of a phonetic syllabary *(kana)* that had earlier helped to bring about a revival of the waka. The famous preface to the *Kokinshū,* diaries, fictional tales, and poem-tales were written in the kana syllabary. By 952 the original version of *Tales of Yamato* had been completed, and in this single work we see reflected the general development of

Japanese literature in which the waka gradually paves the way for the brilliant works of prose by women writers of the imperial court, the supreme examples written a half-century later.

If it is true that *The Tale of Genji,* though written in about 1000, describes life as it was during the reign of Emperor Murakami (947–967), it gives us a picture of the atmosphere at the Heian court at the time *Tales of Yamato* was being written. In this society, imperial consorts and concubines, many of them members of the Fujiwara clan, enjoyed considerable influence. Their ladies-in-waiting, chosen from among the most talented women of good birth, also enjoyed a life of luxury and ease in the inner palace, although there was always the danger of their losing the favor of their mistresses and being sent away in disgrace from the palace, or worse yet, from the capital itself. Nonetheless, despite the vicissitudes in the lives of individuals, an unchanging, almost unearthly, atmosphere of refinement and elegance—the world of courtliness and taste which so influenced the prose and poetry of the period—prevailed. Men and women of taste and talent joined in various literary and artistic pursuits to alleviate the ennui which filled their seemingly uneventful daily lives.

Poetry was of foremost importance in the lives of these people. Because of the great influence of Confucian decorum, the Japanese avoided as being undecorous any expression of deep emotions in their public life, but in poetry they expressed freely their innermost feelings. Miner reminds us, however, that ". . . to Japanese, poetry is less the overspill of welling emotion than it is the constant current of feeling."[7] The superior person was at once sensitive and subdued in manner. To express openly one's deepest emotions was considered vulgar behavior, and in the all-prevailing atmosphere of courtliness and good taste, vulgarity was the grossest sin of all.

The marriage system was exceedingly complex in these times. Three forms of marriage were prevalent: the uxorilocal, in which the husband lived in the wife's home; the neolocal, in which the couple established a new home; and the duolocal, in which both husband and wife continued to reside where they had lived before the marriage, with the husband simply visiting the wife. Moreover, love affairs of varying intensity were extremely common in court circles.

Not only did the courtiers and court ladies compose poems of a private nature, such as might be exchanged by lovers and intimate friends, they also participated in poetry contests and composed poems to be inscribed on screens. One can imagine that they also passed their leisure hours gossiping about well-known poets or influential officials, sometimes relating the circumstances under which poems had been composed, at other times embroidering on the facts or even inventing new tales centering on familiar poems. In the same manner, old legends might be told and retold. Before long people began to make collections of these anecdotes and legends, one of which became *Tales of Yamato.* These manuscripts served as guides to poetry in this society that was so addicted to poetry by giving many examples of how well-known figures responded to different circumstances in composing their poems.

TALES OF YAMATO

1

When Teiji no In[1] was about to abdicate, Lady Ise[2] wrote on the wall of the Kokiden[3] this poem:

(1)	Wakaruredo Ai mo oshimanu Momoshiki o Mizaran koto no Nanika kanashiki	Although I now depart, Not a soul seems to care; Why then does it grieve me To think I shall never see The palace again?[4]

Teiji no In read her poem and wrote beside it:

(2)	Mi hitotsu ni Aranu bakari o Oshinabete Yukikaeritemo Nadoka mizaran	You must realize as well That I am not The only emperor; Why should you not return To see the palace again?[5]

2

In the autumn of the year after Teiji no In abdicated the throne,[1] he entered the priesthood and wandered about from temple to temple, practicing religious austerities. While he was still on the throne, a person by the name of Tachibana no Yoshitoshi,[2] who then held the rank of Secretary of Bizen, served him in the Inner Court. When His Majesty took the tonsure, Yoshitoshi unhesitatingly followed suit. Whenever the Retired Emperor went traveling about incognito, Yoshitoshi always accompanied him. Learning of this, the Reigning Emperor[3] said: "It will not do to have His Majesty travel about in this manner." He thereby commanded several courtiers to accompany the Retired Emperor.[4] However, Teiji no In avoided as best he could the men dispatched from the Imperial Court and continued his wanderings. Upon arriving in the province of Izumi, the Retired Emperor and those men sent by the

Reigning Emperor to accompany him spent the night at a place called Hine.[5] Privately sensing that His Majesty was feeling very depressed and lonely, Yoshitoshi was also saddened. Nevertheless, having been commanded by Teiji no In to compose a poem using the word Hine, Yoshitoshi recited,

(3)	Furusato no	I saw my kinfolk
	Ta<u>bine</u>[6] no yume ni	In a dream I had
	Mietsuru wa	On a distant journey;
	Urami ya suran	They must resent me
	Mata to towaneba	For never once returning.[7]

Everyone was moved to tears upon hearing this poem and unable to compose one of his own. Yoshitoshi was called the Priest Kanren and served Teiji no In for a long time afterward.

3

When Minamoto no Kiyokage,[1] the late Major Counsellor, was serving as an Imperial Adviser, the Kyōgoku no Miyasundokoro[2] declared that there would be a birthday celebration[3] for Teiji no In. "I should like to have baskets tied to single branches,"[4] she said. Kiyokage thereupon had many baskets woven and asked Toshiko[5] to dye them in various colors. He also requested that she dye the cloth linings of the baskets in variegated hues and braid the drawstrings. Working as quickly as she could, Toshiko completed her assigned tasks on the last day of the ninth month. On the first day of the tenth month she had these articles delivered to Kiyokage, who had been most anxious to receive them. She also sent along this poem:

(4)	Chiji no iro ni	Autumn drew to a close
	Isogishi aki wa	While I busily dyed
	Kurenikeri	Cloth into colorful hues;
	Ima wa shigure ni	What am I to dye now
	Nani o somemashi	As the wintry showers fall.[6]

As long as Kiyokage had been in a hurry to get these articles completed, he and Toshiko seemed to have a great many things to talk about. Now, however, as though they no longer had anything in common, he failed to write her a single letter. On the last day of the twelfth month, Toshiko wrote:

(5)	Katakake no	Are you now aboard a boat
	Fune ni ya noreru	With a close-hauled sail?
	Shiranami no	Only when the waves are rough
	Sawagu toki nomi	Do you think of me.[7]
	Omoi izuru kimi	

Kiyokage did not bother to send her an answering poem. Meanwhile the year drew to a close. During the second month he broke off a graceful willow branch, which was remarkably long, from a tree that grew by his mansion and sent it to Toshiko along with this poem:

(6)	Aoyagi no	On this tranquil day in spring
	Ito uchihaete	As the willow branches
	Nodoka naru	Extend gracefully to the ground,
	Haru hi shimo koso	I long for you.[8]
	Omoi idekere	

Deeply impressed, Toshiko talked about this poem for a long time afterward.

4

During Sumitomo's revolt,[1] the Assistant General, Ono no Yoshifuru,[2] was commanded to pursue the rebel and, after being raised to the rank of Minor Captain,[3] he departed from the capital where he had also served at the court.

Yoshifuru was looking forward with anticipation to the New Year's Promotion Ceremony, for this was the year he expected to be promoted to the Fourth Rank. However, he had not heard very much about the outcome from people who had just come from the capital. When Yoshifuru asked one traveler, he received this reply: "Yes, you have indeed been promoted to the Fourth Rank." But upon asking another traveler, he was told: "No, you have not been promoted." Just when he was feeling that he simply had to know what the actual situation was, a messenger arrived from the capital, bearing a letter from Minamoto no Kintada,[4] the Provincial Governor of Ōmi. Very much delighted to hear from him, Yoshifuru opened the letter and read its contents. Kintada had written him of a number of events, and at the very end, after writing in the date, he had inserted this poem:

(7)	Tamakushige	I have not seen you
	Futatose awanu	For two long years—
	Kimi ga mi o	Oh, but I never dreamed
	Akenagara ya wa	I would see you again
	Aran to omoishi	Still dressed in scarlet robes.[5]

No sooner had he finished reading Kintada's poem than Yoshifuru grew despondent and wept bitterly. Kintada had not mentioned a word about Yoshifuru's failing to be promoted to the Fourth Rank in his letter. He had simply inserted the poem at the very end.

5

Upon the demise of the Crown Prince,[1] his former wet nurse[2] was sorely grieved. However, since this happened on the very day that the Crown Prince's mother[3] was made Empress, people thought the nurse's grieving ill became the occasion and hid her away. The grief-stricken woman thereupon composed this poem:

(8)	Wabinureba	As I grieve
	Ima wa to mono o	I think to myself
	Omoedomo	That I must stop;
	Kokoro ni ninu wa	But contrary to my resolution
	Namida narikeri	The tears still flow.[4]

6

The Middle Captain Asatada[1] carried on an illicit love affair with another man's wife. The woman reciprocated his love and they continued to see each other. In time, however, the woman's husband was appointed governor of another province and planned to leave the capital together with his wife. Both Asatada and the woman were made terribly unhappy by this. On the day of her departure from the capital, Asatada composed a poem which he sent to the woman:

(9)	Tagueyaru	I send my spirit
	Waga tamashii o	To accompany you;
	Ika ni shite	How can you abandon it
	Hakanaki sora ni	And forget me
	Mote hanaruran	On your forlorn journey.[2]

7

Once there was a man and a woman who were very fond of each other. Though their relationship had lasted for a number of years, they suddenly parted over a trifling matter. It soon became clear that they had not separated because they had grown tired of each other, for the man, heart-broken, sent her this poem:

(10)	Au koto wa	Though I know in my heart
	Ima wa kagiri to	We shall not meet again,
	Omoedomo	Tears of regret
	Namida wa taenu	Flow ceaselessly.[1]
	Mono ni zo arikeru	

8

When Prince Nakatsukasa[1] used to visit Gen no Myōbu,[2] he once said to her: "I shall not be able to call on you this evening because of a directional taboo."[3] To this Gen no Myōbu replied:

(11)	Au koto no Kata wa sa nomi zo Futagaran Hitoyo Meguri no Kimi to narereba	Because it leads to me That direction is blocked; You seem to be transformed into The deity Hitoyo Meguri.[4]

Upon reading the poem, the prince made his way to her home and spent the night with her, even though it lay in an unlucky direction.

He failed to communicate with her for some time when one day he sent her this message: "I have been to Saga Palace[5] on a hunting trip, and so I have been unable to communicate with you. How lonely you must have been all this time!" Gen no Myōbu sent him this reply:

(12)	Ōsawa no Ike no mizukuki Taenu tomo Nanika ukaran Saga no tsurasa wa	Though your letters Have ceased to come From Ōsawa Pond, Why should I resent Your heartlessness While you were in Saga?[6]

The return poem that Prince Nakatsukasa sent her must have been quite banal, for people have forgotten it.

9

Prince Momozono,[1] the Minister of War, died and, in observing his first death anniversary on the last day of the ninth month, Toshiko[2] sent his widow this poem:

(13)	Ōkata no Aki no hate dani Kanashiki ni Kyō wa ikadeka Kimi kurasuran	One usually feels melancholy When autumn draws to a close; How much sadder it must be for you On this day of days.[3]

Since this poem was sent to her just when she was sorrowing most and weeping constantly, the widow sent Toshiko this answering poem:

(14)	Araba koso	If he were still living,
	Hajime mo hate mo	I would be keenly aware
	Omōeme	Of autumn's beginning and end;
	Kyō ni mo awade	But he has gone away forever
	Kienishi mono o	Before greeting this autumn day.[4]

10

Some time after Gen no Myōbu had sold her house, which had been built on the embankment,[1] she happened to go by it one day on her way to Awata,[2] whereupon she composed this poem:

(15)	Furusato o	Passing by my former home,
	Kawa to mitsutsu mo	I gaze upon it
	Wataru kana	As if it were a river;
	Fuchise ari to wa	How true it is
	Mube mo iikeri	That one's old home
		Is like a river's deep pools and rapids![3]

11

The late Minamoto Major Counsellor[1] had once been deeply in love with his wife, Higashi no Kata, who was the daughter of Tadafusa.[2] He used to visit her frequently for a long period of time. But after he began having an affair with the daughter of Teiji no In,[3] he and his wife became increasingly estranged with each passing day. Since they had several children, he kept in constant touch with his wife and even lived in the same mansion. On one occasion he sent her this poem:

(16)	Sumiyoshi no Matsu naranaku ni Hisashiku mo Kimi to nenu yo no Narinikeru kana	Though it cannot compare With the pines of Sumiyoshi, How long it has been Since last I slept with you![4]

Her answering poem went like this:

(17)	Hisashiku wa Omōenedomo Suminoe no Matsu ya futatabi Oikawaruran	I did not think That it had been so long, But enough time has passed For the Suminoe pines to grow anew And you to find a new love.

12

With the Emperor acting as the go-between, the same Counsellor[1] won the hand of the daughter of Teiji no In. In the beginning, when he used to visit her secretly every night, he once sent her this poem upon his return home:

(18)	Aku to ieba Shizugokoro naki Haru no yo no Yume to ya kimi o Yoru nomi wa min	Though the dawn Has been heralded, My heart is in a turmoil; Why must I meet you only at night, Each night a fleeting spring night's dream?[2]

13

Fujiwara no Chikane,[1] the Secretary of the Right Division of the Bureau of Horses, had a wife named Toshiko. Many children were born to them, and for years they were a devoted couple. When Toshiko died, Chikane was truly grief-stricken, and all he could do was pace about aimlessly. A lady-in-waiting known as Lady Ichijō[2] had been very close to Toshiko, but she failed to even ask after Chikane in his bereavement. Thinking that this was unlike her, Chikane continued to walk about restlessly. He happened to come across a maid-servant of the remiss lady and said to her: "Please recite this poem to your mistress:

(19)	Omoiki ya	Never did I dream
	Suginishi hito no	That when I was torn by grief
	Kanashiki ni	For the departed one
	Kimi sae tsuraku	Even you would prove unkind.
	Naran mono to wa	

This was Lady Ichijō's reply:

(20)	Naki hito o	Thinking I ought not
	Kimi ga kikaku ni	Remind you of the deceased,
	Kakeji tote	I have wept ceaselessly
	Naku naku shinobu	In private—
	Hodo na urami so	Oh, do not think me heartless!

14

There was once a young woman whose childhood name was Ōfune[1] and who was the younger sister of the principal wife[2] of the Hon-in.[3] She was in the service of the Retired Emperor Yōzei,[4] but since he failed to visit her, she composed this poem which she presented to him:

(21)	Aratama no	Though not very many years
	Toshi wa henedomo	Have slipped by,
	Sarusawa no	One can see the beautiful
	Ike no tamamo wa	duckweed—
	Mitsubekarikeri	So like the maiden's tresses—
		Floating in Sarusawa Pond.[5]

15

On another occasion, the Retired Emperor Yōzei summoned into his presence a young woman called Lady Wakasa[1] while he was at the Tsuriden.[2] However, since he failed to call for her again, she wrote:

(22)	Kazu naranu	The jewellike dew
	Mi ni oku yoi no	That settled at night
	Shiratama wa	On one as lowly as myself
	Hikari miesasu	Is no longer visible.[3]
	Mono ni zo arikeru	

16

A lady-in-waiting of the Retired Emperor Yōzei sent this poem to the "Step-father" Minor Captain:[1]

(23)	Haru no no wa	The spring field stretches afar;
	Harukenagara mo	Seeing the forgetting-grass
	Wasuregusa	Growing here and there,
	Ouru wa miyuru	I realize that you
	Mono ni zo arikeru	Have forgotten me.[2]

This was his answering poem:

(24)	Haru no no ni	No forgetting-grass could grow
	Oiji to zo omou	In the spring field,
	Wasuregusa	For there is no seed
	Tsuraki kokoro no	Of an unfeeling heart in me.
	Tane shi nakereba	

17

The same Minor Captain used to visit regularly Lady Idewa,[1] a lady-in-waiting to His Highness, the late Minister of Ceremonial.[2]

Some time after they had gone their separate ways, Lady Idewa attached a letter to some pampas grass and had it delivered to the Minor Captain. In reply he sent her this poem:

(25)	Akikaze ni	The pampas grass,
	Nabiku obana wa	Gently swaying in the autumn wind,
	Mukashi yori	Reminds me of your sleeve
	Tamoto ni nite zo	I often saw in days gone by
	Koishikarikeru	And once again I long for you.[3]

Lady Idewa replied:

(26)	Tamoto tomo	Had you not been startled
	Shinobazaramashi	By the pampas grass
	Akikaze ni	Rustling in the autumn wind,
	Nabiku obana no	You probably would not
	Odorokasazu wa	Have longed for me.[4]

18

The late Minister of Ceremonial stopped visiting Nijō no Miyasundokoro.[1] On the seventh day of the first month of the following year, Nijō no Miyasundokoro presented the late Minister of Ceremonial with some greens,[2] together with this poem:

(27)	Furusato to	These greens were found
	Arenishi yado no	Growing around my cottage
	Kusa no ha mo	Which has fallen to utter ruin—
	Kimi ga tame to zo	See, I have picked these
	Mazu wa tsumitsuru	Just for you![3]

19

The late Minister of Ceremonial had not called on Nijō no Miyasundokoro for some time, and so in the autumn she wrote:

(28)	Yo ni furedo Koi mo senu mi no Yū sareba Suzuro ni mono no Kanashiki ya nazo	I live from day to day With no one to love— Why then does this sadness Press upon my heart Whenever twilight falls?[1]

The poem he returned read:

(29)	Yūgure ni Mono omou koto wa Kaminazuki Ware mo shigure ni Otorazarikeri	Thinking of you As the evening shadows fall, The tears that I shed Are as ceaseless As the rains of the tenth month.

Since he was no longer interested in her, his answering poem was poorly written.

20

Princess Katsura[1] was very much in love with the late Minister of Ceremonial. One night when the moon was breath-takingly lovely, he failed to call on her. Deeply disappointed, she presented him with this poem:

(30)	Hisakata no Sora naru tsuki no Mi nariseba Yuku tomo miede Kimi wa mitemashi	If I were the moon Up in the heavens, I should always be able to see you; And even if I went to you, Not a soul would notice.

21

When Rō Shōshō[1] was still an Assistant Captain of the Middle Palace Guards, he used to visit Gen no Myōbu. One day he received a poem from her:

(31)	Kashiwagi no	Though the grass
	Mori no shitakusa	Under the forest of oaks
	Oinu tomo	Should grow old,
	Mi o itazura ni	I beg of you,
	Nasazu mo aranan	Do not forsake me.[2]

Rō Shōshō replied:

(32)	Kashiwagi no	You should not worry
	Mori no shitakusa	About the uncertain future,
	Oi no yo ni	When the grass
	Kakaru omoi wa	Under the forest of oaks
	Araji to zo omou	Will be old and withered.[3]

22

Rō Shōshō had been searching everywhere for some leather to use as a strap for his sword, whereupon Gen no Myōbu said to him: "Why, I have just the thing you're looking for at home!" However, a long time passed and she still failed to send the thong to him, so he sent her this poem:

(33)	Adabito no	It has been a long time
	Tanome watarishi	Since my fickle friend
	Somekawa no	Made her promise to me;
	Iro no fukasa o	I shall probably never see
	Mide ya yaminan	That colored leather thong.[1]

Gen no Myōbu was so impressed by his poem she immediately sent him the leather strap.

23

The love affair of the second son[1] of the Retired Emperor Yōzei and the daughter of Nochikage, the Middle Captain,[2] lasted for many years. After becoming intimate with the Fifth Princess,[3] however, he no longer visited his former sweetheart. Having given up all hope of his ever coming to see her again, she was feeling very despondent. A long time afterward when she least expected him, he came to call on her. Caught completely off guard, she was struck speechless and fled into an adjoining room. The Prince thereupon returned home and sent her this message the following morning: "I visited you, hoping to talk of the years gone by. Why did you hide from me?" Her only reply was:

(34)	Sekanaku ni Tae to taenishi Yamamizu no Tare shinobe to ka Koe o kikasen	I am like the mountain water Which has ceased to flow From its source; How could you expect me To speak to you again?[4]

24

During the reign of the former Emperor,[1] the daughter of the Minister of the Right[2] went to visit one of the apartments of the Inner Palace.[3] She waited eagerly, thinking that momentarily His Majesty would appear. However, since he failed to make an appearance, she composed this poem:

(35)	Higurashi ni Kimi matsu yama no Hototogisu Towanu toki ni zo Koe mo oshimanu	All day long I waited for you; When you failed to come, I cried my heart out, Like the *hototogisu* in the mountains.[4]

25

When the priest called Nengaku[1] lived in seclusion on Mount Hiei, he saw one day a withered pine near the temple quarters of a priest who had been a famous teacher in his lifetime and who had died a long time ago. Viewing this forlorn scene, the Priest Nengaku composed the following poem:

(36)	Nushi mo naki	When I see the withered pine
	Yado ni karetaru	By the cottage
	Matsu mireba	Whose owner has died,
	Chiyo suginikeru	I feel as though
	Kokochi koso sure	Many generations have slipped by.

The other disciples, who were staying in the same quarters, were deeply moved by the poem. It is said that Nengaku was Toshiko's older brother.

26

Princess Katsura had a secret rendezvous with a man she should not have seen. Afterward she sent him this poem:

(37)	Sore o dani	Please do not tell a soul
	Omou koto tote	That you have seen my house;
	Waga yado o	Even if this is all you do,
	Miki to na ii so	You will have proven
	Hito no kikaku ni	That you truly care.[1]

27

When a man called Kaisen[1] entered the priesthood and was living on Mount Hiei, he had no one to do his laundry. He therefore sent his soiled robes to his father in order to have them cleaned. On one occasion his father became impatient with him and complained, "For someone who entered the priesthood without the family's approval, you have no business making such a troublesome request!" In reply, Kaisen composed this poem which he sent to his father:

(38) Ima wa ware Izuchi yukamashi Yama nite mo Yo no uki koto wa Nao mo taenu ka	Where am I to go now? Even in my mountain retreat Will the troubles Of the world Never cease?[2]

28

In the autumn of the year in which Kaisen's father, the Assistant Captain of the Middle Palace Guards, died, many people gathered at his father's mansion. There they drank saké and feasted from early evening on. Though greatly saddened, both the host and his guests thought fondly of the deceased. At dawning, as mist blanketed the land, one of the guests composed this poem:

(39) Asagiri no Naka ni kimi masu Mono naraba Haruru ma ni ma ni Ureshikaramashi	If he were somewhere In the morning mist, How I would rejoice To see it clear away!

This was Kaisen's reply:

(40) Koto naraba Harezu mo aranan Asagiri no Magire ni miyuru Kimi to omowan	If at all possible I wish the mist Would never clear away; I could then imagine That the autumn mist Concealed him from me.[1]

Among the guests were Tsurayuki[2] and Tomonori.[3]

29

The Minister of the Right[1] went to the mansion of the late Minister of Ceremonial together with several other court nobles. There they played *go* to amuse themselves. As night wore on, they all grew somewhat tipsy and took turns telling stories and presenting one another with gifts. Decorating his cap with a maiden flower,[2] the Minister of the Right composed this poem:

(41)	Ominaeshi Oru te ni kakaru Shiratsuyu wa Mukashi no kyō ni Aranu namida ka	With my own hand I pluck a maiden flower, While on my sleeve the dewdrops fall; Could they be tears I have shed Realizing that today is so unlike The days of long ago?[3]

There were a number of other poems composed by the remaining guests, which, being mediocre, have been forgotten.

30

The late Prince Muneyuki[1] was once terribly disappointed when he failed to get a long-hoped-for promotion. At that time, people were composing poems on the *miru* seaweed which grew on the rocks that had been brought in from the province of Kii[2] and presented to Teiji no In. Prince Muneyuki's poem read:

(42)	Okitsu kaze Fukei no ura ni Tatsu nami no Nagori ni sae ya Ware wa shizuman	I shall sink in the sea Even when the waves in Fukei Bay— Blown high by wind from the offing— Recede from the shore.[3]

31

Prince Muneyuki sent the following poem to Gen no Myōbu:

(43)	Yoso nagara Omoishi yori mo Natsu no yo no Mihatenu yume zo Hakanakarikeru	How fleeting is our brief meeting— So like a dream On a summer's night— Compared to the time Spent longing for you.[1]

32

Prince Muneyuki wrote this poem and presented it to Teiji no In:

(44)	Aware chō Hito mo arubeku Musashi no no Kusa to dani koso Oubekarikere	I wish I were The grass growing On Musashi Plain, For then someone Would look with love on me.[1]

He also composed this poem:

(45)	Shigure nomi Furu yamazato no Ko no shita wa Oru hito kara ya Morisuginuran	I stand under a tree In this mountain village Where the rain never ceases; What is there about me That causes the rain To leak through?[2]

He felt in his heart that he would never receive Teiji no In's patronage. The Retired Emperor read the poems and commented: "What does he mean? I simply cannot understand these poems!" and showed them to a priest. When Muneyuki heard of this, he remarked: "Alas, it was in vain that I presented His Majesty with my poems!"

33

Mitsune[1] composed the following poem which he sent to Teiji no In:

(46)	Tachiyoran Ko no moto mo naki Tsuta no mi wa Tokiwa nagara ni Aki zo kanashiki	I am like an ivy plant Without a tree to cling to; And also like the evergreen, I still wear my robes of green; Oh, how sad the autumn is![2]

34

On one occasion, a woman sent this poem to Prince Muneyuki:

(47)	Iro zo to wa	You may not think
	Omōezu tomo	Its color very attractive,
	Kono hana ni	But I entreat you
	Toki ni tsuketsutsu	To remember now and then
	Omoi idenan	This flower.

35

Tsutsumi no Chūnagon[1] made his way to the palace of Teiji no In on Mount Ōuchi[2] as an imperial messenger. He knew exactly how His Majesty, who was apparently very lonely, was feeling. Since the palace had been built in a high place, it appeared that a great number of clouds were rising from below. Observing this phenomenon, Tsutsumi no Chūnagon composed this poem:

(48)	Shirakumo no	So this is the peak
	Kokonoe ni tatsu	Over which nine-fold layers
	Mine nareba	Of white clouds hover;
	Ōuchi yama to	At last I understand why
	Iū ni zo arikeru	It is called the Great Palace.[3]

36

When the former Priestess of the Ise Shrine[1] was still in the province of Ise, Tsutsumi no Chūnagon came to Ise as an imperial messenger and sent her this poem:

(49)	Kure take no	I have heard
	Yoyo no miyako to	That the Takē Palace
	Kiku kara ni	Has been here for generations;
	Kimi wa chitose no	Surely you too will live
	Utagai mo nashi	Till the end of time.[2]

He received no return poem from the Priestess, who at the time was living in the place called the Takē Palace.

37

When the Provincial Governor of Izumo[1] failed to be appointed to serve in the Inner Palace although one of his brothers was so honored, he composed this poem:

(50)	Kaku sakeru	Some flowers, it would seem,
	Hana mo koso are	Have blossomed splendidly,
	Waga tame ni	But could anyone say
	Onaji haru to ya	The same spring
	Iūbekarikeru	Was as lovely for me?[2]

38

The daughter of the fifth son[1] of Emperor Seiwa was called Lady Ichijō, and she once served the Kyōgoku no Miyasundokoro.[2] However, because of an unfortunate occurrence, she left the court. She composed the following poem after becoming the wife of the Provincial Governor of Iki:[3]

(51)	Tamasaka ni	If anyone should come
	Tou hito araba	To ask after me,
	Wata no hara	Tell them that I have left
	Nageki ho ni agete	For the open sea,
	Inu to kotaeyo	My doleful sails unfurled.[4]

39

When Prince Muneyuki, the Master of the Right Division of the Capital, was arranging the marriage between the daughter of the

Provincial Governor of Ise[1] and Prince Tadaakira,[2] he summoned into his presence a young girl who lived there and exchanged vows of love with her. The next morning he sent her this poem:

(52)	Shiratsuyu no Oku o matsu ma no Asagao wa Mizu zo nakanaka Arubekarikeru	I wish I had not seen The morning glory, Which blooms only while The white dewdrops Linger upon it.[3]

40

When the Minister of Ceremonial used to visit Princess Katsura regularly, a young girl who served in the Princess' mansion fell in love with him, thinking that he was a most attractive man.[1] The Minister of Ceremonial, however, was quite unaware of the tender feelings he had aroused in her.

Once, upon seeing fireflies flitting about, he turned to the girl and said: "Please catch a few of them for me." She therefore complied and gently wrapped them in the sleeve of her outer robe.[2] While she was preparing to show the fireflies to the Minister, she composed this poem:

(53)	Tsutsumedomo Kakurenu mono wa Natsu mushi no Mi yori amareru Omoi narikeri	Although I try to conceal it, The love in my heart, Like the glow Of the summer fireflies, Cannot be hidden.[3]

41

Toshiko often visited the mansion of the Minamoto Major Counsellor. At one time she maintained an apartment in his mansion.[1] One lazy afternoon, the Counsellor, Toshiko, her eldest daughter

Ayakko, who, like her mother, had a pleasant disposition, and Yōko, a young attendant to the Counsellor who was at once sensitive and charming, got together and began telling each other entertaining stories. They also talked at length about worldly matters[2] and of the many sorrows of the world. At one point the Counsellor composed this poem:

(54)	Iitsutsu mo Yo wa hakanaki o Katami ni wa Aware to ikade Kimi ni miemashi	We talk like this But well we know That life is fleeting; As a remembrance of this world What more can I say To express my sadness?[3]

So deeply were they moved by this poem that no one was able to compose an answering poem and could only sob noisily. Indeed, they were a most unusual group.

42

Once there was a priest called Eshū[1] who served as the faith healer of a certain lady. Rumors about them circulated widely, and so he composed this poem:

(55)	Sato wa iū Yama ni wa sawagu Shirakumo no Sora ni hakanaki Mi to ya narinan	Everyone is talking about us Up in the mountains And in the villages; Would that I might disappear Into the heavens Like the white clouds.

He also wrote this poem which he sent to the woman:

(56)	Asaborake Waga mi wa niwa no Shimo nagara Nani o tane nite Kokoro oiken	As lowly as the frost That lies in the garden At break of dawn am I; What seed has caused This love to grow?[2]

43

While Eshū was having a wooden fence[1] put up in front of the priests' temple quarters, he wrote on a shaving:

(57)	Magaki suru	Why this constant din
	Hida no takumi no	Echoing throughout the world–
	Tatsuki oto no	This deafening noise of axes,
	Ana kashigamashi	Swung by the Hida carpenters
	Nazo ya yo no naka	Who busily build the fence?[2]

Eshū walked away, saying, "I am going deep into the mountains to practice austerities." Some time had elapsed when one day a person[3] who had come in search of him asked: "Where has he gone? He must be living in seclusion somewhere on this mountain, but where might it be?" Eshū replied with this poem:

(58)	Nani bakari	This mountain
	Fukaku mo arazu	Is not remote—
	Yo no tsune no	It would only make
	Hiei o toyama to	That famous landmark Mount Hiei
	Miru bakari nari	Seem a mere foothill.[4]

Eshū had been staying at a place called Yokawa.[5]

44

Someone[1] asked Eshū: "Is the day you are to climb the mountain still far off? Tell me, please, when will it be?" Eshū sent this poem by way of reply:

(59)	Noboriyuku	As I climb the mountain
	Yama no kumoi no	High into the clouds,
	Tōkereba	The sun seems closer;
	Hi mo chikaku naru	The day of departure
	Mono ni zo arikeru	Also draws near.[2]

Eshū composed this poem when ugly rumors about him continued to circulate:

(60)	Nogaru tomo	Though one flees
	Tare ka kizaran	Who can escape
	Nuregoromo	False charges
	Ame no shita ni shi	As long as one lives
	Suman kagiri wa	In this world of men?[3]

45

When Tsutsumi no Chūnagon[1] first sent his daughter,[2] who was later to become the mother of the thirteenth prince,[3] to serve in the palace, he was quite anxious about her and asked himself: "I wonder what the Emperor[4] thinks of her?" Very much concerned, he wrote this poem which he sent to His Majesty:

(61)	Hito no oya no	Though it is not dark,
	Kokoro wa yami ni	Truly a parent's heart,
	Aranedomo	For love of his child,
	Ko o omou michi ni	Becomes confused
	Mayoinuru kana	And knows not where it goes.[5]

The Emperor was deeply moved by this poem. Although he sent Tsutsumi no Chūnagon a return poem, no one remembers the lines.

46

A long time after Heichū[1] had stopped seeing Lady Kan'in,[2] he decided to visit her again. Immediately after their reunion, he sent her this poem:

(62)	Uchitokete	I suppose you slept soundly
	Kimi wa netsuran	While I, in my longing,
	Ware wa shimo	Remained awake
	Tsuyu no okiite	Throughout the night
	Koi ni akashitsu	Till morning brought the dewdrops.[3]

Lady Kan'in sent him this reply:

(63)	Shiratsuyu no Okifushi tare o Koitsuran Ware wa kikiowazu Iso no kami nite	For whom had you been longing Awake or sleeping? Surely it could not be me, For long ago You abandoned me.[4]

47

Lady Ichijō[1] of the Yōzei-in composed this poem:

(64)	Okuyama ni Kokoro o irete Tazunezu wa Fukaki momiji no Iro o mimashi ya	Unless you go In search of it Deep into the mountains, How can you see the glorious hue Of the scarlet maple leaves?[2]

48

During the reign of Emperor Uda, a lady of the bedchamber called Lady Gyōbu served in the court. One day she went to visit her family and failed to return to the palace for some time. Missing her presence, His Majesty sent her this poem:

(65)	Ōzora o Wataru haru hi no Kage nare ya Yoso ni nomi mite Nodokekaruran	Do you imagine yourself to be The sun in springtime, Lazily drifting across the skies? All you do is Gaze at us from afar And idly pass the time away.[1]

49

On another occasion, Emperor Uda attached the following poem to a chrysanthemum and sent it to the Priestess of the Kamo Shrine:[1]

(66)	Yukite minu	If it were not for one
	Hito no tame ni to	Who could not come
	Omowazu wa	To view it,
	Tare ka oramashi	Why should I have picked
	Waga yado no kiku	The chrysanthemum from my garden?[2]

This was the Priestess' poem in reply:

(67)	Waga yado ni	If Your Majesty had not picked
	Iro ori tomuru	The chrysanthemum growing
	Kimi naku wa	In the palace garden,
	Yoso ni mo kiku no	How else could I enjoy this flower
	Hana o mimashi ya	So far away from home?[3]

50

Kaisen[1] composed this poem after climbing the mountain:

(68)	Kumo narade	Now that I have abandoned
	Kodakaki mine ni	The floating world,
	Iru mono wa	Apart from the low-flying clouds,
	Ukiyo o somuku	I live alone on this peak
	Waga mi narikeri	Where trees grow tall.[2]

51

This poem from the Priestess of the Kamo Shrine arrived at the palace:

(69)	Onaji e o Wakite shimo oku Aki nareba Hikari mo tsuraku Omōyuru kana	Autumn is here, But how harsh The sunlight seems to me, For even on the same branch The frost lies unevenly.[1]

The Emperor sent back this poem:

(70)	Hana no iro o Mite mo shirinan Hatsushimo no Kokoro yukite wa Okaji to zo omou	When you see the lovely colors Of the flowers You will surely understand; I doubt the first frost of the year Shows any favoritism.[2]

52

The following poem was also composed by Emperor Uda:

(71)	Watatsu umi no Fukaki kokoro wa Okinagara Uramirarenuru Mono ni zo arikeru	With a love As deep as the open sea, I love each of my children; Alas that they should feel Resentful toward me![1]

53

A man called Sakanoue no Tōmichi,[1] who served at the Yōzei-in, was unable to have a rendezvous with a certain young lady who also served there, for she had informed him that she was "indisposed"[2] at the time. Tōmichi thereupon wrote this poem:

(72)	Aki no no o Wakuran mushi mo Waga goto ya Shigeki sawari ni Ne o ba nakuran	The insect which makes its way Through the autumn field Resembles me so; It can only cry forlornly, Seeing the obstacles before it.

54

The third son of Muneyuki, the Master of the Right Division of the Office of the Capital, was scorned by his father and brothers because he loved to gamble. He therefore left for another province, thinking that he would go wherever his feet took him. Some time later he sent his closest friends this poem:

(73)	Shiori shite	As I travel along
	Yuku tabi naredo	I break off branches
	Karisome no	To leave behind as markers;
	Inochi shiraneba	I may not pass this way again,
	Kaerishi mo seji	For I know not when I shall die.[1]

55

A man left the woman with whom he was deeply in love and went to another province. The woman, wondering when he would return to her, waited patiently. Some time later a message arrived notifying her of his death. This is the poem she composed at the time:

(74)	Ima kon to	You left me
	Iite wakareshi	Saying that you would soon return;
	Hito nareba	I shall therefore wait for you,
	Kagiri to kikedo	Though I have heard
	Nao zo mataruru	That you are gone.[1]

56

Kanemori,[1] the Provisional Governor of Echizen, once had a love affair with a woman called Lady Hyōe.[2] After having neglected her for many years, he went to visit her again. On that occasion he composed this poem:

(75)	Yūsareba	When evening shadows fall,
	Michi mo mienedo	No longer is the road visible,
	Furusato wa	But the horse I used to ride
	Moto koshi koma ni	When long ago I called on you,
	Makasete zo yuku	Will lead me to your door.[3]

Lady Hyōe sent him this reply:

(76)	Koma ni koso	So it was your horse
	Makasetarikere	That brought you to me!
	Hakanaku mo	I foolishly thought
	Kokoro no kuru to	Your faithful heart
	Omoikeru kana	Had pointed out the way.[4]

57

Taira no Nakaki,[1] the Assistant Governor of Ōmi, lavished great care upon his daughter. After his death, however, she was reduced to poverty and was forced to live in a desolate spot in another province. Deeply moved by her plight, Kanemori wrote:

(77)	Ochikochi no	Had you ever dreamt
	Hitome marenaru	That you would live
	Yamazato ni	In such a remote spot
	Iei sen to wa	Where visitors
	Omoiki ya kimi	Would be so few?[2]

The wretched woman read this poem and, weeping loudly, failed to send Kanemori a return poem, although she was known to be talented in poetry.

58

At the time Kanemori was living in Michinoku,[1] the daughters of the third son[2] of Prince Sadamoto[3] resided in a place called Kurozuka.[4] One day Kanemori sent this poem to the young ladies:

(78) Michinoku no
Adachi no hara no
Kurozuka ni
Oni komoreri to
Kiku wa makoto ka

I have heard
That demons dwell
In Kurozuka of Adachi Field
In Michinoku province;
Tell me, is this true?[5]

Kanemori approached their father and said: "I would like to marry your daughter." The girls' father replied: "At present, she is much too young to think of marriage. Please wait until she is a little older." Since Kanemori was in a great hurry to return to the capital, he attached this poem to a spray of yellow kerria roses and had it delivered to the young lady:

(79) Hanazakari
Sugi mo ya suru to
Kawazu naku
Ide no yamabuki
Ushiro metashi mo

Thinking that the flower
Will wither while I was gone,
I deeply regret
Having to leave behind
The yellow kerria roses of Ide,
Where the frogs cry.[6]

The wife of Tsunetada,[7] who is said to have composed the poem in which the place name Natori-no-miyu[8] is concealed, was probably the young maiden of Kurozuka whose hand Kanemori had sought. She recited this poem:

(80) Ōzora no
Kumo no kayoiji
Miteshi gana
Tori nomi yukeba
Ato wa kamo nashi

Would that I could see
The pathway through the clouds
In the sky above—
Since only birds travel it,
Not a trace is left behind.[9]

Upon hearing this poem, Kanemori composed another in which he also mentioned the place name Natori-no-miyu:

(81) Shiogama no
Ura ni wa ama ya
Taeniken
Nado sunadori no
Miyuru toki naki

Have the fishermen vanished
From Shiogama Bay?
For if they have not,
Why do I not see
A single soul fishing there?[10]

Having heard that the young girl he had once loved had come to the capital with another man, Kanemori wrote to her, saying, "Why did you not inform me of your arrival in the capital?" To this the woman merely said: "Here is a present for you from Michinoku," and presented him with the slip of paper on which he had long ago written the poem: ". . . I deeply regret having to leave behind / The yellow kerria roses of Ide."[11] Seeing his old poem, Kanemori recited:

(82)	Toshi o hete	My sleeve has continued to be wet
	Nure wataritsutsu	Throughout the years;
	Koromode o	Drenched with the tears
	Kyō no namida ni	I shed today,
	Kuchi ya shinuran	I fear that it will rot away.

59

A man who had grown weary of the world went down to Tsukushi[1] from where he sent this poem to a young woman:

(83)	Wasuru ya to	I came here
	Idete koshikado	Intending to forget my sorrows;
	Izuku ni mo	But no matter where I go,
	Usa wa hanarenu	I cannot escape from them,
	Mono ni zo arikeru	Just as I can never leave Usa.[2]

60

There was once a woman called Lady Gojō.[1] One day she had a sketch drawn of herself, showing her burning with billowing clouds of smoke swirling about her. She sent this sketch to a young man together with this poem:

(84)	Kimi o omoi Namanamashi mi o Yaku toki wa Keburi ōkaru Mono ni zo arikeru	When this body of mine, So full of love for you, Is one day set on fire, How great will be The volume of smoke that rises!

61

A large number of imperial concubines[1] maintained their individual apartments in the Teiji Palace. However, when several years later the Kawara Palace[2] was built in all its splendor, Teiji no In had an apartment readied for the exclusive use of the Kyōgoku no Miyasundokoro[3] and moved into his new residence with her in the spring. The imperial concubines, who were left behind, felt lonelier than they ever imagined they would feel. Courtiers came to visit the old palace and, enjoying the wisteria as they strolled about the palace grounds, said: "What a pity that His Majesty departed without viewing these flowers in full bloom." Just then a slip of paper tied to a branch caught their eye. When they untied it, they found the following poem:

(85)	Yo no naka no Asaki se ni nomi Nariyukeba Kinō no fuji no Hana to koso mire	It is the way of the world That deep pools become shallow rapids; I shall therefore look upon The wisteria as a remembrance Of your love of yesterday.[4]

The courtiers were deeply moved and praised it highly, though no one was able to discover which of the neglected concubines had written it. Nonetheless, the men composed this poem:

(86)	Fuji no hana Iro no asaku mo Miyuru kana Utsuroinikeru Nagori narubeshi	How light is the color Of the wisteria! This is surely a sign That its beauty Has faded away.[5]

62

A woman called Lady Nōsan[1] and the Priest Jōzō[2] were once deeply in love with each other. Exchanging solemn vows of love, they spoke of all that they felt in their hearts. One day Lady Nōsan sent the Priest this poem:

(87)	Omou chō	So this is love—
	Kokoro wa koto ni	How different it is
	Arikeru o	From what I thought it was
	Mukashi no hito ni	When long ago to a former lover
	Nani o iiken	I spoke of love.

The Priest sent her this return poem:

(88)	Yukusue no	Not knowing what the future
	Sukuse o shiranu	Had in store for me,
	Kokoro ni wa	I once promised my former lover
	Kimi ni kagiri no	That I would sacrifice
	Mi to zo iikeru	My life for her.

63

The late Master of the Right Division of the Office of the Capital[1] secretly went to visit the daughter of a certain woman. Presently, the girl's mother learned of their clandestine trysts and, rebuking them severely, did her utmost to keep the lovers apart. Feeling resentful, the man returned to his mansion. The next morning, he composed a poem which he sent to his sweetheart:

(89)	Sa mo koso wa	The storm wind on the mountain peak
	Mine no arashi wa	Blew strongly,
	Arakarame	But I returned home,
	Nabikishi eda o	Resenting the branch
	Uramite zo koshi	Which had bent before it.[2]

64

Heichū[1] brought with him to his wife's home a young girl whom he loved dearly and installed her there. His wife, however, began to speak spitefully of the young girl and finally succeeded in driving her away. Heichū apparently went along with his wife's wishes, for he did not keep the girl from leaving, although he loved her dearly. He was not even able to approach the young girl, since his wife railed against them ceaselessly. He finally managed to sidle up to the four-foot-high silk screen which stood between the girl and himself. Standing up close to it, he said: "I am sorry things did not turn out the way we hoped they would. Though you are far away in a distant province, please do not forget to write me. I too shall write." These were the words he uttered while the girl, with her belongings wrapped up in a bundle, waited for the arrival of the carriage she had summoned. Heichū felt very sad indeed, but before he realized it, the girl had been whisked away. Some time later, he sent her this poem:

(90)	Wasuraru na	Please do not forget—
	Wasure ya shinuru	For I never shall—
	Harugasumi	The promise we made one another
	Kesa tachinagara	This spring morning
	Chigiritsuru koto	In the mist.

65

When Nan-in no Gorō[1] was the Provincial Governor of Mikawa,[2] he fell deeply in love with Lady Iyo, who was serving in the Sokyōden,[3] to whom he said: "I should like to call on you." In reply she sent this message: "I shall soon be leaving for the Imperial Court to serve Her Highness." Upon reading her message, he composed this poem:

(91)	Tamasudare Uchitokakuru wa Itodoshiku Kage o miseji to Omou narikeri	You say you are on your way To the palace Where jewelled blinds Have been lowered, But I think that you are trying To avoid me.[4]

He also wrote:

(92)	Nageki nomi Shigeki miyama no Hototogisu Kogakure ite mo Ne o nomi zo naku	All I do is lament Like the *hototogisu* In the densely wooded mountain; Crying ceaselessly, It hides among the trees.[5]

He had come here eagerly looking forward to meeting her, but she coldly asked him to leave. He thereupon sent her this poem:

(93)	Shine tote ya Tori mo aezu wa Yarawaruru Ito ikigataki Kokochi koso sure	Are you telling me To go and die? No sooner had I come Than you sent me away— Oh, how can I go on living?[6]

The return poem that she sent him was most interesting, but I failed to pay close attention to the lines.[7]

One snowy evening Nan-in no Gorō came to visit Lady Iyo. They were chatting together amiably when Lady Iyo abruptly said: "It is getting very late. Please return to your mansion." However, after he left, he was forced to return to her home.[8] He tried to get back indoors, but found the door latched from the inside. At this point, he composed this poem:

(94)	Ware wa sa wa Yuki furu sora ni Kiene to ya Tachikaeredomo Akenu itado wa	Is this your way Of telling me to disappear Into the snowy heavens? I have been forced to turn back, But you refuse to open the door.

After reciting this poem, he stubbornly refused to budge. Lady Iyo later commented: "He was skillful at composing poetry and spoke with such feeling that, wondering what I should do, I peeked out at him. I then discovered that he was extremely ugly."

66

One night when Toshiko was waiting for Chikane and he failed to come, she composed this poem:

(95)	Sayo fukete Inaōsedori no Nakikeru o Kimi ga tataku to Omoikeru kana	The night deepens, And when the wagtail called, I thought that it was you Knocking at my door.[1]

67

On another occasion, Toshiko waited for Chikane on a rainy night. He failed to appear, doubtless on account of the rain. Meanwhile the rain leaked through, for her house was terribly dilapidated. Some time later, a message arrived in which Chikane said: "I could not visit you because it was pouring. How did you weather the storm in that house of yours?" Toshiko replied:

(96)	Kimi o omou Hima naki yado to Omoedomo Koyoi no ame wa Moranu ma zo naki	I feared that in such a house I would never think of you, But there was no spot Through which the rain that night Did not come through.[1]

68

Lord Biwa[1] sent one of his servants to fetch him a branch of the oak tree growing near Toshiko's home. Toshiko permitted the servant to break off a branch to which she attached a slip of paper containing the poem:

(97) Waga yado o	When did you become
Itsuka wa kimi ga	Familiar with my garden?
Nara no ha no	As though you know me intimately,
Narashigao ni wa	You send a servant
Ori ni okosuru	To break off an oak branch.[2]

Lord Biwa's return poem went:

(98) Kashiwagi ni	Not knowing
Hamori no kami no	That a leaf-protecting deity
Mashikeru o	Lived in the oak tree,
Shirade zo orishi	I have broken off a branch—
Tatari nasaru na	Please do not cast a spell on me![3]

69

At the time Tadabumi,[1] who had been appointed Generalissimo[2] of Michinoku, was about to depart for his new post, Gen no Myōbu was secretly seeing his son Shigemochi.[3] Before the young man's departure with his father, she presented him with farewell gifts, among which were a hunting outfit of dappled cloth,[4] a woman's overrobe, and Shintō offerings.[5] The recipient of her generous gifts composed this poem:

(99) Yoi yoi ni	The hunting outfit
Koishisa masaru	Which you kindly presented me
Karigoromo	Will intensify my love
Kokorozukushi no	With each passing night.
Mono ni zo arikeru	

The woman was moved to tears by his poem.

70

Gen no Myōbu sent Shigemochi some myrica,[1] which he acknowledged with this poem:

(100) Michinoku no	If we could cross together
Adachi no yama mo	The mountains of Adachi
Morotomo ni	In the province of Michinoku,
Koeba wakare no	This parting would not seem
Kanashikaraji o	So very sad.[2]

Gen no Myōbu lived on the Kamo River embankment. Once she caught some trout which she sent to Shigemochi along with this poem:

(101) Kamogawa no	I fished for trout
Se ni fusu ayu no	Which swam in the swift waters
Io torite	Of the Kamo River,
Nede koso akase	Not sleeping until dawn—
Yume ni mietsu ya	Did you see me in your dream?[3]

Shigemochi departed for Michinoku. Whenever he had an opportunity, he sent Gen no Myōbu a letter expressing his wretchedness. Soon afterward, Gen no Myōbu heard that he had fallen ill and had died on his journey. This sad piece of news broke her heart. Some time later, a messenger came from the post town of Shinozuka,[4] bearing a letter in which the deceased had expressed his utter misery. Gen no Myōbu was truly grief-stricken. "When was this letter written?" she asked. One could only guess that it had been delivered long after it had been written.

Gen no Myōbu wrote down these lines:

(102) Shinozuka no	How anxiously I awaited
Umaya umaya to	The day of your return
Machiwabishi	From the post town of Shinozuka;
Kimi wa munashiku	But now that you are gone,
Nari zo shinikeru	My waiting has been in vain.[5]

No sooner had she finished composing the poem than she burst into tears.

When Shigemochi was still called by his childhood name Taishichi, he served in the Imperial Palace. After coming of age,[6] however, he was assigned to the Sovereign's Private Office.[7] Having been appointed a special messenger to bring back the gold,[8] he had gone up north together with his father Tadabumi.

71

The late Minister of Ceremonial died on the last day of the second month when the cherry blossoms were in full bloom. On this sad occasion Tsutsumi no Chūnagon composed this poem:

(103) Saki nioi	The wild cherry blossoms
Kaze matsu hodo no	Will bloom
Yamazakura	Even though they will scatter
Hito no yo yori wa	All too soon—
Hisashikarikeri	And yet they remain longer
	Than man on earth.[1]

The Sanjō Minister of the Right[2] replied:

(104) Haru haru no	Though each spring
Hana wa chiru tomo	Wild cherry blooms scatter,
Sakinubeshi	They will bloom again;
Mata aigataki	How cruel is the world in which
Hito no yo zo uki	One cannot see again
	A dear one who has passed away.[3]

72

Before his death, the same Minister resided in the Teiji Palace.[1] One day Kanemori[2] called on him. The Minister summoned him into his presence and they talked of many things of common interest. Upon the Minister's demise, Kanemori was deeply saddened whenever he saw the Teiji Palace. Moreover, seeing how enchantingly lovely the pond was, Kanemori felt so melancholy he recited these lines:

(105) Ike wa nao	The pond remains
Mukashi nagara no	An unchanged mirror of the past;
Kagami nite	How sad that you,
Kage mishi kimi ga	Who once studied your reflection in it,
Naki zo kanashiki	Are no longer with us![3]

73

Tsutsumi no Chūnagon planned to give a farewell banquet in honor of a friend who, having been appointed governor of a distant province, was about to depart from the capital. He waited for the guest of honor, but the man failed to make an appearance even though night had fallen. Tsutsumi no Chūnagon sent his friend this poem:

(106) Wakarubeki	That we must part is bad enough,
Koto mo aru mono o	But how painful it is
Hinemosu ni	To have had to wait
Matsu to te sae mo	All day for you
Nagekitsuru kana	And have you fail to come!

Upon reading this poem, the guest of honor, very much flustered, rushed to the banquet.

74

Tsutsumi no Chūnagon had uprooted the cherry tree which was growing a trifle too far from the front of the main building of his mansion, replanting it closer to the building. Noting that the tree was beginning to wither, he composed this poem:

(107) Yado chikaku	I have transplanted the tree
Utsushite ueshi	Closer to my mansion
Kai mo naku	But to no avail;
Machidō ni nomi	The blossoms, it would seem,
Miyuru hana kana	Will not bloom for me.[1]

75

On another occasion when an official of the Sovereign's Private Office who had been appointed the Provincial Governor of Kaga was about to leave the capital, Tsutsumi no Chūnagon, feeling very sad about the imminent parting, recited these lines:

(108) Kimi no yuku	Though I do not know
Koshi no Shirayama	Shirayama of Koshi
Shirazu tomo	Whither you are bound,
Yuki no ma ni ma ni	Trudging through the snow,
Ato wa tazunen	I shall follow you there.[1]

76

Yoshitane[1] went to visit Princess Katsura,[2] but her mother, the Miyasundokoro,[3] heard about his arrival and barred the gate. As a result, Yoshitane stood outside all night long. When he was about to leave for home, he called out, saying, "Please relay this poem to the Princess." Then, through an opening in the gate Yoshitane recited:

(109) Koyoi koso	Were you not aware
Namida no kawa ni	That tonight I returned home,
Iri chidori	Shedding a river of tears,
Nakite kaeru to	Like the plover
Kimi wa shirazu ya	By the riverside?[4]

77

Yoshitane also sent Princess Katsura this poem:

(110) Nagaki yo o	All through the endless night,
Akashi no ura ni	The smoke from the salt fires
Yaku shio no	Along the Bay of Akashi
Keburi wa sora ni	Rises into the heavens.[1]
Tachi ya noboranu	

When Princess Katsura and Yoshitane were still seeing each other in secret, Teiji no In made arrangements for a moon-viewing banquet on the night of the fifteenth of the eighth month.[2] Teiji no In had personally commanded that Princess Katsura be present, therefore she felt obliged to make an appearance. However, Yoshitane tried his best to detain her, for he knew very well they could not see each other at the palace. He entreated her, saying, "Please don't go—not tonight of all nights!" Nevertheless, the Emperor himself had summoned her. Thinking it would not do to remain with Yoshitane, Princess Katsura hurried off to the banquet. After her departure Yoshitane composed this poem:

(111) Taketori no	Like Princess Kaguya,
Yoyo ni nakitsutsu	Whom the Bamboo-Cutter
Todomeken	Tried to detain by weeping piteously,
Kimi wa kimi ni to	You leave me tonight
Koyoi shimo yuku	To go to His Majesty.[3]

78

Gen no Myōbu participated in the New Year's Day Ceremony[1] and was one of the lady attendants flanking the imperial throne. The Prince of the Board of Censors[2] beheld her and fell madly in love with her. He wrote her a letter to which she replied:

(112) Uchitsuke ni	I have heard
Madou kokoro to	That you fell in love
Kiku kara ni	At first sight;
Nagusame yasuku	I therefore think
Omōyuru kana	You will forget me
	Just as easily.[3]

I cannot recall the lines of the Prince's return poem.

79

Gen no Myōbu sent the same Prince this poem:

(113) Korizuma no	The floating *miru* seaweed
Ura ni kazukan	In the Bay of Suma
Ukimiru wa	Are swept underwater
Nami sawagashiku	When the waves are rough.[1]
Ari koso wa seme	

80

When the cherry blooms were at their loveliest at the Uda Palace,[1] the sons of the Nan-in[2] got together with a few of their acquaintances and composed poetry to amuse themselves. On this occasion, Prince Muneyuki composed this poem:

(114) Kite miredo	My heart finds no pleasure
Kokoro mo yukazu	In the blossoms
Furusato no	Which I have come to view,
Mukashi nagara no	Even though they scatter
Hana wa chiredomo	At my old home
	As they used to long ago.

A number of other poems were composed by the others in the group.

81

When Ukon, the daughter of the Minor Captain Suenawa,[1] was in attendance upon the late Empress,[2] the late Provisional Middle Counsellor[3] went to call on her. He pledged his love to her, whereupon Ukon immediately left the service of the Empress and returned to her home. The Middle Counsellor never called on her again, but whenever anyone came from the palace, Ukon eagerly asked: "How is he? Does he ever visit the palace?" The person she questioned would usually reply: "Why, yes, he comes to the palace quite regularly." Ukon one day sent the Middle Counsellor a letter in which she had written:

(115) Wasureji to	I have heard
Tanomeshi hito wa	That the man who vowed
Ari to kiku	Never to forget me is well,
Iishi koto no ha	But where have they gone,
Izuchi iniken	Those words he once pronounced?[4]

82

The Provisional Middle Counsellor once sent Ukon a pheasant without a word of explanation. In acknowledging his gift, Ukon sent him this poem:

(116) Kurikoma no	I sought to keep my vows
Yama ni asa tatsu	From being short-lived,
Kiji yori mo	More fearful even than the pheasant,
Kari ni wa awaji to	Rising on Mount Kurikoma
Omoishi mono o	In the morning,
	That fears the hunter.[1]

83

While Ukon was living in an apartment of the Imperial Palace, a certain young gentleman often came in secret to visit her. Being the First Secretary of the Sovereign's Private Office, he made his way to the court quite regularly. One rainy night, he stood outside Ukon's apartment, leaning against the hinged door-leaf,[1] but she was not at all aware of his presence. Meanwhile, thinking that she would turn over a straw mat that had been soaked by the rain, she recited this poem:

(117) Omou hito	If the one I love
Ame to furikuru	Were to come down to me
Mono naraba	As the raindrops do now,
Waga moru toko wa	I would not let him leave
Kaesazaramashi	My rain-soaked bedding.[2]

Deeply moved by her poem, her lover crept silently into her room.

84

A certain gentleman promised Ukon time and again that he would never forget her. Nonetheless, he did forget her in time, and so Ukon wrote:

(118) Wasuraruru	You vowed that you
Mi o ba omowazu	Would never forget;
Chikaiteshi	Now I realize how little
Hito no inochi no	I meant to you,
Oshiku mo aru kana	Even though your life
	Is precious to me.[1]

I do not know what his response was.

85

Rumor had it that the Imperial Adviser Momozono[1] was having a love affair with Ukon, but it was unfounded. Ukon nevertheless composed this poem and sent it to the Imperial Adviser:

(119) Yoshi omoe	Think about it—
Ama no hirowanu	Just as a fisherman
Utsuse kai	Does not pick up an empty shell,
Munashiki na o ba	Would these rumors have arisen
Tatsubeshi ya kimi	Were they not based on fact?[2]

86

Kanemori went to visit the Major Counsellor[1] on New Year's Day, and together they talked about a number of different subjects. At one point the Major Counsellor casually asked Kanemori to compose a poem and in compliance with this request, Kanemori came up with this poem:

(120) Kyō yori wa	Beginning today,
Ogi no yakehara	I shall make my way
Kakiwakete	Through the field of burnt reeds
Wakana tsumi ni to	To gather young greens;
Tare o sasowan	Whom shall I invite along?[2]

The Major Counsellor was delighted with the poem and quickly composed an answer:

(121) Kataoka ni	If we fail to find bracken
Warabi moezu wa	Growing in Kataoka,
Tazunetsutsu	Let us search instead
Kokoro yari ni ya	For young greens
Wakana tsumamashi	To lighten our hearts.[3]

87

The Secretary of the Bureau of Military Storehouses,[1] who often traveled back and forth between the province of Tajima and the capital, once left behind him a young lady in the province and returned to the capital. One snowy day the young lady composed the following poem which she sent to him:

(122) Yamazato ni	You leave me behind
Ware o todomete	In this mountain village,
Wakareji no	Where the snow will bury
Yuki no ma ni ma ni	The road that keeps us apart.
Fukaku naruran	

The Secretary replied:

(123) Yamazato ni	I who depart
Kayou kokoro mo	And you who remain—
Taenubeshi	How wretched we both feel!
Yuku mo tomaru mo	My heart which goes to you
Kokorobososa ni	In the mountain village
	Can no longer bear the pain.

88

Once when the Secretary of the Bureau of Military Storehouses was on his way down to the province of Ki, he complained about the bitter cold and sent a servant to fetch him a robe. The young woman sent him a robe and with it this poem:

(124) Ki no kuni no	You, who depart for
Muro no kōri ni	The district of Muro
Yuku hito wa	In the province of Ki,
Kaze no samusa mo	Will probably not even feel
Omoishirareji	The cold wind that blows.[1]

The Secretary's return poem read:

(125) Ki no kuni no	I am on my way
Muro no kōri ni	To Muro in Ki province,
Yukinagara	But I feel particularly sad
Kimi to fusuma no	At night
Naki zo kanashiki	Since you are not beside me.[2]

89

When the Director of the Right Division of the Bureau of Horses[1] was having a love affair with Lady Suri,[2] he once said to her: "I cannot visit you tonight because it is unlucky for me to travel in that direction. I must first set out in some other direction." In reply, Lady Suri came up with this poem:

(126) Kore naranu Koto o mo ōku Tagaureba Uramin kata mo Naki zo wabishiki	Since you have been inconstant On many other occasions, I no longer resent you; Oh, but I feel so wretched![3]

After some time had elapsed and the Director of the Bureau of Horses no longer called on Lady Suri, she composed these lines:

(127) Ikade nao Ajiro no hio ni Koto towan Nani ni yorite ka Ware o towanu to	How shall I ask The icefish trapped In the bamboo weirs What is keeping my lover From coming to see me?[4]

She received this reply:

(128) Ajiro yori Hoka ni wa hio no Yoru mono ka Shirazu wa Uji no Hito ni toekashi	Does the icefish swim up to Anything beside the bamboo weirs? If you do not know, Please ask the man from Uji.[5]

Early one morning, when the Director of the Right Division of the Bureau of Horses was still visiting Lady Suri, he wrote:

(129) Akenu tote Isogi mo zo suru Ōsaka no Kiri tachinu tomo Hito ni kikasu na	I shall hurry home Since day has dawned, But do not tell a soul That I saw the mist rise At Meeting Barrier.[6]

When this gentleman first began calling on Lady Suri, he sent her this poem:

(130) Ika ni shite	How I long to vanish
Ware wa kienan	Like the white dew;
Shiratsuyu no	Then I would no longer feel
Kaerite nochi no	This aching yearning
Mono wa omowaji	Upon returning home.[7]

Her reply:

(131) Kakio naru	How I long to see
Kimi ga asagao	Your face in the morning!
Miteshigana	I might then see
Kaerite nochi wa	How much you think of me
Mono ya omou to	After leaving me.[8]

Once the Director of the Bureau of Horses spoke intimately with Lady Suri. Upon returning home, he sent her this poem:

(132) Kokoro o shi	Now that I have come away
Kimi ni todomete	After giving you my heart,
Kinishikaba	Shall I continue to long for you
Mono omou koto wa	Though I no longer have
Ware ni ya aruran	A heart to call my own?

Lady Suri sent this reply:

(133) Tamashii wa	Of no interest to me
Okashiki koto mo	Is your soul;
Nakarikeri	All I want
Yorozu no mono wa	In the world
Kara ni zo arikeru	Is you.

90

The late Minister of War[1] corresponded with Lady Suri. In a letter he once said: "I should like to call on you someday." Lady Suri replied with this poem:

(134) Takaku tomo	What else can I do
Nani ni ka wa sen	But refuse to see you,
Kuretake no	Even though you are
Hitoyo futayo no	A high official?
Ada no fushi o ba	What would our meeting
	For a night or two lead to?[2]

91

When the Sanjō Minister of the Right was still serving as a Middle Captain of the Inner Palace Guards,[1] he was appointed the Imperial Envoy to the Kamo Festival[2] and in this capacity set forth from the palace. Before leaving, however, he sent this message to a woman he used to visit but whom he had neglected for some time: "Since I have been appointed the Imperial Envoy to the festival, I am expected to bring a fan[3] with me. I was in such a hurry that I forgot mine, so please send me one." He felt certain that she, being a woman of elegant taste, would send him an appropriate fan. She did indeed send him a fan in a lovely shade of color from which there wafted an exquisite fragrance. On the back of the fan, along the edge, the woman had written this poem:

(135) Yuyushi tote	They say that sending a fan
Imu tomo ima wa	Brings bad luck,
Kai mo araji	But now such taboos are meaningless;
Uki o ba kore ni	I send the fan and with it
Omoi yoseten	All the sadness in my heart.[4]

The Minister of the Right was deeply moved by this poem. This was his return poem:

(136) Yuyushi tote	You should not have sent
Imikeru mono o	The fan I requested;
Waga tame ni	Why did you not reply
Nashi to iwanu wa	That you had none to offer—
Ta ga tsurakinari	Ah, who is suffering now?[5]

92

On the last day of the twelfth month, when the late Provisional Middle Counsellor[1] was courting the daughter[2] of the Minister of the Left,[3] he sent her this poem:

(137) Mono omou to	I was totally oblivious to
Tsuki hi no yuku mo	The passage of time
Shiranu ma ni	As I longed for you;
Kotoshi wa kyō ni	Now I hear that today
Hatenu to ka kiku	Is the last day of the year.[4]

He also sent her this poem:

(138) Ika ni shite	Even if it is only to tell you
Kaku omou chō	How much I care,
Koto o dani	Let me—and no one else—
Hitozute narade	Be the one to speak.[5]
Kimi ni kataran	

The Middle Counsellor continued writing poems in this vein and sending them to her. The morning after he finally succeeded in meeting the woman, he wrote to her:

(139) Kyō soe ni	I know in my heart
Kurezarame ya wa to	That today too will end
Omoedomo	Like yesterday,
Taenu wa hito no	But my aching heart
Kokoro narikeri	Cannot bear this waiting.[6]

93

The same Middle Counsellor had wooed the High Priestess of the Ise Shrine[1] for years. Just when he had been about to make her his, she was selected by divination to serve as the High Priestess. He was sorely distressed but helpless to do anything. He therefore sent her this poem:

(140) Ise no umi	It is in vain
Chihiro no hama ni	That I love you,
Hirou tomo	For you will soon leave me
Ima wa kai naku	To go to gather sea shells
Omōyuru kana	Along the shore at Ise.[2]

94

After his wife's death,[1] the Minister of Central Affairs[2] took his children along with him to live in the mansion of the Sanjō Minister of the Right. At the end of the mourning period, he had had enough of living alone and therefore sought the hand of Ku no Kimi,[3] a younger sister of his deceased wife. Her father and brothers saw no objection to the marriage. Meanwhile, he learned quite by chance that when the Captain of the Left Division of the Middle Palace Guards[4] was serving as a Gentleman-in-Waiting at the palace, he had corresponded with the girl. The Minister must have been extremely upset when he learned of this, for he immediately returned to his own home. Shortly afterward, he received this poem from the Miyasundokoro:[5]

(141) Naki hito no	Though you ought to remain
Sumori ni dani mo	In the empty house,
Narubeki o	You leave us today;
Ima wa to kaeru	How sad you have made us![6]
Kyō no kanashisa	

The Minister of Central Affairs replied:

(142) Sumori ni to	I wished to remain,
Omou kokoro wa	But having heard the rumor,
Todomuredo	I realized how meaningless
Kai arubeki mo	It would be
Nashi to koso kike	To go on living here.[7]

95

After the demise of the Emperor,[1] the Minister of Ceremonial[2] began visiting the Miyasundokoro, the Emperor's widow, who was the daughter of the Minister of the Right. However, just when, for some unknown reason, the Minister of Ceremonial had ceased to call on her, she received a letter from the High Priestess of Ise.[3] The Miyasundokoro wrote back, saying that the Minister no longer came to visit her. At the end of her letter, she added this poem:

(143) Shirayama ni	Just as the traveler's footprints
Furinishi yuki no	Are buried under the snow
Ato taete	That falls on Shirayama,
Ima wa koshiji no	My lover no longer comes to me,
Hito mo kayowazu	Now that I have grown old.[4]

There seems to have been a return poem, but the original text states that there was none.[5]

96

Ku no Kimi eventually married the Gentleman-in-Waiting.[1] At about the same time, the Minister of Ceremonial stopped visiting the Miyasundokoro, whereupon the Minister of the Left,[2] who was then serving as Captain of the Outer Palace Guards, began writing to her. Upon learning that the Gentleman-in-Waiting had become the son-in-law of the Minister of the Right, the Minister of the Left sent the Miyasundokoro this poem:

(144) Nami no tatsu	I do not know
Kata mo shiranedo	Where along the shore
Watatsumi no	The waves rush in,
Urayamashiku mo	Nor do I know
Omōyuru kana	How you feel toward me;
	Oh, but I envy the man.[3]

97

When everyone was busily preparing for the final rites at the end of the mourning period for the wife of the Prime Minister, the Prime Minister[1] himself stepped out onto the veranda, for the moon was especially lovely that night, and, feeling very melancholy, composed this poem:

(145) Kakurenishi	The moon,
Tsuki wa megurite	Which until now was hidden,
Idekuredo	Has come out again,
Kage ni mo hito wa	But even in its light
Miezu zo arikeru	I cannot see her.[2]

98

Princess Sugawara,[1] the mother of the Minister of the Left, passed away. When the mourning period was over, Teiji no In wrote to the Imperial Palace as the result of which the Prime Minister was allowed to wear the imperial colors.[2] Dressed resplendently in a lined robe of crimson,[3] the Prime Minister called on the Empress[4] and said: "Thanks to the letter from the Retired Emperor, I have been permitted to wear these robes." This is the poem he composed on this occasion:

(146) Nugu o nomi	I thought I would be sad
Kanashi to omoishi	Only when I removed my robes,
Naki hito no	But I grieve again,
Katami no iro wa	Seeing these colors that serve
Mata mo arikeri	As a memento of my wife.[5]

He then fell to weeping. At the time he was serving as a Middle Controller.[6]

99

When the Prime Minister accompanied Teiji no In on an outing to the Ōi River,[1] he praised ecstatically the breath-taking beauty of the colorful maple leaves on Mount Ogura, saying, "This is truly a place of great charm worthy of Your Majesty's honoring with an imperial visit. Let us recommend this idyllic spot to the reigning sovereign." He thereupon composed this poem:

(147) Ogurayama	Oh, maple leaves,
Mine no momiji shi	Aflame on Mount Ogura's peak,
Kokoro araba	If you have any feelings,
Ima hitotabi no	Please wait for
Miyuki matanan	Another imperial visit.[2]

They returned to the palace and reported to the Emperor what they had seen. The Emperor himself thought that such an outing would be most enjoyable. This is how the traditional imperial visits to the Ōi River began.

100

When the Minor Captain Suenawa[1] was living in the Ōi region, His Majesty[2] said: "I definitely plan to view the kerria roses when they are at their loveliest." Nonetheless, His Majesty forgot all about them. Deeply disappointed, the Minor Captain recited these lines:

(148) Chirinureba	The yellow kerria roses
Kuyashiki mono o	Are today in full bloom
Ōigawa	Along the banks of the Ōi;
Kishi no yamabuki	How I shall regret it
Kyō sakarinari	When the petals fall![3]

His Majesty was so deeply moved by this poem that he hastily made his way to the Ōi River in order to enjoy the roses.

101

Having fallen seriously ill, the Minor Captain Suenawa suffered terribly. When he was feeling slightly better, he made his way to the palace. At the time Kintada,[1] the Provincial Governor of Ōmi, was serving as both the Sovereign's Private Secretary and Assistant Director of the Housekeeping Office. Suenawa happened to meet Kintada at the palace and said: "I have not yet fully recovered from my recent illness but, feeling depressed and melancholy, I thought I would visit the palace. I do not know how much longer I shall last, but I have managed to survive thus far. I shall be leaving now, but I expect to be back again the day after tomorrow. Please put in a good word for me." So saying, Suenawa departed.

Three days later, Kintada received a letter from Suenawa in which was written this poem:

(149) Kuyashiku zo	I deeply regret having promised
Nochi ni awan to	To see you later;
Chigirikeru	How I wish I had said instead
Kyō o kagiri to	That today is the last time
Iwamashi mono o	I shall ever see you.[2]

Kintada was stunned. He turned to the messenger and, with tears streaming down his face, asked: "How is your master?" "He has become very weak," replied the messenger, who was himself weeping so bitterly Kintada was hardly able to understand him. "I myself shall go to see him immediately," said Kintada, and sent for a carriage from his mansion. He grew increasingly agitated while waiting for it. He went out as far as the Konoe Gate[3] to meet the carriage, and when at last it arrived, he jumped in and hurried off at top speed. Upon arriving at Suenawa's mansion on Gojō,[4] Kintada observed that a state of utter confusion pervailed and that the gate was closed. The Minor Captain had just breathed his last. Although Kintada requested to be ushered in, no one paid any attention to him. Greatly saddened, Kintada wept as he drove away. When he reported the events as they had taken place to the Throne, the Emperor too grieved deeply.

102

A certain gentleman named Sakai no Hitozane,[1] who was then the Provincial Governor of Tosa, fell ill and grew weaker with each passing day. Announcing that he was going to his home in Toba,[2] he composed this poem:

(150) Yuku hito wa	One who goes away
Sono kami kon to	Usually remarks in leaving
Iū mono o	That he will soon return;
Kokorobososhi na	But today's parting
Kyō no wakare wa	Is so very sad![3]

103

Once when Heichū was at the height of his career as a great lover, he went to the market.[1] In those days men of high birth used to visit the market and indulge there in sensual pleasures. That same day the ladies-in-waiting of the late Empress[2] made their way to the market. Heichū dallied with them and fell madly in love with one of the young ladies. Soon afterward he sent her a letter. The ladies, however, said to him: "There were a number of us in the carriage. To whom did you address your letter?" In reply, Heichū composed this poem and sent it to the young ladies:

(151) Momoshiki no	Numerous indeed
Tamoto no kazu wa	Were the sleeves of the ladies
Mishikado mo	I saw today,
Wakite omoi no	But the girl with the scarlet one
Iro zo koishiki	Is the one I love.[3]

The woman to whom Heichū had sent the letter was the daughter of the Provincial Governor of Musashi.[4] He had fallen in love with this woman who, when he first saw her, had been wearing a dark crimson robe of glossed silk.[5] Sometime afterward, the lady answered his letter and so he began to court her. She was an exceedingly lovely young woman, with beautiful features and long black tresses. Many men had fallen deeply in love with her, but she, being very proud, had never yielded to their advances. Heichū, however, courted her so earnestly that she finally consented to meet him.

The next morning Heichū failed to send her the usual letter.[6] Nor did any message come from him, though she waited until nightfall. The wretched young woman remained awake all night long, sorely distressed, but still no letter arrived. The following morning her servants said indignantly: "He is known for being extremely fickle in his attachments, but after finally winning our mistress' heart, how could he fail to write, even if he himself were prevented from coming? How heartless he is!" Because her servants were expressing what she herself had been feeling in her heart, heart-broken and extremely vexed with herself, the poor woman could only weep. That night, thinking that he might possibly come to her, she waited up for her lover, but he failed to appear. The next day too no letter came from him. Already several days had gone by and still she had received no word from him.

The woman wept ceaselessly and refused to eat. Her servants said: "Do not brood over it so! Surely this will not be the only affair a lady like you will ever have! Break with him, without telling anyone about it, then find yourself another man." To their well-meaning advice she made no comment and merely remained in seclusion. When none of her servants were watching her, she, having decided to become a Buddhist nun, cut her long flowing hair with her own hands. When her servants discovered what their mistress had done, they gathered about her and wept but were helpless to do anything. Only then did the lady speak, saying, "I feel so miserable I wish I were dead. Nonetheless, I lack the courage to kill myself. If I must remain alive, I should at least become a nun and live a life of religious austerity. Please do not fuss over me so."

The circumstances which led to this tragic turn of events were as follows. On the morning after their meeting, Heichū was on the point of sending a messenger with a letter to the woman when his superior officer[7] stopped by unexpectedly, thinking he would take

Heichū along with him on an outing. He found Heichū dozing and woke him, saying, "Were you still sleeping?" He then took Heichū along with him on an excursion to a distant spot where they drank saké and joked together. He absolutely refused to allow Heichū to return home.

Heichū managed with great difficulty to arrive home only to set out immediately on an imperial visit to the Ōi River as a companion to Teiji no In. He served His Majesty for two nights, in the course of which he became quite drunk. The imperial party started back late the next night. Heichū had been planning to visit the woman, but because it was unlucky for them to travel in that particular direction, the whole party—including Teiji no In and his attendants—headed in another direction.

All the while Heichū, realizing how upset the young woman must be and how strange she must find his silence, had been filled with longing for her. He thought to himself, as he gradually came out of his drunken stupor: "I cannot wait for it to get dark. I shall go see her myself and explain what happened. Or perhaps I shall send her a letter instead."

At this juncture, someone came and knocked at his door. "Who is it?" he asked. A voice called out, saying, "I have a message for the Junior Lieutenant."[8] When Heichū looked out to see who it was, he recognized the lady's servant. His heart beating rapidly, he said: "Please come in." Opening the letter, he found a lock of hair wrapped in a piece of paper from which there wafted a lovely fragrance. Heichū thought this was very strange indeed. This is the poem he found written there:

(152) Amanogawa	I had often heard
Sora naru mono to	That becoming a nun
Kikishikado	Was an empty act,
Waga me no mae no	But now it is sad reality
Namida narikeri	And I cannot help but weep.[9]

Realizing that she must have become a nun, Heichū was blinded by his tears. His heart in a turmoil, he asked the messenger what had happened. Weeping, the messenger replied: "She has already cut her hair and become a nun. That is why her attendants, in their bewilderment, have been weeping all day long both yesterday and today. Even the hearts of us humble menservants have been filled with deep sorrow. Oh, how could our mistress have cut her hair!'' By now Heichū was feeling utterly wretched. He thought to himself: ''Why did I ever lead such a wicked, debauched life? How can I endure such sorrow?'' Nonetheless, there was nothing he could do about the situation. He wrote this return poem, weeping all the while:

(153) Yo o waburu	You may have heard
Namida nagarete	That the world of reality
Hayaku tomo	Was truly a wretched place,
Amanogawa ni wa	But was it necessary
Sa ya wa narubeki	To become a nun so hastily?[10]

Heichū thereupon remarked: ''All this has been so unexpected that I am at a loss for words. I must go at once to her.'' He immediately made his way to the woman's home. In the meantime, she had shut herself up in a closet.[11] Heichū weeping uncontrollably, briefly explained to her servants why he had failed to come earlier. He then called out to the young woman: ''Please speak to me. Let me hear your voice, if nothing else.'' But she uttered not a word in reply. Heichū must have felt truly wretched, thinking that the young lady, unaware of the difficulties that had hampered him, probably imagined he was speaking merely out of pity.

104

A young woman sent the Minor Captain Shigemoto[1] this poem:

(154) Koishisa ni	My love is so great
Shinuru inochi o	I cannot go on living;
Omoiidete	If someone, remembering,
Tou hito araba	Should ask about me,
Nashi to kotaeyo	Please tell him I have died.[2]

The Minor Captain sent her this return poem:

(155) Kara ni dani	Tell her lifeless body
Ware kitari tee	That I came;
Tsuyu no mi no	We had once promised one another
Kieba tomo ni to	That we would die together.[3]
Chigiri okiteki	

105

When the Daughter of Nakaki,[1] the Assistant Governor of Ōmi, was possessed by an evil spirit and the Priest Jōzō[2] was serving as her faith healer, people began to gossip about them. At first there was no substance to the rumors, but once they began to meet in secret, the rumors grew worse. Thinking that he could not bear to live in such a society any longer, Jōzō disappeared. He sequestered himself in a place called Kurama[3] where he practiced strict religious discipline. In spite of himself, however, he still longed passionately for the woman. Recalling his happier days in the capital, he began to find everything about his austere life most depressing. One day he cried himself to sleep and when he awoke, he found a letter at his side. Wondering what sort of letter it might be, he picked it up and, glancing at it, discovered to his joy that it was from the woman he loved. She had written this poem:

(156) Sumizome no	I wish the priest,
Kurama no yama ni	Who went into
Iru hito wa	The dark mountain of Kurama,
Tadoru tadoru mo	Would come back to me,
Kaeri kinanan	Groping his way in the dark.[4]

Jōzō thought that this was strange indeed and wondered who had been asked to deliver the letter. He could not recall having seen any messenger. So puzzled was he that he found himself wandering back to the capital again. Returning immediately afterward to his mountain retreat, he sent her this poem:

(157) Karaku shite	I thought that I had
Omoi wasururu	At last forgotten you,
Koishisa o	But, alas, I was once again
Utate nakitsuru	Filled with longing
Uguisu no koe	As I read your letter.[5]

This was her reply:

(158) Sate mo kimi	You had forgotten me;
Wasurekerikashi	Is it right
Uguisu no	That you should remember me
Naku ori nomi ya	Only at times
Omoi izubeki	When the nightingale sings?

The Priest also composed this poem:

(159) Waga tame ni	Why should I resent the world,
Tsuraki hito o ba	Which is guiltless?
Okinagara	Except for you,
Nani no tsumi naki	Who have been so unkind to me,
Yo o ya uramin	No one else has hurt me so.[6]

The young woman had been brought up with much love and care. Princes and nobles alike had proposed to her, but her father, wishing to present her to the emperor himself, had not let her marry anyone. As a result of this disgraceful affair, however, even her father abandoned her.

106

The late Minister of War[1] used to visit the same girl[2] before she became involved in that disgraceful affair. On one occasion, the Prince sent her this poem:

(160) Ogi no ha no	I resent your cruel heart,
Soyogu goto ni zo	So like the reed
Uramitsuru	That shows its underleaves
Kaze ni utsurite	As it bends in whichever direction
Tsuraki kokoro o	The wind happens to blow.[3]

The Prince also composed this poem:

(161) Asaku koso
Hito wa mirurame
Sekigawa no
Tayuru kokoro wa
Araji to zo omou

Shallow it may appear
To the eyes of men,
But like Sekigawa
It will never cease—
My love for you.[4]

The girl sent the Prince this return poem:

(162) Sekigawa no
Iwama o kuguru
Mizu asami
Taenubeku nomi
Miyuru kokoro o

The water which flows
Between the boulders
Of the Sekigawa is shallow;
Momentarily, it will cease to flow,
Like your love.[5]

Although she was willing to express herself in this manner, she stubbornly refused to meet the Prince; he therefore went at night to see her. While the moon shone in all its splendor, he composed this poem:

(163) Yona yona ni
Izu to mishikado
Hakanakute
Irinishi tsuki to
Iite yaminan

How like the moon you are—
The moon which nightly appears
But sets all too soon;
No longer shall I seek
To win your love.[6]

On another occasion, the Prince dropped his fan. The girl picked it up and saw this poem written in a woman's hand which she did not recognize:

(164) Wasuraruru
Mi wa ware kara no
Ayamachi ni
Nashite dani koso
Kimi o uramime

I tell myself
That I have been forgotten
Through mistakes
Of my own making,
But I still resent you.[7]

The girl wrote next to it.

(165) Yuyushiku mo
Omōyuru kana
Hito goto ni
Utomarenikeru
Yo ni koso arikere

This world in which
You are bitterly resented
By each woman
From whom you have become estranged
Is a wretched place indeed![8]

She also composed this poem which she sent to the Prince:

(166) Wasuraruru
Tokiwa no yama mo
Ne o zo naku
Akino no mushi no
Koe ni midarete

Now that I am forgotten,
I shall weep on Mount Tokiwa,
My voice blending
With the cries of the insects
In the autumn field.[9]

The Prince's return poem went:

(167) Naku naredo
Obotsukanaku zo
Omōyuru
Koe kiku koto no
Ima wa kakereba

You say that you are weeping,
But I do not know
If you speak the truth,
For I cannot hear your voice
This very moment.

The Prince also sent her this poem:

(168) Kumoi nite
Yo o furu koro wa
Samidare no
Ame no shita ni zo
Ikeru kai naki

Spending my days
At the Cloud-Dwelling Palace,
The summer rain falls;
It is in vain
To go on living.[10]

This was the girl's return poem:

(169) Fureba koso
Koe mo kumoi ni
Kikoekeme
Itodo harukeki
Kokochi nomi shite

Feeling so estranged from you,
I weep loudly;
Surely my voice has been heard
At the Cloud-Dwelling Palace
Where you are.[11]

107

Another woman sent the Prince a poem which went:

(170) Au koto no	All I do now
Negau bakari ni	Is beg you for another meeting;
Narinureba	How nostalgically
Tada ni kaeshishi	I remember the time
Toki zo koishiki	I sent you away so coldly!

108

Princess Nan-in[1] was the daughter of Prince Muneyuki, the Master of the Right Division of the Capital. She served Princess Naishi,[2] the daughter of the Prime Minister. When the Captain of the Middle Palace Guards[3] was still called by his boyhood name Ayagimi, he often visited the Princess in her apartment. When his visits ceased altogether, she sent the following poem, attached to a withered pink:[4]

(171) Karisome ni	For a short while
Kimi ga fushimishi	You came and slept
Tokonatsu no	In my bed of pinks—
Ne mo karenishi o	How could it be
Ikade sakiken	That when the root has withered
	The flower has blossomed?[5]

109

The same woman once borrowed an ox which belonged to Ōki.[1] Some time later when she wanted to borrow the beast again, she was told: "The ox I lent you the other day has died." She thereupon replied with this poem:

(172) Waga norishi	Did the poor beast die,
Koto o ushi to ya	Finding it difficult
Kieniken	To carry me on his back?
Kusa ni kakareru	What a pity his life
Tsuyu no inochi wa	Was as brief as the dewdrops
	That linger on the grass![2]

110

The same woman sent this poem to a certain gentleman:

(173) Ōzora wa	There is not a cloud
Kumorazu nagara	In the vast heavens,
Kaminazuki	But in the Godless Month
Toshi no furu ni mo	I am keenly aware of the passage of time
Sode wa nurekeri	And my sleeve becomes wet once more.[1]

111

The daughters of Kinhira,[1] the Master of the Office of the Palace Table, lived in a place called Agata no Ido.[2] The eldest daughter was called Lady Shōshō and served the Empress.[3] The third daughter's first husband was Saneakira,[4] the Provincial Governor of Bingo, whom she married when he was still a young man. Because they had never lived together, the third daughter composed this poem which she sent to him:

(174) Kono yo ni wa	I shall end my life
Kakute mo yaminu	Resigned to my wretched fate;
Wakareji no	Oh, but whom shall I ask to guide me
Fuchise ni tare o	Across the pools and rapids
Toite wataran	When at last I leave this world?[5]

112

The same woman[1] once had a rendezvous with Morotada,[2] a Lieutenant of the Middle Palace Guards. Soon afterward she sent him a poem in which she described the events of the day:[3]

(175) Kochi kaze wa	All day long
Kyō higurashi ni	The east wind blew,
Fukumeredo	But surely tonight
Ame mo yo ni hata	Will not be
Yo ni mo araji na	Another night of rain.[4]

113

After the Lieutenant of the Middle Palace Guards became estranged from the woman, he made his way to the Kamo Shrine, having been selected to be one of the dancers at the Special Festival.[1] The woman and her attendants were also there to enjoy the festivities. Upon returning home, she sent this poem to the Lieutenant:

(176) Mukashi kite	Today, from afar,
Nareshi o sureru	I saw your patterned sleeve,
Koromode o	Which I had known so well
Ana mezurashi to	In the days gone by,
Yoso ni mishi kana	And thought what a rare sight it was![2]

In reply, the Lieutenant sent her a poem attached to yellow kerria roses:

(177) Morotomo ni	I recall nostalgically
Ide no sato koso	The time we were together
Koishikere	In the village of Ide;
Hitori ori uki	Oh, kerria roses—
Yamabuki no hana	How sad I am in my solitude![3]

The woman's return poem is not known.

When he began seeing her again, she composed this poem:

(178) Ōzora mo	Though I believed
Tada naranu kana	That I alone wept
Kaminazuki	Under the skies of the tenth month,
Ware nomi shita ni	Even the heavens above
Shiguru to omoeba	Now show signs of rain.[4]

She also composed this poem:

(179) Au koto no	Unable to meet you,
Nami no shitakusa	I conceal myself from sight,
Migakurete	Like the water plants,
Shizugokoro naku	And weep aloud,
Ne koso nakarure	My heart in a turmoil.[5]

114

At about the time of the Festival of the Weaver,[1] Princess Katsura[2] had a secret rendezvous with a young gentleman. Afterward she wrote to him:

(180) Sode o shimo	Though I did not
Kasazarishikado	Lend her my robes,
Tanabata no	They are now wet with tears
Akanu wakare ni	As we reluctantly parted
Hijinikeru kana	On the Weaver's Festival Day.[3]

115

When the Minister of the Right[1] was the First Secretary of the Sovereign's Private Office, he composed this poem and sent it to the Wet Nurse Shōni:[2]

(181) Aki no yo o
Mate to tanomeshi
Koto no ha ni
Ima mo kakareru
Tsuyu no hakanasa

"Wait until a night in autumn,"
Were the words I trusted in;
But they seem as empty now
As the ephemeral dew.[3]

She sent back this poem:

(182) Aki mo kozu
Tsuyu mo okanedo
Koto no ha wa
Waga tame ni koso
Iro kawarikere

Autumn has yet to come
And the dew has yet to form,
But we have not met;
Alas, your promises
Have lost their meaning.[4]

116

When the daughter of Kinhira was about to breathe her last, she composed this poem:

(183) Nagakeku mo
Tanomekeru kana
Yo no naka o
Sode ni namida no
Kakaru mi o mote

How I had hoped
That I might live long,
Even though my fate has been
So sad my sleeve
Is drenched with tears.[1]

117

On one occasion, Princess Katsura sent this poem to Yoshitane:[1]

(184) Tsuyu shigemi
Kusa no tamoto o
Makura nite
Kimi matsumushi no
Ne o nomi zo naku

Using as a pillow
My sleeve bedewed with tears,
Which so resembles the dew-laden
grass,
I cry like the cricket,
As I wait here for you.[2]

118

Princess Kan-in[1] composed this poem:

(185) Mukashi yori
Omou kokoro wa
Arisoumi no
Hana no masago wa
Kazu mo shirarezu

Having loved you sc long,
The depth of my love
Is as measureless
As the grains of sand
Along the rocky shore.[2]

119

There is a poem which Fujiwara no Saneki,[1] the late Provincial Governor of Michinoku, sent to the same woman. At the time, he was just recovering from a serious illness. He wrote to her, saying, "I should like very much to see you," and added in his letter this poem:

(186) Karaku shite
Oshimi tometaru
Inochi mote
Au koto o sae
Yaman to ya suru

My life has been saved
With the greatest effort;
Would you still
Keep me from seeing you?[2]

Princess Kan-in sent back this poem:

(187) Morotomo ni
Iza to wa iwade
Shide no yama
Nadoka wa hitori
Koen to wa seshi

Why did you not ask me
To go with you?
How could you have thought
To cross all alone
The Mountain of Death?[3]

On the night he went to her mansion, however, the Princess was apparently too busy to see him, and so he returned home in disappointment.

The next morning, Saneki sent her this poem:

(188) Akatsuki wa	At dawn today,
Naku yūtsuke no	I returned home,
Wabigoe ni	Crying in a voice
Otoranu ne o zo	No less pathetic
Nakite kaerishi	Than the forlorn crowing
	Of the cock.[4]

Princess Kan-in sent him this reply:

(189) Akatsuki no	I awoke from sleep
Nezame no mimi ni	At break of dawn,
Kikishikado	But all I could hear
Tori yori hoka no	Was the crowing
Koe wa sezariki	Of the cock.[5]

120

Although many years had passed since the Prime Minister[1] had been appointed a Minister of State, Lord Biwa[2] had yet to attain a rank of equal prestige. When, however, he was finally appointed to the position of Minister of State, the Prime Minister broke off a plum branch and stuck it in his cap in jubilation over his brother's promotion. He then composed this poem:

(190) Osoku toku	One late, one early,
Tsui ni sakikeru	Both have blossomed at last,
Ume no hana	These plum blossoms—
Taga ueokishi	Who planted the seeds
Tane ni ka aruran	For this glory?[3]

Writing down the events of that day and adding several poems, they decided to send the account to the High Priestess of Ise Shrine.[4]

The daughter of the Sanjō Minister of the Right[5] took this opportunity to write down this poem:

(191) Ikade kaku	How I wish I had
Toshikiri mo senu	The seed of a tree
Tane mo gana	That yearly puts forth blossoms!
Areyuku niwa no	I could then rely on it for shade
Kage to tanoman	In my neglected garden.[6]

I have forgotten the lines of the return poem from the High Priestess.

The young girl's wishes were granted in time. When the Minister of the Left[7] was still a Middle Counsellor, he lived with her, and their union was blessed with many children. At one point the High Priestess of the Ise Shrine sent this poem:

(192) Hanazakari	I have heard that you have planted
Haru wa mi ni kon	The seed of a tree
Toshigiri mo	That never fails to put forth blossoms;
Sezu to iū tane wa	I shall go to view it in the spring
Oinu to ka kiku	When they are at their loveliest.[8]

121

The lover of the daughter of Sanetō no Shōni[1] composed this poem:

(193) Fuetake no	Even when I spend
Hitoyo mo kimi to	A single night away from you,
Nenu toki wa	My cries, as I weep,
Chigusa no koe ni	Sound like the notes
Ne koso nakarure	Played on a flute.[2]

The woman replied:

(194) Chiji no ne wa	You exaggerated when you said
Kotoba no fuki ka	That you wept loudly,
Fuetake no	For I have yet
Kochiku no koe mo	To hear you say
Kikoe konaku ni	That you will come to me.[3]

122

Once when Toshiko visited the Shiga Temple,[1] a priest by the name of Zōki[2] happened to be there too. This priest was then living on Mount Hiei and often visited the court of Teiji no In. Since he arrived in Shiga on the very day of Toshiko's arrival, they became acquainted. In that they were both lodged in the *hashidono,*[3] they had occasion to exchange vows of every kind. Later, when Toshiko was preparing for her return journey, Zōki composed this poem:

(195) Aimite wa	If there were no parting
Wakaruru koto no	Following a lovers' meeting,
Nakariseba	I do not think
Katsugatsu mono wa	I would love you so dearly.[4]
Omowazaramashi	

This is the poem Toshiko sent in reply:

(196) Ikanareba	Oh, why did you say
Katsugatsu mono o	That you did not love me?
Omouran	Since you told me,
Nagori mo naku zo	I have been overcome
Ware wa kanashiki	By a deep sadness.[5]

A brief note accompanied the poem.

123

On another occasion, Zōki composed a poem and sent it to a young woman whose identity was not known:

(197) Kusa no ha ni	Is it because
Kakareru tsuyu no	My frail body resembles
Minareba ya	The dew on the grass
Kokoro ugoku ni	That my tears flow
Namida otsuran	At each beat of my heart?[1]

124

When the wife of the Hon-in[1] was still the wife of the Governor-General and Major Counsellor,[2] Heichū sent this poem to her:

(198) Haru no no ni	Green grow the clinging vines
Midori ni haeru	In the spring field—
Sanekazura	I want you to be my wife
Waga kimizane to	So that I might cling to you forever,
Tanomu ika ni zo	But how do you feel about me?[3]

On and on they corresponded, promising to love one another forever. Some time later she became very influential as the wife of the Minister of the Left. Heichū thereupon addressed this poem to her:

(199) Yukusue no	Do you recall
Sukuse mo shirazu	That I once pledged
Waga mukashi	My love to you long ago
Chigirishi koto wa	When I little dreamed
Omōyu ya kimi	Your future would be so bright?

The woman's return poem and other poems written earlier were numerous, but I have never heard them recited.

125

One day the Major Captain of Izumi[1] went to visit the late Minister of the Left.[2] He had had some saké on his way there and was quite inebriated when he unexpectedly showed up in the middle of the night. Surprised by this late visit, the Minister asked: "Where have you come from?" When his servants, making a great deal of racket, raised the upper half of the lattice door, the Minister saw that the Major Captain had Mibu no Tadamine[3] with him. Tadamine, holding aloft a burning pine torch at the foot of the stairs, knelt and said: "This is what my master wishes to say to you:

(200) Kasasagi no	Over the frost,
Wataseru hashi no	On the bridge formed by the
Shimo no ue o	magpies,
Yowa ni fumiwake	Have I trod
Kotosara ni koso	In the hush of night
	Especially to see you.[4]

The Minister, their host, was at once touched and amused by the poem. That night he held a drinking party for his guests at which musical entertainment was provided. He also presented gifts to the Major Captain and a reward to Tadamine.

A young gentleman, having heard that Tadamine had a daughter, said: "I wish to marry your daughter." Tadamine replied: "What a splendid match!" Soon afterward a message came from the man which said: "I hope that in the near future you will carry out your promise." In reply, Tadamine composed this poem:

(201) Waga yado no	Since my only daughter
Hitomura susuki	Is still as young as the pampas grass
Urawakami	Growing in my garden,
Musubi toki ni wa	It is not yet time
Mada shi karikeri	For her to marry.[5]

Indeed, she was still a very young girl.

126

Lady Higaki,[1] who lived in Tsukushi, was extremly witty and led a life of elegance and refinement until Sumitomo's revolt[2] when her house was destroyed by fire and all her furniture looted. What a pity this was!

Unaware of this misfortune, Ono no Yoshifuru,[3] the Senior Assistant Governor-General, arrived from the capital at the head of a punitive force. He looked for Lady Higaki's house where it had earlier stood and said: "I wish to locate the person called Lady Higaki. I wonder where she is living now." The men accompanying him said: "She used to live in this neighborhood." "What could have happened to her during the disturbances?" asked Yoshifuru. "I wish to see her again." Just then a gray-haired woman, who had gone to draw some water, passed by before them and went into a wretched-looking hovel. Someone then exclaimed: "Why, is that not Lady Higaki?" Feeling sorry for the woman, Yoshifuru called to her, but embarrassed to be seen in such a pathetic state, Lady Higaki refused to come out. Instead, she recited aloud this poem:

(202) Mubatama no	My jet-black hair
Waga kurokami wa	Has turned as white
Shirakawa no	As the waters of White River;
Mizu hagumu made	I at last realize
Narinikeru kana	How old I have grown.[4]

Yoshifuru was so moved by her pitiful state that he took off one of his robes[5] and presented it to her.

127

On another occasion, the same person[1] was induced to compose a poem on the autumn maple leaves at the mansion of the Senior Assistant Governor-General:

(203) Shika no ne wa	No sooner does the deer
Ikura bakari no	Begin to bell
Kurenai zo	Than the mountain to crimson turns;
Furiizuru kara ni	I wonder how much of the red
Yama no somuran	Is contained in its call.[2]

128

Lady Higaki was reputed to be a talented poetess. Once, when some men of taste had gathered together, they gave her what they believed was a difficult poem to complete. The poem began:

(204) Watatsumi no	In the midst of the ocean
Naka ni zo tateru	Is standing
Saoshika wa	A stag—

Lady Higaki added these lines:

Aki no yamabe ya	The autumn mountainside
Soko ni miyuran	May be seen there in the depths.[1]

129

A woman who lived in Tsukushi[1] composed this poem when sending off her lover to the capital:

(205) Hito o matsu	The house is which
Yado wa kuraku zo	I await your return
Narinikeru	Has grown dark and gloomy,
Chigirishi tsuki no	For I have yet to see you
Uchi ni mieneba	In the month you promised to return.[2]

130

The woman who lived in Tsukushi also composed this poem:

(206) Akikaze no	Is the heart
Kokoro ya tsuraki	Of the autumn wind so cruel
Hana susuki	That the pampas grass
Fukikuru kata o	Turns away from
Mazu somukuran	Whence it comes?[1]

131

During the reign of the former Emperor,[1] His Majesty, on the first day of the fourth month,[2] gave the command for those present to compose poems on a nightingale that would not sing. Kintada[3] composed this poem:

(207) Haru wa tada	Spring ended only yesterday
Kinō bakari o	And yet today the nightingale
Uguisu no	No longer sings,
Kagireru goto mo	As if it were confined
Nakanu kyō kana	To a given season.[4]

132

Once, during the reign of the same Emperor, His Majesty summoned Mitsune[1] into his presence, and on a night when the moon was exceedingly lovely, he made arrangements for various forms of entertainment to be provided.[2] His Majesty said: "What do people mean when they remark that the moon is bow-shaped? Please compose a poem in answer to this question." Mitsune, who was attending upon His Majesty at the foot of the stairs, recited these lines:

(208) Teru tsuki o	The crescent moon
Yumihari to shimo	Is called the Bow-Shaped Moon,
Iū koto wa	For it sets behind the mountain
Yamabe o sashite	As if it had been shot
Ireba narikeri	From a tautly drawn bow.[3]

As a reward, Mitsune received a specially tailored underrobe.[4] He then composed this poem:

(209) Shirakumo no	This robe covers my shoulders
Kono kata ni shimo	Like a white cloud—
Oriiru wa	How fully conscious I am
Amatsu kaze koso	Of having been favored
Fukite kitsurashi	By His Majesty![5]

133

One night, when the moon was especially lovely, the same Emperor stealthily made a round of the women's apartments, accompanied by Kintada. Suddenly a very attractive woman, who was wearing a dark crimson robe, emerged from one of the rooms crying bitterly. His Majesty had Kintada approach her to see what was the matter, whereupon the woman let her long hair fall forward to conceal her face and continued to weep. Kintada asked: "Why are you crying so?" But the young woman made no reply. Even His Majesty thought that her behavior was very strange. At this point, Kintada composed the following poem:

(210) Omouran	Though I know not
Kokoro no uchi wa	What she feels in her heart,
Shiranedomo	Seeing her cry so bitterly
Naku o miru koso	Makes me feel sad too.[1]
Wabishikarikere	

Deeply moved, the Emperor praised highly Kintada's verse.

134

During the reign of the former Emperor, a pretty little girl lived in one of the palace apartments. His Majesty beheld her one day and secretly summoned her into his presence. He told not a soul about this and thereafter often had her come to him. One day he recited this poem to her:

(211) Akade nomi	It is surely
Mireba narubeshi	Because I have not seen
Awanu yo mo	Enough of you;
Au yo mo hito o	Whether I see you or not,
Aware to zo omou	I long for you each night.[1]

The young girl was so touched that she was unable to keep the words of His Majesty to herself. One day she blurted out to her companions: "This is what His Majesty said to me!" Her mistress, the Empress, heard of this and dismissed the young girl. How severe she was!

135

When the daughter of the Sanjō Minister of the Right first began having a love affair with Tsutsumi no Chūnagon,[1] he was then the Assistant Director of the Bureau of Palace Storehouses and served in the Inner Palace. Since she did not seem very enthusiastic, she probably did not care much for him. At any rate, Tsutsumi no Chūnagon could not always be with her, for he had duties to perform at the Imperial Palace. Once while he was away, the woman sent him this poem:

(212) Takimono no	Although I regret
Kuyuru kokoro wa	Ever having met you,
Arishikado	When I am alone,
Hitori wa taete	I cannot get a wink of sleep.[2]
Nerarezarikeri	

His return poem was undoubtedly good, since he was an outstanding poet, but not having listened closely to it, I am unable to quote it here.

136

On another occasion, the man[1] sent this message to the woman: "Being very busy these days, I have not called on you. But even as I hurry about performing my duties, I am deeply troubled, thinking of how you must feel about my not being able to come to you." In reply the young woman wrote:

(213) Sawagu naru	You think of me
Uchi ni mo mono wa	Even when you are busy;
Omounari	To what then shall I compare
Waga tsurezure o	My endless yearning
Nani ni tatoen	As I live each day
	In utter boredom?

137

His Highness, the late Minister of War,[1] had a magnificent mansion built at Iwae on the road to Shiga Pass[2] and occasionally visited the place. There were also times when he made his way to the mansion in the utmost secrecy and watched the women go by on their way to worship at Shiga Temple. The surrounding scenery was exceedingly lovely, and the mansion itself stately.

One day Toshiko stopped by on her way to the temple and, walking around the mansion, gazed about her. Deeply impressed, she expressed her admiration in a poem:

(214) Kari ni nomi	How sad the autumn is
Kuru kimi matsu to	On Mount Shiga
Furiidetsutsu	Where the deer belling loudly
Naku Shigayama wa	Awaits your coming
Aki zo kanashiki	On a hunting trip.[3]

Before departing, Toshiko wrote down her poem.

138

A young man called Koyakushi courted a young woman. One day he sent her this poem:

(215) Kakurenu no	My love for you—
Soko no shitakusa	Hidden like the plants
Migakurete	Growing at the bottom
Shirarenu koi wa	Of the grassy swamp—
Kurushikarikeri	Brings me naught but pain.[1]

The young woman's return poem:

(216) Migakure ni	I do not believe
Kakaru bakari no	That the water plant
Shitakusa wa	Is very long,
Nagakaraji tomo	For it is so easily concealed
Omōyuru kana	In the waters of the swamp.[2]

Koyakushi was extremely short in stature.

139

During the reign of the former Emperor,[1] a young woman called Lady Chūnagon[2] served in the apartment of the Sokyōden no Miyasundokoro.[3] When His Highness, the late Minister of War, was a young man and still called by his childhood name Ichinomiya, he lived near the Sokyōden, having one love affair after the other. Having heard that there were women in the Sokyōden who were at once experienced and fascinating, he often went to converse with the ladies. At about this time he secretly began to spend his nights with Lady Chūnagon. At first the Prince visited her regularly, but in time he hardly ever called on her. It was then that Lady Chūnagon sent him this poem:

(217) Hito o toku	People say that you soon tire
Akutagawa chō	Of each new love;
Tsu no kuni no	Indeed you are
Naniwa tagawanu	As fickle as
Kimi ni zo arikeru	You are reputed to be.[4]

Unable to eat and weeping unceasingly in her longing, Lady Chūnagon fell gravely ill. One day she broke off a snow-covered branch of a pine tree growing in front of the Sokyōden and recited:

(218) Konu hito o	As I await my lover
Matsu no ha ni furu	Who fails to come,
Shirayuki no	I feel that I shall pine away,
Kie koso kaere	Vanishing like the snow
Awanu omoi ni	On the pine needles.[5]

She handed the branch to the messenger to be delivered, saying, "See that you do not shake off the snow."

140

His Highness, the late Minister of War, once had a love affair with the daughter of Noboru,[1] the Major Counsellor. One night, instead of sleeping in the usual bedchamber, he spread his bedding out in one of the adjoining rooms[2] and slept there. The next day he returned to his mansion and did not come again to visit the young lady for some time. Presently he sent this message to her: "Is the bedding which I had spread out in the adjoining room just as I left it, or have you folded it away?" By way of reply she sent him this poem:

(219) Shikikaezu	Your bedding is left
Arishinagara ni	Just as it was,
Kusamakura	But the dust lies thickly
Chiri nomi zo iru	On your pillow,
Harau hito nami	Since there is no one here
	To brush it away.[3]

His reply:

(220) Kusamakura	I shall soon be there
Chiri harai ni wa	To brush the dust from my pillow,
Karagoromo	But please wait until
Tamoto yutaka ni	I have made a Chinese robe
Tatsu o mate kashi	With sleeves cut wide.[4]

The daughter of Noboru thereupon sent him this poem:

(221) Karagoromo	While I wait for you
Tatsu o matsu ma no	To have your sleeve made wider,
Hodo koso wa	The dust will continue
Waga shikitae no	To collect
Chiri mo tsumorame	On your bedding.[5]

When he called on her again, he said: "I shall soon be off on a hunting trip to Uji." To this the woman replied:

(222) Mikari suru	More forlorn am I
Kurikomayama no	To have to spend
Shika yori mo	The night alone
Hitori nuru mi zo	Than the deer on Mount Kurikoma
Wabishikarikeru	Where you go a-hunting.[6]

141

Among the brothers of the Imperial Adviser called Yoshiie[1] was the Secretary of Yamato province.[2] He once brought back with him a young woman from Tsukushi[3] whom he installed in his principal wife's house.

Fortunately for him, his principal wife got along very well with the new wife. The two women often found themselves living together, for the Secretary was forever going off to one province or another. In time the woman from Tsukushi began having a secret love affair. Since people gossiped a good deal about her affair, she composed this peom:

(223) Yowa ni idete	If only the moon
Tsuki dani mizu wa	Had not observed me
Au koto o	Stealing out into the night;
Shirazugao ni mo	I could then feign innocence
Iwamashi mono o	And declare that we had never met.[4]

Although the young woman was behaving indiscreetly, the principal wife, who was a person of great tact and refinement, did not mention the new wife's unfaithfulness to her husband. Nevertheless, he himself learned from another source that the woman had a lover. The Secretary was troubled by the report, but instead of becoming terribly upset, he allowed her to stay on in his home, even after discovering what she was really like.

Now that he knew about the woman's lover, he asked her one day: "Which of us do you really love—your new lover or me?" The woman replied:

(224) Hana susuki	It appears
Kimi ga kata ni zo	That the flowering pampas
Nabikumeru	Still bends in your direction,
Omowanu yama no	Though an undersirable wind
Kaze wa fukedomo	Comes blowing
	From the mountain-top.[5]

Shortly afterward, another gentleman came to court her, but the woman said: "I shall never take on another lover. The relationship between a man and a woman is much too painful!'' Despite her emphatic declaration, she gradually was attracted to this particular man, for she began answering his letters. The woman wrote to the principal wife, folding a knot at one end of the rolled stationery.[6] The letter held this poem:

(225) Mi o ushi to	Once again I am falling in love
Omou kokoro no	With someone new;
Korineba ya	Have I not learned by now
Hito o aware to	The heartaches
Omoisomuran	Love can bring?[7]

This poem clearly indicated that she had failed to learn from her past experience.

The Secretary had once loved this woman with all his heart, and she in turn had admired him greatly. However, his passion for her gradually cooled, and when she indicated her desire to return to her family in Tsukushi, the man, no longer enamored of her, allowed her to go. He made no effort to detain her, for he knew that things could never be the same again. The principal wife, having by now grown accustomed to living with the woman, was very sad to see her go. She accompanied the woman as far as Yamazaki[8] to see that she boarded the boat safely. The Secretary also accompanied them.

The principal wife and the secondary wife spent the entire day discussing a number of topics, and early the next morning the latter boarded the boat. Thinking that they ought to be getting back, the Secretary and his wife got into their carriage. They, as well as the woman on board the boat, were greatly saddened by the imminent parting. Just then a messenger made his way up to the Secretary and his wife and handed them a letter from the woman about to depart. All that she had written was:

(226) Futari koshi	This does not look like
Michi tomo mienu	The road we had once taken;
Nami no ue o	Little did I dream
Omoikakedemo	That you would coldly
Kaesumeru kana	Send me back over the waves.[9]

The Secretary and his principal wife were so deeply moved that they could not suppress their tears. Meanwhile, because the boat had already left the shore, they were unable to send the woman a return poem. Their carriage remained where it was as they watched the boat sail off into the distance. On board the boat, the woman sought hard to catch one last glimpse of the carriage. On the shore, the Secretary and his wife, feeling very forlorn, watched until the woman's face became a tiny dot.

142

The elder sister[1] of the late Empress was the eldest daughter in the family. She was a woman of experience, and her poetic talents far surpassed that of any of her younger sisters, including the Empress herself. When she was young, she lost her mother. There were times when she could not always have her way, since she was brought up by her step-mother. On one occasion, she composed this poem:

(227) Arihatenu	While waiting for
Inochi matsu ma no	The end of my life,
Hodo bakari	I hope that I shall know
Ukikoto shigeku	Little of sorrow.[2]
Nagekazu mo gana	

Breaking off a flowering plum branch, she recited still another poem:

(228) Kakaru ka no	If the fragrance
Aki mo kawarazu	Of the plum blossoms
Nioiseba	Were as sweet in the fall,
Haru koishi chō	Would I long so much
Nagame semashi ya	For the perfumed spring?[3]

The elder sister of the Empress was most elegant and beautiful. Many men courted her, but she refused even to answer any of their letters. Her father and step-mother complained to her, saying, "It would not do for a woman to remain unmarried. You really should answer a gentleman's letter now and then.'' Thus reproached by her parents, she sent her latest suitor this poem:

(229) Omoedomo	Though I long for you,
Kai nakarubemi	I know that I love in vain;
Shinobureba	But since I conceal
Tsurenaki tomo ya	My true feelings,
Hito no miruran	How heartless I must seem!

She had nothing more to say apart from the poem. The reason why she had written the poem in the first place was that she had overheard her parents say: ''We must find a husband for our daughter.'' Nevertheless, she kept insisting: ''I shall never marry as long as I live.'' Just as she had predicted, she died in her twenty-ninth year still single.

143

Long ago there lived a woman who later became the wife of a man called Zaiji-gimi,[1] the son of Zai Chūjō.[2] The woman was the niece of the Middle Counsellor Yamakage[3] and was called Lady Gojō. Zaiji-gimi met her for the first time when he went to visit his younger sister, who was then the wife of the Provincial Governor of Ise.[4] Lady Gojō was then serving as the Provincial Governor's personal attendant. In spite of this, Zaiji-gimi, the elder brother of the Provincial Governor's wife, began having a secret love affair with Lady Gojō. He seriously believed that he was her only lover, but he soon discovered, to his dismay, that his own brothers[5] were also visiting her. He therefore wrote:

(230) Wasurenan to	The sadness I feel
Omou kokoro no	At the thought
Kanashiki wa	That I must forget you
Uki mo ukaranu	Is so great my other griefs
Mono ni zo arikeru	Are not so painful.[6]

All this happened a long time ago.

144

It was probably because Zai Chūjō had gone to the Eastland that Zaiji-gimi and the other sons of Zai Chūjō traveled widely from province to province. At any rate, Zaiji-gimi was very poetic by nature and, whenever he found himself in an unfamiliar province and was feeling lonely and sad, he would compose a poem and write it down. The post-town of Ofusa[1] was located on the seacoast. Once, when Zaiji-gimi was visiting there, he wrote down this poem:

(231) Watatsumi to
Hito ya miruran
Au koto no
Namida o fusa ni
Nakitsumetsureba

I suppose people
Look upon this place as the sea
Because I have shed in grief
An ocean of tears
Over not being able to see you.[2]

Some time later, when Zaiji-gimi was at a place called Minowa Village,[3] he jotted down this poem:

(232) Itsu wa to wa
Wakanedo taete
Aki no yo zo
Mi no wabishisa wa
Shirimasarikeru

I always feel
A vague sadness,
But I feel far more keenly
My deep melancholy
On a night in autumn.[4]

Zaiji-gimi traveled from one province to another until he finally arrived in the province of Kai[5] where he remained for some time. While there, he fell seriously ill. Realizing that he was about to die, he composed this poem:

(233) Karisome no
Yukikaiji to zo
Omoishi o
Ima wa kagiri no
Kadode narikeri

I thought that this would be
A short trip to Kai,
But I have a feeling
That this is the last journey
I shall ever go on.[6]

Zaiji-gimi died soon after writing the above poem.

A gentleman who had formerly accompanined Zaiji-gimi in his distant wanderings happened to stop over at the same post-town on his way to the capital from the province of Mikawa.[7] Recognizing Zaiji-gimi's hand as he read the poem, the man was stricken with grief.

145

Teiji no In once made his way to the mouth of the Yodo River. A courtesan[1] named Shiro was living there at the time. His Majesty sent a messenger to summon her into his presence, whereupon Shiro immediately went to serve him. However, since there were a great many nobles, courtiers, and princes present, Shiro withdrew to a spot far away from His Majesty. Teiji no In thereupon gave this command: "Compose a poem on the theme of waiting on me from afar." In compliance with His Majesty's request, Shiro recited these lines:

(234) Hama chidori	Since a plover can fly
Tobiyuku kagiri	Only so far,
Arikereba	It gazes vacantly
Kumotatsu yama o	At the cloud-covered mountain
Awa to koso mire	In the distance.[2]

His Majesty was delighted with her poem and bestowed upon her a prize.

It is said that Shiro also composed this poem:

(235) Inochi dani	If my life
Kokoro ni kanau	Could be fashioned
Mono naraba	Exactly as I wished,
Nanika wakare no	Why should parting
Kanashikaramashi	Be so sad?[3]

146

Teiji no In once made his way to Torikai Palace.[1] As always, various forms of entertainment were provided for his amusement. Meanwhile His Majesty casually asked if any of the many courtesans of the district who had come to wait on him had an especially pleasing voice and was of good birth. The courtesans replied: "We happen to have among us today a woman known as the daughter of Ōe no Tamabuchi.[2] His Majesty was impressed by the woman's beauty and summoned her to his side. He asked the courtesan: "Are you really the daughter of Tamabuchi?" Immediately afterward he commanded everyone present to compose a poem on the place named Torikai. His Majesty then turned to the young courtesan and said: "Tamabuchi was known to have been very talented and excelled especially in poetry. Therefore, only if you are able to compose a verse mentioning Torikai shall I believe that you are his daughter." The girl responded with this poem:

(236) Asa midori	Now that I have seen
Kai aru haru ni	The fertile spring
Ainureba	In her light greenery,
Kasumi naranedo	I appear before Your Majesty,
Tachinoborikeri	Though of humble birth am I.[3]

This poem pleased His Majesty who was moved to tears. Everyone was feeling quite tipsy by this time, and so they too began to weep. Teiji no In presented the courtesan with a set of robes and a divided skirt. To the various nobles, princes, and holders of the Fourth and Fifth Ranks, His Majesty said: "Those of you who refuse to offer a robe to this young woman must leave the room." Then, one after the other, starting at one end of the room, those of high as well as low rank presented their robes to the girl. The robes were far too many in number for her to carry and had to be stacked up in two different piles. When Teiji no In and his retinue were about to return to the capital, a man called His Lordship Nan-in no Shichirō[4] was summoned into his presence. Having heard that he had built his house in the young courtesan's neighborhood, His Majesty gave Shichirō the following instructions: "Please report to me her every move. I shall be sending gifts for her to your mansion. Above all, see that no harm befalls her." Shichirō obeyed His Majesty's request and often visited the courtesan to see that all went well.

147

Long ago, there was a young maiden who lived in the province of Settsu.[1] Two young men courted her. One of them, who belonged to the Mubara clan,[2] lived in Settsu province; the other was from the province of Izumi.[3] His clan was called Chinu. These two youths were alike in age, looks, and social status. The maiden thought that she would marry the one whose love for her was the greater, but then even their love for her was of the same intensity. When darkness fell, the two young men came together to call on her. And even when they sent her presents, they sent the same articles. Since she had no way to determine which of the youths was the superior, she found herself in a terrible predicament. If their affection for her had been tepid, she could have turned them both down. However, since the two men, for a long period of time, faithfully came and stood at her gate, demonstrating in countless ways how great was their love, she was at a loss what to do.

Although she refused the gifts brought to her by her admirers, they brought her still more, of every kind, and patiently stood outside with them. One day her mother said: "How sorry I feel for those men. You have made them both suffer in vain for so long. If you marry one of them, the other will surely abandon his suit." The girl replied: "That is the way I feel, but I find myself in such an awkward position. Their love for me seems about equal. Oh, what am I to do?"

The girl was living at this time in a pavilion[4] which had been set up on a bank of the Ikuta River.[5] Her mother summoned the two youths who were trying to win her daughter's hand and said: "It seems that both of you love my daughter equally well. She has therefore been sorely troubled as to which of you she should choose. I would like to settle the matter this very day. One of you has come from a distant place; the other lives in this province. Nonetheless, both of you have suffered greatly. Let me express my deepest sympathy for you two. When the men heard the girl's mother speak to them in this way, they felt extremely pleased. The mother continued: "What I would like you to do is to shoot that waterfowl floating on the river. I shall offer my daughter to the man who succeeds." "A splendid idea!" exclaimed the young men. But, alas! they both hit the target—one of them managed to strike the bird's head, the other its tail. Since no one could, in all fairness, say which one had won, the girl was more perplexed than ever and composed this poem:

(237) Sumiwabinu	How weary I am of life!
Waga mi nageten	Let me cast myself into the Ikuta—
Tsu no kuni no	The River of Living Fields—
Ikuta no kawa wa	Of Tsu province;
Na nomi narikeri	Then will Ikuta be but a name.[6]

Because the pavilion was built over the river, the girl threw herself directly into the water. Greatly alarmed, her mother called for help, whereupon the two youths immediately threw themselves into the river where the girl had jumped in. One of the young men grasped the girl's feet and the other her hands. Thus, in this tragic manner, all three drowned. Terribly distraught, the mother retrieved their bodies. Soon afterward, overcome by tears though she was, she made arrangements for the funeral service for the two youths and her daughter.

The fathers of the young men also attended the funeral. When they were about to bury the youths in the mounds raised for them alongside the maiden's grave-mound, the father of the young man from Settsu province objected, saying, "The young man from the same province as the girl has every right to be buried here, but is it fitting for his rival from another province to defile the earth of this province by being buried here too?" The father of the young man from Izumi province thereupon shipped in some earth from his province to the spot set aside for his son and buried him next to the maiden. Thus, even today, the maiden's grave, located in the middle, is flanked on the right and on the left by the grave-mounds of her admirers.

Someone depicted this tragic tale of long ago in a detailed painting and presented it to the late Empress.[7] Everyone present tried to imagine themselves in the place of one of the three tragic people and composed a number of poems. Lady Ise,[8] expressing the feelings of one of the youths, composed this poem:

(238) Kage to nomi	Our shadowy forms
Mizu no shita nite	Are now united
Aimiredo	At the river's bottom,
Tama naki kara wa	But of what use to me
Kai nakarikeri	Is your body
	Without a soul?[9]

Onna-ichi no Miko,[10] pretending to be the maiden, recited this poem:

(239) Kagiri naku	My soul,
Fukaku shizumeru	Which has sunk deep beneath
Waga tama wa	The river's surface,
Ukitaru hito ni	Will never be united
Mien mono ka wa	With a drifting, faithless lover.

Onna-ichi no Miko also recited:

(240) Izuku ni ka	Not even knowing
Tama o motomen	Whether it is here or there
Watatsu umi no	In the vast stretches
Koko kashiko tomo	Of the sea,
Omōenaku ni	Where shall I search for her soul?[11]

Hyōe no Myōbu[12] then composed this poem:

(241) Tsuka no ma mo	Though to others it may seem
Morotomo ni to zo	That we had never met,
Chigirikeru	We promised to stay together,
Au to wa hito ni	Even in our graves,
Mienu mono kara	Never parting for a moment.[13]

The Head of the Sewing Department[14] recited,

(242) Kachimake mo	Though we vied
Nakute ya haten	To win your love,
Kimi ni yori	Must we die
Omoikurabu no	With neither of us
Yama wa koyutomo	Emerging victorious?[15]

She went on to express what might have been the feelings of the maiden before she died:

(243) Au koto no	It grieves me so
Katami ni uuru	To hear that you
Nayotake no	Were forced to stand outside,
Tachiwazurau to	Finding it impossible
Kiku zo kanashiki	To come to me.[16]

She also came up with this poem:

(244) Mi o nagete	I do not recall promising
Awan to hito ni	I would be united with him
Chigiranedo	By throwing myself into the river,
Ukimo wa mizu ni	But now our bodies
Kage o narabetsu	Lie side by side in the water.[17]

Picturing herself in the place of the rival, the Head of the Sewing Department composed the following poem:

(245) Onaji e ni	It is my happy fate
Sumu wa ureshiki	To be able to dwell with you
Naka naredo	In the same bay,
Nado ware to nomi	But why did you not
Chigirazariken	Pledge yourself to me alone?[18]

This is a return poem the maiden might have come up with:

(246) Ukarikeru	I wish I had not promised you
Waga mi na soko o	That my wretched body
Ōkata wa	Would sink
Nakaru chigiri no	To the river's bottom.[19]
Nakaramashikaba	

Imagining herself to be one of the youths, the Head of the Sewing Department composed this poem:

(247) Ware to nomi	Not only to me
Chigirazu nagara	Did you promise yourself,
Onaji e ni	But I feel content
Sumu wa ureshiki	Dwelling with you
Migiwa to zo omou	At the river's edge.[20]

To continue with our story, the father of one of the young men cut down some tall bamboos and set up a fence around his son's grave. He buried together with his son's body a hunting cloak, a divided skirt, a cap, and a sash. He also added to these a bow, a quiver, and a sword. The father of the other youth was probably not so thoughtful, for he failed to do the same for his son. These mounds are known today as the Maiden's Tomb.

A traveler once spent the night at the foot of these burial mounds. Hearing unusual sounds of violent quarreling, he thought this very strange and called his companion's attention to the sounds. However, his companion said: "You should not be disturbed by them." Still feeling uneasy, the traveler fell asleep. Presently a man, smeared with blood, appeared before him and, kneeling, said: "I have been attacked by my rival and am in grave danger. Please lend me your sword for a while. I wish to take vengeance on that hated enemy of mine."

The traveler was alarmed, but he lent the young man his sword. When he awoke, he tried to convince himself that it had all been a terrible nightmare. However, he realized that he must have actually handed over his sword, for it was gone. He strained his ears for some time when again, as before, he heard a heated argument and an ensuing scuffle. Soon afterward, the man reappeared and triumphantly said: "I have you to thank for having been able to kill a man I have hated for many years past. Henceforth, I shall be your protector." The young man proceeded to relate the whole story from the beginning. The traveler thought that the tale was at once eerie and fascinating. As he listened to the story, day began to dawn and before he was aware of it the young man had vanished.

When it grew a little lighter, he noticed blood stains at the foot of the grave-mounds and on his sword. This is a rather gory tale, but I have written it down exactly as it was told to me.

148

There once was a man who lived in a house which he had built in the Naniwa district of Settsu province.[1] This man was intimate with a young woman for many years. Neither he nor the woman was of particularly humble birth, but as the years went by, they fell on difficult times. As their house gradually grew dilapidated, one by one their servants deserted them for mansions of the rich. Eventually they found themselves living all alone. Being of good birth, they could not very well be employed by other people or become servants. They felt truly unhappy and, in their desperation, said to each other: "We cannot go on enduring such hardship indefinitely." The man said: "How could I ever desert you and go elsewhere when I see you looking so sad?" And the woman, in her turn, insisted: "I should have nowhere to go if I left your side."

Nonetheless, the man said resolutely: "I can get along somehow, but it would be a pity for a woman as young as you to live out your life so wretchedly. Please make your way to the capital and enter the service of a nobleman. When you have attained a position of importance, come and visit me. As for myself, I shall certainly seek you out if ever I regain my position." Weeping, the couple made their promises to each other. The woman asked a relative to escort her to the capital.

Having no particular destination in mind, she stayed at the home of the relative with whom she had traveled, all the while yearning for her husband far away. Reeds and pampas grass grew luxuriantly in front of the house. Whenever the wind rustled through the tall growth, she nostalgically thought of Settsu province. In her anxiety over her husband, she grew increasingly melancholy. It was then that she composed this poem, which she recited softly to herself:

(248) Hitori shite	In my solitude,
Ika ni semashi to	I sadly wonder what to do,
Wabitsureba	But the only reply
Soyo tomo mae no	Is the rustling
Ogi zo kotauru	Of the reeds before me.[2]

The young woman wandered about from place to place before obtaining a position in a nobleman's household. Being in service in so grand an establishment, she dressed elegantly. Furthermore, since her daily life was one of relative comfort, she became strikingly beautiful. Nevertheless, she did not for a single moment forget Settsu province and sadly longed for her old home. Whenever anyone happened to be going to her native province, she would ask him to deliver a letter to her former husband, but each time she would receive the disheartening news that no one knew of such a man. To make matters worse, since she had no intimate friend, she could not discreetly send messengers as often as she wished. Feeling gravely concerned about the welfare of her former husband, she constantly wondered how he was getting along.

Meanwhile the principal wife of the nobleman in whose mansion she served passed away. From among the women attendants, it was with this woman that the lord of the mansion fell in love. She too was attracted to her master and in time became his wife. The woman seemed to be free from anxiety and quite content, but deep in her heart, one thought, unknown to others, plagued her night and day. She never ceased to worry about her former husband and wondered if he had met with bad times or had prospered. She thought of sending someone to ask after him, since he could not possibly know where she was now living. However, fearing that her present husband would undoubtedly hear of it and be extremely displeased, she contained her impulse. The young woman thus endured patiently each day that went by.

In time, however, she could no longer restrain her anxiety over the welfare of her former husband. One day she turned to her present husband and said: "I would like to go to Settsu province which is said to be a very scenic place. It will give me an opportunity to participate in the purification ceremony at Naniwa."[3] Her husband replied: "Splendid! I will go with you." "Oh, please don't. I would like to go alone," insisted the wife and departed.

When she was about to return home after having offered prayers during the ceremony at Naniwa, she said: "There is something here I have to see. Please drive the carriage as I direct you." After they had traveled some distance, they reached the site of her former home. She searched the area in vain for the house and her first husband. "I wonder where he has gone," she thought sadly. The woman had come all the way expressly to see her former husband once again, but since she had no confidante among her attendants, she had absolutely no way of asking after the man. Despairing, she stopped the carriage and gazed blankly about her.

The woman's attendants said: "It will soon grow dark. Let us be on our way." "Wait a while longer," entreated their mistress. Just then a man carrying a bundle of rushes on his shoulder and looking for all the world like a beggar passed in front of their carriage. The woman scrutinized his face but could not say for certain that he was her former husband, for this man looked so wretched. But she noticed a distinct resemblance, and desiring to get a closer look at the man, the woman said to her attendants: "Please summon that man with the rushes. I wish to buy his bundle of rushes."

Hearing their mistress' request, her attendants wondered why she wanted to purchase something which would be of no use whatsoever. However, this was after all what their mistress wished, and so they asked the man to come up to the carriage so that she could make her puchase. The lady said: "Please bring your bundle of rushes here and let me have a closer look at it." The man did as he was requested. All the while the woman carefully scrutinized his face and saw that he was indeed her former husband. "How wretched he must feel to have to eke out a scanty existence by selling rushes!" exclaimed the woman and began to weep. Her attendants thought that she was merely displaying compassion toward an unfortunate.

The lady directed her waiting women: "Please offer the man

something to eat. And when you pay him for the rushes, give him more than the amount he asks." "Why should we pay a total stranger more than he asks for?" protested her attendants. She could not insist on anything so unreasonable, so the woman tried to think of a way in which she might slip something more to the man.

Meanwhile, he had been staring at her through an opening in the silk curtains[4] and saw that the woman resembled his former wife. "How very strange," he thought, but he somehow managed to calm the turmoil in his heart and studied her further. He decided by her face and voice that she was none other than his former wife. However, when he compared his wretched appearance with her splendor, he suddenly lost his composure and, unable to remain in her presence, threw down the bundle of rushes and fled.

"Wait!" cried the woman, but the man ran into a nearby house and crouched at the far corner of the hearth. The woman called out from her carriage: "Search for him and bring him here!" Her attendants scattered and noisily carried out their search for the man. Someone presently reported: "He's in that house." The lady's attendants called out to the man: "We have been requested by our mistress to fetch you. We shall not mistreat you in any way. All we want to do is present you with a little gift. What a silly man you are to run away like that!" The man asked for an inkstone and proceeded to write a letter in which he included this poem:

<table>
<tr><td>(249)</td><td>Kimi nakute
Ashikarikeri to
Omou ni mo
Itodo Naniwa no
Ura zo sumiuki</td><td>When I think of
How I have gathered rushes
In your absence,
I find it most unbearable
To live near Naniwa Bay.[5]</td></tr>
</table>

After sealing the letter, the man said: "Please deliver this to the lady in the carriage." The attendants thought his request very strange but did as they were told. When their mistress unsealed the letter and read her former husband's poem, she was greatly saddened and sobbed aloud. I do not know what she wrote by way of a return poem. She sent him the outer robe she had been wearing together with a letter she had written. The unhappy woman then made her way home. It is not known what became of the two thereafter.

(250) Ashikaraji	We went our separate ways,
Tote koso hito no	Thinking that things
Wakarekeme	Could not become worse;
Nanika Naniwa no	Why, then, should I feel forlorn,
Ura mo sumiuki	Living here at Naniwa Bay?[6]

149

Long ago there lived a man and a woman in the Katsuragi district[1] of Yamato province. The young woman was strikingly beautiful. The two were deeply in love with each other and had lived together for many years, but as time went by the woman lost her looks. Although the man took great pains to help her and was extremely fond of her, he found himself another wife. The new wife was wealthy. He did not love her especially, but she treated him kindly whenever he visited her and provided him with magnificent robes. He gradually grew so accustomed to her lavish household that his first wife seemed to him very wretched indeed. Nevertheless, he felt sorry for the poor woman, especially since outwardly she showed no signs of jealousy.

Deep in her heart, however, his first wife was terribly jealous but was careful to conceal her true feelings. Even on nights when he planned to stay away, she would cheerfully say: "Please have a good time." Because of her strange attitude, her husband thought: "Although I do as I please, she does not seem to be jealous. She must be having a secret love affair of her own; otherwise, she would certainly resent my being unfaithful to her."

One evening he pretended to leave for the other woman's house, only to hide among the shrubbery in the front garden to watch for her lover. Presently the woman stepped out onto the veranda and, in the light of the moon which was especially lovely that night, she began to comb her hair. The night deepened, and still she had not retired for the evening. Sighing forlornly and lost in reverie, she appeared to be waiting for her lover. Turning to her servant who was standing in front of her, the woman recited this poem:

(251) Kaze fukeba	When the wind blows,
Okitsu shiranami	The white waves rise—
Tatsutayama	My lover is probably crossing
Yowa ni ya kimi ga	Mount Tatsuta all alone
Hitori koyuran	In the hush of night.[2]

Realizing that his wife was longing for him and for no one else, her husband felt more tenderly toward her than ever before. (His new wife's mansion was located on the road leading over Mount Tatsuta.[3]) While he was still watching her, she burst into tears. Throwing herself down, she poured some water into a metal bowl which she pressed to her breast. "How curious! Why is she doing that?" he wondered and continued his watch. Soon the water was boiling furiously. She emptied it, then filled the bowl once again with cold water. The sight moved him so greatly he ran up to her, crying, "What grief drove you to do this?"[4] He took her into his arms and remained with her that night. Spending all his time with his first wife, he ceased altogether to visit his new wife.

Many days and months slipped by when one day he thought: "My wife appeared outwardly serene, although she was suffering greatly deep within. I wonder how my new wife feels now that I have stopped visiting her." He went to her mansion. Not having visited her for a long time, he felt embarrassed and stood uncertainly outside. Finally he peeped through the fence and saw that, though she had always dressed attractively for him, she was now wearing an extremely shabby robe and that her hair was held in place at her forehead with a large comb.[5] She was helping herself to her meal. "What a disgusting sight," he thought, and hastily returned home, never to visit her again. It is said that this man was an imperial prince.[6]

150

Long ago there was a lady attendant[1] who served the Nara Emperor.[2] She was a very attractive woman, and many men—among whom were several courtiers—wooed her, but she refused to accept any of their proposals. The reason why she kept herself so aloof was that she was deeply in love with His Majesty, admiring him above all other men.

The Emperor had once summoned her to him, but since he failed to call for her again, she felt truly wretched. Night and day she brooded over her unhappy fate, never ceasing to feel unhappy and to long for him.

His Majesty had indeed summoned the lady attendant on one occasion, but he had not been particularly attracted to her. Nevertheless, she continued to appear as usual before him. Realizing that she loved him in vain, the woman had no desire to go on living and one night stole out of the palace and threw herself into Sarusawa Pond.[3]

The Emperor did not learn of her tragic death for some time. One day, however, someone happened to mention the tragedy. Deeply saddened by her untimely death, His Majesty made an imperial visit to the banks of the pond where he had the members of his retinue compose poems in her memory. Kakinomoto no Hitomaro[4] composed this poem:

(252) Wagimo ko no	How sad it makes me
Nekutaregami o	To see the disheveled hair
Sarusawa no	Of my beloved,
Ike no tamamo to	Resembling so the water plants
Miru zo kanashiki	In Sarusawa Pond.[5]

His Majesty composed this poem:

(253) Sarusawa no	How I detest Sarusawa Pond!
Ike mo tsurashi na	I wish its waters had vanished
Wagimo ko ga	When my beloved
Tamamo kazukaba	Threw herself in and was enveloped
Mizu zo hinamashi	By the water plants.[6]

It is said that His Majesty gave her a proper burial near the pond before returning to the palace.

151

On the day that the same Emperor went to view the maple leaves at their loveliest along the Tatsuta River, Hitomaro composed this poem:

(254) Tatsutagawa	The maple leaves float
Momijiba nagaru	Down the Tatsuta River;
Kaminabi no	Yonder, on Mount Mimuro—
Mimuro no yama ni	Also known as Kaminabi—
Shigure fururashi	It seems to be raining.[1]

His Majesty's poem:

(255) Tatsutagawa	The maple leaves in gay profusion
Momiji midarete	Float down the Tatsuta River;
Nagarumeri	If I cross the river now,
Wataraba nishiki	I fear I shall cut in two
Naka ya taenan	The lovely brocaded pattern.[2]

152

The same Emperor enjoyed falconry. The falcon from the district of Iwate in Michinoku, which had been presented to him, was a truly magnificent creature and in no time became a favorite pet of His Majesty, who named it Iwate. The Emperor put his beloved pet under the care of a Major Counsellor, who knew a great deal about the sport and who was in charge of organizing falconry parties. Night and day the Major Counsellor tended the falcon, but one day unwittingly allowed it to escape. Terribly upset over the loss, he searched desperately for it, but his efforts proved to be futile. Although he sent a party of men into the mountains to look for the creature, it was nowhere to be found. Finally the Major

Counsellor himself made his way deep into the mountains in search, but to no avail.

For the moment he did not have to report the missing falcon, but he knew that His Majesty never failed to look in on his pet every two or three days. Wondering what to do about the situation, he reluctantly made his way to the palace. When at last he reported the disappearance of the falcon to the Emperor, His Majesty made no comment. Thinking that perhaps he had not been heard, the Major Counsellor repeated his report, whereupon the Emperor stared speechlessly into his face. "His Majesty must think me totally irresponsible," thought the Major Counsellor with dismay. Feeling faint in the awesome presence of the Emperor, he continued with his report: "I have searched high and low for the falcon but have failed to find it. I will do anything you suggest. Please say something, Your Majesty." At this point the Emperor recited two lines of poetry:

Iwade omou zo	What one feels but does not express
Iū ni masareru	Is far more intense
	Than any word uttered.[1]

This was all that His Majesty had to say—not a word more. He must have been assailed by such remorse that words failed him. In subsequent years people composed what they felt to be appropriate opening lines, but originally this was all there was to the poem.

153

Once, when the Nara Emperor[1] was still on the throne, the Crown Prince, who later became Emperor Saga,[2] composed this poem:

(256) Mina hito no	Today we picked
Soko ka ni mezuru	For our noble lord
Fujibakama	Some agrimony
Kimi no mitame to	Whose fragrance
Taoritaru kyō	We all enjoy.[3]

This was His Majesty's return poem:

(257) Oru hito no	The richly colored agrimony
Kokoro ni kayou	Is indeed worthy
Fujibakama	Of my loyal subjects
Mube iro fukaku	Who have gathered
Nioitarikeri	The flowers.[4]

154

Once there lived in the province of Yamato a man who had a beautiful daughter. A man on horseback, who had come from the capital, happened to catch a glimpse of her one day and, enchanted by her loveliness, kidnapped her. Sweeping her up into his arms, he galloped away. The poor woman was terribly frightened.

When it grew dark, they stopped near Mount Tatsuta. The man unfastened the saddle flaps[1] and spread them out on the ground; then, gathering the woman into his arms, he lay down. The woman was petrified with fear. She felt so wretched that when the man addressed her she responded only with her weeping, whereupon the man composed this poem:

(258) Taga misogi	Who released this fowl
Yūtsukedori ka	In all its splendor
Karagoromo	Following the purification rite?
Tatsuta no yama ni	It cries without let-up
Ori haete naku	On Mount Tatsuta.[2]

The woman's reply:

(259) Tatsutagawa	Flowing past the boulders,
Iwane o sashite	The waters of the Tatsuta
Yuku mizu no	Know not their destination,
Yukue mo shiranu	And, like me,
Waga goto ya naku	Weep forlornly.[3]

No sooner did she recite this poem than she breathed her last. Deeply shaken, the man took her body into his arms and wept bitterly.

155

Long ago a Major Counsellor had a very beautiful daughter upon whom he lavished great care, for he wished to present her to the emperor. One day a man who served as an imperial attendant[1] happened to catch a glimpse of her. Finding her extraordinarily attractive, he was completely entranced and forgot all else. He pined for her night and day. Thinking that he would surely become ill if he remained silent, he one day addressed the young woman, saying, "There is something I must tell you." The woman replied: "How curious! What is it?" As she said this, she appeared before him.

Since the imperial attendant had been planning to kidnap the young lady all along, he immediately swept her up into his arms, set her before him on his horse, and galloped off in the direction of Michinoku, keeping on the move both night and day. At a place called Mount Asaka in the district of Asaka[2] he built a little hut for her. He occasionally went to the neighboring village to buy provisions, and in this manner the months slipped by.

Whenever the man left their hut, the woman remained all alone up in the mountains, not eating any food and feeling terribly despondent. In time the woman discovered that she was pregnant. Soon afterward the man went off for some provisions and failed to return home for several days. In the meantime, the woman, waiting anxiously for his return, ventured forth and made her way to the mountain spring. Studying her reflection in the water, she saw that she had become extremely ugly. Because she had been without a mirror all this time, she had been unaware of how greatly altered her looks were. This sudden glimpse came as a tremendous shock to her and she felt terribly mortified. It was then that she composed this poem:

(260) Asakayama	My love for him
Kage sae miyuru	Was far from being
Yama no i no	As shallow as the waters
Asaku wa hito o	Of the mountain spring
Omou mono ka wa	In which Mount Asaka is reflected.[3]

Attaching the poem to a tree, she returned to the hut and died. Presently the man returned with the provisions he had purchased and was greatly distressed to find the woman lying there dead. He had earlier read the woman's poem. Grief-stricken, he lay down beside her and breathed his last. This incident is said to have taken place a long time ago.[4]

156

Once there lived a man in a place called Sarashina[1] in the province of Shinano. His parents died when he was very young; therefore, his aunt, who had lived with him since he was little, was like a mother to him. The man's wife was extremely cruel and hated intensely the old aunt who was now bent with age. She constantly complained to her husband about being unkindly treated by the old woman. Soon he began to believe his wife's reports and, contrary to the gentle manner in which he had always treated his aunt before, he was very harsh with her on numerous occasions.

In time the old woman grew still more decrepit and bent. His wife thought of the poor old aunt as a nuisance and often wondered why she had not yet died. She never ceased to slander the aunt and one day went as far as to say: "Take her deep into the mountains and abandon her." Her husband was sorely troubled by his wife's request but decided to carry it out.

One night when the moon shone brightly the man said to his aunt: "Come, Aunt. There is to be a service at the temple, and I would like to take you there so that you can participate in it." The old woman was delighted and let herself be carried on his back.

Since they lived at the foot of a high mountain, the man carried his aunt a great distance up. Before turning back, he set her down at the summit, certain that she could not possibly make her way back on her own. The old woman called pathetically after him, but he ignored her and did not answer her cries. Upon arriving home, however, he brooded over what he had done simply because he had been angered by his wife's reports. He now remembered that for many years his aunt had been like a mother to him and felt more wretched than ever for having abandoned her.

Gazing at the moon which shone brightly high above the mountain, he lay sleepless. Feeling utterly miserable, he recited this poem:

(261) Waga kokoro	As I gaze at the moon
Nagusamekanetsu	Shining on Mount Obasute
Sarashina ya	In Sarashina,
Obasuteyama ni	My heart cannot be consoled.[2]
Teru tsuki o mite	

He thereupon got out of bed and climbed the mountain to fetch his aunt. Ever since that time, the mountain has been known as Mount Obasute and has been used in poetry to suggest inconsolable grief.[3]

157

There once lived a man and a woman in the province of Shimotsuke.[1] After living together for many years, the man found himself a new wife. Since his feelings for his first wife had grown cold, he moved everything that had been in the old house into the new wife's place. Although deeply hurt by her husband's cruel treatment, his first wife let him do as he wished. He took everything with him, not leaving a single thing in the house they had shared. The only item left behind was the trough for the horses, and to fetch this last item which belonged to his wife, he sent his servant, a young boy named Makaji.

The woman turned to the boy and remarked: "I suppose you will no longer come to visit me." "Why should I not come? Even though my master no longer visits you, I certainly will,'' insisted the child as he stood before her. The woman then said: ''I have something I wish to say to my husband. Would you please deliver the message? I am sure he will refuse to read any letter I might write, so please relay my message to him verbally.'' ''Indeed I shall,'' promised the boy. The woman said: ''Please recite this poem:

(262) Fune mo inu	Now that the trough is gone,
Makaji mo mieji	I shall probably
Kyō yori wa	Never see Makaji again;
Ukiyo no naka o	How can I go on living
Ikade wataran	In this world of sorrow!''[2]

When the boy recited the poem, his master, who had carried off all of his first wife's possessions, immediately moved the things back. He returned to live together with his faithful wife, never again glancing at another woman.

158

Once there was a man and a woman who lived in the province of Yamato.[1] They had been very much in love with each other for many years when, for some reason or other, the man found himself a mistress and even brought her home with him. Although there was only a wall separating them, he no longer visited his wife in her room.

His wife was very much saddened by this arrangement but did not display any sign of jealousy. One night in autumn she awoke to hear the doleful belling of a deer. As she listened in silence to this mournful sound, her husband called out from the other side of the wall, ''You there in the West Room, did you hear that sound?'' ''What sound?'' asked his wife. ''Did you not hear the belling of a deer?'' her husband queried. ''Yes, I did,'' replied his wife. ''Well, what did you associate it with?'' asked her husband. In reply, the neglected wife recited this poem:

(263) Ware mo shika	Separated from him,
Nakite zo hito ni	All I hear is his voice,
Koirareshi	But he once loved me so
Ima koso yoso ni	He cried in his longing
Koe o nomi kike	As does the deer.[2]

So deeply moved was the man by her poem that he immediately sent his mistress away and once again lived with his wife.

159

There once was a woman called Lady Somedono[1] upon whom Minister Yoshiari[2] occasionally called. Since the lady was reputed to be skillful in sewing and dyeing, the Minister sent her a large roll of damask, requesting her to make a robe for him. She asked: "Should I dye the damask in a cloud-and-crane design?" Failing to hear from him, she sent him another message, saying, "I am at a loss what to do. Please let me know your wishes." The Minister sent back this poem:

(264) Kumotori no	So many years have slipped by
Aya no iro o mo	Without a single glimpse of you
Omōezu	That I can no longer
Hito o aimide	Distinguish one color from another
Toshi no henureba	In a cloud-and-crane design.[3]

160

Once when Zai Chūjō was having a love affair with the same lady, she sent him this poem:

(265) Aki hagi o	Now that the wind which turns
Irodoru kaze no	The bush clover in autumn
Fukinureba	To different shades of color
Hito no kokoro mo	Has begun to blow,
Utagawarekeri	I begin to wonder
	If you really love me.[1]

This was his answering poem:

(266) Aki no no o	Though the wind that tints
Irodoru kaze wa	The autumn fields
Fukinu tomo	Comes blowing my way,
Kokoro wa kareji	My heart will never wither,
Kusaba naraneba	As it is not a leaf.[2]

Some time after he stopped visiting her, Zai Chūjō asked her to sew some robes for him. To this request he added a note which said: "I have been feeling most wretched, for I have no one who will do my laundry. Please perform the task for me." Lady Somedono wrote back, saying, "It is all your own doing," and added:

(267) Ōnusa ni	How sad it is that you,
Narinuru hito no	Having no one to rely on
Kanashiki wa	Have become a sacred wand
Yoru se tomo naku	And can only weep.[3]
Shika zo nakunaru	

He answered with this poem:

(268) Nagaru tomo	Though the cotton strips
Nani to ka mien	Float downstream,
Te ni torite	Only those who had held them
Hikiken hito zo	Can recognize the offerings
Nusa to shiruran	For what they are.[4]

161

Zai Chūjō used to court Empress Nijō[1] when she was an ordinary subject and had not yet become the Emperor's consort. Once he sent her some *hijiki* seaweed together with this poem:

(269) Omoi araba	If you really love me,
Mugura no yado ni	Surely you would not mind
Ne mo shinan	Sleeping with me,
Hijiki mono ni wa	Our sleeves for bedding,
Sode o shitsutsu mo	In a cottage overgrown with weeds.[2]

No one remembers the lines of her return poem.

When the Empress became an imperial concubine,[3] she made a pilgrimage to Ōhara Field.[4] A number of courtiers and court nobles accompanied her. Zai Chūjō was also in attendance. He stood by her carriage in the semidarkness. Earlier, the concubine had bestowed gifts upon everyone at the shrine. From the back of the carriage, she personally presented Zai Chūjō with the unlined robe she had been wearing. He graciously accepted her gift, murmuring in a low voice:

(270) Ōhara ya	On this day of days
Oshio no yama mo	Mount Oshio in Ōhara
Kyō koso wa	Surely recalls
Kamiyo no koto o	Events that occurred
Omoiizurame	In the Age of the Gods.[5]

A wave of nostalgia swept over the lady when she remembered the past.

162

Once when Zai Chūjō was serving in the palace, he received some grass of oblivion from the Empress, who asked him: "What is this plant called?" He replied:

(271) Wasuregusa	Grass of oblivion
Ouru nobe to wa	Seems to carpet the meadow,
Miruramedo	But it is none other than
Ko wa shinobu nari	The herb of remembrance,
Nochi mo tanoman	And I shall look hopefully
	To the future.[1]

He composed this poem because another name for the grass of oblivion is the herb of remembrance.[2]

163

Her Majesty asked Zai Chūjō for a chrysanthemum, so he presented her with one, attaching to it a slip of paper on which he had written:

(272) Ueshi ueba	If you plant it with care,
Aki naki toki ya	It will fail to bloom
Sakazaran	Only when autumn forgets to come,
Hana koso chirame	And though the petals should fall,
Ne sae kareme ya	Its root will never wither.[1]

164

To one who presented him with some prettily decorated rice cakes wrapped in leaves,[1] Zai Chūjō sent in return a pheasant to which he attached this poem:

(273) Ayamegari	While you, who went to gather irises,
Kimi wa numa ni zo	Were distressed in the marshes,
Madoikeru	I went a-hunting
Ware wa no ni idete	In the fields
Karu zo wabishiki	And suffered great hardship.[2]

165

During the reign of the Mizu-no-o Emperor,[1] there lived a woman called Ben no Miyasundokoro, the daughter of the Major Controller of the Left.[2] After His Majesty took the tonsure, the woman lived all alone until Zai Chūjō secretly began to visit her. Some time later, he fell seriously ill and suffered terribly. His former mistresses flocked to his bedside, but since they had been meeting in secret, Ben no Miyasundokoro was unable to visit him. However, day after day she sent him letters inquiring after his health.

One day she failed to write. By this time his illness had taken a turn for the worse, and he was on his deathbed. Zai Chūjō sent the woman this poem:

(274) Tsurezure to	As my pain grows in intensity,
Itodo kokoro no	The moments slip slowly by;
Wabishiki ni	Ah, must this day
Kyō wa towazute	Draw to a close
Kurashiten to ya	Without your asking after me?[3]

"Poor man, how weak he has become!" exclaimed Ben no Miyasundokoro and fell to weeping. Just when she was about to send him a return poem, she received word of his death and was grief-stricken. In his last moments, Zai Chūjō composed this poem:

(275) Tsui ni yuku	I had heard that this is a road
Michi to wa kanete	We all must take in the end,
Kikishikado	But little did I dream
Kinō kyō to wa	I would be taking it today.[4]
Omowazarishi o	

166

Once Zai Chūjō went sight-seeing and found himself standing next to the carriage of a young woman who appeared to be of noble birth. Through an opening in the curtains, he could distinctly see the woman's features, and they conversed for a while before returning to their respective homes. The next day he sent her this poem:

(276) Mizu mo arazu	I cannot say that I really saw
Mi mo senu hito no	The one I love,
Koishiki wa	And so I shall idly
Ayanaku kyō ya	Spend the day
Nagame kurasan	Lost in longing.[1]

The woman sent him this reply:

(277) Mi mo mizu mo	If you did not really see me,
Tare to shirite ka	How can you know my identity?
Koiraruru	Your longing for me today
Obotsukanasa no	Is quite unconvincing.
Kyō no nagame ya	

These poems have been transmitted in old tales and are known to everyone.

167

A certain man, having borrowed some robes from his wife, went off wearing them to his new wife's house and was never again seen in his old home. When all the robes had become tattered through wear, he decided that it was time to return them. He therefore sent them back along with a pheasant, a wild goose, and a wild duck. These tokens of gratitude, however, were hardly of value to anyone living in the countryside, and so the woman wrote:

(278) Ina ya kiji	No, I shall not wear this robe
Hito ni naraseru	Which someone else has worn,
Karigoromo	For if it touches me,
Waga mi ni fureba	I, too, shall be tainted
Uki ka mo zo tsuku	By its unpleasant odor.[1]

168

During the reign of the Fukakusa Emperor,[1] a man called Rō Shōshō[2] was influential in court circles. Moreover, he was known to be a great lover. At this time, there lived in the palace a young woman whom he occasionally visited in secret. One night he promised her: "I shall come to you tonight without fail." The woman therefore made herself up as attractively as possible and eagerly awaited his coming, but he failed to appear. She remained awake all night and was thinking to herself, "It must be very late," when she heard a voice announcing the hour, "Three in the morning!"[3]

The woman wrote down the first half of a poem and sent it to Rō Shōshō. Her lines read:

(279) Hitogokoro Ushi mitsu ima wa Tanomaji yo	It is already three And still you fail to come— No longer shall I rely on you.

Startled awake by the woman's messenger, he replied by adding the closing lines:

Yume ni miyu ya to Ne zo suginikeru	Thinking I shall see you In my dreams, I slept past midnight.[4]

Although Rō Shōshō had dozed off with the intention of resting for a short while only, he had overslept.

He was considered a man of great talent and enjoyed His Majesty's patronage when suddenly the Emperor died. When other government officials were busy attending to various matters on the night of the imperial funeral, Rō Shōshō vanished mysteriously and was not seen from that night on. His wives and friends worried about him and for a long time searched everywhere for him, but no one knew his whereabouts.

People began to wonder: "Has he entered the priesthood—or has he drowned himself? We would surely have heard about his becoming a priest, so he must have drowned himself." At this thought, even strangers—let alone his wives and children—felt very sad. Night and day they purified themselves through severe abstinence and thorough cleansing of both body and spirit. Lamenting unceasingly, they offered prayers to the gods and buddhas but did not receive any news regarding the man.

Rō Shōshō had three wives, two of whom he cared for in an ordinary way. To them he had said: "I am thinking of abandoning this world." But to the third, who had borne him children and whom he loved very dearly, he had not uttered a single word of what he intended to do. He must have felt that she would be deeply saddened if he told her beforehand and that he himself would no longer be able to go through with his plans if he saw her in such a distraught state. At any rate, he suddenly disappeared without even saying goodbye.

Whatever his reasons may have been, his wife was deeply hurt by his not having confided in her and wept unhappily. The wretched woman made a pilgrimage to the temple at Hatsuse.[5] In the meantime, her husband had become a Buddhist priest and, dressed in a straw raincoat, had been traveling throughout the land practicing religious austerities. At this particular time, he was busy at his devotions after having also made his way to Hatsuse Temple. While he was fervently praying near the room in which his wife was meditating, she turned to the priest who was in charge of the memorial service and said: "My husband has disappeared. If he still lives in this world, please let me see him once more; if he has drowned himself, I beseech you to pray for his salvation. Even if he is dead—be it in dream or in reality—please let me see his face and hear his voice again." She presented her husband's robes, ceremonial dress, obi, and long sword as temple offerings. Unable to express in words her innermost feelings, she could only weep.

Rō Shōshō, who was eavesdropping, was curious as to what manner of woman had come to worship at the temple. He soon realized, however, that she was referring to himself and that the offerings she was presenting to the temple were his personal belongings. Needless to say, he was shaken by this discovery and profoundly moved. He thought a thousand times of running to her side, but checking his initial impulse, he wept bitterly throughout the night. He imagined hearing the beloved voices of his wife and children and felt utterly wretched.[6]

Enduring with fortitude the ache in his heart, he wept all night long. When he looked about him in the morning, he saw that his raincoat and other belongings were spattered with the tears of blood he had shed. He thought to himself, "It really is true that when one weeps violently enough, one sheds tears of blood." He then recalled, "Oh, how I wanted to rush to her side when I heard her speak!" Despite all the trouble she had gone through, his wife was still without any news of her husband as the period of national mourning came to an end.[7]

On the day everyone was to change from his mourning robes, numerous courtiers made their way to the Kawara River.[8] A strange-looking child suddenly appeared, bearing a message written on an oak leaf. Someone took up the message and read it aloud, noting that the poem was in Rō Shōshō's hand.

(280) Mina hito wa	Everyone has changed
Hana no koromo ni	Into their gaily colored robes;
Narinu nari	Oh, sleeve
Koke no tamoto yo	Of my priest's robe,
Kawaki dani se yo	It is time you became dry.[9]

"Where did the child go?" cried the people. Although they looked high and low for the boy, he was nowhere to be found. They now knew that Rō Shōshō had taken the tonsure, but they did not have the faintest idea where he was.

Hearing that he was still alive, the Empress[10] dispatched a palace attendant as a messenger to go to search for the priest in the mountains. Before long, the messenger heard that Rō Shōshō could be found in a certain place, but when the messenger sought him there, Rō Shōshō had disappeared. At long last the messenger chanced upon the very spot in which the priest had sequestered himself. No longer able to conceal his identity, Rō Shōshō saw the messenger.

"I have come as a messenger from the Empress," said the palace attendant. "Her Majesty had these words to say to you. 'The Emperor lives no longer, but it grieves me sorely that you with whom His Majesty had been so intimate and who ought to serve me in his memory should disappear, hiding yourself from the rest of the world. Moreover, even though you may be practicing religious discipline in the mountains and forests, why have you failed to send me word of your whereabouts? Furthermore, you have not been in touch with your own family, who weep and grieve over your sudden disappearance. Please tell me why you have been so heartless.' Thus spoke Her Majesty. As for myself, I have come here after searching everywhere for you."

The messenger's words moved Rō Shōshō to tears. "I am deeply honored to have heard the words of Her Majesty,'' he said. ''Since the Emperor's demise, I, who had been accustomed to serving him, no longer wished to go on living in this world. I therefore secluded myself deep in the mountains, hoping I too would die. But strangely enough, I have managed to survive. It was most gracious of Her Majesty to have inquired after me. Please rest assured that I have not forgotten my children.'' He then added, ''Recite this poem to her Majesty:

(281) Kagiri naki	Though I go infinitely far
Kumoi no yoso ni	From the palace
Wakaru tomo	Where you are,
Hito o kokoro ni	How could I fail to take you
Okurazarame ya wa	With me in my heart.''[11]

The messenger was deeply moved as he gazed at the wretched-looking priest. A mere shadow of his former self, the priest was now dressed in a straw raincoat and no longer resembled the man he used to be. Recalling how handsome he had been when he had served as a Minor Captain, the messenger wept.

The attendant thought that the situation was truly pathetic. However, since this spot deep in the mountains was a place where one could not remain for very long, he tearfully bade him farewell and returned to the palace. He reported to Her Majesty what had transpired after he had located the priest. The Empress wept bitterly, joined by her attendants, who were very much saddened and wept aloud. By the time the messenger, bearing Her Majesty's reply as well as letters from various people, made his way back to where he had left the priest, the man had again vanished.

During the first month, a person by the name of Ono no Komachi[12] made a pilgrimage to Kiyomizu Temple.[13] While attending a Buddhist service, she heard a priest intoning the sutras and chanting magical incantations[14] in a strangely awe-inspiring voice. Komachi was surprised and casually sent someone to investigate who it was. ''There was a priest dressed in a straw raincoat sitting in the corner with a tinderbox tied to his waist,'' reported the person she had sent.

As Komachi listened on, the priest's voice sounded even more distinguished and impressive. She thought that surely he was no ordinary priest and might even possibly be the former Minor Captain. "I wonder what he will say to me," thought Komachi, and had this message delivered: "I have come from afar to worship at this temple, but it is so cold, I should like to borrow one of your robes for a while." She added:

(282) Iwa no ue ni	When sleeping on boulders
Tabine o sureba	Along my journey,
Ito samushi	I shall feel cold;
Koke no koromo o	Do lend me
Ware ni kasanan	Your priest's robe.[15]

His return poem went:

(283) Yo o somuku	Having abandoned the world,
Koke no koromo wa	My sole possession
Tada hitoe	Is a single priest's robe;
Kasaneba tsurashi	Since you will think me cruel
Iza futari nen	If I do not lend it to you,
	Come, let us sleep together.[16]

Komachi was more convinced than ever that this priest was none other than Rō Shōshō. Since they used to talk to one another in the past, she thought that she ought to speak with him, but by then he had disappeared. She searched for him throughout the temple grounds, but he had fled, never to be seen again.

The priest who had vanished eventually became an archbishop and lived in a temple called Kazan.[17] He had several children who had been born when he was still a layman. His eldest son[18] at one time served in the palace as a Lieutenant of the Left Division of the Inner Palace Guards. Having heard that his father was alive, he was most eager to see him. Obtaining his mother's consent, he went to look for him and when at last father and son met, the father said: "A priest's son should also become a priest." Thus the young man entered the priesthood. It is said that this poem was composed by the archbishop:

(284) Oritsureba	If you pick the flower
Tabusa ni kegaru	It will stain your wrist—
Tatenagara	Let us offer it then
Miyo no hotoke ni	Just as it grows
Hana tatematsuru	To the Buddha of Three Worlds.[19]

Since the young priest had been forced into taking the tonsure and had not truly wanted to become a priest, he, unlike his father, often went to the capital and became involved in numerous love affairs. On one occasion, he secretly seduced the daughter of a relative, a young woman who had been brought up strictly in order that she might serve in the palace. Learning of this affair, her father denounced them both and forbade the priest ever to visit her again. The priest thereupon built a little cottage up in the mountains and lived there alone, unable even to correspond with his sweetheart.

A long time afterward the older brothers of the woman whose conduct had induced such a commotion climbed the mountain for a Buddhist service in memory of an acquaintance. They made their way to the priest's hut, spending some time chatting and relaxing in his company. It was during their visit that the priest wrote this poem on the neckband of the cloak of the eldest brother:

(285) Shirakumo no	I go on living
Yadoru mine ni zo	On this cloud-covered peak
Okurenuru	With no hope of seeing you—
Omoi no hoka ni	Alas, this world
Aru yo narikeri	Is not what I expected![20]

Unaware of what the priest had done, the brother of the young lady, who was then serving as a Lieutenant of the Middle Palace Guards, returned to the capital. How sad his sister must have felt when she discovered the writing on his neckband! In time this young priest rose to the rank of bishop and was called the Bishop of Kyōgoku.

169

Long ago a palace attendant went to the province of Yamato as an imperial messenger to the Ōwa Shrine.[1] At a place called Ide, several women and children came out of a neat little cottage and watched him go by. An attractive young woman, who was carrying in her arms a very pretty child, stood by the gate. Drawn to the child with the adorable face, the messenger said: "Please bring the child here." Obeying, the young woman drew closer with the child. The messenger studied the girl closely and saw that she was truly lovely. "Promise me you will not marry anyone else but me," said he. "I shall come for you when you have grown up." Untying his obi, he handed it to her, saying, "Please keep this to remember me by." He then untied the obi which the child was wearing and, after tying it to the letter he had with him, gave it to his servant before continuing on his way.

The girl was about six or seven at the time of the incident. Being an amorous man, the messenger had glibly made his flattering little speech. The child, however, never for a moment forgot his words, cherishing them deep in her heart.

Seven or eight years went by when the same man was once again sent as a messenger to the Ōwa Shrine. On his way to the province of Yamato, he stopped for the night at Ide Crossing. In front of his lodgings was a well and several women were drawing water from it, one of whom said:[2]

170

When the present Counsellor Korehira[1] was a Middle Captain, he was also serving as a steward to the late Minster of Ceremonial.[2] He often went to the palace and spent his time conversing with the court ladies. As soon as he left service in the palace, Korehira caught a cold and suffered terribly. To show their concern for him, the court ladies prepared some medicinal saké and a variety of delicacies which Lady Hyōe[3] delivered. In acknowledging their gifts, he said: "How delighted I am to have you come to see me. It is distressing to have come down with a miserable cold." He then recited this poem:

(286) Aoyagi no	Though far from being
Ito naranedomo	The threadlike leaves
Harukaze no	Of the green willow,
Fukeba katayoru	My body bends before
Waga mi narikeri	The spring wind that blows.[4]

She composed this answering poem:

(287) Isasame ni	Why should you bend
Fuku kaze ni ya wa	Before a wind that blows
Nabikubeki	But for a moment,
Nowaki sugushishi	For have you not lived
Kimi ni ya wa aranu	Through the typhoons of autumn?[5]

171

When the present Minister of the Left[1] was serving as a Minor Captain, he often visited the Minister of Ceremonial. A woman by the name of Yamato was in the service of the Minister, and since she was an amorous woman, she was truly thrilled when the Minor Captain pledged his love to her. However, the lovers always found it difficult to meet. One day Yamato sent this poem to her lover:

(288) Hito shirenu	The flame of love in my heart
Kokoro no uchi ni	Burns unknown to others,
Moyuru hi wa	And though no smoke can be seen
Keburi wa tatade	Rising from it,
Kuyuri koso sure	It burns unceasingly.[2]

This was the Minor Captain's return poem:

(289) Fuji no ne no	My love for you,
Taenu omoi mo	Like the smoke that rises
Aru mono o	From Mount Fuji,
Kuyuru wa tsuraki	Is eternal;
Kokoro narikeri	Oh, how it pains my heart
	That you regret you loved me![3]

When the Minor Captain failed to call on her for some time, Yamato became very impatient waiting for him. It is difficult to imagine the emotional state that prompted her to get into a carriage one day—without informing anyone of her plans—and make her way to the palace. Coming to a halt at the guardhouse of the Left Division of the Outer Palace Guards, she called out to man passing by, saying, "I should like to speak to the Minor Captain." As the man, ignoring her, went on in, he muttered to himself: "How very odd! Who does she think she is, behaving in such a brazen manner?"

When other men sauntered by, Yamato called out to them. Passing through the gate, the men said to her: "Well now, he is probably in the Inner Palace so you cannot possibly speak to him at this moment."

Finally, Yamato called out imploringly to a gentleman, dressed in a formal coat, who was about to enter. Thinking that it was most unusual to have a woman address him in this manner, he approached her carriage. Yamato asked: "Is the Minor Captain there?" "Yes, he is," replied the gentleman, whereupon Yamato said: "Please tell him that someone has come from his mansion with an urgent message for him."

The gentleman then said: "That is easy enough to do, but be sure not to forget the man who delivered your message. What a pity you should be without a companion so late at night!" He went inside but failed to emerge again even after a long time had elapsed. Meanwhile Yamato was kept waiting for what seemed to her an eternity. Just as she was beginning to think that he had probably left without delivering her message and was wondering what she should do next, the gentleman reappeared.

Said the man: "As the Minor Captain was performing for His Majesty, it was with great difficulty that I finally managed to speak to him. This is what he said: 'Who could have come from my mansion? How very odd! Please ask her to identify herself.' " "The reason why I have not disclosed my name is that I am of humble birth. Please tell the Captain that I must speak to him in person," said Yamato.

The gentleman made a full report to the Minor Captain. Realizing that she could be none other than Yamato, the Minor Captain was at once puzzled and amused. He told the gentleman to ask Yamato to wait awhile, then excused himself in order to consult the Hirohata Middle Counsellor,[4] who was then serving as a Gentleman-in-Waiting. "What should I do in this particular situation?" asked the Minor Captain.

Soon afterward the Minor Captain brought a silk screen and a straw mat from the night duty room to the guardhouse of the Left Division of the Outer Palace Guards and asked Yamato to be seated. "Why have you come here?" he queried. Yamato replied: "I have no special reason except that you have treated me abominably . . . "[5]

It is said that the present Minister of the Left sent this poem to a woman by the name of Yamato, who lived in the mansion of Prince Atsuyoshi:

(290) Ima sara ni	I try my utmost
Omoiideji to	To drive you from my mind,
Shinoburu o	But loving you as I do
Koishiki ni koso	I cannot forget you
Wasure wabinure	And continue to suffer.[6]

172

Teiji no In often went on a pilgrimage to Ishiyama Temple.[1] One day His Majesty heard that the Provincial Governor[2] had been worried that the continuation of these visits would cause the people to become exhausted and the province to be ruined. Teiji no In thereupon decreed: "Let the expenses be shouldered by the estates in other provinces." Numerous goods were thus transported into the province and various preparations made for the next imperial visit to the temple.

Meanwhile the Provincial Governor of Ōmi, anxious and fearful, wondered how the former Emperor had heard of his complaints. As he could not very well pretend that he had not complained, he built a magnificent temporary villa for His Majesty at Uchide Bay, a place the imperial procession would pass on its return journey and, planting some beautiful chrysanthemums, made elaborate preparations to receive the former Emperor. The Provincial Governor, however, dreaded an encounter with His Majesty and remained out of sight, leaving Kuronushi[3] to welcome him.

When the imperial entourage went by, a courtier asked: "Why are you standing there, Kuronushi?" The former Emperor himself had the carriage come to a halt and also inquired: "Why, indeed, are you here?" Kuronushi replied:

(291) Sazara nami	The tiny ripples wash
Mamonaku kishi o	The lake's shore endlessly;
Araumeri	Because it longs for
Nagisa kiyokuba	Your Majesty to stay,
Kimi tomare to ka	The shore keeps itself immaculate.[4]

Much pleased by this poem, His Majesty paused awhile to bestow gifts upon those present before continuing his homeward journey.

173

It began to pour as Yoshimine no Munesada, the Minor Captain, was once walking along Gojō Avenue. Seeking shelter in the gateway of a dilapidated house, he peered inside. Under a thirty-foot-square roof thatched with cypress bark were tiny storehouses but not a soul in sight. He made his way inside. Looking about him, he noticed a plum tree in full bloom near the steps leading to the main building. A nightingale[1] was singing. Although he had assumed that no one was there, he caught a glimpse of the graceful figure of a woman dressed in a robe of light violet over one of dark crimson through the rattan blinds. With her hair trailing to the ground, the woman softly murmured to herself:

(292) Yomogi oite	At this old cottage,
Aretaru yado o	Overgrown with mugwort,
Uguisu no	The nightingale cries,
Hitoku to naku ya	"Someone approaches!"
Tare to ka matan	Ah, but I have no one to wait for![2]

Speaking gently, the Minor Captain recited:

(293) Kitaredomo	Though I have come here,
Iishi nareneba	I remain silent,
Uguisu no	Unused to addressing you;
Kimi ni tsugeyo to	But the nightingale cries,
Oshiete zo naku	Informing you of my presence.[3]

Having thought that no one was near, the woman was startled and, mortified to have been seen in such a state of disarray, was at a loss for words. Meanwhile the man made his way onto the veranda. "Why do you not speak to me? It is pouring outside, so please let me stay here until the weather clears," said he. The woman replied: "I am afraid you will find that the rain leaks through so badly it would be better out on the highway."

It was about the tenth day of the first month. The woman slipped him a cushion from behind the rattan blinds which the man drew toward him and on which he seated himself. He studied the blinds and noticed that pieces along the edge had been gnawed off by bats. He also saw that the room had seen better days in that the straw mats, though now worn with age, were of a superior quality.

The day was gradually drawing to a close, whereupon the man slipped into the room and kept the woman from escaping into the inner chamber. Terribly embarrassed, the woman found herself unable to ward off his advances and at a loss for words.

Although it rained all night long, it cleared by morning. When the woman tried to flee, the man restrained her, saying, "Stay where you are!"

When at last the sun had risen high up in the heavens, the woman's parents, though far from wealthy, wished to entertain the Captain. They had his young attendants remain a while longer, serving them saké with lumps of salt as a side dish. They offered the Captain some tender young greens, which had come from their spacious garden; the greens had been steamed and served attractively in a bowl. For chopsticks, they broke off branches of plum blossoms in full bloom. On the petals, written beautifully in a woman's hand, was this poem:

<table>
<tr><td>(294) Kimi ga tame
Koromo no suso o
Nurashitsutsu
Haru no no ni idete
Tsumeru wakana zo</td><td>The hem of my robe was wetted
As I made my way
To the spring fields
To gather these greens
For you alone.[4]</td></tr>
</table>

Upon reading this poem, he felt truly sorry for the woman and, drawing the dish closer to him, ate it with relish. In her embarrassment, the woman crouched in a corner. Presently the Captain stood up and sent a young attendant to fetch several useful articles from the carraige.

"I must go now, as someone has come for me, but I shall soon return," said the Minor Captain and departed. Indeed, from that time on he visited them constantly. Although he was to taste a great variety of dishes in his lifetime, he felt deep in his heart that the one he had been served at the house on Gojō Avenue was the most unusual and tastiest of all.

Many years later, the Minor Captain, having outlived the Emperor[5] whom he had served faithfully and no longer desiring to be a part of the new reign, entered the priesthood. On one occasion, he sent his Buddhist robe which he wished to have laundered to the woman mentioned above. This poem accompanied the robes:

<table>
<tr><td>(295) Shimo yuki no
Furuya no moto ni
Hitori ne no
Utsubushizome no
Asa no kesa nari</td><td>I sleep all alone
In an ancient house
Into which frost and snow
Have made their way;
Here, I offer you
My black robe of hemp.[6]</td></tr>
</table>

I

Long ago two men[1] fell in love with the same woman. The man who first began to court her was a high official in attendance upon the Reigning Emperor. The other man who began to woo her later was a relative of the Emperor's mother and was of low rank.[2] Although it is not known how the woman personally felt about the latter, she nevertheless yielded to him. The first suitor was resigned that her decision had been predestined. Nonetheless, whenever he had the opportunity, the unsuccessful suitor fabricated stories about his rival in order to slander him—stories which would doubtless make His Majesty believe that the man had no sense of propriety.

In the meantime, the successful suitor began to find serving at the court most trying; his greatest pleasure lay in taking long walks. Because he neglected his duties at the Headquarters,[3] he was dismissed. Feeling that this world was a world of sorrow, he shut himself up in his house and brooded over his unhappy fate. He reminded himself that life was ephemeral. When one was sorely distressed, of what importance was a petty office?

No longer wishing to have anything to do with this world of sorrow, he became obsessed with the idea of going deep into the mountains—far from worldy cares—to practice religious discipline. However, his father and mother so doted on him that they would not allow him to go very far. Thus, because of their all-consuming love, he was prevented from doing anything to solve the many wretched and trying problems plaguing him.

It was autumn, and everything surrounding him filled him with a heavy sadness. One evening, he softly murmured to himself:

(1)	Ukiyo ni wa	Though the gate
	Kado saseri tomo	To this world of sorrow
	Mienaku ni	Appears not to be locked,
	Nado waga yado no	Why do I hesitate to leave my home
	Idegate ni suru	For the priesthood?[4]

He was feeling embittered toward the world when he received

some beautifully tinted ivy from a woman who, admiring him from afar, had spoken to him on several occasions. She had written on the ivy: "Of what do these remind you?" She also sent this poem:

(2)	Uki Tatsuta Yama no tsuyu no Momijiba wa Mono omou aki no Sode ni zo arikeru	The dew-laden maple leaves On Mount Tatsuta Resemble my sleeve Which this autumn is wetted With tears of longing.[5]

Since he failed to send back an answering poem, the affair did not develop into anything serious.

Upon learning of his troubles, his friends gathered together and tried to console him. They offered each other saké to drink and had some light musical entertainment. As the night deepened, the unhappy man composed this poem:

(3)	Mi o umi no Omoinagisa wa Koyoi kana Ura ni tatsu nami Uchiwasuretsutsu	My sorrows are as countless As the waves that rise In the bay; And though they distress me, I shall forget them tonight.[6]

Deeply moved by this poem, everyone sadly awaited the coming of dawn. He received no answering poem.

Since the moon was exceedingly lovely the following night, he stood out on the veranda and gazed up at the heavens as the night deepened and the wind blew coldly. His brooding caused him to become terribly depressed. To his friends, who were men of feeling, he wrote: "I suppose we are the only ones who have been gazing all this time at the moon." Added to this message was this poem:

(4)	Nagekitsutsu Sora naru tsuki to Nagamureba Namida zo Ama no Kawa to nagaruru	Grieving, I gaze up at The moon in the sky, And my tears flow unceasingly As does the Heavenly River.[7]

Shortly afterward, he was again entrusted with his former responsibilities, since his offense had not been a serious one. Among his friends were Mitsune and Tomonori.[8]

The same man[9] often visited a certain woman with whom he was intimate. A very ugly girl lived in the house. Although, as a rule, when a girl matures she acquires considerable poise, he was so sure this one was a hopeless case that he could only be amused. Nonetheless, each time he saw her she seemed more beautiful. As she had become far more attractive than he ever dreamed possible, he sent her this poem:

(5)	Numa mizu ni	Though you do not live
	Kimi wa aranedo	In the waters of the marsh,
	Kakaru mo no	You resemble the water plants
	Miruma miruma ni	And grow more lovely
	Oimasarikeri	Each time I see you.[10]

This was her return poem:

(6)	Kakaru mo no	Since your heart is
	Miruma miruma zo	As shallow as the marsh
	Utomaruru	Where the water plants grow,
	Kokoro asama no	You become more estranged from me
	Numa ni oureba	Each time you gaze at me.[11]

She also sent him this poem:

(7)	Itsuwari o	If you really love me
	Tadasu-no-Mori no	Swear that you do
	Yūdasuki	By the God of Tadasu Woods,
	Kakete o chikae	Who investigates
	Ware o omowaba	All lies.[12]

Shortly afterward, the woman found herself a new lover. Having actually seen her send her lover on his way, her earlier admirer sent her this poem:

(8)	Arawanaru Koto aragō na Sakurabana Haru wa kagiri to Chiru o mietsutsu	Do not deny What is crystal clear; It is as clear to me As the scattering of cherry blooms, Announcing the end of spring.[13]

She replied:

(9)	Iro ni idete Ada ni miyu tomo Sakurabana Kaze no fukazu wa Chiraji to zo omou	The cherry blossoms Appear so fragile; If no wind came blowing, They would not scatter.[14]

Along Rokujō Avenue in the west side of the capital, the earthen walls[15] had crumbled here and there, and the grass grew thickly. Nonetheless, there stood a mansion with its many shutters raised in a neat row.[16] A young man who happened to be passing by could not resist stopping after having glimpsed several women through the opening below the rattan blinds. He immediately sent his young attendant to ask them: "Why is this place so run down?" Insulted, one of the women called out: "Who dares to ask such a rude question?" "A mere passer-by," replied the man, whereupon the women emerged from the ruins, reciting this poem:

(10)	Hito no aki ni Niwa sae arete Michi mo naku Yomogi shigereru Yado to ya wa minu	Here at this neglected mansion Where the mugwort grows thickly, No pathway is visible; Can you not see that it belongs To one who has been abandoned?[17]

The man instructed his servant to recite this poem:

(11) Taga aki ni	Who could have grown weary
Aite aretaru	Of the mansion
Yado naran	To so neglect the garden?
Ware dani niwa no	If you permit me to visit you,
Kusa wa ousaji	I shall see to it
	That the grass never grows.[18]

Although the man visited the lady of the mansion from time to time, the suspicion that someone was trying to play a trick on him made him feel uneasy. He continued to visit her but he did not inform anyone of his destination. One day the women moved away. The only one who had remained behind said: "I have been instructed to hand this letter over to anyone who inquires after my mistress." The letter which she handed him contained this poem:

(12) Waga yado wa	My home is in Nara;
Nara no miyako zo	Do come and visit me
Otokoyama	If you ever
Koyu bakari ni wa	Chance to cross over
Araba sate toe	Mount Otoko.[19]

Disappointed to learn of the lady's departure, the man presented a number of gifts to the woman who had been left behind in the mansion. He continued to question her about her mistress' whereabouts, but all she would say was: "Her Ladyship has set out for Nara." He could think of no way to extract any additional information.

In time he managed to forget about the woman. One day, however, as he was accompanying his parents, who were making a pilgrimage to Hatsuse, he thought: "Did such a thing really happen? If, indeed, I had met that woman, I wonder which of these houses might be hers?" He thereupon related the above story to his traveling companions.

The party visited the Hatsuse Temple and, on the way back, traveled along Sanjō Avenue. At a place called Asuka-moto[20] the man and his parents ran into a priest, with whom the man was acquainted, and a number of laymen. The priest said: "The day is drawing to a close. Beyond Nara Slope[21] you will be unable to find a house where you can seek lodgings, so please spend the night here."

They were offered rooms in a charming house which had originally been two separate dwellings. Very pleased with the place, they decided to spend the night. Their hosts prepared an elaborate feast in their honor to which they cheerfully helped themselves. All too soon their merry-making ended and evening was upon them.

The man made his way to the doorway, pausing for a moment to study the scene before him. A few Japanese oak trees were growing at the northern end of the adjoining buildings. "How strange that there is no other variety of trees planted there," he commented as he peered into the adjoining house. The charming shutters of the house were raised, and several women could be seen seated within. They murmured among themselves: "My, but he is inquisitive!" Their mistress summoned the man's attendant to her and asked: "Has your master been given lodgings in the South House?"

The man, who had some time ago caught a glimpse of the women through the broken-down section of the earthen wall, thought: "Ah, she remembers me after all![22] I wonder if she came here accompanied by a man." These confused thoughts were running through his head when the woman sent him this poem:

(13)	Kuyashiku mo	How I regret having told you
	Nara zo to dani mo	That my destination was Nara,
	Iitekeru	For you have never called on me,
	Tamaboko ni dani	Though you often
	Kite mo towaneba	Come this way.[23]

The poem was in the hand of the woman who had composed the previous poem on the neglected garden.[24] Since the man had been longing to see the capital on his journey, he asked for an inkstand and wrote down this poem:

(14) Nara no ki no	Though you did not inform me
Narabu hodo to wa	That oak trees grew nearby,
Oshienedo	I sought lodgings here
Na ni ya ou tote	Where the trees bear
Yado wa karitsuru	The same name as your home.[25]

"What nonsense!" exclaimed the woman and promptly retorted with this poem:

(15) Kado sugite	If you happened to pass by my gate
Hatsusegawa made	And cross the Hatsuse River,
Wataru se mo	You would probably say
Ware ga tame to ya	That you did so to see me.[26]
Kimi wa kotaen	

He spent the night at the house and early the next morning sent her this poem:

(16) Asa madaki	I am most reluctant
Tatsu sora mo nashi	To leave this morning,
Shiranami no	But like the white waves
Kaerugaeru mo	That never cease to ebb and flow,
Kaerikinu beshi	I shall return again and again.[27]

II[1]

Prince Muneyuki,[2] the Master of the Right Division of the Capital, had designed for his mansion a lovely garden with an air of elegance about it. Growing here and there were maiden flowers[3] and chrysanthemums. The members of the household eagerly awaited the time when the master would be away. One night, when the moon was shining in all its glory, several lady attendants gathered together and strolled leisurely through the garden, enjoying the beauties about them. They wrote a poem on a tall signboard which they planted in the midst of the flowers. The poem read:

(17)	Kitemireba Mukashi no hito wa Sudakikeri Hana no yue aru Yado ni zo arikeru	As we view the garden, We see gathered here Friends of old; How lovely the flowers are At this mansion![4]

Although their master did not know who was responsible for the signboard, he was sure that someone would come to take it away and so he added this poem on the signboard, then planted it in place again:

(18)	Waga yado no Hana wa ueshi ni Kokoro areba Mamoru hito nomi Sudaku bakari zo	Since my mansion Has an elegant air Now that flowers have been planted, Only those who watch over it May gather here.[5]

Certain that someone would come to remove the signboard, he had an attendant watch over the garden. Because no one came for it during the first few nights, the attendant became somewhat careless and failed to guard it closely. It was only then that someone crept in and ran off with it. The master, much to his chagrin, was never able to discover who had been responsible for this mischievous deed.

On another occasion, the Ninna Emperor[6] summoned him into his presence and gave this command: "Bring me some of your beautiful chrysanthemums so that I might have them planted at Omuro."[7] The man did as he was ordered, but just as he was excusing himself, he was again summoned and told by the Emperor: "If the flowers are not labeled, I cannot accept them." The man thereupon arranged the chrysanthemums neatly and labeled them before presenting them once more to His Majesty. Accompanying the flowers was this poem:

(19)	Shigure furu Toki zo orikeru Kiku no hana Utsurou kara ni Iro no masareba	I gathered these chrysanthemums While the autumn showers fell; Wet with rain, The colors will seem Still more beautiful.[8]

It is difficult to determine whether or not this poem is a good one.

The same man received a letter from the Major Counsellor Kunitsune,[9] which contained little news of importance. He felt obligated, however, to send a reply to which he attached a lovely chrysanthemum, wondering how Kunitsune would react to it. This was the poem Kunitsune sent in return:[10]

He was surprised that Kunitsune could compose such a poem. Thinking that he would waste a great deal of time if he pondered too seriously over his reply and realizing that the messenger must be wondering what was causing the long delay, he quickly dashed off a poem which he handed to the messenger:

(20)	Hanagoromo	If you in a bright-colored robe
	Kimi ga ki oraba	Should come to gather the chrysanthemums
	Asajū ni	Growing amidst the miscanthus,
	Majireru kiku no	They would become
	Ka ni masarinan	Still more fragrant.[11]

A woman about whom the man had often heard but whom he had never courted lived in a certain place. Wondering how he might make her acquaintance, he passed by her house as often as he possibly could but failed to find the right opportunity to begin courting her. One night, as he was going by her gate where the lamplight shone brightly, he saw several women standing there. Dismounting, he spoke with them. Since they readily answered his questions, he was truly delighted and remained standing at the gate for some time.

The ladies had someone ask the man's attendant who he was,

whereupon the attendant was instructed to reveal his master's name. Learning who it was they were speaking to, the women exclaimed: "We have heard so much about you! Come with us into the garden to view the moon." Thinking that this was a marvelous idea, the man said, "That would be wonderful!" and accompanied them into the garden.

Afterward, they invited the man to join them on the veranda where all the women had gathered. Oddly enough, although they hardly knew him, they chatted amiably about a number of topics. The man as well as the women participated in the conversation and thoroughly enjoyed each other's company. The women spoke up occasionally, for they found the man most congenial. As for the man, he felt strangely elated in their company and carried on a lively conversation with the ladies, thinking that he would like to form a liaison with at least one of them.

At this juncture, someone came to interrupt them, saying to the man, "Your horse has broken loose. No one seems to know to where it has run off!" Irritated, the man replied: "Oh, let it go where it will!" and dismissed him. "What has happened?" queried the women as they looked on anxiously. The man replied: "There is nothing to worry about. It is just that my horse, startled by something, has run off." But the women cried: "Oh, no. Your wife probably planned this, since you failed to return home even after it had grown so late. How frightening! We must not speak to a man whose wife becomes so upset over a trivial matter." Terrified at the thought of what might happen to them, they railed against the poor man before going into hiding.

"How sad this makes me! I wish I were dead. Oh, it is not at all what you think," he said, but the women refused to listen. There was now no one left with whom he could become intimate. Realizing that it was in vain to remain where he was, he departed.

Early the next morning as the showers of late autumn fell, the man composed this poem:

(21) Sayonaka ni Uki Natorigawa Wataruran Nurenishi sode ni Shigure sae furu	Did I cross the Natori River, Where rumors about me fly, In the middle of the night? The autumn showers fall, Wetting my sleeve all the more.[12]

A woman replied with this poem:

(22) Shigure nomi Furu ya naraba zo Nureniken Tachikakuretaru Koto ya kuyashiki	Since this is a house Upon which the autumn rains Beat unceasingly, You have become soaked to the bone; Do you now regret That you sought refuge here?[13]

Charmed by the poem, the man wrote several letters to the woman, but she failed to respond. As it was futile to say anything more, he made no further attempt to communicate with her.

The same man had another woman with whom he had secretly become intimate. One day he sent her a message, lamenting that such a long time had elapsed since their last meeting. The woman replied: "I, too, feel the same way. Please send someone over to fetch me." The man therefore went to her house accompanied by an elegant friend of his.[14] When they arrived there, his friend said: "Now that I have escorted you here, I shall be returning home." "Please spend the night here," pleaded the man. His friend protested, saying, "Oh, but it is much too eerie here! Why do you insist that I stay?" He then composed this poem:

(23) Naniwa-gata Okite mo yukan Ashitazu no Koe furitatete Ikite todomeyo	I shall now leave Naniwa Bay— Oh, crane among the reeds, Please entreat me to stay With your loud cries![15]

The man recited:

(24)	Naniwa-e no	How can you abandon
	Shio mitsu made ni	The crane that sheds
	Naku tazu o	Such a flood of tears
	Mata ika nareba	That it causes the tide to rise
	Sugite yukuran	In the Bay of Naniwa?[16]

No sooner had the man finished reciting the poem than his friend exclaimed: "That is not true. You have not shed a single tear." Although he did not reveal how he personally felt about the situation, he consented to stay overnight.[17] No one knows what words were exchanged between the man and the woman.

The man once had a secret love affair with a woman whose father lived in Ōmi.[18] Her father soon learned of it and thereafter watched his daughter with special care, latching the gate each night. Studying her face, he could see that she was lost in thought and sorely distressed.

For a long time, her lover was unable to go to her. One night, however, with a great deal of effort on his part, he managed to get in and had his attendant announce to her that he had climbed in over the walls. Having seen his daughter go up to the messenger and speak with him, her father reproved her severely. The woman thereupon said to her lover: "This cannot go on. We must not see each other anymore, since my father has found out about us and disapproves. Please go home immediately." Disappointed, her lover said: "You must not say such things. Please let me in!" But terrified of her father, the woman said beseechingly: "If you care about my future welfare, please do as I ask you." Her lover then said: "I see that you really mean what you say. All right, I shall return home just this once." Before leaving, he composed this poem:

(25)	Miru me nami	Without seeing you,
	Tachi ya kaeran	I shall return home,
	Ōmiji wa	Resenting all the while
	Nani no ura naru	That the Meeting Road
	Ura to uramite	Is but a name.[19]

The woman's return poem went:

(26)	Sekiyama no	Since the storm wind
	Arashi no koe no	On Mount Seki
	Arakeraba	Sounded threatening,
	Kimi no ōmi	Ōmi—where I was to meet you—
	Na ni nomi narikeri	Is but a name.[20]

Her lover failed to send her a reply. In everything she did, she showed herself unworthy of her noble birth. Because the woman continued to fear her father, the lovers saw no more of each other.

On still another occasion, the same man went on a pilgrimage to Shiga. Several women, who had unhitched the oxen from their carriage, were standing by a bubbling spring near the Meeting Barrier. The man rode up and dismounted. Seeing that a stranger was present, the women immediately hitched the carriage to the oxen and started on their way. "Where are you off to?" inquired the man. The carriage attendant replied for the ladies, "To Shiga Temple," whereupon the man followed the carriage, keeping at a discreet distance.

When they crossed the Meeting Barrier and began their descent to the shore, one of the occupants of the carriage sent him this poem:

(27)	Ōsaka wa	True to its name—
	Na ni tanomarenu	The Meeting Barrier—
	Sekimizu no	I have at long last met the man
	Nagarete oto ni	About whom rumors are as ceaseless
	Kiku hito o mite	As the waters flowing at the barrier.[21]

At once impressed and amused by her poem, the man sent back this poem:

(28)	Na o tanomi	Trusting in its name,
	Ware mo kayowan	I, too, shall cross
	Ōsaka o	The Meeting Barrier;
	Koyureba kimi ni	When I arrive in Ōmi
	Ōmi narikeri	I am sure to see you.[22]

The woman had her attendant ask: "Where are you heading?" The man replied, "I am on my way to Shiga Temple." "As I am also heading that way, let us go together," said the woman and off they went.

The man and the woman thought that this was indeed a happy turn of events. Obtaining quarters near each other, they stayed at the temple, conversing to their hearts' content.

It happened to be a time when it was unlucky for the man to travel in a given direction away from the temple. Since he could not stay until the following day, he departed in another direction. As he went off he declared: "My life is precious to me now that I care about our future relationship."[23] In her unhappiness the woman said: "There must be another alternative to parting. Oh, what am I to do? Promise me you will visit me in the capital." In that they both served in the Imperial Palace, she informed him of the location of her apartment and the names of the women who were with her.

Although their encounter had been brief, the man was reluctant to part from the woman. Before taking his leave, he composed this poem:

(29)	Tachite yuku	Though I know not
	Yukue mo shiranu	My destination,
	Kaku nomi zo	I now depart,
	Tabi no sora ni wa	Hoping to call on you
	Toubekarikeru	At the end of my journey.[24]

This was the woman's answering poem:

(30) Kaku nomi shi	Because you are uncertain
Yukue madowaba	About your destination,
Waga tama wa	I should like to send
Tague yaramashi	My spirit to guide you
Tabi no sora ni wa	On your journey.[25]

He thought of sending her a return poem, but his attendants warned him, saying, "It will be unlucky for you to travel away from the temple once day breaks." Unable to linger any longer at the temple, the man made his way to a nearby mansion.

The next morning, thinking that he would meet her carriage as it went by, he asked a fisherman for permission to draw the fishing nets in to the shore. As he was pulling them in, a friend came by, inviting him for a walk in the direction of Seta.[26] The man immediately accepted the invitation. In the meantime, the woman returned to the palace and told her friends about her adventure in Shiga. In the audience was a woman whom the man had once courted but whom he had stopped seeing altogether. Hearing this story, she inquired: "What was the man's name?"[27] "He is a rogue!" she exclaimed and fabricated the most preposterous stories about him. The woman who was involved with the man this time cried: "If you had not told me, I would never have known what he is really like! I am so heart-broken!" She then instructed the other women: "I forbid you to accept any of his letters."

Completely ignorant of all this, the man who had gone for a walk to Seta returned and promptly made his way to the woman's palace apartment. He sent his messenger to announce to the ladies that the man they had met in Shiga was here to see them. One of the lady attendants said: "I am sorry, but the young lady is still in the country. Before she left, she informed us that she would be going on a pilgrimage to Shiga and has not yet returned." Although she spoke kindly to the messenger, she refused to accept his master's letter.

When the messenger reported what had happened, his master thought that the woman's behavior was very strange. Even after he was unsuccessful in discovering the reason for this behavior, he kept sending messengers to the palace with his letters day after day. Alas, no one would accept them! Among the men who had visited the Shiga Temple with him was a friend who knew why the ladies were behaving so strangely. The man summoned his friend. Since the latter had witnessed everything from the very beginning and knew exactly what had happened, he said: "I am afraid someone has been speaking unfavorably about you."

Sadly viewing his garden, the man composed this impromptu verse:

(31)	Tasukubeki	The trees and plants
	Kusaki naranedo	Fail to console me;
	Aware to zo	They seem so forlorn
	Mono omou toki no	As I gaze at them,
	Me ni wa miekeru	Lost in longing for my love.[28]

His friend commented: "Indeed, it seems that way." Meanwhile, night had fallen and the moon was breathtakingly lovely. The man said: "Please accompany me to the woman's residence in the west side of the capital; I usually go there whenever I have something I want to discuss with her. I will make her talk to me this time." "It would not seem proper at night," protested his friend. Nevertheless, the two men started off for the west side of the capital, traveling along Nijō Avenue.

Fondly recalling what had happened in Shiga, he recited in a loud voice full of longing the first poem the woman had composed.[29] A carriage happened to pass by just then. The man followed it, reciting the poem all the way to Suzaku Avenue.

The woman in the carriage had someone ask him: "Who dares to recite my poem?" Taken aback by this question, the man replied: "I am reciting this poem as I travel along, hoping to come across its writer." The woman called out: "It is you! I was so hurt to hear that you had formerly been intimate with someone else. I do not wish to see you just now." As he listened to her words, the man wondered what he should do about his present predicament. Feeling truly remorseful, he asked: "Was that what was troubling you all this time?" "Yes," replied the woman.

The man said: "Please stop your carriage for a moment." "Well, I am anxious to hear what you have to say," replied the woman and had her carriage come to a halt. The man dismounted and, approaching the carriage, asked: "Where are you heading?" "Home," answered the woman.

Ever since his letters had been refused, the man had borne a bitter grudge against her. Because he spoke to her in such a pitiful manner, the woman, hardly able to say anything from her side, sounded truly wretched whenever she responded. Reluctantly he withdrew from the carriage, thinking to himself: "I suppose she was just being a little stubborn. Although people have probably been saying unkind things about me, what they said could not have been all that bad." But as the carriage rumbled off, he began thinking that the whole affair had been quite irrational. He called out to her to stop so that they could discuss their misunderstanding. Eager to learn who had told her such stories about him, he had his friend say for him: "I came here with the intention of drowning myself, since I had been feeling positively wretched and hated myself. However, I had one more thing to say to you, and so I was unable to throw myself into any other river[30] but this." The man thereupon composed this poem:

(32)	Mi no usa o	Weary of my misery,
	Itoi sute ni to	I came here
	Idetsuredo	Intending to drown myself,
	Namida no kawa wa	But alas, I was unable to cross
	Wataru to mo nashi	The River of Tears.[31]

The woman sent back this poem:

(33)	Makoto nite	Though there is no ford
	Wataru se naraba	Where one might cross,
	Namidagawa	Seeing your swiftly flowing
	Nagarete hayaki	River of Tears,
	Mi to o tanoman	I shall trust in you.[32]

She then added: "Please come up closer. I have something I wish to say to you." Approaching the carriage, the man began to exchange words with her. When at last day began to dawn, the woman said: "I must be going now. Do not tell a soul what we have said to one another tonight. I certainly will not forget a thing that has happened, but as for you, I hope you think of it all as being nothing but a dream." So saying, she started to leave when the man recited this poem:

(34)	Aki no yo no	It is said
	Yume wa hakanaku	That an autumn night's dream
	Ari to ieba	Is unrealiable;
	Haru ni kaerite	I wish spring would come
	Masashikaranan	To make my dreams come true.[33]

By this time it had grown very light. Worriedly the woman said: "You must return home," but the man refused to leave her side, for he was determined to find out where she lived. As neither was about to give in to the other, the man recited this poem:

(35)	Koto naraba	It matters very much to me,
	Akashi hatete yo	So please wait until
	Koromode ni	Day has dawned—
	Fureru namida no	I want you to see the color
	Iro mo mizubeku	Of my tear-stained sleeve.[34]

The woman sent back this poem:

(36)	Koromode ni	Were I to wait
	Furan namida no	Until it grew light enough
	Iro min to	To see the stain of the tears
	Akasaba ware mo	That fell on your sleeve,
	Arawarenu kana	You would discover where I live.[35]

It was becoming lighter and lighter with each passing moment, and so he had a young servant remain behind, saying to him, "Follow that carriage and be sure to take note of where it turns in." He himself went on home. As he had been instructed, the young servant observed carefully where the carriage turned in. However, it is not known what happened afterward.

Once there was a woman with whom the same man had secretly become intimate. In that she lived in a house which could easily be seen by passersby, the man had to take great pains to leave before it grew light. This morning, too, he had left early, and because it was still quite dark, he had to grope his way out. Being reluctant to leave his sweetheart's home, however, he stood for some time on the bridge which extended in front of the gate. This is the poem he had his attendant deliver to the woman:

(37)	Yo ni wa idete	Though I steal out in the night,
	Wataru zo waburu	I cannot cross the River of Tears
	Namidagawa	I shed in my unhappiness,
	Fuchi to nagarete	For it looks so deep
	Fukaku miyureba	As it flows along.[36]

The woman, unable to sleep, was still wide awake when she received the poem. She therefore replied:

(38)	Sayonaka ni	All alone
	Okurete waburu	In the middle of the night,
	Namida koso	I shed tears of sorrow;
	Kimi ga atari no	I believe my tears have turned into
	Fuchi to narurame	The deep pools near you.[37]

As people were beginning to travel back and forth along the highway, he could not very well remain standing there indefinitely and thus returned home.

The man happened to catch a glimpse of a woman who was far above him in social status and fell madly in love with her. He realized all too well how far apart they were but one day he had an opportunity to communicate with her. Afterward, he wondered how he might begin to court her. Some time had elapsed since he had first communicated with her, and so he wrote again to her, saying, ''I should like very much to speak to you directly without any intermediary or having to resort to letter-writing.'' The man sounded so earnest that the woman wondered: ''What am I to do? Perhaps I ought to listen to what he has to say, even though I should be seated behind a screen.''

Meanwhile, her mother, who was a spiteful old woman, discovered what was going on between them. Since she was very strict, as soon as she learned that they had been exchanging letters, she forbade them to continue their correspondence. Her daughter became very much distressed when the man insisted upon seeing her, knowing that her mother, who had forbidden her to see him, was watching her every move.

At a loss as to what to do, the woman confided in her friend, saying, ''I have been sorely troubled lately, for my mother is determined to keep us apart. Since my lover does not know of this, he insists on seeing me. I now find myself in a terribly awkward situation. I wish to tell him to give up any hope of ever being anything more than a casual acquaintance.'' Her confidante exclaimed: ''Oh, why did you not speak to me sooner? Before he upsets your mother any more than he already has, you must discuss this problem like two sensible adults. Go out onto the veranda to view the moon in all its loveliness. You will soon have forgotten most of your worries. Meanwhile, I shall summon the man here, so please speak to him when he comes.'' The confidante then went to the man's house and said: ''Please make your way cautiously to the veranda. Remember, you have me to thank for arranging this rendezvous.'' The man waited anxiously for it to grow dark before setting out for the woman's house.

When he arrived, the woman's friend said: ''Remember that this meeting was made possible because of my efforts.'' The lovers were delighted to see each other, for they were deeply in love. All went well for them as they chatted the time away, for the woman's grouchy old mother had been asleep since early evening. As the night deepened, however, the girl's mother awoke with a start and sat up on the bedding, saying, ''Ah, this is very strange. I wonder why I am unable to sleep? Is there a special reason for my restlessness?" With these words, she jumped out of bed and rushed out. The man immediately hid himself under the veranda, while the girl's mother carefully checked to see if all was well. Observing that no one else was there, she breathed a sigh of relief and went back inside.

No sooner had she gone inside than the man emerged from his hiding place and continued speaking to his sweetheart. He said: "Just look at me. Because of such a close call, I have to speak to you as desperately as I do. After all, a man lives only once." While he was exchanging vows of love with the young woman, her mother said in a loud voice: "How odd that she has not come in." Hearing these words, the young woman said to her lover: "I promise to come out to see you some other time, but you must leave now." Unhappy that he had to part from his beloved, the man composed this poem:

(39)	Tamasaka ni	We play the koto
	Kimi to shiraburu	In perfect harmony
	Koto no ne ni	Whenever we happen to meet;
	Aite mo awanu	Oh, why must our meetings
	Koi o suru kana	Be so few?[38]

Amused by the situation he found himself in, the man lingered a while longer and said: "Please tell your mother that I have already left." Meanwhile, the mean old woman, who had secretly been peering out at them, said: "Just where did you come from, you thief! Now I know why people say that there is a reason for sleeplessness." She then attempted to tie him up, but he fled into the night without even bothering to put his sandals on properly. As for the frightened girl, she lay prone, not daring to breathe. Because she was forbidden to communicate with the man who no longer came to call on her, it was in vain . . .[39]

Appendix: Early Heian Literature

EARLY HEIAN WAKA

In spite of the overwhelming influence of things Chinese during the early ninth century, Heian courtiers maintained the Japanese language in its purity, largely because of the indispensable role that poetry played in courtship. A man who became interested in a woman would at once address her a poem, written in Japanese because she was unlikely to know Chinese, and because Chinese was considered the language of the intellect rather than of the heart. The lady in turn would reply with a similar verse. Japanese poetry now meant almost exclusively the waka, written in five lines arranged 5, 7, 5, 7, and 7 syllables. Earlier there had been other verse forms, such as the *chōka* ("the long poem"), but in the ninth and tenth centuries the waka reigned supreme, presumably because the functions of Japanese poetry were now restricted to brief expressions of feeling, whereas poetry had sometimes served in earlier times such public functions as mourning the death of a royal personage or celebrating the discovery of gold.

There is a possibility that the preference for 5- or 7-syllable lines may have been influenced by the 5-character *shih,* first popular during the Six Dynasties period in China, and the 7-character *shih,* which came into vogue during the T'ang period. The language of the waka, however, was little affected by Chinese poetry. Indeed, there was a surprising absence of Chinese loanwords in the Japanese poetic diction, even during the periods when Chinese influence was at its height. Early Heian works of prose were also written in the pure "Yamato" language, though later we find Chinese loanwords gradually creeping into prose writings.

The nature of the Japanese language makes rhyme or meter based on stress or quantity impossible, so poetry came to be based on syllabics. The general adoption of the waka form did not preclude the use of a number of important poetic conventions found especially in the *chōka,* including the pillow-word *(makura kotoba),* the pivot-word *(kakekotoba),* the associated word *(engo),* the preface *(jo),* and the allusive variation *(honkadori).* The waka form being as short as it was, some of these poetic devices may seem to us to have been a waste of precious syllables, but others, especially the pivot-words, enabled the poet to compress by the use of puns several levels of meaning into one poem.

THE DEVELOPMENT OF THE WAKA

Since the Nara period the waka, also known as *tanka,* has been the classic verse form of Japan.[1] Ninety percent of the poems in the eighth-century anthology *Man'yōshū* (c. 759) are waka, indicating that from about a century earlier this form was considered the most appropriate for expressing a Japanese poet's sentiments. Other poetic forms, such as the *chōka,* existed in Man'yō times, but Brower and Miner state that "soon after the age of the first primitive songs and the emergence of a literary sense, the tanka form was realized, and that although it was to undergo many vicissitudes, and other forms were to have their hour, the formal constant of the Japanese prosodic tradition is this verse of 31 syllables."[2]

The poems in the *Man'yōshū* were written in an extremely cumbersome script in which Chinese characters were used sometimes phonetically, sometimes ideographically. The main reason the *Man'yōshū* was almost forgotten in the years following its compilation was that the people in the Heian court were no longer able to read the difficult script. A break in poetic tradition had been occasioned by the change to the *kana* script, and also by the dominance of Chinese culture during the first half of the ninth century. The hiatus in native poetry coincided with the period of the greatest vogue of Chinese poetry (800–850).[3] As we shall later see, this hiatus, however, was by no means complete, and even when the composition of Chinese poetry was at its height, waka were still being composed.

Since it was considered unladylike for women to study Chinese, those who managed somehow to acquire a knowledge of Chinese normally did not boast of their accomplishments.[4] Instead, they kept alive the tradition of waka. A courtier therefore found it necessary to compose waka in order to communicate with a woman he fancied in the conventional manner of Japanese courtship at the time. Thus, though the men immersed themselves in Chinese studies for the sake of their careers, they nevertheless kept up the waka tradition in their private lives.

For about a century following the compilation of the *Man'yōshū,* there was an eclipse of Japanese culture; this period is sometimes referred to as the "Dark Age of National Customs and Manners" *(kokufū ankoku).* However, shortly after the last official embassy to T'ang China in 838, many signs indicated that the Japanese were becoming interested once again in their own culture. Chinese influence remained great, but the Japanese increasingly sought to modify whatever they imported to suit their own taste. Developments within the sphere of Japanese poetry were to result in the "golden age" of waka in the tenth century.

In the early ninth century, waka were composed by emperors and courtiers at banquets and on hunting excursions as a form of light entertainment. Two notable early Heian waka poets were Ono no Takamura (802–852) and the Emperor Heizei (774–824, r. 806–809); somewhat later Ariwara no Yukihira (818–893) appeared upon the scene. From the mid-ninth to late-ninth century a group of poets known as the Six Poetic Geniuses brought about a revival of the waka. The rebirth of waka was closely related to the increasing importance of women in the courts of the reigning and retired emperors as the Fujiwara family, by marrying their daughters into the imperial family, came into prominence.

During the Engi era (901–923), a number of courtiers were expert in both Chinese studies and Japanese poetry. Among the outstanding men of talent were Ki no Haseo (845–912), Ki no

Yoshimochi (d. 919), Miyoshi no Kiyotsura (847–918), Ōe no Chisato (dates unknown), Fujiwara no Tokihira (871–909), and Fujiwara no Tadahira (880–949). It was during this era that the waka began to be considered almost as important to the cultivated man as Chinese studies, though the latter retained its supremacy until the end of the Heian period. Chinese continued to be used in official and private writings of the courtiers even after the invention of the Japanese phonetic script, but the first half of *Tales of Yamato* illustrates the importance of the waka in the daily lives of the imperial family and the ladies and gentlemen of the Heian court.

To be discussed in the following sections are the various developments in poetry that eventually culminated in a great flowering of the waka: (1) the poetry contests *(utaawase),* (2) the poems on silk screens *(byōbu-uta),* (3) the private collections *(shikashū),* and (4) the first three of the twenty-one imperial anthologies *(chokusenshū)*—the *Kokinshū,* the *Gosenshū,* and the *Shūishū.*

The Poetry Contests

In the eighth century, waka figured in poetry competitions; however, these informal tests of poetic ability are not classed as *utaawase,* a court activity that flourished from the ninth century on. The poetry contests are believed to have originated in the second half of the ninth century, about the time the Six Poetic Geniuses were bringing about the waka revival. The oldest known poetry contest is the *Zai Mimbukyō no ie no utaawase* which was held at the mansion of Ariwara no Yukihira some time between 884 and 887. The *Koresada no Miko no utaawase*—from which Sugawara no Michizane borrowed in compiling a collection of waka known as the *Shinsen man'yōshū* in 893—were two other early Heian poetry contests.[5] The first poetry contest to be transcribed, however, was the *Teiji no In no utaawase* (913),[6] which was sponsored by the Retired Emperor Uda about whom many of the episodes in *Tales of Yamato* revolve. A number of poetry contests were held during the lifetime of Emperor Uda, but they were chiefly ceremonial, with entertainment rather than a serious consideration of poetry being the main purpose of the gatherings. Many poetry contests were held at the court of a reigning or retired emperor or at a private mansion of a high-ranking official; poetry contests were also sponsored by the High Priestesses of the Ise and Kamo shrines and by the leading poets of the day. Abe Akio states that between the *Kokinshū* (905) and the *Gosenshū* (952), there were over a hundred known *utaawase*.[7]

Participants in these contests—men as well as women—were divided into two teams, designated "left" and "right." In the earlier competitions the participants were assigned a theme, usually on an aspect of one of the seasons or on a stage in courtship, on which they were expected to compose extemporaneously an appropriate poem using the accepted poetic diction and suitable imagery. The atmosphere of the earlier competitions was light-hearted and casual; this is reflected in accounts of such poetry contests as the *Teiji no In no utaawase* (913) and the *Kyōgoku no Miyasundokoro Hōshi no utaawase* (921).[8] In the latter contest, for example, the Retired Emperor called a draw in judging two poems so as not to hurt the feelings of one of the contestants.[9] Nevertheless, even as early as the *Teiji no In no utaawase* there was a suggestion of serious literary competition.

By the time of the *Tentoku yonen Dairi no utaawase* in 960,[10] the poetry contests had begun to be taken seriously indeed. Brower and Miner mention some interesting details of this contest which set the standard for later competitions, concluding that "it is clear that what was once a mere pastime was now a contest involving social and literary reputations."[11]

The fact that this contest was held shortly after the completion of *Tales of Yamato* reflects the importance of the waka to the aristocrats of the time, not only in their private lives but in their public lives as well. Together with the compilation of imperial anthologies, these contests played an important role in developing a sense of critical consciousness in the early Heian courtiers. In the tenth century, Japanese poetry was of the greatest importance in social circles, though only shortly before it had been obscured because of the emphasis on Chinese studies.

A detailed study of the poetry contests reveals that in the competitions held at the courts of the reigning and retired emperors up to the *Saki no Dajō Daijin no ie no utaawase*[12] held in 1094, the emphasis was on the ceremonial aspects, and not on the serious poetic criticisms of the poems submitted.[13] Later, however, the emphasis shifted to the critical decisions made by the judges, written down either during the contest or at a later date. These judgments were important in formulating the poetic standards of the age. And since the golden age of poetic criticism coincides with the flourishing of the *utaawase* (late twelfth to early thirteenth centuries), it is clear that these poetry contests were central to the development of Japanese literary criticism.[14] The reputations of the participating poets were at stake in these contests, which were therefore conducted with great seriousness. This has been said of the later contests: "the judges' decisions were sometimes repealed in formal letters of protest to the sponsors and occasionally changed. In general a desperate atmosphere prevailed."[15]

A "desperate atmosphere" certainly did not prevail at the contests held during the first half of the tenth century. The *utaawase* were social gatherings where courtiers and court ladies were entertained. They provided outstanding poets with the opportunity to associate with one another and form close ties of friendship. A greater part of the first half of *Tales of Yamato* deals with historical figures who moved in the court circle of the Retired Emperor Uda; many of them participated in the poetry contests sponsored by him or a member of his court. Nothing suggests that the competition was intense; rather, the atmosphere at these contests was informal and congenial. Nonetheless, even these earlier contests indicate the importance of waka composition in the social as well as the private lives of the aristocracy.

Poems on Silk Screens

The ideal Heian courtier was expected to be an amateur painter as well as a poet; this suggests how intimately art and poetry were related at this time. The combination, then in vogue, of silk-screen paintings *(byōbu-e)* and waka which accompanied them *(byōbu-uta)* illustrates the close relationship of art and poetry. The *byōbu-*

uta were written attractively on thick, cardboardlike paper *(shikishi)* and pasted directly onto the painting, with both the calligraphy and the meaning of the poem enhancing the beauty of the screen. Silk screens were originally imported from China, but the demand for them grew along with the increase in the number of mansions of the Heian aristocrats; it eventually became necessary for the Japanese themselves to produce them.

Tamagami Takuya has made a detailed study of the relationship of silk-screen paintings to the development of poetry and various *monogatari* in which he stressed the importance of the Enthronement Ceremony *(Daijōkai),* at which screens from various provinces were presented, in the development of the waka during the late ninth and early tenth centuries.[16] On these ceremonial occasions, five-foot-high screens decorated with Chinese poems and four-foot-high screens decorated with waka—the two varieties of screens produced by Japanese artists—were displayed.

Screen poems were also composed for other formal occasions, such as the celebration of special birthdays of members of the imperial family or high-ranking officials. The *Kokinshū* contains a group of seven poems composed for a silk screen painted on the occasion of the fortieth birthday of Fujiwara no Sadakuni in 906 (KT 357–363).[17]

The earliest screen poems were composed with the poet in the role of one viewing the painting. As an example Tamagami cites a poem which appears in the *Kokinshū* (KT 930). According to the headnote, the poem was composed by Sanjō no Machi, a court lady serving in the court of Emperor Montoku (r. 850–858):

Omoi seku	I wonder if this waterfall
Kokoro no uchi no	Is the waterfall of love
Taki nare ya	Concealed in my heart;
Otsu to wa miredo	Though I see it fall,
Oto no kikoenu	Not a sound do I hear.[18]

Here in this poem, the court lady is expressing her sentiments upon seeing the waterfall in a painting. However, as composing poems for the numerous screen paintings became a popular pastime in the Heian court, the courtiers and court ladies—instead of expressing their feelings as mere spectators—began to compose screen poems imagining themselves to be figures in the paintings. We have an example of this practice in episode 147 of *Tales of Yamato.* The empress and a number of her ladies-in-waiting compose poems on the Ikuta legend of the maiden courted by two young men, the subject of a screen painting, each participant pretending to be one of the tragic figures and composing an appropriate poem. Tamagami cites this as an example illustrating the close relationship of the waka and the monogatari to the art of painting.[19] A similar series of poems in the *Ise shū* was composed for the *Chōgonka no byōbu*—a silk-screen painting depicting the tragic love story of a Chinese emperor and his beloved consort—presented to the Retired Emperor Uda (ZKT 18155–18164).

Of great importance in the development of the *tsukuri-monogatari* (fictional tales) and the *uta monogatari* (poem-tales) were the sets of screen poems consisting entirely of love poems exchanged by the lovers depicted in a painting. A group may be found in the *Ise shū* (ZKT 18138–18154). Tamagami believes that the poems in this particular group were written early in the reign of Emperor Uda (887–897). If this is true, these poems are the earliest examples of screen poems consisting entirely of love poems.[20]

From these examples we see that during the early tenth century the art of painting and the art of story-telling were intimately associated with the composition of poetry. Because of the great demand for decorative screens, professional poets were kept busy composing screen poems, their chief duty being to satisfy their patrons. Thanks to their efforts, the waka came to occupy a place of such importance in Heian court society that a special governmental bureau—the *Wakadokoro*—was created in 951. A total of 443 *byōbu-uta* were included in the imperial anthologies and the following poets were most active as contributors: Ki no Tsurayuki (99), Taira no Kanemori (24), Ōshikōchi no Mitsune (22), and Lady Ise (15).[21]

The Imperial Anthologies

The compilation of the first of the twenty-one imperial anthologies, the *Kokinshū,* was ordered by Emperor Daigo in 905 and was completed in about 913. This anthology of 1,111 poems—arranged by seasons and other subject headings, such as love and travel—was extremely important in that it established an elegant and refined poetic diction for the waka that changed very little up to the end of the nineteenth century. Moreover, it established the importance of the waka after a long period of obscurity; the waka, now recognized as a literary form of the highest quality, could no longer be dismissed merely as a vehicle for private communication between lovers or friends. The *Kokinshū* poems, influenced by Chinese poetry of the Six Dynasties period, are often described as being artificial, burdened with conceits, and altogether lacking the genuine emotion and freshness of the *Man'yōshū* poems. Nevertheless, the *Kokinshū* was of immense importance and its poems were memorized and alluded to for centuries.

The compilers of the *Kokinshū*—Ki no Tsurayuki, Ki no Tomonori, Ōshikōchi no Mitsune, and Mibu no Tadamine—were court officials of middling rank. Nonetheless, they had gained a position of prominence because they were professional court poets active in poetry contests and known for their poems for silk-screen paintings. A number of their poems are included in the *Kokinshū:* Ki no Tsurayuki (102), Mitsune, (60), Tomonori (46), and Tadamine (35). Ki no Tsurayuki was the most prolific poet of his age, though he is often considered a greater literary critic than a poet. Through his efforts, the waka came to be recognized in court circles as a dignified form of literary expression, suitable for both social and private purposes. Tsurayuki's famous preface to the *Kokinshū,* written in kana, is the first work of Japanese poetic criticism. Late in his life, he also compiled the *Shinsen wakashū,* a privately compiled anthology *(shisenshū),* at the command of Emperor Daigo. In this anthology, Tsurayuki included 360 waka selected from the *Kokinshū* and other sources. The preface to the *Shinsen wakashū,* unlike his better-known works, was written in Chinese, proof that he was proficient enough in Chinese studies to express himself gracefully in Chinese.[22] Nevertheless, Tsurayuki, the leading literary figure of his day, normally chose to write in Japanese, using the kana syllabary. By writing in kana, considered until this time "a woman's hand" and an unworthy medium for serious expression, Tsurayuki gave the phonetic syllabary a new prestige. No doubt his example influenced other men; henceforth many prose works were composed in Japanese.

The second imperial anthology, the *Gosenshū,* was compiled by command of the Emperor Murakami in 951. Because this was a project of the newly created *Wakadokoro,* the "Five Poets of the Pear-Jar Room"—Ōnakatomi no Yoshinobu, Kiyowara no Mototsuke, Minamoto no Shitagō, Ki no Tokibumi (Tsurayuki's son), and Sakanoue no Mochiki—all worked on this anthology. Some of the notable characteristics of this collection are that: (1) the head-notes are extremely long, often containing fictional elements; (2) there are no poems by any of the compilers; (3) a great number of love poems are scattered throughout the anthology.[23] It is interesting to note that the *Gosenshū* dates from about the same time as *Tales of Yamato.* In that the prose in the second half of *Tales of Yamato* is of more importance than the poetry, both works suggest the marked development in Japanese prose which was to culminate in the masterpieces of a half-century later.

The *Shūishū* (c. 996), the third imperial anthology, was compiled by Fujiwara no Kintō at the command of the Retired Emperor Kazan. *Tales of Yamato* includes a number of poems from these anthologies: *Kokinshū* (19), *Gosenshū* (33), and *Shūishū* (16). The imperial anthologies played an essential role in preserving and making known the best poems of the day; it was considered a great honor for a poet to have his waka included. A privately compiled collection of 4,500 waka called the *Kokin rokujō* ("Six Notebooks of Old and New Poetry") also deserves mention. Brower and Miner state that the collection was "unofficial" but widely read.[24] Forty-two poems in *Tales of Yamato* are included in this collection.

The Private Collections

The private collections *(shikashū* or *kashū)* differ from the imperial anthologies *(chokusenshū)* and privately compiled anthologies *(shisenshū)* in that the poems are all by a single poet. Various private collections were dipped into by the compilers of the *Man'yōshū;* mention is made of such private collections as the *Ka-*

kinomoto no Hitomaro shū and the *Takahashi no Mushimaro shū*, evidence that private collections were already in existence in the eighth century.[25] Although the private collections mentioned in the *Man'yōshū* have all been lost, Hisamatsu Sen'ichi believes that they must have resembled the extant collections compiled in later years.[26]

Numerous private collections were compiled during the tenth century, the period of the first three imperial anthologies. The private collections featuring love poems tended to have fictional elements in the headnotes to the poems and thus played an important role in the development of the monogatari genre. The private collections were sometimes compiled by the poet himself, sometimes by an admirer of a particular poet. At times the emperor ordered the compilation of a private collection.

The work known as the *Sanjūrokuninshū* ("Collection of Thirty-six Poets") is comprised of the private collections of thirty-six outstanding poets of the Nara and Heian periods. These private collections are conveniently located in this work, but other versions of the original collection have been preserved in private libraries in manuscript form. A number of poems in *Tales of Yamato* also appear in private collections,[27] but it is difficult to determine which came first, the private collections or *Tales of Yamato*. Moreover, there may have been other sources. Nonetheless, it should be noted that about the time *Tales of Yamato* was being compiled, the composition of waka was at its peak in aristocratic circles, and numerous anthologies of poetry appeared on the literary scene. The compilation of private collections and imperial anthologies played an important role in developing the critical consciousness of the Japanese courtiers and paved the way for the great works of fiction of the next generation.

EARLY HEIAN JAPANESE PROSE

Prefaces to Poetry Collections

The elegant style of Ki no Tsurayuki's Preface to the *Kokinshū* (early tenth century) was admired and imitated for centuries and, as the first work of literary criticism, it occupies a place of great importance in the history of Japanese literature. Tsurayuki also wrote in Japanese the preface to a collection of poems composed when the Retired Emperor Uda visited the Ōi River in 907.[28] In this preface Tsurayuki again expressed his views concerning the functions of the waka. Mibu no Tadamine, another compiler of the *Kokinshū,* also wrote a preface in Japanese for the same group of poems.[29] Now that the leading literary figures of the day had written criticism in Japanese, other men soon followed suit.

Another variety of work intimately associated with poetry was the diary in kana describing the circumstances of different poetry contests preceding the transcriptions of the poems submitted. An interesting example, the diary of the *Kyōgoku no Miyasundokoro Hōshi no utaawase* (921), treats the ceremonial aspects of the contest, giving particularly detailed descriptions of the splendid robes worn by the participants.[30] These diaries, however, belong to a class apart; the works which eventually led to the development of Heian literary prose were the poetic diaries.

The Poetic Diaries

Tsurayuki, when an old man in his sixties, wrote *The Tosa Diary,* or *Tosa nikki* (c. 935),[31] a work of fiction based in part on a diary kept in Chinese of his journey back to the capital from the province of Tosa where he had served as provincial governor. Although written in a prose style far simpler than that of the preface to the *Kokinshū* written two decades earlier, the combination of pathos and humor gives *The Tosa Diary* an enduring charm. Poetry plays an important part in this work; moreover, Tsurayuki touches on some of his poetic theories. Miner writes of Japanese literary diaries, the genre of which *The Tosa Diary* was the first example:

> . . . the diaries combine, or poise, two formal energies: the ceaseless pressure of time implied by the diary form itself and the enhancement of the moment, or related moments, usually demonstrated in poetry. It is the flow of time rather than the concatenation of events or architecture of design that is important, and the sudden glowing of poetic experience rather than the order of a well-lighted city that gives the diaries their sense of depth of experience.[32]

Miner continues:

> Poetry and time are also the two chief thematic bases of the diaries. After prose has said all it can, or all that it is decent for it to attempt, poems rise to have their say. . . . The prose of the diary is not merely an excuse for the poem; but the poems are not also a mere decoration.[33]

In subsequent literary diaries, the daily-entry form, which *The Tosa Diary* maintained, was abandoned. The diaries tended, as Miner points out, to "pass over long periods of time with a phrase or, on the other hand, devote to a single night the most detailed description."[34] Nevertheless, waka continued to play an indispensable role in the later examples of this genre.

A work entitled the *Takamitsu Diary (Takamitsu nikki),* also known as the *Tale of the Minor Captain of Tōnomine (Tōnomine Shōshō monogatari),* was written shortly after 962. The work itself covers a period of nine months and tells of how Fujiwara no Takamitsu, the son of the Minister of the Right Morosuke (d. 994), enters the priesthood and builds himself a hut at a place called Tōnomine. It contains eighty-five waka—those of Takamitsu, his wife, his younger sister, and others. This work is often referred to as a poem-tale, but since it describes an important event in the life of a historical figure, it may more properly be considered a variation of the poetic diary.

The Gossamer Diary (Kagerō nikki),[35] the first of the literary diaries by a woman, was written in 974, approximately twenty years after the compilation of *Tales of Yamato.* The writer—a bitterly jealous woman married to Fujiwara no Kaneie (929–990), a high-ranking official—candidly reveals her innermost thoughts and feelings in this work. This psychological probing into a woman's heart and mind foreshadows the great works of prose that were to appear several decades later.

The poetic diary, however, had to combine with two other genres, the fictional tales *(tsukuri-monogatari)* and the poem-tales *(uta monogatari),* before it was possible to create the supreme prose classic of Japanese literature, *The Tale of Genji.*

The Fictional Tales

It is not known exactly when *The Tale of the Bamboo-Cutter,*[36] the earliest example of the *tsukuri-monogatari,* was written, but a version must have existed before the compilation of *Tales of Yamato* in the mid-tenth century, for a poem in episode 77 of this work alludes to the tale of the old bamboo-cutter and Princess Kaguya, the lovely creature he found in a bamboo stalk and raised as his child. Furthermore, *The Tale of the Bamboo-Cutter,* though heavily indebted to Chinese literature and folklore, presents certain aspects of the life of the Heian aristocracy. The heroine is the beautiful adopted daughter of the bamboo-cutter, and the theme is the tasks she sets her suitors, five courtiers. The tale is given charm by the elegance of the prose style and by the humor in the passages relating the hardships the five men undergo in their impossibly difficult missions. When all five have failed, the emperor himself is attracted to Princess Kaguya, but despite his efforts to win her love, she refuses his favors and eventually returns to the moon.

Waka are scattered throughout *The Tale of the Bamboo-Cutter,* as they are, even more conspicuously, in such later examples of the fictional tales as the lengthy *Utsubo monogatari* and *Ochikubo monogatari.* The emphasis in these works is clearly on the prose passages, unlike the poem-tale where, as a rule, there is a delicate balance of prose and poetry.

The Poem-Tale

The *uta monogatari* flourished during the tenth century and ceased to exist as a genre soon afterward. A general characteristic of this genre is that each work consists of a collection of anecdotes revolving around one or more waka. Although some of these anecdotes are united by a central hero—as in *Tales of Ise* and *Tales of Heichū*—this is not true of *Tales of Yamato* which lacks any outward semblance of unity. In the earliest examples of this genre, the waka is essential to each anecdote; the prose passages are often little more than headnotes to the poems.

However, by the time of *Tales of Yamato* the prose passages had grown longer and become more interesting. Greater care was taken in the descriptions of circumstances leading to the composition of the poems and the emotions of the writer or recipient of the poems. In the *Tale of Takamura,* the last example of this genre (it is believed to have been written after *The Tale of Genji*), we find not a collection of anecdotes, but two distinct plots sustained throughout the work, somewhat at the expense of the waka.

Sanekata Kiyoshi states in his study of the poem-tale that *Kojiki* ("Record of Ancient Matters," 712), a quasi-historical work, contains stories that resemble the tenth-century *uta monogatari* anecdotes. These stories are related in several *chōka* exchanged by a man or woman (or two deities) and connected by brief prose passages; in these episodes we find what seems to be the beginnings of the lyrical narrative.[37] Among the numerous examples found in *Kojiki* are: (1) the story of the deity Yachihoko who woos Princess Nunakawa;[38] (2) the tragic tale of Princess Saho and Emperor Suinin;[39] and (3) the adventures of Yamato-Takeru no Mikoto.[40] Although Sanekata feels that the emphasis in these episodes is on the description of what were believed to be historical events, he considers these stories to have been the sources of later monogatari, principally the *tsukuri-monogatari.*[41]

Sanekata believes that the beginnings of the poem-tale may be found in the love stories contained in the *Man'yōshū.* This is particularly true of some of the poetic selections in volumes 9 and 16. Mentioned by Sanekata are the following selections: "Of the Maiden Tamana at Sué of the province of Kazusa" (KT 1738–9),[42] "Urashima of Mizunoé" (KT 1740–1),[43] "Of the Maiden Mama of Katsushika" (KT 1807–8),[44] and "On Seeing the Tomb of the Maiden Unai" (KT 1809–11).[45] These poems, all in the *chōka* form, tell a romantic story, often based on legendary material; they are rich in description, especially that of feminine beauty and charm.

In volume 16 we find examples in which the headnotes in Chinese and the poem combine to form a unit, just as they do in the later *uta monogatari.* Sanekata points out the fact that the prose and poetry are connected in a harmonious and natural manner and, as an example, he cites the poem entitled "The Cherry-Flower Maid" (KT 3786–7).[46]

According to Sanekata, "The Old Bamboo-Cutter" (KT 3791–3)[47] could very well have served as the model for such works as *The Tale of the Bamboo-Cutter* (although the *Man'yōshū* poem tells a story that differs altogether from that of Princess Kaguya) and *Tales of Ise.*[48] Besides these examples, there are waka exchanged by lovers, such as the series in volume 15 of the *Man'yōshū* which recounts the tragic love story of Nakatomi no Yakamori and the Maiden Sano no Chigami (KT 3723–3785).[49]

T'ang short stories[50] may have influenced the development of the *uta monogatari;* furthermore, in this section we have seen in the *Man'yōshū* and *Kojiki* examples of the lyrical narrative of the eighth century. It is difficult to trace the development of the poem-tale, particularly during the ninth century when Chinese influence was at its greatest. Nonetheless, scholars have concurred that *Tales of Ise,* the first of the poem-tales, was completed sometime during the first half of the tenth century. Within two centuries following the compilation of this classic, three other works considered to be examples of this genre—*Tales of Yamato, Tales of Heichū,* and the *Tale of Takamura* (the first half)—were compiled.

Tales of Ise

This work is generally believed to be the earliest and best example of a poem-tale; in the usual printed texts, it is made up of 125 episodes. Because the waka are indispensable to each episode, *Tales of Ise* constitutes the perfect example of the *uta monogatari,* which literally means "stories about poems." Although both the authorship and date of this classic are unknown, it has often been treated as a kind of biography of Ariwara no Narihara (825–880), the hero of most of the episodes, and formerly was thought to have been written by him. Today, however, *Tales of Ise* is believed to have been a product of the early tenth century, the work of an anonymous writer. Apart from the beauty of its style, it is important for the insights it gives the readers into the society of Heian Japan.

Some of the anecdotes consist of little more than a poem or two introduced by a brief prose passage, differing only slightly from poems and prefaces found in the various anthologies of poetry. This is not surprising, considering that at about the time *Tales of Ise* was being compiled (about the third or fourth decade of the tenth century), a great number of poetry collections were also being compiled.

Various reasons have been suggested for the compilation of *Tales of Ise.* McCullough, in the introduction to her translation of this work, states that "it is probably best to think of the work as a response to contemporary interest in the waka—the poems themselves, the circumstances of their composition, their authors—and in the emerging possibilities of the prose medium."[51]

Noting the similarity of certain passages to those in poetry anthologies, one may conclude that the anecdotes in *Tales of Ise* were drawn from them. However, as in the case of the anecdotes in *Tales of Yamato,* the poetry anthologies and the poem-tales may have drawn from a common source, not from each other.

Tales of Yamato

The second example of the *uta monogatari* genre is *Tales of Yamato.* The compiler-editor is unknown, but the work has been attributed to a number of people, ranging from a retired emperor to an obscure court lady. Scholars who have investigated the historical personages appearing in the first half of the work believe that it was completed between 951 and 952. The prose of *Tales of Yamato,* notably in the latter half where the emphasis is more on the narrative than the waka, shows a development from the simple elegance and charm of *Tales of Ise.*

This poem-tale consists of 173 main episodes and may be divided into two major sections: the first dealing with actual historical personages, the second with legends. Some unity is given *Tales of Ise* by the biography of Narihira; unity of this kind is altogether lacking in *Tales of Yamato.* Over a hundred characters are presented, many episodes dealing with historical figures who moved in the court circle of Emperor Uda.

Namba Hiroshi, speculating on how *Tales of Yamato* came to be written, attempts to trace the development of various genres following the composition of the poems themselves:

1) Poems were written down in memo form *(uta hōgo).*

2) Stories centering on certain poems were established *(utagatari)* and were: (a) transmitted orally or (b) recorded in kana.

Namba concludes that this process resulted in the creation of private collections and *Tales of Yamato.*[52] I believe that the imperial anthologies and other poem-tales came to be compiled in this manner.

Tales of Heichū

Also known as *The Sadabumi Diary (Sadabumi nikki),* this poem-tale consisting of 39 episodes[53] is believed to have been compiled some time between 959 and 965.[54] The work deals with the life and adventures of a minor court official, Taira no Sadabumi (d. 923), popularly known as Heichū. His father, Yoshikaze, was the nephew of Princess Hanshi, the mother of Emperor Uda. Yoshikaze was reputed to have been an amorous man and in time his son acquired the same reputation.

Many of the poems in this work were exchanged by Heichū with young ladies. There is ample evidence, both in *Tales of Heichū* and in the anecdotes about Heichū in *Tales of Yamato,* that he was indeed involved in many love affairs. The numbers of the episodes in *Tales of Yamato* and those of the corresponding episodes in *Tales of Heichū* are listed in a section that follows entitled "The Influence of *Tales of Yamato* on Later Literary Works." It is quite clear that the anecdotes related in I and II of my translation of *Tales of Yamato* are highly condensed and sometimes corrupt versions of those in *Tales of Heichū.*

Nonetheless, the anecdotes included in *Tales of Yamato* give us some idea of Heichū's character. Far from being an all-conquering lover, he emerges as a rather pathetic figure: in episode 46 he has an inconclusive affair with Lady Kan'in; in episode 64 he brings home with him a young girl, who is treated cruelly and eventually driven from the house by his wife; in episode 103 he is responsible for a young woman becoming a nun; and in episode 124 he has an affair with a married woman who eventually becomes the wife of still another man. A more detailed account of the ill-fated Heichū may be found in I and II of *Tales of Yamato.*

In *The Tale of Genji,* Heichū is referred to as a comical figure. One story about him known in Lady Murasaki's time relates that he used to splash his face with water in order to convince the lady he was courting that her cruelty made him weep. To expose him, the lady mixes some ink with the water and when next he plays his little trick, his face is blackened. In the novel by Lady Murasaki, Genji alludes to this incident when Murasaki, Genji's young ward, rubs a red spot of paint on his nose with a piece of paper dipped in water. Genji comments: "Take care . . . that you do not serve as Heichū was treated by his lady. I would rather have a red nose than a black one."[55]

Tales of Heichū has not enjoyed a high reputation among Japanese scholars, but stories about Heichū—whether included in the work itself or in other works, such as *Tales of Yamato, Konjaku monogatari,* and *Uji shūi monogatari*—have provided such modern authors as Tanizaki Jun'ichirō and Akutagawa Ryūnosuke with material for their stories.

The Tale of Takamura

This poem-tale, also known as *The Diary of Takamura (Takamura nikki),* concentrates on Ono no Takamura (802–852), a talented *kanshi* poet who was even compared to the great T'ang poet, Po Chü-i (772–846).[56] Takamura's poems are included in the *Keikokushū* (827) and his prose in Chinese has been compared to that of Han Yü (768–824) and Liu Tsung-yüan (773–819).[57] So highly was his knowledge of Chinese rated that he was chosen to be one of the compilers of the *Commentary for the Legal Code (Ryō no gige).* A number of waka by Takamura, known for his poetry, are included in various imperial anthologies. It was therefore fitting that Takamura, who excelled at waka composition even during the period when Japanese poetry was neglected, should have been chosen as the subject of a poem-tale.

Tradition has it that Takamura as a youth spent much time roaming the countryside on horseback, sadly neglecting his studies. However, after Emperor Saga expressed his dismay over Takamura's indifference to learning, the young man threw himself into his studies and eventually rose high in the bureaucracy.[58] In 838 he was appointed deputy leader of the embassy to China; however, he declined to go, so angering the emperor that he was exiled to the islands of Oki. It was at this time that he composed the famous waka:

Wata no hara	Oh, fisherman on yonder boat,
Yasojima kakete	Tell her
Kogi idenu to	That I have sailed out
Hito ni wa tsugeyo	Between the many islands
Ama no tsuribune	To the open sea.[59]

Takamura was released from exile in 840 shortly after the mission of 838—the last official one for several centuries—returned from China. Advancing in rank, he served in the court as an Imperial Adviser.

The Tale of Takamura has two parts. The first half relates the tragic story of the love between Takamura and his half-sister. While still a student at the university, Takamura is ordered by his father to teach Chinese to his half-sister. The two young people fall in love, and the girl soon finds herself pregnant. Her mother learns of the affair and in order to keep the lovers apart, locks the girl in her room. She, desperately longing for her lover, refuses to eat and dies of starvation. Her ghost later appears to Takamura and several waka are exchanged.

The second half of the poem-tale relates how years later Takamura marries the third daughter of the Minister of the Right after having sent her father a kanshi, which displayed his mastery of Chinese, asking for the hand of one of his daughters. Shortly afterward Takamura disappears for about a week, during which he stays at the home of his dead half-sister and communicates with her ghost. Takamura then returns to his wife and tells her of his earlier love-affair. Although she realizes she can never take the place of his first love in his affections and is apprehensive about the future, their marriage turns out to be a happy one. Takamura treats his devoted wife with great kindness, his thoughtfulness even extending to her sisters.

The first half of the work contains 29 of the 32 waka contained in the entire work, the large number of poems giving the rather scanty prose the appearance of a poetry collection with headnotes. In contrast to the first half, which is romantic and highly imaginative, the latter half tends to be prosaic, describing realistically Takamura's life. The fact that the poems by Takamura included in this work appear only in such post-Heian anthologies as *Shinkokinshū* (2), *Shoku kokinshū* (1), *Gyokuyōshū* (5), and *Shinsenzaishū* suggests that *The Tale of Takamura* was probably written during the early part of the Kamakura period (late twelfth or early thirteenth century.)[60] However, Endō Yoshimoto feels that the first half must be older, possibly having been written at the beginning of the eleventh century, not long after Sei Shōnagon's *Pillow Book*.[61] The anonymous compilers of this poem-tale were doubtless admirers of Ono no Takamura, who wove a story around the poems attributed to him.

In *Tales of Heichū* and the latter half of *The Tale of Takamura* there is a greater stress on the prose; the poetry ceases to play the indispensable role it did in *Tales of Ise* or *Tales of Yamato,* both appearing in the mid-tenth century when the primacy of the waka was just beginning to be threatened by prose writings in pure Japanese.

Tales of Yamato

Authorship and Dating

Numerous theories have been presented by scholars throughout the centuries regarding the title of this classic. After studying the painstaking research conducted by Namba Hiroshi and Abe Toshiko, I believe that Yamato refers to both the name of the ancient

Japanese province (in contrast to Ise province, as *Tales of Ise* was already known) and Japan, either interpretation being valid in view of what is presently known through the extant texts of this poem-tale.

As for the authorship of *Tales of Yamato,* Abe Toshiko concludes that the compiler-editor was probably a Heian courtier who had a special interest in poem-tales and was familiar with old poems and legends included in the *Man'yōshū* and the *Kokinshū.*[62] Moreover, Abe notes that the compiler-editor seemed to know some intimate details about Toshiko who is mentioned in episodes 3, 9, 13, 25, 41, 67, and 68. It is possible that he had heard these anecdotes from a lady-in-waiting serving in the court of either Emperor Daigo (r. 897–930) or Emperor Suzaku (r. 930–946) who was close to Toshiko. It is fairly certain that someone else revised and enlarged the original text shortly after the compilation of the *Shūishū* (c. 996), the third of the imperial anthologies,[63] so that the work we know today as *Tales of Yamato* is not the product of a single writer. This opinion of Abe Toshiko is shared by most Japanese scholars today.

The fact that neither the compiler nor the original form of *Tales of Yamato* is known makes it extremely difficult to date the work. The stories are taken from different sources: anecdotes about famous people preserved orally or with the aid of memos; manuscript copies of works; legends and folk tales. None of these sources provides detailed information on the date of compilation of *Tales of Yamato.* Although some of the poems included in this work appear also in imperial anthologies and private collections, we cannot definitely state that the relevant episodes of *Tales of Yamato* derived from those sources. One can only suggest tentatively that brief outlines of anecdotes giving the circumstances of the poems were jotted down by men and women of the court and only later collected in the form of private anthologies or poem-tales.

Thus far, studies concerning the dating of *Tales of Yamato* have been based primarily on the contents of the episodes. A few of the episodes derive from factually verifiable stories or gossip circulated at the court; the mention of events involving actual historical figures has for centuries encouraged scholars to attempt to date the entire work.

The dating of *Tales of Yamato* proposed by scholars during the past 800 years has ranged from the middle to late tenth century, with certain later additions. The differences in the dates proposed are less striking than the similarities; indeed, it is nothing short of remarkable that a conglomerate work by an unknown compiler can be dated so precisely. The mention of historical personages in the first half of the work provides the essential clues which have enabled scholars to reach their conclusions by a comparative study of such information as official court ranks and death dates. I accept the view of Abe, as modified by Namba, that the work was completed between 951 and 952 and that additions were made either by the compiler himself or by someone else in the form of annotations that eventually came to be considered part of the original text.[64]

I agree with both Abe and Namba that episode 173, whose writing style is highly sophisticated compared to the other episodes of *Tales of Yamato,* was added before the twelfth century. Fujiwara Kiyosuke (1104–1177), who completed copying the *Kokinshū* in about 1157, mentioned that a *Kokinshū* poem (KT 1068) was included in *Tales of Yamato;* he was referring to poem 295 in episode 173.

Finally, I concur with Abe and Namba that the appended sections (I included in a number of Nijō texts and II in the Rokujō texts) were added during the Muromachi period (1336–1573) or even later; these sections are not included in the Shōmei text, whose parent text is believed to be the oldest copy of *Tales of Yamato.*[65]

Intrinsic Literary Importance

Tales of Yamato is an anonymous work written in the mid-tenth century shortly after *Tales of Ise,* the first and foremost example of the *uta monogatari* genre. *Tales of Ise* may be considered to be a kind of biography of the great ninth-century poet, Ariwara no Narihira, but *Tales of Yamato,* lacking the unity of its predecessor, consists instead of a number of anecdotes about many men like Narihira.

Over a hundred different historical figures, ranging from emperors to courtesans, are introduced. Many of the historical figures are men and women active in the court of the Retired Emperor Uda. The anecdotes about court life in the first half of *Tales of Yamato* provide us with a picture of Heian society during the early ninth century, when the waka was at its height of prosperity. After compilation, *Tales of Yamato* may well have been circulated as a kind of poetry handbook. Because of the indispensable role played by the waka in the aristocratic society of the time, the work was undoubtedly studied as well as read for pleasure.

The importance of poetry in the lives of the court aristocrats of the mid-tenth century is suggested by a passage from Sei Shōnagon's *Pillow Book.* Empress Sadako, disappointed that her ladies-in-waiting had not learned by heart all the *Kokinshū* poems, related the following anecdote about an incident which occurred during the reign of Emperor Murakami (946–969).

> When the daughter of Fujiwara no Morotada (920–969) was a young girl, her father advised her to do three things: to study calligraphy, to learn to play the zither well, and to memorize all the poems of the *Kokinshū.* The young girl in time became the concubine of Emperor Murakami. The emperor heard of the advice her father had given her and decided to test the girl's memory. He spent the entire night quizzing her on all twenty volumes of the *Kokinshū.* Not once did her memory fail her.

The Empress, continuing her story, said:

> During all this time His Excellency, the lady's father, was in a state of great agitation. As soon as he was informed that the Emperor was testing his daughter, he sent his attendants to various temples to arrange for special recitations of the Scriptures. Then he turned in the direction of the Imperial Palace and spent a long time in prayer. Such enthusiasm for poetry is really rather moving.[66]

When the Empress finished telling her story, Emperor Ichijō (r.

986–1011), amazed that Emperor Murakami could have read so many poems in a single night, remarked:

> I doubt whether I could get through three or four volumes. But of course things have changed. In the old days even people of humble station had a taste for the arts and were interested in elegant pastimes. Such a story would hardly be possible nowadays, would it?[67]

In the "old days"—actually only about fifty years before Sei Shōnagon's time—the lives of men and women of high birth were immersed in poetry. They memorized the *Kokinshū* poems and were familiar with countless other poems as well. The anecdotes centered on poems in *Tales of Yamato* had probably been transmitted orally before being recorded. Poetry contests flourished, and outstanding poets were called upon to compose poems for the silk screens used to decorate the apartments of the palace buildings and the mansions of the aristocrats. Numerous private anthologies and the second anthology, the *Gosenshū,* were being compiled. With the first *uta monogatari* available as a model, it did not take long before *Tales of Yamato* achieved written form.

Tales of Yamato consists of two distinct parts: the first half emphasizes the waka and the second half, the stories told in prose. One might say that the shift of emphasis within the work itself is indicative of the development of classical Japanese literature in the direction of prose after a long period when it meant only poetry. However, one must always remember that poetry continued to be considered the highest form of literature in Heian Japan, even after the great prose masterpiece, *The Tale of Genji,* had appeared on the literary scene. Barbara Ruch writes about the role of fiction in Heian times:

> In early Japanese aristocratic circles the prevalent attitude towards the reading and writing of fiction was that it was a pleasant diverting pastime. Skill in poetic composition was an absolute necessity to a cultured aristocrat, and an essential part of his education, but no one studied how to write *monogatari.* Members of the court enjoyed reading whatever *monogatari* were available, and some even attempted to write them, but the light-hearted enthusiasm of their approach to fic-

tion cannot compare to the seriousness they exhibited towards the composition of poetry.[68]

Nevertheless, prose was to flourish in Japan, and in *Tales of Yamato* we see one of the earliest signs of movement away from the complete domination by poetry.

Tales of Yamato lacks unity; there is no central figure, such as Ariwara no Narihira in *Tales of Ise* or Taira no Sadabumi in *Tales of Heichū* to sustain our interest in the seemingly unconnected episodes, some of which are so brief as to leave little impression. Japanese scholars have speculated as to why *Tales of Yamato* is so unlike other *uta monogatari*. Sanekata believes that the *uta monogatari* of the tenth century developed in two different directions:

1) Those which use a historical figure as the main character to tie the episodes together, such as *Tales of Ise,* merged with the *tsukuri monogatari,* or fictional tale, two examples of which are *Utsubo monogatari* and *Ochikubo monogatari.* This line of *uta monogatari* furthermore combined with the *uta nikki,* or poetic diary, and ultimately resulted in *The Tale of Genji,* which is a synthesis of the above elements.

2) *Tales of Yamato* is the only example of the *uta monogatari* genre which lacks the unity found in *Tales of Ise.* A careful study of the work suggests that it merged with another genre, known as *setsuwa bungaku* of which *Konjaku monogatari* (eleventh century) and *Kara monogatari* (thirteenth century) are well-known examples. Other examples of the *setsuwa bungaku* genre are *Ima monogatari* (thirteenth century), *Jikkinshō* (1252), and *Kokon chomonjū* (1254).[69]

Abe Toshiko, a Japanese authority on *Tales of Yamato,* also believes that the nature of the work indicates a development in the direction of *setsuwa bungaku.*[70] The contents of the above examples of *setsuwa bungaku* show striking resemblances to *Tales of Yamato.* Although it is true that the tales in *Kara monogatari* concern historical personages in China and that many tales in *Konjaku monogatari* were derived from Indian and Chinese sources, the *Kara monogatari* tales contain waka and a few tales in *Konjaku monogatari* seem to be based directly on episodes taken from *Tales of Yamato*.

Thus *Tales of Yamato*, though invariably mentioned in studies of classical Japanese literature in conjunction with *Tales of Ise*, is in fact a unique example of a poem-tale. It deserves to be translated and carefully studied not only because of the picture it gives of Heian society in the early tenth century but also because of the influence it exerted on later works. The latter episodes in particular have genuine literary interest and have retained their appeal for Japanese throughout the thousand years since the work was first compiled.

Influence on Later Literary Works

What is the relationship of *Tales of Yamato* to two other contemporary poem-tales, *Tales of Ise* and *Tales of Heichū*? Listed below are the episodes in *Tales of Yamato* and the corresponding episodes in *Tales of Ise*. The page numbers of the latter as they appear in McCullough's translation, *Tales of Ise*, are also given for the convenience of the reader:

Tales of Yamato	*Tales of Ise*	*McCullough*
episode 149	episode 23	87–89
episode 161	episodes 3, 76	70–71, 120–121
episode 162	episode 100	138
episode 163	episode 51	104–105
episode 164	episode 52	105
episode 165	episode 125	125

A careful comparison of the corresponding passages shows that the writer of *Tales of Yamato* did not borrow directly from *Tales of Ise*, for the two versions differ considerably. Moreover, episodes 160 and 166 in *Tales of Yamato* which are about Narihira are not included in *Tales of Ise*. Vos is probably correct in stating that both narratives seem to be based on the same or similar tradition.[71]. The unnamed "man" of the *Tales of Ise* episodes is called Zai Chūjō (referring to Ariwara no Narihira) in all the *Tales of*

Yamato episodes mentioned above except episode 149. The fact that the name is not given in that particular episode, continued Vos, "shows that the author of this part of the *Yamato monogatari* was aware that episode 23 of the *Ise monogatari* was based on a popular tradition and had nothing to do with Narihira's life."[72]

Tales of Yamato also contains passages in common with *Tales of Heichū*, a work believed to have been compiled some time after 952 when the original *Tales of Yamato* was completed. The page numbers of the *Tales of Heichū* episodes as they appear in the NKBT printed edition are listed below.

Tales of Yamato	*Tales of Heichū*	*NKBT, Vol. 77*
episode 46	episode 9	65–66
episode 64		
episode 103	episode 38	103–105
episode 124		
I	episode 1	51–52
	episodes 37, 34	103, 96–97
	episode 36	98–102
II	episode 19	74
	episode 20	75
	episode 21	75
	episode 22	76–77
	episode 23	78
	episode 24	78–79
	episode 25	79–84
	episode 26	85
	episode 27	85–87

It is quite possible that the passages in I (Nijō texts) and II (Rokujō texts) of *Tales of Yamato* were based on *Tales of Heichū*, for these sections were added to the main text of 173 episodes some time after the Muromachi period. However, a careful comparison of *Tales of Yamato* and *Tales of Heichū* versions reveals that they differ greatly; the appended sections of *Tales of Yamato* are much condensed and sometimes corrupt.[73]

It should be noted that two episodes about Heichū in *Tales of Yamato*, episodes 64 and 124, have no corresponding version in

Tales of Heichū. This could indicate that the episodes appearing in the main text of *Tales of Yamato* and the stories included in *Tales of Heichū* were based on the same traditions of the historical figure known to have been a great lover. Stories about celebrated amorous men continued to be transmitted either orally or in written form even after the compilation of *Tales of Yamato* and doubtless influenced Lady Murasaki, who described the ideal Heian lover in *The Tale of Genji.*

Evidence of the influence of *Tales of Yamato* may be found in *Ōkagami,* a historical tale believed to have been written in the eleventh century, and in *Konjaku monogatari,* a collection of legends from India, China, and Japan compiled in the twelfth century. A comparative study of eight passages in *Ōkagami* and eight episodes in *Tales of Yamato* has been made by Matsumura Hiroshi.[74] The numbers of the episodes in *Tales of Yamato* and the page numbers of the corresponding passages in Professor Yamagiwa's translation of *Ōkagami* are provided below.

Tales of Yamato	*Ōkagami*
episode 1	223
episode 2	28
episode 5	31–32
episode 99	226
episode 120	63
episode 132	247–248
episode 145	246
episode 146	246–247

After carefully comparing these passages, Matsumura concludes that most of them could not have been derived directly from *Tales of Yamato.* Nevertheless, in that it is certain that the writers of *Ōkagami* borrowed from *Tales of Ise,* it is possible that they used *Tales of Yamato,* a work of the same genre, as a source for their work. Matsumura believes that passages 7 and 8 are the only ones that resemble the *Tales of Yamato* versions closely enough to be considered direct derivatives.[75]

In the collection of legends known as *Konjaku monogatari,*

seven tales in volume 30 seem to have been borrowed from *Tales of Yamato.* Listed below are the numbers of the *Tales of Yamato* episodes and the page numbers of the NKBT printed edition of *Konjaku monogatari* on which the corresponding tales may be found.

Tales of Yamato	*Konjaku monogatari*	*NKBT, vol. 26*
episode 103	tale 2	215–217
episode 105	tale 3	218–220
episode 148	tale 5	224–226
episode 155	tale 8	233–235
episode 156	tale 9	236–237
episode 157	tale 10	237–238
episode 158	tale 12	240–241

Two reasons suggest that the *Konjaku monogatari* versions were based on the *Tales of Yamato* versions. First, the order in which the stories appear in volume 30 of *Konjaku monogatari* is exactly the same as the order of corresponding episodes in *Tales of Yamato.* Second, these seven are all among the fourteen tales comprising a single volume of *Konjaku monogatari.* Nonetheless, since the *Konjaku monogatari* versions sometimes differ markedly from the *Tales of Yamato* versions and since both works contain other stories as well, it is possible that these stories were drawn from other sources that are no longer extant.

Let us consider, for example, tale 1 in volume 30 of *Konjaku monogatari.*[76] This episode, about Heichū and Hon-in no Jijū, a lady-in-waiting to Tokihira, the Minister of the Left, is found neither in *Tales of Yamato* nor in *Tales of Heichū.* Heichū falls madly in love with Hon-in no Jijū but is rejected by her. On one occasion, he finds himself alone with her in her room and is ecstatically happy. The young lady slips away, however, and latches the door from the outside. Some time later, he manages to get hold of her chamber pot, hoping that by seeing its contents he will be cured of his obsessive love. This incident was skillfully retold by the short story writer, Akutagawa Ryūnosuke (1892–1927), in *Kō-*

shoku.[77] Heichū's affair with Hon-in no Jijū is also described in the novel *Shōshō Shigemoto no haha*[78] by another outstanding Japanese writer, Tanizaki Jun'ichirō (1886–1965). Although the story may have been made up by the writer of *Konjaku monogatari,* it is even more likely that there was another source which is no longer extant.

On the other hand, tale 2 recounts an anecdote about Heichū, apparently based on episode 103 of *Tales of Yamato,* in which the amorous man wins the affection of a young woman, who becomes a Buddhist nun when he fails to write her a morning-after letter.

The first two passages deal with actual historical figures, Heichū and the Priest Daitoku—but the remaining five are based on legends: the Ashikari legend (episode 148), the legend of Mount Asaka (episode 155), the legend of Mount Obasute (episode 156), and two others—a tale of Shimotsuke province (episode 157) and a tale of Yamato province (episode 158), both about a neglected wife who wins back the affection of her unfaithful husband.

Tales of Yamato in all likelihood influenced not only *Konjaku monogatari* but other works belonging to the *setsuwa bungaku* genre, such as *Uji shūi monogatari* and *Jikkinshō.* The latter work in particular contains anecdotes about famous historical figures; some of them belong to the same period as those mentioned in *Tales of Yamato,* and it would have been natural to borrow from a work accepted as an authentic source of information on Heian court life.

The Nō drama flourished during the Muromachi period under the patronage of the political leaders and aristocrats of Japan. Six Nō plays still in the active repertory were influenced by stories in *Tales of Yamato.* A brief synopsis of these plays are given below.

1) *Adachigahara* (Adachi Field), or *Kurozuka* (The Black Mound)—a demon play, author unknown.[79] This play is based on a legend alluded to in episode 58 of *Tales of Yamato:* an ogress, who lived on human flesh, was reputed to live in Kurozuka of Adachi Field in the province of Mutsu.

In the Nō play version, a party of priests, headed by the Priest Yūkei, arrives at Adachi Field one evening in early autumn. The priests see a light in the darkness; approaching it, they discover that it comes from a dilapidated house. The old woman who lives there allows them to spend the night.

She tells them that she earns her livelihood by spinning and demonstrates her craft, singing spinning songs about the many kinds of thread she uses. Presently she excuses herself to go to fetch some firewood. Before leaving, she forbids them to look into the adjoining room. Nonetheless, one of the priests, unable to contain his curiosity, peeps into the forbidden room and is horrified to see a mountain of human bones and the remains of a half-eaten man. Yūkei then recalls having heard about the ogress of Kurozuka who fed on human flesh. Realizing that the old woman is none other than the ogress, the party flees in terror.

The old woman returns to find her guests gone. Furious because they had disobeyed her instructions, she rushes out in pursuit. Assuming the shape of an ogress, she catches up with the priests; however, Yūkei invokes the aid of Buddha and begins chanting incantations. Thanks to the efficacy of his prayers, the ogress is unable to harm the priests and is soon compelled to disappear.

A modern dance play based on the Nō play *Kurozuka* was created by Kimura Tomiko (1890–1944). It was first performed at the Tokyo Gekijō in November 1939.[80]

2) *Higaki* (The Woman within the Cypress Fence)[81]—a woman play by Zeami (1363–1443). This Nō play is based on episode 126 of *Tales of Yamato* which is about the courtesan Higaki. An important character in this play is a priest who lives on Mount Iwado in Higo province. He describes an old woman who comes daily to draw water which she offers to the god of the mountain, known for his many miracles. Soon afterward the old woman enters, lamenting her old age and seeking forgiveness for her past sins. She has been offering water to the god in the hope that she might thereby atone for her many sins. She asks the priest to pray for her when she is dead.

Upon being asked her name, she gives a vague reply, saying that it was she who composed the *Gosenshū* poem (KT 1220):

Toshi fureba	I have grown old . . .
Waga kurokami mo	My hair, once dark, is white
Shirakawa no	Like the River White;
Mizu hagumu made	And my shape resembles the man
Okinikeru kana	Who, stooping, draws water from the river.[82]

The old woman proceeds to tell the priest her story. Years ago, she had been a court dancer and lived in a house surrounded by a cypress fence in the Dazaifu, the government headquarters in Kyushu. When she grew old, she moved to the shore of "the White River." The priest recalls having heard of how a courtier, Lord Okinori, had once passed by her house built on the riverbank and asked for water. It was when she was drawing water for him that she composed the above poem.

The old woman explains the pun on the phrase *mizu hagumu,* meaning "to scoop up water" but also describing a person bent with age like herself. Entreating the priest to go to the shore of the White River to pray for her, the woman disappears into the darkness.

While searching for the woman's old home, the priest sees a dim light in the dark and as he approaches he hears the voice of a woman thanking him for his prayers. She speaks of the transience of life and the imminence of death. Recognizing her voice, the priest asks her to come out, whereupon the old woman reveals herself in the form of a ghost. The priest, realizing that it was because her soul was still attached to the world that her ghost haunted the place, advises her to forget her passions and begins praying for her. The woman's ghost, however, laments her lost youth and past sins and tells of the agonies of hell; she then performs a graceful court dance, the same one she had once performed for Lord Okinori. The play ends with the ghost of the old woman beseeching the priest to cleanse her of her sins so that she may enter into the Buddhist heaven.

A dance play based on two Nō plays, *Sekidera Komachi* and

Higaki, with lyrics by Sakurada Jisuke I (1734–1806) and music by Namisaki Tokuji I was performed in 1776. The first half of this work is about Ono no Komachi and a Minor Lieutenant, better known as Fukakusa no Shōshō. Higaki, with whom the Minor Lieutenant is said to have fallen in love when he first saw her in front of Sekidera, is murdered by him. Her ghost appears in the second half of the dance play and keeps the Minor Lieutenant and Komachi apart.[83]

3) *Motomezuka* (The Sought-for Grave)—a play of the fourth class by Kannami (1333–1384).[84] This Nō play is based on episode 147 of *Tales of Yamato,* which in turn seems to be based on two long poems in the *Man'yōshū.*[85]

According to an ancient legend, there once lived by the Ikuta River in Settsu province a maiden called Unai who was courted by two equally gifted men. Unable to decide between them, she promises to marry the one who shoots a water-bird. Both men succeed in striking the bird, and she finds herself at a loss what to do. Blaming herself for the death of the innocent bird and the strife between the two youths, she drowns herself. Heartbroken, her suitors kill each other beside her grave. Their deaths only add to the girl's wretchedness, and she is doomed to suffer forever in hell.

The Nō play opens on a day in early spring. A traveling priest with his attendants passes by the Ikuta River on his way to the capital. Several village girls are out gathering young herbs in the field, and among them is the spirit of Unai, who appears as a young girl. The priest wishes to see the famous Maiden's Tomb and asks where it is. At first Unai's spirit feigns ignorance, but later when the other village girls have left, she leads him to the mound and tells him her tragic story. Before vanishing, she begs the priest to say prayers for her restless soul.

The priest, complying with her request, recites the Lotus Sutra. The maiden's ghost presently appears and thanks him for his prayers. She vividly describes the tortures she undergoes in hell—the water-bird, killed by her suitors, pecks at her skull, and hell fiends pursue her ceaselessly with rods. In vain the priest tries to convince the ghost that her sufferings are all delusions. The play closes with the chorus describing her tortures in hell.

4) *Ashikari* (The Reed-Cutter)—a play of the fourth class adapted by Zeami.[86] The latter half of this work is said to have been revised by Komparu Zenchiku (1405–1468). This Nō play, earlier called *Naniwa,* is based on episode 148 of *Tales of Yamato.* It is an unusually long Nō play and, unlike the *Tales of Yamato* version (which does not reveal what becomes of the couple), the Nō version ends happily with the couple united after three years of separation.

The Nō play takes place in Settsu province on the shore of Naniwa Bay. It is spring. A woman, accompanied by her attendants, arrives at the village of Kusaka in search of her former husband. They had parted three years earlier because their poverty made it impossible to stay together. Meanwhile she had become the nurse of a nobleman's child in the capital and had prospered, but no one knew what had become of her former husband.

A villager tells them of a market on the shore of the bay where people buy and sell different products. He mentions an entertaining reed-cutter, who sells the famed reeds of Naniwa. Shortly afterward the reed-cutter himself appears. He lyrically describes the lovely spring scene and dances for the party. He is asked to show his reeds to the lady, but as he draws near, he recognizes his former wife. Mortified to be seen in so menial a guise, he rushes into a nearby hut. The lady informs her attendants that the man is her former husband and, approaching the hut, she reminds him of how they had once pledged their love.

After a long poetic discourse on the role that poetry plays in bringing men and women together, the man emerges from the hut. The play ends on a happy note with the reunited couple bound together for the capital.

5) *Uneme* (The Palace Attendant)—a woman play by Zeami.[87] This play is based on the legend of Sarusawa Pond told in episode 150 of *Tales of Yamato* in which an *uneme,* or palace attendant, bitter at having lost the emperor's favor, casts herself into Saru-

sawa Pond in Nara. It is spring. A priest, who is making a circuit of the provinces, arrives at the Kasuga Shrine in Nara. A woman appears and tells him of the shrine's origin. On the bank of Sarusawa Pond she reveals to him that she is the ghost of the palace attendant, then disappears into the pond.

In the second half of the play, the ghost reappears in the form of a young woman while the priest is chanting sutras for her. She thanks him, then gives a detailed explanation of the duties of a palace attendant and reminisces about her own days of glory. Once at a Winding-Water Banquet, the emperor himself, intoxicated with wine, had commanded her to perform a court dance. Before vanishing into the pond, she performs the dance for the priest.

6) *Obasute* (The Abandoned Aunt)—a woman play by Zeami.[88] This play is based on episode 156 of *Tales of Yamato,* which in turn has its origin in a Buddhist tale known in Japan since the sixth or seventh century. Unlike the *Tales of Yamato* version in which the old aunt is brought back home by her nephew, in the Nō play the old woman eventually perishes on the mountain and turns into stone.

The play begins as a traveler and his companions appear. The traveler describes his journey to Sarashina to see the autumn moon over Mount Obasute. It is night. Soon an old woman in the guise of a peasant woman makes her appearance. When the traveler asks her about the abandoned aunt of the legend, the old woman tells him that the aunt lies buried beneath a nearby tree. Before vanishing into the night, she reveals to him that she herself is the ghost of the deserted crone.

A villager happens along and tells the traveler the legend of Mount Obasute. The abandoned aunt, he says, had died, turning into stone.[89] The nephew, despite his wife's objections, returned to rescue his aunt only to find the stone. Filled with deep remorse, he became a priest. The villager then tells the traveler that the old woman who had appeared earlier was probably none other than the spirit of the abandoned woman.

In the second scene of the play, while the traveler and his companions are enjoying the beauty of the full moon, the old woman reappears and performs a dance. The poetry that is recited extols the loveliness of the moon over Sarashina. She also sings of the wonders of the Buddhist paradise, but unable to break away from her attachment to the world, the ghost is doomed to wander restlessly in limbo.

As stated in episode 156 of *Tales of Yamato,* the moon shining over Mount Obasute in Sarashina has been associated with inconsolable grief since the origin of the legend. Due to its association with this haunting legend, Sarashina was considered by Zeami to be the loveliest spot of all for moon-viewing. In 1688 the famous haiku poet Bashō (1644–1694), who traveled widely in his lifetime to see places famed in poetry, made a special journey to Sarashina to view the famous autumn moon. The account of this journey is entitled *Sarashina kikō.*[90] Inspired by the legend of Mount Obasute, Bashō composed the haiku:

Omokage ya	I can see her face—
Oba hitori naku	The aunt weeping, all alone,
Tsuki no tomo	The moon her companion.[91]

Besides Bashō's "Journey to Sarashina," *Tales of the Spring Rain* by Ueda Akinari (1734–1809), a scholar of the National Learning School and writer of short stories, also shows the influence of *Tales of Yamato.* Ueda's work is comprised of ten groups of stories, each of which deals with a literary or historical figure. One group of stories entitled "Amatsu otome" contains anecdotes about Sōjō Henjō, one of the Six Poetic Geniuses of the early Heian period. One of the stories tells of how Ono no Komachi met Henjō at the Kiyomizu Temple in the capital and exchanged poems with him.[92] Henjō was reputed to be a great lover in court circles before he took the tonsure, and he figures in this capacity in episode 168 of *Tales of Yamato* which specifically mentions the chance encounter of Komachi and Henjō. Although this incident is only a small part of what *Tales of Yamato* relates about

Henjō, Ueda Akinari, a scholar of Japanese classics who had made a careful study of *Tales of Yamato,* may well have used it as a source for his tale.[93] However, other historical information has been added, suggesting that he drew from other sources.

Several modern works show the influence of the anecdotes concerning historical figures and the ancient legends included in *Tales of Yamato.*

1) *Ikutagawa*—a modern play in colloquial Japanese by Mori Ōgai (1862–1922).[94] This drama, first performed in 1910, is based on episode 147 of *Tales of Yamato,* which tells the tragic story of the maiden Unai courted by two men. Ōgai follows closely the legend recorded in the earlier work. The girl, unable to decide between the two youths, is instructed by her mother to accept the one who shoots a swan floating on the Ikuta River. Much to her dismay, the arrows of both men strike the swan—one its head, the other its tail. The choice between the two suitors falls upon the girl, but rather than choosing one over the other, she throws herself into the river and drowns. In the course of the play, Ōgai attempted to impart by means of the dialogue a distinct personality to each of the characters. He was especially successful in evoking the girl's anxiety over her own fate and guilt over the death of the swan.

A mendicant priest appears to the girl in her wretchedness but he fails to cheer her. Instead, his visit seems to decide the girl to drown herself. Nothing is mentioned of the fate of the two young men.

2) *Shōshō Shigemoto no haha*[95]—a novel by Tanizaki Jun'ichirō (1886–1965), serialized in *Mainichi Shimbun* from November 1950 to March 1951. Episodes 14, 104, and 124 of *Tales of Yamato* are about the historical personages that figure in this story. Episode 124 tells of the love affair between the Daughter of Muneyana, then the wife of the Major Counsellor Fujiwara no Kunitsune (828–908), and Heichū. They exchange love poems and promise to love one another forever. Later, when she has become the wife of Fujiwara no Tokihira (871–909), the Minister of the Left, Heichū sends her this poem:

Yukusue no	Do you recall
Sukuse mo shirazu	That I once pledged my love to you
Waga mukashi	A long long time ago
Chigirishi koto wa	When I little dreamed
Omōyu ya kimi	How successful you would be?

Fujiwara no Shigemoto (d. 931), the son born to Kunitsune and the Daughter of Muneyana, is mentioned in episode 104. In this episode he and a young woman exchange love poems. Episode 14 is about a young woman whose childhood name was Ōfune; she is believed to have been the younger sister of the principal wife of Tokihira (the daughter of Muneyana). In that Muneyana was the son of Ariwara no Narihira, who is said to have been a handsome man, it is conceivable that his daughters—Narihira's granddaughters—were attractive. To Tokihira and the daughter of Muneyana was born a son, Atsutada (906–943), who grew up to be a poet of note. Episodes 81, 82, 92, and 93 of *Tales of Yamato* are about Atsutada and his love affairs.

Tanizaki, making use of a number of historical facts and anecdotes obtained from various sources, weaves a fascinating story. Each of his main characters is vividly described. Moreover, in that Tanizaki also gives the reader an insight into the innermost workings of the characters' minds, the novel is most engrossing.

The novel opens with a description of Heichū, the great lover, and his numerous amours. One of his lovers was the daughter of Muneyana. Although in her early twenties, she was married to Kunitsune, a man over three times her age. Their child Shigemoto is the principal figure in the latter part of the work. Having heard of the woman's beauty from Heichū, Tokihira, the Minister of the Left and Kunitsune's nephew, becomes interested in her. Soon afterward Tokihira begins to treat Kunitsune with special kindness. In return Kunitsune entertains him at an elaborate banquet; at the end of the banquet he offers Tokihira the young wife upon whom he so doted. Tanizaki gives us a detailed account of what induced the old man to surrender his beloved wife and then describes his anguish when he realizes that he has lost her.

The unhappy old man lives for a few years beyond this incident, and it is during this time that little Shigemoto witnesses the sufferings of his decrepit father as he attempts in vain to forget his beautiful wife. For a short while, Shigemoto also recalls having been able to visit his mother in her new home, and on one occasion shows her a poem written on his arm by Heichū, whose passion for her had been aroused again, now that she was unattainable. The mother writes an answering poem on Shigemoto's arm, instructing him to show it to Heichū. However, not long after this incident, Shigemoto's visits to his mother cease. From then on his memories are of his aged father, and the last two chapters of the novel describe Kunitsune's desperate efforts to forget his former wife.

Throughout the work Tanizaki skillfully makes his characters live against the historical background of the period. Tokihira, who is generally depicted as a villain because of the part he played in exiling his rival, Sugawara no Michizane, is described as an attractive, fun-loving man in the prime of his life. Heichū, on the other hand, emerges as a rather weak, unfortunate man, a failure in his relations with Shigemoto's mother and Hon-in no Jijū. As for Kunitsune, he is a pathetic old man, who, despite his wishes to promote the happiness of his lovely young wife, cannot bear living without her. So obsessed is he by her memory that he ignores his son, who sadly and with knowledge far beyond his years, observes the activities of the adults moving about him.

3) *Obasute*[96]—a short story by Inoue Yasushi (b. 1907), which appeared in the January 1955 issue of *Bungei shunjū.* In this story a young newspaperman, who from childhood had been fascinated by the legend of the abandoned aunt, imagines what it would be like to be taking his own mother up the mountain and abandoning her. Once, in fact, she had jokingly suggested she would leave home when she grew old. He sees himself carrying his mother on his back and searching for an appropriate place to abandon her. He is unsuccessful in finding a place to her liking and begs his mother to return home, but she adamantly refuses.

In the course of the story, the hero notes a very peculiar trait running through several members of his family, a strange desire to escape from the world. His younger sister leaves her husband and two children; his younger brother leaves a secure position with a newspaper company to work in a small bank in the country; an uncle, who had been the president of an engineering firm, goes off to try his luck in a small business. This trait, the hero believes, is associated with the desire once expressed by his mother to abandon the family. The story ends with the hero visiting Mount Obasute where he views the stone believed to be the metamorphosed form of the old woman of the legend.

4) *Narayama bushi-kō* (The Songs of Oak Mountain) by Fukasawa Shichirō (b. 1914), which in November 1956 won the New Writer's Prize awarded by *Chūō kōron.*[97] The setting of this story is Shinano province about the year 1850. In this province men and women who reached the age of seventy were taken up Oak Mountain and abandoned. For years Orin, a woman sixty-nine years old, has been preparing for her pilgrimage. Before making preparations for her own farewell banquet, she sees to it that her son, Tatsuhei, is remarried. On the day her son reluctantly takes her up Oak Mountain, it begins snowing, just as Orin had predicted all along.

The character of the old woman as she cheerfully looks forward to being taken up the mountain is touchingly portrayed by the author. The other characters are also memorable—her devoted son, the warm-hearted and hard-working widow he marries, his selfish son, and his son's lazy, pleasure-loving young wife. This short story was warmly received by the public and was later made into a prize-winning film. Although contrasting greatly with the *Tales of Yamato* version of the legend, the theme of the abandonment of an old woman remains unchanged.

As we have seen in this section, the anecdotes and legends in *Tales of Yamato* have been used as sources for later, often more effective, works by writers throughout the centuries. The fact that three works written in the past twenty years have been influenced by the stories in *Tales of Yamato* clearly indicates that the work still has the power to inspire modern writers and the general public. This may be the reason why scholars are today giving more attention than ever before to the study of the original work.

Texts

At the end of the Heian period, Fujiwara no Kiyosuke (1104–1177) mentioned in his work on poetics, *Fukuro zōshi* (1159), that *Tales of Yamato* contained 270 waka, among which were three *tanrenga,* or short linked-verse. He also wrote that there were many different texts, no two of which were alike.[98] One can therefore reasonably conclude that the text Kiyosuke used was shorter than the one used in modern editions consisting of 173 episodes and containing 295 poems. However, it may be that the episodes in the text he knew differed so considerably from the *Tales of Yamato* texts known today as to make such conjectures meaningless.

The Priest Kenshō (1130–c. 1210), a brother-in-law of Kiyosuke, quoted from various sections of *Tales of Yamato*—sections which are not included in extant editions—in the *Shūchūshō* which he wrote between 1185 and 1189. The text he used is now lost.

There are two classes of extant texts: the Nijō and the Rokujō.

Nijō texts

These texts were copied by Fujiwara no Teika (1162–1241), Fujiwara no Tameie (1198–1275), and Fujiwara no Tameuji (1222–1286) and have been widely circulated since the Kamakura period. The popular editions printed and circulated since the Tokugawa period have been based on these texts which may be subdivided into the following:

Tameie (Maeda) text, which dates from the mid-twelfth century. The postscript bears the date Kōchō 1 (1261) and the signature of Enkaku. The colophon states that Enkaku was the name Tameie assumed upon taking the tonsure. This is considered to be a reliable text and has been widely circulated since the Tokugawa period. Abe Toshiko selected this text to work with, as there are comparatively few errors in copying and an insignificant number of misplaced annotations. Moreover, the date of the completion of the manuscript is clearly indicated.[99] Together with the Tameuji text, it is the oldest extant copy of *Tales of Yamato* belonging to the Nijō line.

Tameuji (Sanjōnishi) text, which has no postscript but is believed to date from the Kamakura period. According to Ikeda Kikan's study, it differs in minor details from the Tameie text in 725 different instances.[100] In that Abe Toshiko had already annotated the Tameie text, Namba Hiroshi chose to work with this text.

Teika texts:

1. Kangi text, which states in the postscript that Teika copied it in Kangi 3 (1231). Extant copies, however, date from the Muromachi period. Some important manuscripts are:
   a. Tawa Bunko (Asukai Masatoshi) text
   b. Hōsa Bunko (Tametomo) text
   c. Sanjōnishi text
   d. Ueno Kokuritsu Hakubutsukan text
   e. Ryūmon Bunko text
   f. Keian text
   g. Kokugakuin Daigaku text. This is the text used by Takeda Yūkichi and Mizuno Komao in *Yamato monogatari shōkai.*
2. Tempuku text, which is said to have been copied by Teika in Tempuku 1 (1233). Important manuscripts are:
   a. Itsukushima Jinja (Toshimori) text
   b. Mukyūkai Shinshū Bunko text
3. Karitani (Konoe Taneie) text. This manuscript, dating from the end of the Muromachi period, is kept in the Kyōto Daigaku Kokugo Kokubungaku Kenkyū Shitsu.
4. Gunsho ruijū text.
5. Kitamura Kigin's *Yamato monogatari shō* text. This text, which contains the short episodes in appended section I of my translation, can be traced to the Kangi text. Tokugawa scholars based their studies on this text: Sairin—*Yamato monogatari*

shusho; Kamo no Mabuchi—*Yamato monogatari chokkai;* Kisaki Masaki—*Yamato monogatari kyoseishō;* Ueda Akinari—*Ueda Akinari kōseibon;* Maeda Natsukage—*Yamato monogatari kinshōshō;* Inoue Fumio—*Kanchū Yamato monogatari.*

6. Katsura no Miya text (also known as the Kyōto Daigaku Kenkyūshitsu Nakagawa text). This manuscript is similar in many respects to both the Teika and Tameie texts. Besides being influenced by the Rokujō texts, it contains the anecdotes included in appended section I of my translation. This manuscript, copied in the late Tokugawa period, may be found today in the Kunaichō Shoryōbu Collection.

Rokujō texts

These texts differ from the Nijō texts in minor details as well as the content. In that the Rokujō and Nijō texts differ considerably, one should avoid using a Rokujō text to elucidate obscure points in the Nijō texts. Rokujō texts were already quite rare by Tokugawa times; modern printed editions of *Tales of Yamato* are based mainly on Nijō texts.

Shōmei text. This text was introduced by Kyūsojin Hitaku in 1957; it is the only printed edition of a Rokujō text. Some of the characteristics of this late Muromachi manuscript are that: 1) it contains only 172 episodes and, following episode 142, there is an episode which is not found in other texts; 2) it is very much like the Hōsa Bunko and Karitani texts up to episode 133 but thereafter it is similar to the Mikanagi and Suzuka texts; 3) from episode 141 on, it shows signs of having been collated with other Rokujō texts. The latter half of this manuscript differs greatly from the Nijō texts. Its parent text, as indicated in the postscript, was the manuscript copied by Kōamidabutsu (the Priest Sokō) in Shōji 2 (1200), the oldest copy referred to in an extant text. All earlier copies have been lost. In their studies, scholars such as Kenshō and Fujiwara no Kiyosuke used copies of the Rokujō texts, which probably resembled the Shōmei text.

Mikanagi and Suzuka texts. The Mikanagi text, which may be seen in the Tenri Library, differs from the Nijō texts discussed above. Between episodes 172 and 173 are inserted additional episodes from *Tales of Heichū* in a greatly modified form (appended section II of my translation). At the end of episode 173, it is stated that this collection of tales is believed to be the work of the Retired Emperor Kazan. This statement is followed by what is episode 169 in the modern printed editions. This manuscript bears no postscript; it mentions, however, that it had been copied by a man named Mototsuna. Abe Toshiko identifies the copyist as Anekōji Mototsuna, who studied poetry under the great *renga* master Sōgi (1421–1502).

The Suzuka text, which resembles closely the Mikanagi text, also states that it had been copied by Mototsuna. If indeed these two manuscripts were copied by Anekōji Mototsuna, they date from shortly after the middle of the Muromachi period.

The Rokujō texts are older than the Nijō texts and are important in investigating the earliest form of *Tales of Yamato.* However, with the rise of Nijō scholars, works by Rokujō scholars were ultimately neglected and by Tokugawa times the Rokujō texts of *Tales of Yamato* had all but disappeared. Nevertheless, included in most modern printed editions of this classic are sections based on *Tales of Heichū* as they appear in the Mikanagi and Suzuka texts of the Rokujō line.[101]

Notes

Introduction

1. Although Michizane was able to remain in Japan, he was soon sent to Kyushu in virtual exile as Viceroy of the Dazaifu Military Headquarters, despite the fact that he enjoyed imperial favor. The action was the result of pressures from Fujiwara no Tokihira (871–909) and other members of the powerful Fujiwara clan.

2. An account of the period between 889 and 1092, centering upon the rule of Michinaga, is given in *Tales of Glory (Eiga monogatari)*.

3. Two English translations of this work are available: a partial translation by Arthur Waley entitled *The Pillow-Book of Sei Shōnagon* and a complete one in two volumes by Ivan Morris also entitled *The Pillow Book of Sei Shōnagon*.

4. Two English translations are available: one by Arthur Waley (1960), the other by Edward G. Seidensticker (1976).

5. See Brower and Miner, *Japanese Court Poetry*, p. 163.

6. Helen McCullough has provided an excellent study of the Six Poetic Geniuses in her introduction to *Tales of Ise*, pp. 34–55.

7. Miner, *An Introduction to Japanese Court Poetry*, p. 9.

Tales of Yamato

1

1. Emperor Uda (867–931, r. 887–897), who, upon abdicating the throne on the third day of the seventh month of Kampyō 9 (897), was called Teiji no In.

2. Ise no Go, who lived from about 877 to about 938. She served in Emperor Uda's court and, through a union with the Emperor, gave birth to Prince Yukiakira (926–948). Lady Ise is one of the Thirty-six Poetic Geniuses who lived before the eleventh century.

3. A part of the Imperial Palace reserved for the Empress, the imperial concubines, and their attendants.

4. At the time, it was customary for members of the court of an abdicating emperor to leave the palace with him.

5. This incident is mentioned in the following anthologies of Japanese poetry: the *Gosenshū* (KT 1323, 1324), *Ise shū* (ZKT 18343, 18344), and *Teiji no In gyoshū* (*Katsura no Miya-bon sōsho,* vol. 20, p. 71), with the second line of the first poem given as *Ai mo omowanu.* This incident is also mentioned in *Ōkagami* (KT, *Rekishi,* 932, 933). The Emperor is trying to console Lady Ise, hinting to her that she could readily live in the palace again if she returned to serve the new sovereign.

2

1. Actually two years after his abdication, that is, the tenth month of Shōtai 2 (899).

2. Tachibana no Yoshitoshi was born in 874 in the province of Bizen, a part of modern Okayama prefecture. His death date is unknown.

3. Emperor Daigo (885–930, r. 897–930).

4. According to the entry of the tenth month of Engi 7 (907) in the *Daigo Tennō gyoki* (*Zoku zoku gunsho ruijū,* vol. 5, p. 27), Ariwara no Tomoyuki, Fujiwara no Nakahira, and others were sent to join the Retired Emperor.

5. Located in present-day Osaka-fu.

6. In the original poem, the place name Hine is found in the last two syllables of the word *tabine* ("sleeping on one's journey").

7. This poem is also included in the *Shinkokinshū* (KT 912).

3

1. Minamoto no Kiyokage (884–950), son of Emperor Yōzei (868–949, r. 877–884).

2. The daughter of Fujiwara no Tokihira and consort of Teiji no In, her given name was Hōshi.

3. His sixtieth birthday, which fell on the twenty-eighth day of the ninth month of Enchō 4 (926). There were special celebrations at ten-year intervals after a man's fortieth birthday. Later, these celebrations were held on a man's forty-second, sixty-first, seventy-seventh, and eighty-eighth birthdays.

4. It was customary for a bamboo basket to be attached to a pine, cherry, or plum branch. Some article of value was then placed into the basket and offered as a gift.

5. Toshiko, referred to as Sokyōden no Shunshi in the *Shūishū,* was the wife of Fujiwara no Chikane, the Provincial Governor of Hizen. Chikane and Kiyokage were related by marriage.

6. A version of this poem appears in the *Kokin rokujō* (ZKT 31368). The poem is given as follows: Chiji no iro ni/ Utsurishi aki wa/ Suginikeri/ Kyō no shigure ni/ Nani o somemashi.

7. The word *sawagu,* which means "to rise (of ocean waves)" also has two other meanings: "to make a great deal of noise" and "to busily go about doing one's work." Toshiko is accusing Kiyokage of thinking of her only when there is work to be done.

8. Denying that he thinks of her only when he needs her help, Kiyokage says that he thinks constantly of her, even on a balmy day in spring. There is a pun on the word *ito,* which means both "very much" and "thread."

4

1. A revolt which took place between the years 939 and 941; it was led by Fujiwara no Sumitomo, who invaded Harima (a part of modern Hyōgo prefecture), Bizen, and the entire San'yō area. Sumitomo was eventually defeated at Hakata, whereupon he fled to Iyo (Ehime prefecture), where he was finally arrested and put to death.

2. Ono no Yoshifuru (884–967) was placed at the head of a fleet of warships and pursued Sumitomo during his revolt.

3. Of the Left Division of the Inner Palace Guards.

4. Minamoto no Kintada (889–948), one of the Thirty-six Poetic Geniuses.

5. There is a pun on the word *futatose,* which means "two years" and "a box and its cover." There is also another pun on *ake (aka),* meaning "scarlet" and "to open." These are all *engo* (an associated word) for *tamakushige* ("a beautiful box"), which is also a pillow-word (a kind of epithet) for *futa.* This poem appears in the *Kintada shū* (ZKT 16413) and in the *Gosenshū* (KT 1124). According to the *Gosenshū,* however, Yoshifuru had first expressed his disappointment in not having been promoted to Kintada. Kintada then sent him the above poem. Yoshifuru's answering poem went:

Akenagara	Two years have slipped by
Toshi furu koto wa	While I wore
Tamakushige	My scarlet robes—
Mi no itazura ni	For two years
Nareba narikeri	I have lived in vain.

5

1. Prince Yasuakira (903–923), son of Emperor Daigo.

2. The daughter of Minamoto no Tasuku, who was also recognized as a talented poetess.

3. Fujiwara no Shizuko (885–954), daughter of Fujiwara no Mototsune.

4. This anecdote and poem are also recorded in the section dealing with Emperor Murakami (926–967, r. 946–967) in *Ōkagami* (KT, *Rekishi,* 880) and in the *Shinchokusenshū* (KT 886). In the latter work, the poem (with the fourth line reading *Kokoro shiranu wa* instead of *Kokoro ni ninu wa*) is attributed to Ōshikōchi no Mitsune.

6

1. Fujiwara no Asatada (910–966), who held the rank of Middle Captain of the Inner Palace Guards in 951 and 952. He was one of the Thirty-six Poetic Geniuses.

2. This poem appears in the *Asatada shū* of the *Nishi Honganji-bon Sanjūrokuninshū* (p. 236 n.33), with the first line reading *Taguetsutsu.* In the *Shinsenzaishū* (KT 740), the poem is attributed to Fujiwara no Koretada, with the fourth line reading *Harukeki sora ni.*

7

1. This is an anonymous poem in the *Shinchokusenshū* (KT 936), with the first line reading *Au koto o.*

8

1. Emperor Daigo's son, also known as Prince Tsuneakira (907–966).

2. Although her real name is unknown, she was probably a daughter of a Lieutenant of the Inner Palace Guards who served as a lady-in-waiting at the court.

3. Based on the *yin-yang* principles which the Japanese had adopted from the Chinese, there was a belief that on certain days it was considered bad luck for a person to travel in the direction in which one of the moving divinities happened to be at the time. To prevent anything unpleasant from happening to him, the traveler would start out in some other direction, and later progress toward his original destination. Bernard Frank discusses in greater detail this practice known as *katatagae* in *Kata-imi et katatagae; étude sur les interdits de direction à l'époque Heian.*

4. This poem in which one of the moving deities, Hitoyo Meguri or Taihaku, is mentioned is discussed on pp. 152–153 of Frank's work.

5. It had earlier been the detached palace of Emperor Saga (786–882, r. 809–823) and was located in the province of Yamashiro, a part of modern Kyoto. In Jōgan 18 (876), its name was changed to Daikaku-ji.

6. Ōsawa Pond is located in Saga. There is a pun on the word *saga*, which means "one's nature" as well as being a place name. Gen no Myōbu is saying that since she has forgotten him altogether, there is now no reason for her to resent him. This poem, together with the previous one, may be found in the *Motoyoshi no Miko shū* (ZKT 21254, 21255). The fourth and fifth lines of ZKT 21255 read Saga no tsurasa o/ Nanika uramin. It is believed that Gen no Myōbu had sent this poem to either Prince Nakatsukasa or Prince Motoyoshi (890–943). There is a greater possibility that she had sent this poem to Prince Motoyoshi, for nowhere else is there any mention of an affair between Prince Nakatsukasa and Gen no Myōbu. The anonymous compiler-editor of *Yamato monogatari* probably confused the two names.

9

1. Emperor Daigo's son, also known as Prince Katsuakira (903–927). His widow was the daughter of Fujiwara no Tokihira.

2. See episode 3.

3. The word *hate* may be interpreted in two ways: "the end (of the year)" and "the end of the mourning period." This poem also appears in the *Shoku gosenshū* (KT 1244).

4. The widow is saying that she is so grief-stricken that she was unaware of the seasonal change.

10

1. The embankment along the Kamo River in Kyoto.

2. Located in present-day Awataguchi, Sakyō-ku, Kyoto.

3. There is a pun on the word *kawa*, meaning either "river" or "that." There is also a pun on *wataru*, meaning "to cross (a river)" and "to go by (a house)." The anonymous poem alluded to in this poem may be found in the *Kokinshū* (KT 933):

Yo no naka wa	What is there in this world
Nanika tsune naru	That remains unchanged?
Asukagawa	Why, look at the Asuka River—
Kinō no fuchi zo	The deep pools of yesterday
Kyō wa se ni naru	Have become the rapids of today!

A poem by Lady Ise in the *Kokinshū* (KT 990) is also on the same theme. According to the prose introduction, it was probably composed after seeing her house:

Asukagawa	Though my home
Fuchi ni mo aranu	Is not a deep pool
Waga yado mo	In the Asuka River,
Se ni kawariyuku	I have exchanged it
Mono ni zo arikeru	For a sum of gold.*

*There is a pun here on the phrase *se ni,* which means either "into rapids" or "money *(zeni)*."

11

1. Minamoto no Kiyokage. See episode 3.

2. Fujiwara no Tadafusa (d. 928), who was one of the Thirty-six Poetic Geniuses and excelled both as a musician and as a composer.

3. This young woman was probably Princess Shōshi (918–980), the daughter of Teiji no In. The relationship of the three individuals mentioned in episode 11 to other people already mentioned may be shown by the following chart:

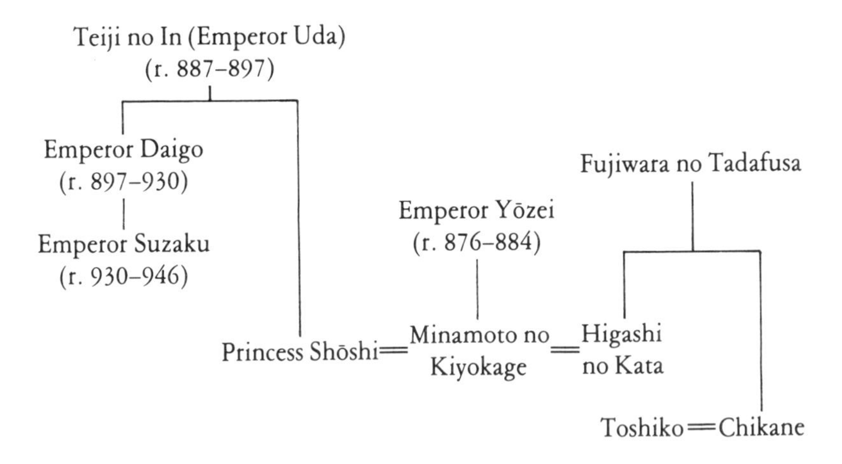

4. This poem appears in the *Shūishū* (KT 740), with the second line reading *Matsu naranedomo.* The pines of Sumiyoshi (Suminoe) are a symbol of the many years that have gone by in endless succession.

12

1. Minamoto no Kiyokage.

2. This poem appears in the *Shinkokinshū* (KT 1177).

13

1. Chikane was the son of Tadafusa and a talented musician.

2. Ichijō no Kimi, the daughter of Prince Sadahira (d. 913), son of Emperor Seiwa (850–880, r. 858–876).

14

1. Not very much is known about her except for the fact that three of her poems appear in the *Gosenshū* (KT 635, 660, 697). In the *Gosenshū* she is called Ōtsubune.

2. The daughter of Ariwara no Muneyana. It is said that she had first been the wife of Fujiwara no Kunitsune but that later she became the wife of Tokihira. See episode 124.

3. Fujiwara no Tokihira (871–909), the Minister of the Left. He was one of the men who plotted to have Sugawara no Michizane (845–903) banished to Kyushu.

4. His reign was from 877 to 884, but he lived on in retirement until 949.

5. *Aratama no* is a pillow-word for *toshi* ("year"). *Mi* ("to see") has two possible interpretations: (1) the Emperor of long ago seeing the young maiden's dark tresses in the pond; (2) the maiden herself seeing the duckweed in the pond. This poem alludes to the legend in which a young girl commits suicide by throwing herself into the Sarusawa Pond in Nara because the Emperor had forgotten her. Ōfune, like the maiden in the legend, is finding it unbearable to be so completely ignored by the Retired Emperor.

15

1. No information about this woman's background is available.

2. The palace of Princess Yasuko (d. 925), the daughter of Emperor Kōkō (830–887, r. 884–887).

3. This poem appears in the *Gosenshū* (KT 1170) and is attributed to Musashi. Lady Wakasa and Musashi are probably the same person. The jewellike dew symbolizes the Retired Emperor who no longer visits her.

16

1. His background is not known except for the fact that he held the rank of Minor Captain of the Inner Palace Guards. He is called Mamachichi no Shōshō in the original, which was probably a nickname, since *mamachichi* means "step-father."

2. *Harukenagara* can be interpreted as meaning "far" or "estrangement." The *wasuregusa* is an ancient name for the yellow day lily.

17

1. Idewa no Go. There is no further information on this young woman.

2. Prince Atsuyoshi (887–930), the fourth son of Emperor Uda (Teiji no In). He was a man of culture and a very talented musician.

3. This poem is based on one by Ariwara no Muneyana, which appears in the *Kokinshū* (KT 243):

Aki no no no	Are the flowering pampas grass
Kusa no tamoto ka	Sleeves blowing among the wild grass
Hanasusuki	In an autumn field?
Ho ni idete maneku	Each swaying ear seems to beckon
Sode to miyuran	To a loved one.

4. There is a pun on the word *akikaze,* which means "the autumn wind," and *aki,* which means "to weary of," hinting at the man's inconstancy.

18

1. This was probably Sanjō no Miyasundokoro, the concubine of Emperor Daigo.

2. On the seventh day of the first month, a person was supposed to eat the seven spring herbs. By doing so, it was believed that one could ward off sickness during that particular year.

3. This poem is based on a poem by Emperor Kōkō, the late Minister of Ceremonial's grandfather, which appears in the *Kokinshū* (KT 21):

Kimi ga tame	I went out into the spring field
Haru no no ni idete	To gather the young greens
Wakana tsumu	Just for you;
Waga koromode ni	While I was gathering them,
Yuki wa furitsutsu	Snow fell gently on my sleeves.

19

1. In her poem, Nijō no Miyasundokoro declares that she is not in love with anyone. She hints, however, that the Minister's heartlessness makes her feel sad.

20

1. Princess Fushi (d. 954), the daughter of Emperor Uda. She was a half-sister of Prince Atsuyoshi, the late Minister of Ceremonial.

21

1. Yoshimine no Yoshikata (915–957). He later became Middle Captain of the Right Division of the Inner Palace Guards and served as Minor Captain between 936 and 945.

2. Kashiwagi was another name for both the Outer Palace Guards and the Middle Palace Guards. Since Rō Shōshō was serving as a Minor Captain of the Middle Palace Guards, in this poem *kashiwagi* is substituted for his name. There is a pun on the word *oinu,* meaning "to grow old" as well as "to grow." The grass under the oaks is a symbol for Gen no Myōbu.

3. In the *Shoku kokinshū* (KT 1134, 1135), these two poems are respectively attributed to Gen no Myōbu and the Priest Henjō (816–890), whose name before he entered the priesthood had been Yoshimine no Munesada. The second poem is erroneously attributed to Henjō. In the *Kakaishō* (*Kokubun chūshaku zensho,* vol. 3, p. 229), the second poem is attributed to Yoshimine no Nakatsura, the elder brother of Yoshikata.

22

1. *Somekawa* means "dyed leather," but it is also the name of a river in the province of Chikuzen, a part of present-day Fukuoka prefecture in Kyushu. The words *watari(shi)* ("to cross") and *fukasa* ("depth") are *engo* for *kawa* ("river"). This poem has been wrongly attributed to Yoshimine no Munesada in the *Shoku goshūishū* (KT 1122).

23

1. Prince Motohira (d. 958), who at one time held the rank of President of the Board of Censors of the Third Order.

2. Fujiwara no Nochikage (d. 921). No further information on his daughter is available. At the time of the episode, he held the rank of Middle Captain of the Inner Palace Guards.

3. Princess Yoriko (895–936), the daughter of Emperor Uda.

4. The young woman is saying that the Prince has no right to expect a civil greeting from someone he no longer loved. This poem appears in the *Shoku gosenshū* (KT 986).

24

1. Emperor Daigo (r. 897–930).

2. Yoshiko, the daughter of Fujiwara no Sadakata. After the death of Emperor Daigo, she was married first to Prince Atsumi and then to Fujiwara no Saneyori. See episode 120.

3. The room in which she found herself was probably a small room in the Seiryōden, one of the buildings in the Imperial Palace compound.

4. The *hototogisu* is a kind of cuckoo. There is a pun on the word *higurashi,* meaning "all day long" as well as "a cicada." There is also a play on words on *matsuyama* ("a pine-covered mountain") and *matsu* ("to wait").

25

1. Except that he was the older brother of Toshiko, nothing else is known about him.

26

1. *Yado o miru* means "to see one's house" as well as "to exchange vows of love under cover of darkness." This poem appears in the *Kokinshū* (KT 811). It also appears in the *Kokin rokujō* (ZKT 33819), with the first line reading *Kore o dani.* There is, moreover, an allusion to it in *Genji monogatari* (see Waley, *Tale of Genji,* p. 42; see also NKBT, vol. 14, p. 97).

27

1. The name Kaishō is given in the original text, but the author was probably referring to the Priest Kaisen, whose poems appear in the *Gosenshū* (KT 743, 1045, 1414). In another episode, the name Kaisen does appear in the original text, and so I shall consistently refer to him as Kaisen.

2. This poem may have been based on Ōshikōchi no Mitsune's poem, which appears in the *Kokinshū* (KT 956):

Yo o sutete	You, who abandoned the world
Yama ni iru hito	And now live alone
Yama nite mo	On a mountaintop,
Nao uki toki wa	Where can you go
Izuchi yukuran	When troubles beset you?

This poem was sent to a Buddhist priest living in seclusion in the mountains.

28

1. The two poems in this episode appear in the *Kokin rokujō* (ZKT 31533, 31534) in different versions. ZKT 31533 reads: Koto naraba/ Harezu mo arinan/ Asagiri no/ Magire ni mienu/ Kimi to omowan.

ZKT 31534 reads: Kawagiri no/ Naka ni kimi masu/ Mono naraba/ Haruru ma ni ma ni/ Ureshikaramashi.

2. Ki no Tsurayuki (868–946), one of the compilers of the *Kokinshū,* whose preface to this anthology of Japanese poetry is well known. The *Tosa Diary* is also another famous work of his.

3. Ki no Tomonori (845?–905) was another compiler of the *Kokinshū.*

29

1. Fujiwara no Sadakata (873–932), the father of Yoshiko who appears in episode 24. He was a talented musician and poet.

2. The Japanese name for the flower is *ominaeshi.* It is a light yellow flower that blooms in the summer and autumn.

3. This poem appears in the *Shinchokusenshū* (KT 243). In the *Sanjō no Udaijin shū* (*Katsura no Miya-bon sōsho,* vol. 2, p. 53), the second line reads *Oru te ni utsuru.* The general meaning of the poem is that since the Minister of Ceremonial is dead, the place no longer seems the same.

30

1. Minamoto no Muneyuki (d. 939), the grandson of Emperor Kōkō and son of Prince Koretada. Another theory is that he was the grandson of Emperor Nimmyō (810–850, r. 833–850) and the son of Prince Motoyasu. He is one of the Thirty-six Poetic Geniuses. An anthology of his poetry is entitled the *Muneyuki shū.* At one point in his life, he was the Master of the Right Division of the Office of the Capital.

2. Present-day Wakayama prefecture.

3. *Okitsu kaze* ("the wind from the offing") is the *jo* (or preface) for Fukei Bay, named after the village Fukei in the Sennan district of Osaka. The poet, likening himself to the *miru* seaweed, is complaining to Teiji no In about not having been promoted. The *miru* seaweed is a popular poetic image dating back to the *Man'yōshū,* an anthology of Japanese poetry compiled in the eighth century. This poem appears in the *Shinsenzaishū* (KT 1448).

31

1. Included in the *Gosenshū* (KT 171) as an anonymous poem.

32

1. This poem appears in the *Shoku gosenshū* (KT 848), with the second line reading *Hito mo ya aru to.* It is mistakenly said to have been written by Gen no Myōbu and presented to Emperor Uda. The poem also appears in the *Teiji no In gyoshū* (*Katsura no Miya-bon sōsho,* vol. 20, p. 72), with the second and last lines reading Hito mo ya aru to/ Omoubekarikere. It had probably been based on a poem in the *Kokinshū* (KT 867) which goes:

Murasaki no	Because of a single *murasaki,* *
Hitomoto yue ni	All the other plants
Musashi no no	Growing on Musashi Plain
Kusa wa minagara	Appear enchanting.
Aware to zo miru	

* A plant from whose root a purple dye was extracted. Growing to a height of about two feet, it bears a white flower which resembles a plum blossom. The flower blooms in summer.

2. The poet is wondering whether something unattractive about his personality is preventing him from being promoted. In this poem, the word *morisugi* ("to leak through") can also be interpreted as "to continue to lose one's chance of promotion." There is a pun on the word *oru,* which means "to break off" as well as "to be."

33

1. Ōshikōchi no Mitsune, one of the compilers of the *Kokinshū.*

2. The poet is saying that, being of no consequence, he has to greet the

autumn without being promoted and still dressed in the green robes of the Sixth and Seventh Ranks. The red robes are for the holders of the Fifth Rank. Autumn makes him feel especially sad, for the red maple leaves constantly remind him of the red robes of the rank to which he had failed to be promoted. Moreover, he likens himself to the evergreen which reminds him of the color of his robes. There is a pun on the word *tsuta,* which means "the ivy" and "clumsy *(tsutanashi).*"

35

1. Fujiwara no Kanesuke (877–933). A number of his poems appear in the imperial anthologies. There is also a private collection of his poems entitled the *Kanesuke shū.* He was called Tsutsumi (meaning "embankment") because he lived on the embankment of the Kamo River in Kyoto.

2. Located in Saga, a district in present-day Kyoto. The Ninna-ji, where Teiji no In lived for a time after his abdication, was built on this mountain.

3. This poem appears in the *Shinchokusenshū* (KT 1267). The version given in the *Kanesuke shū* (ZKT 16182) goes: Shirakumo no/ Kokonoe ni shimo/ Tachitsuru wa/ Ōuchi yama to/ Ieba narikeri.

The word "nine-fold *(kokonoe)*" was often used to describe or indicate the Imperial Palace. Moreover, the *uchi* in the place name Mount Ōuchi is another word for the Imperial Palace.

36

1. Princess Jūshi (d. 959), the daughter of Emperor Uda. She served as the Priestess of the Ise Shrine *(Saigū)* during the reign of Emperor Daigo and left the shrine in 930. The Ise Shrine is located on the Ise peninsula of Mie prefecture. The Ise Priestess was chosen from among the unmarried princesses of royal blood upon the enthronement of a new emperor. This practice is said to have begun during the time of Emperor Sujin (148–30 B.C., r. 97–30 B.C.) and to have ended during the reign of Emperor Daigo (1288–1339, r. 1318–1339).

2. *Kuretake no* ("bamboo") is a pillow-word for *yoyo,* meaning "generations." The name of the palace, Také, is mentioned as a part of the phrase. There is a pun on the word *yoyo,* which means both "for generations" and "the nodes of a bamboo."

37

1. The man himself has not been identified, but the province of Izumo is a part of modern Shimane prefecture.

2. The flowers in bloom represent the men who, like his brother, had been picked to serve in the Imperial Palace.

38

1. Prince Sadahira (d. 913).

2. Fujiwara no Hōshi, Emperor Uda's consort.

3. An island off the coast of Kyushu, obviously a place far beneath the dignity of the granddaughter of an emperor.

4. *Ho* ("sail") is an *engo* for *wata no hara* ("the open sea"). This poem has the same theme as the one by Ariwara no Yukihira which appears in the *Kokinshū* (KT 962) and in the *Kokin rokujō* (ZKT 23647):

Wakuraba ni	If at anytime
Tou hito araba	Anyone asks for me,
Suma no ura ni	Please tell him
Moshio taretsutsu	That I shed tears of sorrow
Wabu to kotaeyo	On the shore of Suma Bay.

39

1. Although the name Moromichi is given in the original text, the author probably meant Morofuji, the son of Fujiwara no Morokuzu.

2. Minamoto no Tadaakira (903–958), the son of Prince Koretada and brother of Muneyuki. He served as Middle Captain of the Inner Palace Guards from 934 to 951.

3. The first two lines of the poem read as follows in Takeda's *Yamato monogatari shōkai:* Oku tsuyu no / Hodo o mo matanu. Prince Muneyuki Hodo is lamenting the fact that their meeting had been so brief. The white dew *(shiratsuyu)* represents himself, while the morning glory *(asagao)* is a symbol for the young girl. This poem reveals that they had indeed met and exchanged vows as lovers.

40

1. According to tradition, the Minister of Ceremonial (Prince Atsuyoshi) was a handsome man and a great lover.

2. Called a *kazami,* it was an outer robe worn by a young girl in early

summer. It had originally been an underrobe worn next to one's skin to absorb perspiration.

3. There is a pun on the word *omoi* ("to love") and *hi* ("a light"), which is the last syllable in the word *omoi.* In the *Gosenshū* (KT 209), this poem is attributed to a young child, who presented it to Princess Katsura.

41

1. The following sentence is omitted in the NKBT text: "Okashiki hito nite yorozu no koto o tsune ni iikawashi tamainikeri (She was a fascinating creature, who always had many topics to talk about)."

2. Takeda suggests that the phrase *Yo wa hakanaki o,* which ordinarily meant "trivial worldly matters," here refers to the seemingly short-lived relationship of man and wife.

3. This poem appears in the *Shinchokusenshū* (KT 1215), with the fourth line reading *Aware to iwade.*

42

1. Possibly Enshō (880–964), a priest of the Tendai sect of Buddhism. On the other hand, he may be a priest named Eshū about whom nothing is known.

2. There is a pun on the word *shimo,* meaning both "lowly" and "frost."

43

1. Called a *kirikane,* it is a type of fence with wooden planks placed horizontally on posts in the manner of blinds.

2. The province of Hida, a part of modern Gifu prefecture, was a mountainous, thickly forested area famed for its expert carpenters and architects who were called upon to build and repair the buildings in the capital.

3. According to the *Yamato monogatari shōkai,* the person mentioned here is probably the woman with whom Eshū's name had been linked in the widely spread rumors.

4. This poem is alluded to in the section covering the second month of Ten'en 2 (974) in *Kagerō nikki* (NKBT, vol. 20, p. 297; see also Seidensticker, *The Gossamer Years,* p. 148). Eshū is trying to discourage any visitor from coming by saying that his mountain retreat is located so far

away that even Mount Hiei, which was far enough away, lay back toward the capital.

5. Located on a mountain peak northeast of Mount Hiei.

44

1. Again, this was probably the same person mentioned in the earlier episode.

2. There is a pun on *hi,* meaning "the sun" as well as "day." In a light-hearted and flippant manner, he is trying to discourage the person who seems to be overly concerned about his private affairs.

3. There is a play on words on *ame,* meaning both "the heavens" and "rain." *Nure* ("to become wet") and *ame* ("rain") are *engo. Nuregoromo* (literally meaning "wet robes") is a word meaning "false accusations."

45

1. Fujiwara no Kanesuke. See episode 35.

2. Fujiwara no Kuwako.

3. Prince Shōmei (924–990), the son of Emperor Daigo.

4. Emperor Daigo.

5. This poem appears in the *Kanesuke shū* (ZKT 16285), in the *Kokin rokujō* (ZKT 32272), and in the *Gosenshū* (KT 1103). The last line of the poem as it appears in the *Gosenshū* reads *Madoinuru kana.*

46

1. Taira no Sadabumi (d. 923), who attained the Fifth Rank and held the post of Assistant Captain of the Left Division of the Middle Palace Guards. He was a great lover and one of the Thirty-six Poetic Geniuses. It is around his poems that the various tales of the *Heichū monogatari* were written.

2. The daughter of Prince Muneyuki.

3. There are a number of puns in this poem: *uchitokete* ("completely at ease") and *tokete* ("to melt"); *ware wa shimo* ("I") and *shimo* ("frost"); *oki,* meaning "to deposit (dew)" and "to wake up"; *koi* ("love") and *hi* ("the sun"), which is the last syllable in the word *koi.* Moreover, these are all *engo* for the word *tsuyu* ("dewdrops"). The two poems in this episode appear also in episode 9 of *Heichū monogatari* (NKBT, vol. 77, pp. 65–66); however, the wording of the poems is slightly different. The first poem goes: Uchitokete/ Kimi wa nenuran/

Ware wa shimo/ Tsuyu to okiite/ Omoi akashitsu. The second poem differs in that the second line reads *Okiite tare o.*

4. *Shiratsuyu no* ("the white dew") is a *jo* for the word *oki,* meaning "to deposit" and "to awaken." *Iso no kami* is a pillow-word for *furu,* meaning "to grow old." Lady Kan'in is saying that she could not be the one Heichū has been yearning for because, having been abandoned by him long ago, she has grown old and unattractive.

47

1. See episode 38.

2. Lady Ichijō is probably addressing this poem to a man who was complaining about it being difficult for him to visit her. In her poem, she accuses him of not loving her sincerely enough to surmount the difficulties standing in their way.

48

1. Emperor Uda is asking her to hurry back to the palace. This poem appears in the *Shinkokinshū* (KT 1019), with the fourth line reading *Yoso ni nomi shite.* It also appears in the *Teiji no In gyoshū* (*Katsura no Miya-bon sōsho,* vol. 20, p. 70).

49

1. Princess Kimiko (d. 902), the daughter of Emperor Uda, who was the Priestess of the Kamo Shrine *(Saiin)* in Kyoto from Kampyō 5 (893) to her death in 902. The Priestess of the Kamo Shrine was chosen from among the unmarried royal princesses to serve at the shrine. This practice began with Princess Uchiko (807–847), the daughter of Emperor Saga (786–882, r. 809–823), and ended with Princess Reishi, the daughter of Emperor Gotoba (1180–1239, r. 1184–1198).

2. This poem appears in the *Shoku kokinshū* (KT 499), with the third and fifth lines reading: Omowazuba/ Niwa no shiragiku.

3. The Priestess is saying that if her father, the Emperor, had not picked the flower and sent it to her, she would never have been able to enjoy the chrysanthemum from home. There is a pun on *kiku,* meaning both "chrysanthemum" and "to hear." *Waga yado* refers to either "her former home (the Imperial Palace)" or "her present residence (the Kamo Shrine)." *Waga yado, kimi* ("the Emperor"), and *yoso* ("another place") are *engo.*

50

1. See episode 27.

2. This poem appears in the *Shinshūishū* (KT 1806). There are two meanings for the adjective *kodakashi:* (1) slightly elevated and (2) having tall trees growing. The mountain must have been extremely high to have clouds surrounding its peak.

51

1. The Priestess is lamenting the fact that her father shows favoritism among his own children. She resents having been chosen from among all the royal princesses to lead this lonely life away from the palace. The word *e* is vague enough to suggest both *eda* ("branch") and *en* ("relation").

2. The *hatsushimo* ("the first frost of the year") is a symbol for the Emperor himself, who denies that he is impartial to any one of his children.

52

1. There is a pun on the word *oki,* meaning both "the open sea" and "to deposit." There is also a pun on *urami,* meaning "to be resentful" and "to view the bay." This poem appears as an anonymous poem in the *Shūishū* (KT 983), with the third line reading *Arinagara.* It also appears in the *Kokin rokujō* (ZKT 32956), again with the third line reading *Arinagara.* Still another version of the poem appears in the *Teiji no In gyoshū* (*Katsura no Miya-bon sōsho,* vol. 20, p. 70): Watatsumi no/ Fukaki kokoro to/ Shirinagara/ Uramiraruru zo/ Wabishikarikeru. According to the prose introduction, the poet composed this poem upon hearing the cry of a *hototogisu.*

53

1. Nothing more is known about this man.

2. This probably meant that she was having her menstrual period.

54

1. The word *shiori* may be interpreted in two ways: (1) "to break off branches as markers," and (2) "to be ill-treated."

55

1. This poem appears in the *Shoku goshūishū* (KT 1252). However, the third and fourth lines read Kimi nareba/ Naki yo to kikedo.

56

1. Taira no Kanemori (d. 990). He was the son of Atsuyuki, a great-grandson of Emperor Kōkō. Kanemori was also one of the Thirty-six Poetic Geniuses. He served as the Provisional Governor of Echizen, a part of modern Fukui prefecture, from 950 to 961.

2. Hyōe no Kimi, the daughter of Fujiwara no Kaneshige (d. 923). Kaneshige once served as an Imperial Adviser. Two of Lady Hyōe's poems appear in the *Gosenshū* (KT 740, 921).

3. A different version appears in the *Gosenshū* (KT 979): Yū yami wa/ Michi mo mienedo/ Furusato wa/ Moto koshi koma ni/ Makasete zo kuru.

4. This poem also appears in the *Gosenshū* (KT 980) as a return poem to the preceding one, but the fourth line reads "Ayanaku mo" instead of "Hakanaku mo."

57

1. Taira no Nakaki (d. 930), who later held the rank of Provisional Assistant Captain of the Left Division of the Outer Palace Guards. He was the Assistant Governor of Ōmi from 915 to 922. No information is available on his daughter.

2. This poem appears in the *Gosenshū* (KT 1173). The woman's return poem (KT 1174) which follows (not given in *Yamato monogatari*) runs:

Mi o ushi to	Thinking it would be distressing
Hito shirenu yo o	To be seen in this wretched state,
Tazunekoshi	I have sought a place
Kumo no yaetatsu	Unknown to others;
Yama ni ya wa aranu	And here I shall live
	On this cloud-covered mountain.

58

1. Also called Michinokuni, it is the ancient province of Mutsu (modern Aomori prefecture).

2. Minamoto no Kanenobu.

3. Prince Sadamoto (880–909), the third son of Emperor Seiwa. He is called Kan'in in the original text.

4. An ancient name for a spot in what is present-day Adachi-gun, Fukushima prefecture.

5. This poem appears in the *Shūishū* (KT 559), with the fifth line

reading *Iū wa makoto ka.* In the prose introduction, it states that Kanemori composed this poem upon hearing about the sisters of Shigeyuki, who were living in Kurozuka in the Natori district of Mutsu. In a teasing mood, he refers to the young women as demons. The Nō play *Adachigahara* (also called *Kurozuka*) is based on the legend about a female ogre living in Kurozuka of Adachi Field who fed on human flesh.

6. Ide, the name of a river, is famous in poetry for the yellow kerria roses *(yamabuki)* growing on its banks. The river flows through Tsuzukigun of modern Kyoto. In this poem, the kerria roses represent the young girl. Ide also calls to mind the word *oide* ("to be" or "to reside in"). *Kawazu naku* ("where the frogs cry") is a pillow-word for Ide. This poem is based on an anonymous poem which appears in the *Kokinshū* (KT 125):

Kawazu naku	The petals of the kerria roses
Ide no yamabuki	Of Ide where the frogs cry
Chirinikeri	Have scattered;
Hana no sakari ni	If only I had come
Awamashi mono o	When they were in full bloom!

7. Nothing more is known about the man.

8. The Natori Hot Spring, located in the Natori-gun of Miyagi prefecture.

9. This poem appears in the *Shūishū* (KT 386), with the first line reading *Obotsukana.* The place name, Natori-no-miyu, has been skillfully incorporated into the poem. The young woman is referring to the fact that ever since he had returned to the capital, he had not written to her. *Ato* ("trace") is an *engo* for *tori* ("bird"), and *tori* suggests the wild geese that were traditionally thought of as letter-bearers.

10. Once again the place name, Natori-no-miyu, can be seen in the underlined portion of the original poem. In the previous poem the woman had said that she sees no trace at all of the birds. Here, the poet says that he sees no fisherman. There is a pun on *sunadori* ("fisherman") and *tori,* a part of the word which means "birds."

11. See poem 79.

59

1. Kyushu.

2. *Usa* is a word meaning "sorrows" and is also a place name in Kyushu. Both meanings are suggested in the general meaning of the poem.

60

1. Gojō no Go, the daughter of Fujiwara no Yamakage. See episode 143.

61

1. Among the identified concubines of Teiji no In were: Fujiwara no Onshi (872–907), the daughter of Mototsune; Fujiwara no Inshi (d. 896), the daughter of Takafuji; Tachibana no Yoshiko, the daughter of Hiromi; Sugawara no Nobuko, the daughter of Michizane; Tachibana no Fusako (d. 893); Minamoto no Sadako, the daughter of Noboru; Fujiwara no Hōshi, the daughter of Tokihira; and Ise no Go, the daughter of Fujiwara no Tsugukage.

2. The mansion of Minamoto no Tōru (822–895), the Minister of the Left. He had the garden of the Kawara Palace landscaped after the breathtaking view of Shiogama Bay in Michinoku. After Tōru's death, Teiji no In moved into the Kawara Palace.

3. Fujiwara no Hōshi. See episodes 3 and 38.

4. In the original poem, there is a pun on the word *fuji* ("wisteria") and *fuchi* ("deep pools"). This poem refers to the deep pools and rapids of the Asuka River, which symbolize the impermanence of things (see episode 10). The neglected concubine is lamenting the fact that His Majesty's love has now grown cold.

5. The courtiers, by noting that the color of the wisteria has faded, are implying that the imperial favor has been transferred to someone else.

62

1. Nothing more is known about her; she was probably a lady-in-waiting at the palace.

2. The son of Miyoshi no Kiyotsura (847–918).

63

1. Prince Muneyuki. See episode 30.

2. He resents his lover for submitting so readily to her mother's command. The storm wind represents the girl's mother, and the branch, the daughter. There is a pun on *uramite,* which means both "to resent" and "to look back."

64

1. Taira no Sadabumi. See episode 46.

65

1. The fifth son of Prince Koretada, Emperor Kōkō's son.

2. Present-day Aichi prefecture.

3. A building within the grounds of the Imperial Palace, occupied at this time by one of the concubines of Emperor Daigo, Minamoto no Kazuko (d. 947), the daughter of Emperor Kōkō. Also pronounced Jōkyōden.

4. There is a pun on the word *uchi to,* which means "the Imperial Palace" and also "inside and outside." There is another pun on the word *kaku,* which can be interpreted as either *kuchi ni suru* ("to say") and *kakeru* ("to hang up").

5. Longing for her so, he can only cry as does the *hototogisu.* The word *nageki* ("to lament") contains the word *ki* ("tree"); the word *kogakure* ("hiding among the trees") brings to mind *kogare* ("to long passionately for"). The *hototogisu* is a bird which is rarely seen.

6. There is a pun on *tori,* meaning "bird" (referring to the *hototogisu* in the previous poem) and *tori mo aezu,* meaning "at once."

7. The compiler-editor of *Yamato monogatari* interjects at this point in his capacity as narrator, apologizing for not including the answering poem.

8. He was probably forced to turn back by the heavy snowfall.

66

1. The *inaōsedori* ("the wagtail") is one of the *sanchō* ("three birds") in the *Kokinshū* Secret Tradition, the other two being the *yobukodori* ("the cuckoo") and the *momochidori* ("the plover"), sometimes substituted by the *miyakodori* ("the curlew").

67

1. She is implying that she thought constantly of him.

68

1. Fujiwara no Nakahira (875–945), the third son of Mototsune. He was also the Minister of the Left. It is said that the nickname "Lord Biwa (Lord Loquat)" had been given to him because he had planted loquat trees on his property.

2. This poem appears in the *Gosenshū* (KT 1183). However, the second and third lines read Itsu nara shita ka/ Nara no ha o. Although the

nara tree and the *kashiwagi* are different species of oak, in these poems they are interchangeable.

3. This poem also appears in the *Gosenshū* (KT 1184), with the first line reading *Nara no ha no.* There is an ancient Japanese belief that a "leaf-protecting deity" resided in certain trees like the oak. Lord Biwa, in his poem, addresses Toshiko as the "leaf-protecting deity" and asks her not to torment him.

69

1. Fujiwara no Tadabumi (873–947), who once served as an Imperial Adviser.

2. The Barbarian-Subduing Generalissimo *(Sei-i-tai-shōgun).* Tadabumi attained this rank in the first month of Tengyō 3 (940) during the revolt of Taira no Masakado.

3. Also mentioned in episode 70.

4. A *kariginu.* It was originally a silk garment worn by nobles when hawking; it was later worn daily by court officials of the Sixth Rank and above. The edges of the sleeves and trousers had drawstrings which were tightened when worn. The *kariginu* that Shigemochi received had been tie-dyed.

5. These offerings often consisted of polished rice, the *sakaki* (the sacred Shintō tree), and strips of cloth or paper. Offerings were made along a journey to ensure the traveler's safety.

70

1. Or wax myrtle. In the spring it bears yellow blossoms and in the summer a purplish-red fruit resembling strawberries.

2. The underlined portion of the original poem gives the Japanese word, *yamamomo,* for the myrica.

3. There is a pun on the word *io,* meaning "fish," and *i* (of *inu*), meaning "to sleep." The words *fusu* ("to sleep"), *nede* ("without sleeping"), and *yume* ("dream") are *engo.* The *ayu,* a certain species of trout, are usually caught at night. It was believed that one whose heart is distressed appears in the dreams of his beloved, thus Gen no Myōbu asks Shigemochi if he had seen her in his dream.

4. What is today Kosakai-chō in Hōi-gun, Aichi prefecture.

5. *Umaya* ("a post-station") suggests *ima ya* ("any moment now"), which expresses the anxiety and impatience of a person waiting for a lover's return.

6. A young boy of noble birth had to go through a formal coming-of-age ceremony *(gempuku)* between the ages of twelve and fifteen. Thereafter the youth was called by his adult name and allowed to wear the cap and robe of an adult.

7. The *Kurōdodokoro* was a bureau of the ancient Imperial Court which had charge of private records, judged and determined litigated cases brought before the court, and had the authority to report directly to the emperor on various matters. It had originally taken care of the more personal aspects of the emperor's life. Later it expanded to include pronouncements, court records, and court ceremonies. Still later, it acquired legislative powers, becoming the most important organ of government under the Fujiwara.

8. Gold from the general northeastern section of Japan called Ōshū, which included the five ancient provinces of Mutsu, Rikuchū, Rikuzen, Iwashiro, and Iwaki (the modern prefectures of Aomori, Iwate, Miyagi, and Fukushima).

71

1. This poem appears in the *Shinchokusenshū* (KT 1227) and in the *Sanjō no Udaijin shū* (*Katsura no Miya-bon sōsho,* vol. 2, p. 58), as a poem by Kanesuke (Tsutsumi no Chūnagon). In the latter work, the first and third lines read *Saki niou* and *Yaezakura.* In the *Kokin rokujō* (ZKT 33312), the first through third lines read Fuku kaze ni/ Makasete mireba/ Sakurabana. In the *Kanesuke shū* (ZKT 16229), the poem is attributed to Fujiwara no Sadakata. The poet is lamenting the fact that man's life is so brief.

2. Fujiwara no Sadakata. See episode 29. He was also known as Sanjō no Udaijin. The relationship of the historical figures may be seen in the following chart:

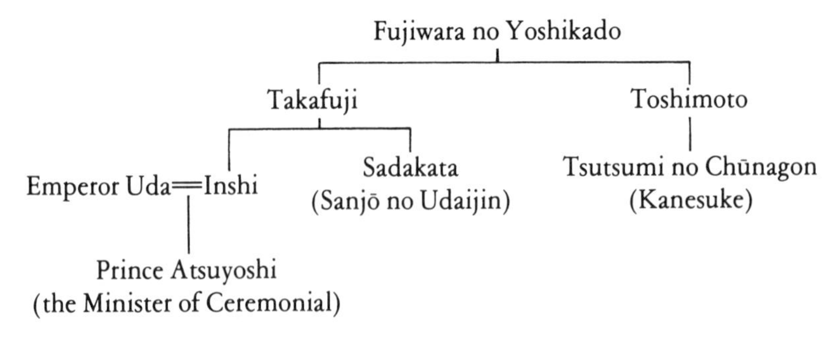

3. This poem appears in the *Shoku kokinshū* (KT 1402), with the first line reading *Haru goto ni.* It also appears in the *Sanjō no Udaijin shū* (*Katsura no Miya-bon sōsho,* vol. 2, p. 59).

72

1. Also mentioned in episode 61. It had originally been the residence of Onshi, Emperor Uda's concubine, but later it became the residence of the Emperor himself upon his abdication.

2. See episode 56.

3. A poem on a similar theme appears in the *Sakaki* (The Sacred Tree) chapter of *Genji monogatari* (KT, *Monogatari,* 904):

Sae wataru	How sad it is
Ike no kagami no	Not to see reflected
Sayakeki ni	In the cold mirror
Minareshi kage o	Of the still pond
Minu zo kanashiki	You whom I knew so well.

See also Waley, *The Tale of Genji,* p. 199.

74

1. This poem appears in the *Gosenshū* (KT 17) and in the *Kanesuke shū* (ZKT 16320). According to the prose introduction, the poem is said to have been written when the plum blossoms were late in blooming. In both anthologies, the fourth line of the poem reads *Niou hana kana.* Moreover, in the *Kanesuke shū* (ZKT 16321), an answering poem to the above is given:

Hitoyo nomi	I stayed for one night only
Neteshi kaereba	Before returning home,
Fujigoromo	But already the color
Kokoro tokete no	Of my robe of wisteria*
Iro misen ya wa	Has faded.

*A coarse robe made of wisteria vines.

75

1. This poem appears in the *Kokinshū* (KT 391), with the first and third lines reading *Kimi ga yuku* and *Shiranedomo.* In the *Kanesuke shū* (*Nishi Honganji-bon Sanjūrokuninshū,* p. 232, poem 93), it is said that Tsutsumi no Chūnagon had sent it to Ōe no Chifuru. However, the

first and third lines read *Kimi ga yuku* and *Shiranedomo.* There is a pun on the word *yuki,* which means either "to go" or "snow." There is also another pun on the phrase *ma ni ma ni,* meaning either "as it is" or "through (a space)." *Koshi* is the ancient name for the Hokurikudō, one of the eight circuits of Japan. It was made up of the following provinces located in central Japan: Wakasa, Echizen, Noto, Kaga, Etchū, Echigo, and Sado. Shirayama (now called Hakusan) is a dormant volcano northwest of Nagoya. It, Mount Fuji, and Tateyama (in the Japan Alps) are the three famous mountains of Japan.

76

1. Minamoto no Yoshitane, the son of Emperor Seiwa's son Nagakazu (d. 918). Yoshitane attained the Senior Fifth Rank, Lower Grade, and was appointed Governor of Mimasaka.

2. See episode 20.

3. The daughter of the Imperial Adviser Prince Tōyo (833–916), who was the grandson of Emperor Kammu (737–806, r. 781–806). She was one of the many concubines of Emperor Uda. See episode 61 for the names of other known concubines.

4. In this poem, there is a pun on the word *namida* ("tears") and *nami* ("waves"). The *engo* for *nami* are *kawa* ("river"), *chidori* ("plover"), and *kaeru* ("to return").

77

1. This poem also appears in the *Shoku gosenshū* (KT 731), with the last line given as *Tachi ya noboran.* The word *yaku* ("to burn") is used in the sense of the "the burning salt fires" and a person's "burning with passion." There is, moreover, a pun on the word *akashi,* meaning "to waken to" and Akashi, a place name for a seaside area in modern Kobe.

2. The full moon on this particular night of the year, according to the lunar calendar, was thought to be the most beautiful of all. In this episode, a moon-viewing banquet at the Teiji Palace had been arranged.

3. This poem alludes to *Taketori monogatari (The Tale of the Bamboo-Cutter).* At the end of this tale, the old bamboo-cutter weeps in order to detain his adopted daughter, the lovely Princess Kaguya. In spite of his weeping, on the night of the fifteenth, when the moon was at its loveliest, she was escorted back to her home in the moon by the heavenly angels who had come for her. The phrase *kimi ni* refers to her father, Teiji no In. Moreover, the princess' name, Katsura, is also the name of a leg-

endary tree believed to be growing on the moon and often stood for the moon itself. The word *yoyo* describes the sound of weeping, but it also means "the nodes of a bamboo" as well as "night."

78

1. A colorful, impressive ceremony held on New Year's Day during which the Emperor and Empress received the New Year's greetings of their subjects.

2. Oka Kazuo believes that this was Prince Shōmei (see episode 45), who became President of the Board of Censors in Kōhō 1 (964). Hazama Tetsurō, however, believes that the man mentioned in this episode was Prince Motohira (d. 958), the son of Emperor Yōzei.

3. This poem appears in the *Shinsenzaishū* (KT 1027), with the second line reading *Mayou kokoro to.*

79

1. On another level, the poem may be translated: If, never tiring of you, / I were to meet you time and again, / How miserable we would be / With all the world / Gossiping about us!

Korizuma means "without becoming disgusted." Suma, taken from the last part of the word *korizuma,* is the name of a bay. *Ukimiru* means "the floating *miru* seaweed" as well as "to come to grief." There are *engo* in the words Suma, *kazuku* ("to be submerged"), and *miru* ("a kind of seaweed").

80

1. Located in the western half of the capital, it had originally been the mansion of Minamoto no Tatae, the Minister of Justice, but was later used as one of the residences of the Retired Emperor Uda.

2. The sons of Prince Koretada, called the Nan-in in this episode. Two of them have appeared in earlier episodes: Prince Muneyuki (episode 30) and Nan-in no Gorō (episode 65).

81

1. Fujiwara no Suenawa (d. c. 919), the son of Chishige. He served as the Minor Captain of the Right Division of the Inner Palace Guards and was nicknamed Katano no Urin (*Urin* being the Chinese term for the Inner Palace Guards). He was skillful at hawking.

2. Fujiwara no Shizuko (see episode 5).

3. Fujiwara no Atsutada (906–943), the son of Tokihira and the daughter of Ariwara no Muneyana. He was very good at playing the *biwa,* a four-stringed lute. One of the Thirty-six Poetic Geniuses, his poems are recorded in a private collection entitled the *Atsutada shū.*

4. This poem appears in the *Gosenshū* (KT 666), with the first line reading *Omowan to.*

82

1. This poem appears in the *Kokin rokujō* (ZKT 32048), with the fourth and fifth lines reading Ware o bakari ni/ Omoikeru kana. Mount Kurikoma in Kyoto is mentioned in *Nihon kōki* as a hunting park: (1) The entry for the twenty-first day of the ninth month of Enryaku 15 (796) (see *Kokushi taikei,* vol. 3, p. 4). (2) The entry for the twenty-fifth day of the first month of Kōnin 3 (812) (see *Kokushi taikei,* vol. 3, p. 111). In this poem, there is a pun on the word *kari,* meaning both "temporary" and "a hunt." Though Ukon had tried to be true to her vows, she regrets her efforts, for he has not treated her very kindly.

83

1. A *shitomi.* Boards were nailed in place behind a lattice-work, the top of which was a hinged door-leaf that could be opened or closed by elevating or lowering it. The *shitomi* served to keep out sunlight, wind, and rain.

2. There is a pun on the word *moru,* meaning both "to leak" and "to look after" (actually the word *mamoru*). Two meanings are also possible in the word *kaesazaramashi:* "I would not let him go home" and "I would not turn over (the bedding)." Thus, the poem may also be translated: If the one I love/ Were to come down to me/ Like the rain,/ I would leave unturned/ My rain-soaked bedding.

A poem by Ki no Tsurayuki in which he uses similar imagery appears in the *Kokin rokujō* (ZKT 31357):

Omou hito	If the one I love
Ame to furikuru	Were to come down to me
Mono naraba	Like the rain,
Moru waga yane wa	My leaky roof
Awasezaramashi	Would not let us meet.

84

1. This poem appears in the *Shūishū* (KT 870) and in the *Kokin rokujō* (ZKT 33813).

85

1. Fujiwara no Morouji (913–970), the son of Tokihira, who is called Momozono no Saishō in the original text. *Saishō* is the Chinese term for the Imperial Adviser *(Sangi)*, and Morouji served in this position from 944 to 955. According to *Yamato monogatari shōkai*, the *Saishō* in this episode was Minamoto no Yasumitsu (924–995), the son of Prince Yoshiakira (Emperor Daigo's son).

2. Ukon was probably in love with the Imperial Adviser and wished that the rumors were based on fact.

86

1. Fujiwara no Akitada (897–965), the son of Tokihira. He served as Major Counsellor from 948 to 959 and then later became the Minister of the Right.

2. This poem appears in the *Gosenshū* (KT 3). Kanemori is indirectly inviting Akitada to accompany him. In at least one variant text the word *hagi* ("bush-clover") appears instead of *ogi* ("miscanthus").

3. Kataoka is a hill with a steep slope on one side and is located in Kita-Katsuragi, Nara prefecture.

87

1. Nothing is known about the man.

88

1. The ancient province of Ki (also pronounced Kii) is presently known as Wakayama prefecture. *Muro,* besides being a place name, also means a kind of hothouse. The woman is thus saying that he will probably not feel cold in a place called Muro.

2. *Fusuma* means both "the time during which one sleeps" and "a coverlet (in this case, a robe with which he could cover himself)."

89

1. The man is not identified.

2. Her father was probably an official in the Office of Palace Repairs (*Surishiki,* also pronounced *Shurishiki*). According to the *Yamato mono-*

gatari shōkai text, she is believed to have been the daughter of Fujiwara no Naoyuki.

3. There is a pun on the word *kata,* meaning both "way or method" and "direction."

4. This poem appears in the *Shūishū* (KT 1134). The *hio* ("icefish") are small smeltlike fish, also known as whitebait, which are plentiful in the Uji River in late autumn and throughout the winter. The *ajiro,* a kind of fishing contraption made of bamboo or brushwood, is set up along the rapids of a river. Straw matting was placed at the ends in place of fishing nets to catch the icefish. The line *Nani ni yorite ka* means either "for what reason" or "where he (the woman's lover) has gone." Therefore, the last two lines of the poem may also be translated: . . . Where my lover has gone to/ That he does not come to see me.

5. In this poem, the bamboo fishing device is a symbol of the woman, and the icefish that of the man. Moreover, the word *Uji* may be interpreted as either the place name famous for the icefish or *uchi,* meaning "one's home." This poem may also be translated: Apart from you,/ Whom can I go to?/ If you have any doubts,/ Ask anyone/ Living in my house.

6. Ōsaka, the name of a mountain at the foot of which was a barrier—the famous "Meeting Barrier" in Japanese poetry—between the provinces of Yamashiro and Ōmi (the former is a part of modern Kyoto and the latter, modern Shiga prefecture).

7. In this poem, the verbs *kienan* ("to disappear") and *kaerite* ("to return home"), taken together, form a new verb *kiekaeru,* which means "to be so overwhelmed by one's emotion that one could die."

8. *Asagao* means both "one's face in the morning" and "the morning glory." The line *Kakio naru,* meaning "on the fence," is a *jo* for the word *asagao* with the meaning "morning glory."

90

1. Prince Motoyoshi (890–943), the son of Emperor Yōzei. He was known to have been a man of talent and refinement. A private collection of his poems is entitled the *Motoyoshi no Miko shū.*

2. This poem appears in the *Shinchokusenshū* (KT 737) and in the *Motoyoshi no Miko shū* (ZKT 21241). *Kuretake no* is a pillow-word for a bamboo joint. It is also the name for a kind of bamboo which grows in the garden of the Imperial Palace. There is a pun on the word *fushi,* meaning "a bamboo joint" or "matter."

91

1. Fujiwara no Sadakata served as a Middle Captain of the Inner Palace Guards between the years 906 and 913.

2. An annual festival held at the Kamo Shrine in Kyoto. It used to be held on the second Day of the Bird of the fourth month, according to the lunar calendar. Because people would decorate the front of the Kamo Shrine, their carriages, and their caps with hollyhock, it was also known as the Hollyhock Festival *(Aoi Matsuri)*. Still another name for it was *Kita Matsuri*.

3. The importance of fans in religious ceremonies and in the daily lives of courtiers is discussed in U. A. Casal's article "The Lore of the Japanese Fan."

4. This poem appears in the *Shūishū* (KT 1270), with the last two lines reading Uki o ba kaze ni/ Tsukete yaminan. It also appears in the *Sanjō no Udaijin shū* (*Katsura no Miya-bon sōsho,* vol. 2, p. 56), with the last two lines reading Uki o ba kore ni/ Omoi yoseken. The young woman is saying that she really had not wanted to send him the fan, for a fan, sent as a gift between a man and a woman, expressed the fact that their relationship had come to an end. The often-used phrase *aki no ōgi* ("the autumn fan")—the fan discarded once the chilly winds of autumn begin to blow, thus symbolizing a woman abandoned by her lover—alludes to this tradition. See the Nō play *Hanjo* in which a courtesan and her lover exchange fans as pledges of their love. Hanjo refers to Pan Chieh-yü, the concubine of Emperor Ch'eng Ti (r. 32–6 B.C.), who likened herself to a fan abandoned in autumn in her poem entitled *Yüan ko hsing* in the *Wen hsüan* and *Yüan shih* in the *Yü-t'ai hsin-yung*. A translation of this poem may be found on page 89 of Casal's article.

5. This poem appears in the *Sanjō no Udaijin shū* (*Katsura no Miya-bon sōsho,* vol. 2, p. 57), with the last line reading *Tsuraki narikeri.* A similar poem appears in the *Kokin rokujō* (ZKT 34292): Yo no hito no/ Imikeru mono o/ Waga tame ni/ Nashi to iwanu wa/ Tare ga ukinari.

The Minister of the Right is implying that he is suffering because, by sending him the fan, the young woman has indicated that their relationship has come to an end.

92

1. Fujiwara no Atsutada. See episode 81.

2. Fujiwara no Kishi (904–962), who served as the Head of the Sewing Hall for the Costume of the Imperial Consort.

3. Fujiwara no Tadahira (880–949), who later became Prime Minister and Regent. His posthumous name was Teishin Kō. He served as the Minister of the Left from 924 to 936.

4. This poem appears in the *Gosenshū* (KT 507), with the second line reading *Suguru tsuki hi mo.* It also appears in the *Kokin rokujō* (ZKT 31101), with the second line reading the same as the *Gosenshū* version. Again, the following version appears in the *Atsutada shū* (*Nishi Honganji-bon Sanjūrokuninshū,* p. 243, poem 138): Mono omou to/ Suguru tsuki hi mo/ Shiranaku ni/ Kotoshi wa kyō ni/ Narinu to ka kiku.

5. This poem appears in the *Gosenshū* (KT 962) and in the *Atsutada shū* (*Nishi Honganji-bon Sanjūrokuninshū,* p. 243, poem 142). In the *Shūishū* (KT 635), the first line reads *Ikade ka wa* and the last, *Kimi ni shirasen.*

6. This poem appears in the *Gosenshū* (KT 883) and in the *Atsutada shū* (ZKT 16351). The poet is declaring that even though he was going to meet her again tonight, as he had done the night before, he is so much in love with her that he can hardly wait for night to fall.

93

1. Princess Gashi (910–954), the daughter of Emperor Daigo. She was appointed High Priestess of Ise in 931.

2. This poem appears in the *Kokin rokujō* (ZKT 33970), with the first line reading *Ise no umi no.* It also appears in the *Gosenshū* (KT 928), with the first line reading the same as the *Kokin rokujō* version and the last two lines reading Ima wa nani chō/ Kai ka arubeki. In the *Atsutada shū* (*Nishi Honganji-bon Sanjūrokuninshū,* p. 242, poem 118), the first line reads *Ise no umi no* and the last two lines read *Ima wa nani shite/ Kai ka arubeki.* The first three lines in the original are all used as a *jo* to the phrase *kai naku* ("in vain"). The word *kai* also means "sea shell," hence the use of all the imagery of the seashore in the poem. The poet is trying to say that since the one he loves has been chosen to serve as the High Priestess of Ise, he realizes that to continue to long for her would be in vain.

94

1. The daughter of Fujiwara no Sadakata, the Sanjō Minister of the Right.

2. Prince Yoshiakira (d. 937), the son of Emperor Daigo. His relationship to Sadakata and his family is shown below:

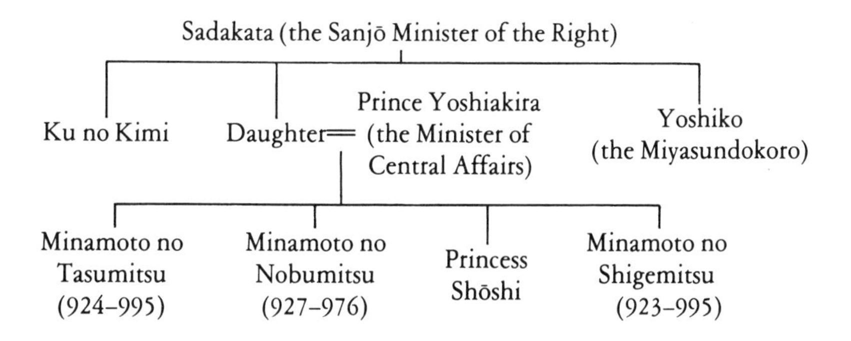

3. The ninth daughter of Sadakata. She later became the wife of Fujiwara no Morotada (920–969) and mother of Naritoki (941–995).

4. Fujiwara no Morotada was the fifth son of Tadahira and eventually attained the position of the Minister of the Left. He served as the Captain of the Left Division of the Middle Palace Guards from 947 to 953. Earlier, he had served as a Gentleman-in-Waiting at the palace from 935 to 937.

5. Fujiwara no Yoshiko (d. 964), the daughter of Sadakata and consort of Emperor Daigo. She was the older sister of Ku no Kimi.

6. The Miyasundokoro feels that in remembrance of his wife, Prince Yoshiakira should remain at his father-in-law's home. The word *sumori* has two meanings: "the egg which remains unhatched in the nest" and "to watch over a desolate spot." There is also a pun on the verb *kaeru,* which means both "to return home" and "to hatch."

7. In this poem, the Minister of Central Affairs is saying that he is returning home, for he now realizes that Ku no Kimi is interested in someone else and that it would be in vain for him to remain. This entire episode is quoted in the *Kakaishō* (*Kokubun chūshaku zensho,* vol. 3, p. 395).

95

1. Emperor Daigo.

2. Prince Atsumi (893–967), the son of Emperor Uda. He and Emperor Daigo were half-brothers. Prince Atsumi is known to have been a talented musician.

3. Princess Jūshi, Prince Atsumi's half-sister. See episode 36.

4. This poem appears in the *Gosenshū* (KT 471) and in the *Kokin rokujō* (ZKT 31722), with the second line reading *Yuki furinureba.* There are numerous puns: *furi,* meaning "to fall" and "to grow old"; *yuki,* meaning "snow" and "to go"; and *koshi,* meaning "to cross" and

"to come." There is also a pun on the place name *Koshiji,* where Shirayama is located.

5. This is probably a note written in by an early copyist of the original text which was later copied as a part of the work itself.

96

1. Fujiwara no Morotada.

2. Fujiwara no Saneyori (900–970), the son of Tadahira. He ultimately became Regent and Prime Minister and was posthumously known as Teishin Kō. A private collection of his poems is entitled the *Seishin Kō shū.* Saneyori served as the Minister of the Left from 947 to 967. The following chart shows how the different historical figures are related:

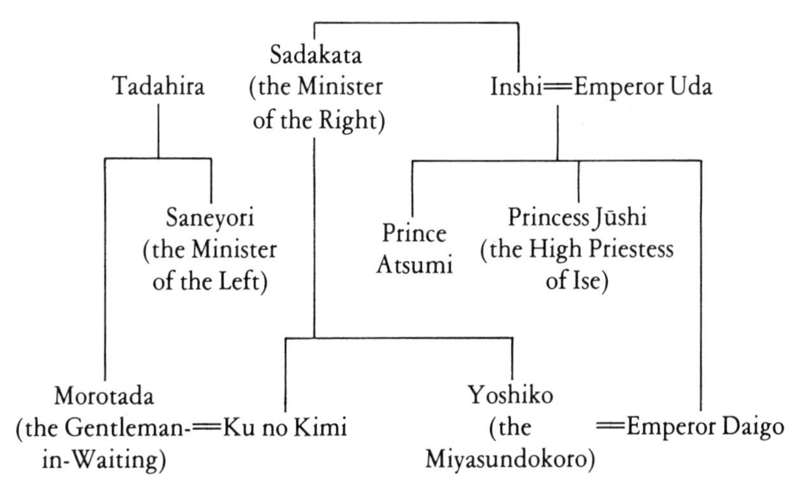

3. There is a pun on the word *kata,* which means both "direction" and "beach." A part of the word *urayamashi* ("to envy") is *ura,* meaning "a bay." *Watatsumi* ("the open sea") is a *jo* for the word *ura;* it is also an *engo* for *nami* ("waves") and *ura.*

In this particular poem, Saneyori is expressing his jealousy toward his younger brother for having become the brother-in-law of the Miyasundokoro.

97

1. Fujiwara no Tadahira. See episode 92. His wife was Yoshiko, the daughter of Emperor Uda and Sugawara no Nobuko. She was the mother of Saneyori, the Minister of the Left.

2. This poem appears in the *Shoku gosenshū* (KT 1245). The word *kage* is an abbreviation for either *tsukikage* ("moonlight") or *hitokage* ("a figure"). The following words are *engo: kakure* ("to hide"), *tsuki* ("the moon"), *meguri* ("to come around"), and *kage.*

98

1. Sugawara no Kimi, or Yoshiko. The following chart shows the relationship of a number of historical figures to each other:

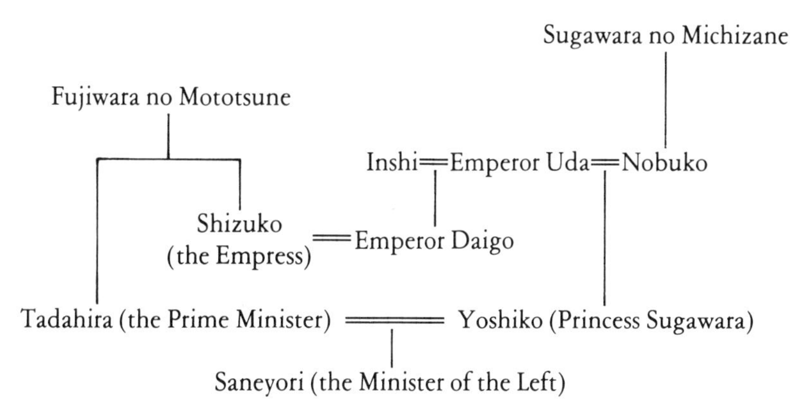

2. Robes of either dark purple or dark crimson. A courtier had to receive the Emperor's permission to wear such robes.

3. *Suōgasane,* a lined robe that was light crimson on the outside and dark red on the inside.

4. Fujiwara no Shizuko. See episode 5.

5. *Nugu,* meaning "to take off (clothes)," refers to the court robes he put aside when the mourning period began following his wife's death. The cheerful color he now wears reminds him of his wife, making him feel sad. Moreover, it had been Teiji no In, his wife's father, who, though grief-stricken, had given him permission to wear crimson robes.

6. *Chūben,* or Magistrate of the Council of State. According to historical records, however, Tadahira never held the office of Middle Controller.

99

1. Teiji no In often went on an imperial excursion to the Ōi River, which flowed along the southwestern foot of Mount Ogura in Kadano district in the ancient province of Yamashiro. Arashiyama loomed on the other side of the river.

2. This poem appears in the *Shūishū* (KT 1128), with the second line reading *Mine no momijiba.* It also appears in the *Ogura hyakunin isshu* (*Ogura hyakunin isshu no kōgi,* pp. 68–69), with the second line also reading *Mine no momijiba.* Moreover, it is included in *Ōkagami* (KT, *Rekishi,* 935), with the second line reading *Momiji no iro mo.*

100

1. See episode 81.
2. Teiji no In.
3. This poem appears in the *Shinshūishū* (KT 179), with the last line reading *Ima sakarinari.* It is erroneously attributed to Fujiwara no Suetsuna, an eleventh-century poet. It also appears in *Fubokushō,* a fourteenth-century poetry anthology, with the last line given as *Ima sakarinari* (*Sakusha bunrui Fuboku wakashū-Honbunhen,* p. 196, poem 145).

101

1. Minamoto no Kintada. See episode 4.
2. This poem appears in the *Shinkokinshū* (KT 854).
3. The Yōmei-mon, one of the twelve gates opening into the Inner Palace, which was located in the east side of the capital.
4. One of the avenues running from east to west in the capital.

102

1. Hitozane died in 917.
2. In Fushimi-ku, a part of the city of Kyoto.
3. One of the poems in the original *Kokin rokujō,* which is not included in extant texts but quoted in *Ōgishō,* a twelfth-century critique on poetry (*Nihon kagaku taikei,* vol. 1, p. 360), with the last two lines reading Kokorobososhi ya/ Kyō no wakare yo. The poet is bewailing the fact that he is seriously ill and that he does not know if he will ever be back again.

103

1. There used to be an Eastern Market *(higashi no ichi)* and a Western Market *(nishi no ichi)* in the capital, both of which opened for business on certain days of the month.
2. Princess Hanshi (833–900), the daughter of Prince Nakano.
3. This poem appears in the *Shoku gosenshū* (KT 698), with the second and third lines given as Amata no sode wa/ Mieshikado. In the

Kokin rokujō (ZKT 33488), the first through third lines read Momoshiki ni/ Amata no sode wa/ Mieshikado. It also appears in episode 38 of *Heichū monogatari* (NKBT, vol. 77, p. 104), with the third line reading *Shiranedomo.* Moreover, it appears in *Konjaku monogatari* (KT, *Monogatari,* 1885), with the fourth line given as *Naka ni omoi* and the last line missing. The word *momoshiki* means either "numerous layers" or "the Imperial Palace." There is a pun on the word *omo(h)i,* meaning "to love," and *hi,* meaning "scarlet."

4. The general area of modern Saitama prefecture and the municipality of Tokyo combined. The governor is unidentified.

5. According to *Yamato monogatari shōkai,* both the robe and its lining were of a material dyed a deep crimson.

6. The *kinuginu no fumi,* or the "morning-after" letter, in which the man customarily expressed his deep regret in having had to part with his sweetheart at dawn and which he sent off to her immediately upon returning home. It was most embarrassing and agonizing for a woman not to receive such a letter by noon at least, for she could then assume that he had lost interest in her.

7. According to Hagitani Boku, this was Fujiwara no Kiyotsune, who was then Captain of the Right Division of the Middle Palace Guards.

8. Heichū was then serving as a Junior Lieutenant of the Right Division of the Middle Palace Guards.

9. This poem appears in episode 38 of *Heichū monogatari* (NKBT, vol. 77, p. 105). This poem also appears in *Konjaku monogatari* (KT, *Monogatari,* 1859), with the second line reading *Yoso naru mono to. Amanogawa* (literally, "the Heavenly River") refers to the Milky Way, and *ama* alone means "a Buddhist nun." *Sora* means both "sky" and "to be meaningless." On a completely different level, the poem may be translated: I have heard/ That the Heavenly River/ Can be seen up in the sky,/ But it is actually/ The tears streaming from my eyes.

10. This poem appears in episode 38 of *Heichū monogatari* (NKBT, vol. 77, p. 105). It also appears in *Konjaku monogatari* (KT, *Monogatari,* 1860), with the fourth and fifth lines reading Amanogawa ya wa/ Nagarubekaran. The following words are *engo* for *namida* ("tears"): *nagare* ("to flow"), *hayaku* ("swiftly"), and *kawa* ("river"). This poem may also be translated: Thinking that the world/ Is a wretched place indeed,/ You may have shed a river of tears,/ But they could hardly flow rapidly enough/ To become the Heavenly River.

11. A *nurigome,* which is a small room with lacquered walls, used to

store away clothing and various household items. It was sometimes used as a bedroom.

104

1. Fujiwara no Shigemoto (d. 931), the son of the Major Counsellor Kunitsune and the daughter of Ariwara no Muneyana. Shigemoto attained the Junior Fifth Rank, Upper Grade, and served as the Minor Captain of the Left Division of the Inner Palace Guards. He was appointed Minor Captain of the Right Division of the Inner Palace Guards in Enchō 6 (928). The Minor Captain Shigemoto is the main figure in Tanizaki Jun'ichirō's novel, *Shōshō Shigemoto no haha.* A partial translation of this novel by Edward Seidensticker may be found in Professor Keene's *Modern Japanese Literature,* pp. 387–397.
2. This poem appears in the *Shinkokinshū* (KT 1236).
3. This poem is written as though it were addressed to the servant of the young lady, who, according to the previous poem, had died of love.

105

1. Taira no Nakaki. See episode 57.
2. See episode 62.
3. A mountain located north of Kyoto. The Kurama Temple, dedicated to Bishamonten (Vaisravana), was built on the mountainside.
4. This poem appears in the *Gosenshū* (KT 833). In the *Kokin rokujō* (ZKT 31760), the second through fourth lines read Kurabu no yama ni/ Irishi hito/ Madou madou mo. It also appears in *Konjaku monogatari* (KT, *Monogatari,* 1861). There is a pun on Kurama, a place name, and *kura(i),* meaning "dark." *Tadoru* ("to grope for") is an *engo* for *kura(i). Kurozome* calls to mind the monk's robe dyed black and is used as a *jo* for *kura(i).*
5. This poem, along with poem 158, appears in *Konjaku monogatari* (KT 1862, 1863). The phrase *uguisu no koe* (literally, "the nightingale's cry") stands for the woman's letter. *Uguisu* is also an abbreviation for the Japanese phrase *Uku (namida ni) hizu,* which means "Sadly, one is drenched with tears."
6. This poem appears in the *Shikashū* (KT 199). It also appears in *Konjaku monogatari* (KT, *Monogatari,* 1864), with the last line reading *Yo o uramuran.*

106

1. Prince Motoyoshi. See episode 90.

2. The daughter of Nakaki.

3. This poem appears in the *Motoyoshi no Miko shū* (ZKT 21256), with the fourth line reading *Kaze ni kaeshite.* The prose introduction states that it was addressed to the daughter of Naoki (not Nakaki), the Assistant Governor of Ōmi. There is a pun on the word *urami,* meaning "to feel bitter toward" as well as "to see the underside of." The Prince is accusing the young woman of accepting the advances of the numerous eligible men who, one after the other, come to woo her. The reed bending with the wind represents a fickle young woman.

4. This poem appears in the *Shinchokusenshū* (KT 877), with the second line reading *Hito wa miru tomo.* It also appears in the *Motoyoshi no Miko shū* (ZKT 21257), with the third line reading *Sekimizu no.* The Sekigawa, a river which flowed in the province of Ōmi near the famous Meeting Barrier, was known for its clear waters.

5. This poem appears in the *Motoyoshi no Miko shū* (ZKT 21258). The young woman is saying that, although the Prince may declare that he will never stop loving her, she knows that he soon will, for due to the boulders in the river that keep them apart, they can neither see nor speak to one another. There is a pun on the name of the river Sekigawa and *seki,* meaning "to dam up"; the words *iwama* ("between the boulders") and *iū ma* ("while someone is speaking"); and the word *mizu,* meaning "water" as well as "without seeing."

6. This poem appears in the *Motoyoshi no Miko shū* (ZKT 21259). There is a pun on the word *izu* ("to come out") and *itsu* ("when"). The Prince states that every night his heart has been in a turmoil, wondering if that night she would let him come to her. Now, however, he will give up all hope of ever winning her affection.

7. This poem appears in the *Motoyoshi no Miko shū* (ZKT 21260), with the last line reading *Omoi taename.* In the *Kanesuke shū* (ZKT 16200), the first line reads *Kazu naranu* and the last line, *Kimi o wasureme.*

8. This poem appears in the *Motoyoshi no Miko shū* (ZKT 21261), with the first line reading *Yukashiku mo* and the last line, *Yo ni zo arikeru.* According to *Yamato monogatari shōkai,* the girl thinks this is a wretched world because she, like her many predecessors, is destined to be abandoned by her lover.

9. There is a pun on the word Tokiwa, the name of a mountain in Ukyō-ku, Kyoto, and also meaning "evergreen pine," and *toki wa,* meaning "a time." There is another pun on the word *aki,* meaning "autumn" as well as "to weary of."

10. *Kumoi* ("Cloud-Dwelling Palace") is a poetic name for the Imperial Palace. There are puns on the following words: *fu,* meaning "to elapse (of time)" and *furu,* meaning "to fall (of rain)"; *samidare* (literally "the rain of the fifth month," which refers to the early summer rain) and *midare* ("to be in disorder"); *ame* ("rain") and *ama* ("heaven"). *Yo,* meaning "night" and *hi* (of *kai naku*), meaning "day," *ama,* and *samidare* are *engo* for *fu.*

11. There is a pun on the word *fureba,* which represents the phrase *furitatete naku* ("to raise one's voice in crying") and *furu* ("to reject"). *Harukeki* ("far-off") is an *engo* for *kumoi.*

108

1. Nothing more is known about this woman. The annotators of *Yamato monogatari shōkai* believe that since the Nan-in was Prince Koretada, Princess Nan-in (Nan-in no Imagimi, in the original) was probably his daughter. If this were true, she would then be Prince Muneyuki's sister and not his daughter.

2. Fujiwara no Kishi (904–962), the daughter of Tadahira. She later became the wife of Prince Yasuakira, and after his death, she served as the Head of the Palace Attendants Office at the court of Emperor Suzaku (923–952, r. 930–946). She was the sister of Morotada. See episode 94.

3. Fujiwara no Morotada.

4. The *tokonatsu* ("the Japanese pink"), one of the Seven Herbs of Autumn in the Japanese poetic tradition.

5. Princess Nan-in is heartbroken, for Morotada had never again come to see her after having spent some time with her. The *tokonatsu* is her love which blossomed even though the root (his love) had dried up. The word *toko* means "bed." There is a pun on *ne,* meaning simultaneously "root," "to sleep," and "sound." The word *kare* ("to wither") suggests two other verbs: *hanare* ("to grow distant") and *tsukire* ("to dry up").

109

1. Minamoto no Ōki.

2. This poem appears in the *Kokin rokujō* (ZKT 32283), with the last two lines reading Kusaba ni kakaru/ Tsuyu no inochi o. There is a pun on

the word *ushi,* meaning "ox" as well as "to be miserable." The words *kusa* ("grass") and *tsuyu* ("dewdrops") are *engo* for *kiyu* (the dictionary form of *kieniken*), meaning "to disappear."

110

1. This poem appears in the *Kokin rokujō* (ZKT 33331), with the third line reading *Nagametsutsu.* There is a pun on the word *fu,* meaning "to elapse" (of time) and *furu,* meaning "to fall (of rain)." Princess Nan-in states that her sleeve has become wet, not with the early winter showers, but with the tears that she has shed because they have not met for so long a time.

111

1. According to the annotators of the NKBT text, the father's name may have been Kinhiko, who was the son of Hiromi, and who, attaining the Senior Fifth Rank, Upper Grade, once served as Master of the Office of the Palace Table.
2. Located northeast of Ichijō (First Avenue) in the capital.
3. Fujiwara no Shizuko, the consort of Emperor Daigo. See episode 5.
4. Minamoto no Saneakira (910–970), the son of Kintada. He served as the Provincial Governor of Bingo, a part of present-day Hiroshima prefecture, from 947 to 953. Saneakira is one of the Thirty-six Poetic Geniuses and a collection of his poetry is entitled the *Saneakira shū.*
5. It was popularly believed that after a woman's death she was guided across the "River Styx *(Sanzu no kawa)*" by her first lover. Having now been abandoned by her first husband, the third daughter of Kinhira is expressing her wretchedness by alluding to this tradition.

112

1. The third daughter of Kinhira.
2. Fujiwara no Morotada, the son of Kanesuke (Tsutsumi no Chūnagon), who served as a Lieutenant of the Left Division of the Middle Palace Guards.
3. In Takeda's text, this line appears introducing the poem: *Kaze fuki ame furikeru hi no koto ni nan* (It was a day when the wind blew and rain fell).
4. She had waited for him all day and kept hoping that tonight he would come. If he comes, she hints to him in her poem, he will surely drive the rain away. The east wind was believed to forecast rain. There is a

pun on *ame no yo* ("a rainy night") and *yo ni* ("at night"). *Kochi* ("the east wind") also suggests the phrase *Kochira e koi* ("come here").

113

1. A festival held at a shrine on a day other than that of the main annual festival. At the Kamo Shrine, the main festival was held on the second Day of the Bird of the fourth month; the Special Festival was held on the last Day of the Bird of the eleventh month. At the Iwashimizu Hachiman Shrine, it was held on the second Day of the Horse of the third month. Dancers performed on these two festival days. There was also a Special Festival at the Gion Shrine on the fifteenth day of the sixth month, but no dance was performed. In this episode, the Special Festival was that held at the Kamo Shrine.

2. The verb *sureru* means "to rub a print (on cloth)" by using an indigo or dayflower plant in making the design. There are puns on the words *kite,* meaning "to come" as well as "to wear," and *nare,* meaning "an article of clothing which has been worn many times" and "to be accustomed to seeing." The word *mezurashi* ("unusual") contains the word *tsurashi* ("to be painful"), thus the woman is saying that it was painful to see her former lover again at the festival.

3. This poem appears in the *Kokin rokujō* (ZKT 34458). The place name Ide may also be interpreted as the verb *ite* ("to be"). There is a pun on *ori,* meaning "to pluck" or "to be." As mentioned earlier, Ide is a place famous for the yellow kerria roses.

4. The phrase *shita ni* may be interpreted as "deep in my heart" or "under the skies."

5. This poem appears in the *Shinkokinshū* (KT 1359). There are puns on the words *nami,* which means "waves" as well as "not"; *ne,* meaning "root" and "sound"; and *migakurete,* meaning "to hide oneself" and "to hide in water." There is also a pun on *nakaru,* meaning "to cry," and *nagaru,* meaning "to flow." The words *migakurete* and *nagaru* are *engo* for *nami* ("waves").

114

1. The *Tanabata Matsuri,* which was celebrated on the seventh day of the seventh month. According to an ancient Chinese legend, the Weaver Maiden (the star Vega) crossed the Heavenly River (the Milky Way) once a year to meet her lover, the Herdsboy (the star Altair). This summer festival was held in their honor.

2. See episode 20.

3. Although she did not lend her robes to the Weaver Maid, who crosses the Heavenly River to meet her lover, her robes have become wet with her tears of sorrow. A poem by the Retired Emperor Kazan on a similar theme appears in the *Shikashū* (KT 83):

Tanabata ni	Though I should remove this robe
Koromo mo nugite	And lend it to the Weaver Maid,
Kasubeki ni	She will probably find
Yuyushi to yamin	My black priest's robe
Kurozome no sode	Most unbecoming.

There seems to have been an ancient practice in which a person offered his robe to the Weaver Maid, leaving it outside for the rain and dew to wash away the body's impurities.

115

1. Fujiwara no Morosuke (908–960), the son of Tadahira, who was talented in poetry composition and koto playing. A private collection of his poetry is entitled the *Kujō no Udaijin shū.* Morosuke served as the First Secretary of the Sovereign's Private Office from 931 to 935 and was appointed Minister of the Right in Tenryaku 1 (947).

2. Shōni no Menoto was also called Shigeno no Naishi. She was the wet nurse of Emperor Murakami (926–967, r. 946–967) when he was a young child. One of her poems appears in the *Gosenshū* (KT 1138).

3. This poem appears in the *Shoku gosenshū* (KT 788), but according to the prose introduction, it was addressed to Shōni no Myōbu, not Shōni no Menoto. The phrase *koto no ha* ("words") and *kakareru tsuyu* ("the dewdrops that have formed") are *engo.*

4. Shōni is lamenting the fact that even before the coming of autumn, his promises have become empty. The phrase *aki mo kozu* may be interpreted as either "autumn has not yet come" or "I have not yet grown tired of you (implying that she still loves him)." The phrase *tsuyu mo okanedo,* meaning "though no dewdrops have formed," can also be interpreted "though we have not met at all."

116

1. There is a pun on the word *kakaru,* meaning "to be splashed (with tears)" and "such." *Kakaru mi* (literally, "such a body") emphasizes her weakened physical state as she lies dying.

117

1. Both Princess Katsura and Minamoto no Yoshitane have appeared earlier in episodes 76 and 77.

2. This poem appears in the *Shinchokusenshū* (KT 890), with the first line given as *Tsuyu shigeki.* There is a pun on the words *matsumushi* ("a species of cricket") and *matsu* ("to wait").

118

1. Kan-in no Ōigimi, the daughter of Minamoto no Muneyuki. Her poems are included in the *Gosenshū* (KT 737, 1249) and in the *Shūishū* (KT 986).

2. This poem appears in the *Shoku kokinshū* (KT 1115). There is a pun on *arisoumi,* meaning "a rocky shore" or "a shore buffeted by rough waves," and *ari* alone, meaning "to have." The following poem, using the same nature imagery, is quoted in the *kana* preface to the *Kokinshū* (NKBT, vol. 8, p. 96):

Waga koi wa	Even though you could count
Yomu to mo tsukiji	The grains of sand
Arisoumi no	Along the rocky shore,
Hama no masago wa	You cannot possibly gauge
Yomi tsukusu tomo	The depth of my love for you.

And still another poem based on the poem appearing in the *kana* preface appears in the *Kokinshū* (KT 818):

Arisoumi no	When you alluded to
Hama no masago to	"The grains of sand
Tanomeshi wa	Along the rocky shore,"
Wasururu koto no	I thought you meant you loved me;
Kasu ni zo arikeru	Alas, you simply meant
	You would forget me!

119

1. Probably Fujiwara no Saneki, who attained the Junior Fourth Rank, Upper Grade; he served as the Provincial Governor of Michinoku (Mutsu). He was active during the Engi era (901–923). Another possibility is that he was Minamoto no Saneakira (d. 970). Still another possibility, according to *Yamato monogatari shōkai,* is that he was Fujiwara no Saneki, the son of Takamarō.

2. This poem appears in the *Saneakira shū* (ZKT 20171). There is a

pun on *yaman,* meaning "to come to an end" and "to become sick." *Yaman,* meaning "to come to an end" is an *engo* for *tometaru,* meaning "to stop."

3. This poem appears in the *Gosenshū* (KT 1249) and in the *Saneakira shū* (ZKT 20172), with the fourth line reading *Ikadeka hitori.* In the *Atsutada shū* (ZKT 19398), this version is given: Morotomo ni/ Iza to iwazu wa/ Shide no yama/ Koyu to mo kosan/ Mono naranaku ni.

There is a pun on the word *Shide* ("death") and *shi* ("four"). *Shi* ("four") is an *engo* for *hitori* ("alone").

4. This poem appears in the *Saneakira shū* (ZKT 20173), with the first line reading *Akatsuki ni* and the third line reading *Waga koe ni.* The *Yūtsukedori* is another name for the cock. The name comes from the ancient practice of tying cotton *(yū)* to a cock and offering it to the deities in hopes for peace whenever a disturbance broke out.

5. This poem appears in the *Saneakira shū* (ZKT 20174), with the third line reading *Kikishikaba.*

120

1. Fujiwara no Tadahira. See episode 97. Both Tadahira and Nakahira were sons of Mototsune, Nakahira being the older by five years.

2. Fujiwara no Nakahira (875–945). See episode 68. The following chart is given to show the relationship of the historical figures:

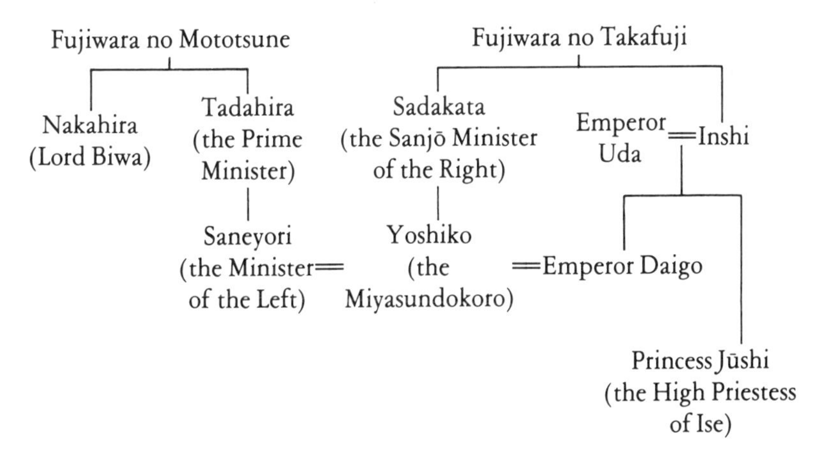

3. This poem appears in the *Shinkokinshū* (KT 1442), with the second line reading *Tsui ni sakinuru.* In *Ōkagami* (KT, *Rekishi,* 898), the poem, with the second line reading *Tsui ni sakinuru,* is attributed to Tadahira.

In poem 190, the Prime Minister is saying that thanks to their deceased father Mototsune, who had given them life, both he and his brother have attained the important position of Minister of State. Nakahira was appointed Minister of the Right on the third day of the second month of Jōhei 3 (933).

4. Princess Jūshi. See episode 36.

5. Fujiwara no Yoshiko, the daughter of Sadakata. See episode 94. She was a cousin as well as sister-in-law of the High Priestess of the Ise Shrine.

6. This poem appears in the *Gosenshū* (KT 1110) in a slightly different version: Ikade kano/ Toshigiri mo senu/ Tane mo gana/ Aretaru yado ni/ Uete mirubeku.

According to the prose preface, this poem was written in the spring of the year after the death of the Minister of the Left (933). In her poem, Yoshiko is expressing her hope that their family too will prosper in the years to come. The phrase *Toshigiri mo senu* describes a tree that never fails to bring forth blossoms and bear fruit annually.

7. Fujiwara no Saneyori. See episode 96. He served as a Middle Counsellor from 934 to 939 and was Minister of the Left from 947 to 967.

8. This poem appears in the *Gosenshū* (KT 1111), with the first and second lines reading Haru goto ni/ Yukite nomi min. The tree mentioned in the two poems above is probably that of the plum.

121

1. Sanetō no Shōni is not identified, but whoever he was, he once served as the Junior Assistant Governor-General of the Government Headquarters in Kyushu.

2. There is a pun on the word *yo,* meaning "the nodes of the bamboo" and "night." The words *chigusa* ("varied") and *hitoyo* ("one night") are *engo. Fuetake no* (literally, "the bamboo flute") is a *jo* for the word *yo,* meaning "a node."

3. There is a pun on the word *kochiku,* which is a variety of bamboo and at the same time meaning "to come here." *Fuki* means "to blow" or "to brag." *Fuki,* meaning "to blow," is an *engo* for *fue* ("a flute").

122

1. This temple was also called the Sōfuku-ji and was located in what is present-day Shiga-gun in Shiga prefecture.

2. One of his poems appears in the *Gosenshū* (KT 454). However, he is not the Zōki who left behind the Heian travelogue entitled *Io nushi.*

3. A building constructed over a little valley in a bridgelike fashion.

4. This poem appears as an anonymous poem in the *Gosenshū* (KT 729), with the first line reading *Aimite mo*.

5. This poem appears in the *Shoku kokinshū* (KT 1008). Zōki had implied in his poem that he loved her very much, but Toshiko purposely twists his meaning to mean the complete opposite: that he did not love her at all. In her return poem, she claims that she is heartbroken that he does not care for her.

123

1. *Ugoku* ("to move") is an *engo* for *ha* ("leaf") and *tsuyu* ("dew").

124

1. Fujiwara no Tokihira. See episode 14. The chart below shows the relationship of the historical figures mentioned in this episode:

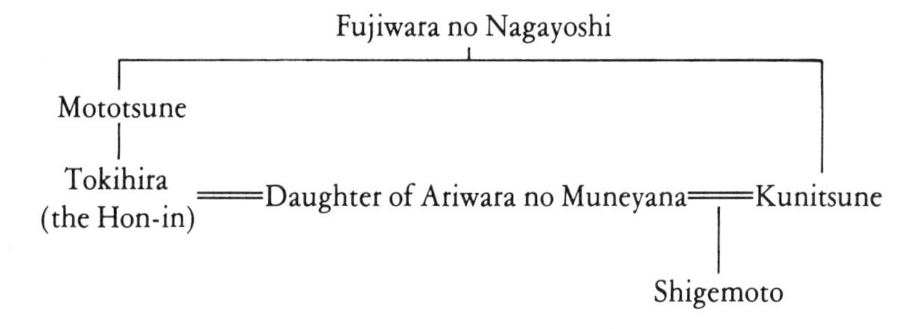

A part of Tanizaki Jun'ichirō's novel *Shōshō Shigemoto no haha* is woven around the characters mentioned above. Shigemoto has already been mentioned in episode 104.

2. Fujiwara no Kunitsune (828–908). See episode 14. At the time of this incident, he was holding concurrently the offices of Governor-General of the Government Headquarters in Kyushu and Major Counsellor.

3. The first three lines (literally meaning "the vines growing in the spring field") are a *jo* for *zane* of *waga kimizane*, meaning "my beloved wife." There is a pun on *kimizane* ("beloved wife") and *ne* ("to sleep"). The *sanekazura* is a kind of vine which bears a lemon-colored flower. There is yet another pun on *haeru*, meaning "to grow (of a vine)" and "to extend far (into the future)."

125

1. Fujiwara no Sadakuni (867–906), the son of Takafuji and grandson of Fuyutsugu. He was also the elder brother of Sadakata. At this time, he was serving as the Major Captain of the Right Division of the Inner Palace Guards and later became a Major Counsellor.

2. Fujiwara no Tokihira.

3. Mibu no Tadamine (868–920), one of the compilers of the *Kokinshū*. There is an anthology of his poetry entitled the *Tadamine shū* and also a work of poetic criticism entitled *Tadamine juttei.*

4. According to the ancient legend about the Weaver and the Herdsboy, once a year magpies spread their wings and form a bridge so that the lovers may meet. The bridge formed by the magpies also refers to the steps leading to the Imperial Palace. Thus, in reply to the Minister's question, the poem says that they had come directly from the palace.

5. The pampas grass symbolizes the young daughter. The literal meaning of the poem is: Since the pampas grass is still green, it is too early to tie it up in bundles. The verb *musubu* means "to tie up (in bundles)" as well as "to tie (the nuptial knot)."

126

1. Higaki no Ōna, a courtesan who lived in Tsukushi (present-day Kita-Kyushu). A collection of her poems, compiled posthumously, is entitled the *Higaki no Ōna shū*. One of her poems is included in the *Gosenshū* (KT 1220).

2. See episode 4.

3. See episode 4. Ono no Yoshifuru attained the rank of Senior Assistant Governor-General of the Government Headquarters in Kyushu.

4. This poem, said to have been composed by Lady Higaki when Fujiwara no Okinori passed by asking for water, appears in the *Gosenshū* (KT 1220) in a slightly different version: Toshi fureba/ Waga kurokami mo/ Shirakawa no/ Mizu hagumu made/ Oinikeru kana.

In the *Higaki no Ōna shū* (*Gunsho ruijū,* vol. 15, p. 521), the first two lines read Oihatete/ Kashira no kami wa. Annotators have discussed at great length the meaning of the phrase *mizu hagumu,* but it ultimately describes someone who is very old. The phrase could also be taken to mean *mizu wa kumu* ("to draw water"). The Shirakawa (White River) has its source in Mt. Aso in Kumamoto prefecture; it is said that its waters were cloudy white. *Mubatama no* (literally, "a blackberry lily") is a pillow-word for *kuro* ("black").

5. The *akome,* a garment worn between the robe called the *shitagasane* and the unlined robe called *hitoe,* is worn closer to the body in ceremonial court dress.

127

1. Lady Higaki.
2. This poem appears in the *Higaki no Ōna shū* (*Gunsho ruijū,* vol. 15, p. 521). The process of dying cloth red consisted of infusing the root of such plants as the *akanegusa* ("the madder") and the *murasakigusa* ("the gromwell") in hot water. There is a pun on the word *furiizu,* meaning "to infuse in hot water" and also "to raise (one's voice)."

128

1. This poem appears in the *Higaki no Ōna shū* (*Gunsho ruijū,* vol. 15, p. 521), with the fourth line reading *Aki no yamabe zo.* This is an example of *tanrenga,* or "short linked verse," with two different parties composing the two parts of the poem—the gentlemen composing the first three lines and Lady Higaki adding the last two. The deer is usually pictured in an autumnal mountain setting, but the men have made the poem difficult by having it stand in the sea. Lady Higaki, however, displays her skill as a poet by bringing into the poem the imagery of the mountain in autumn. The deer is on the mountain which in turn is reflected in the water. There is a pun on the word *soko,* meaning "there" and "the bottom."

129

1. Probably Lady Higaki, for the poem given here appears in the collection of her poetry.
2. This poem, attributed to Gen no Myōbu, appears in the *Shingoshūishū* (KT 1114) in a slightly different version: Hito o matsu/ Kado wa kuraku zo/ Narinikeru/ Tanomeshi tsuki no/ Uchi ni mieneba.

It also appears in the *Higaki no Ōna shū* (*Gunsho ruijū,* vol. 15, p. 521). There is a pun on the word *uchi,* meaning "within a certain length of time" and "in one's house."

130

1. This poem appears in the *Higaki no Ōna shū* (*Gunsho ruijū,* vol. 15, p. 522).

131

1. Emperor Daigo.
2. The first day of summer, according to the lunar calendar.
3. Minamoto no Kintada. See episode 4.
4. This poem appears in the *Kintada shū* (ZKT 16392).

132

1. Ōshikōchi no Mitsune. See episode 33.
2. Forms of entertainment such as poetry contests and the music of various reed and string instruments.
3. This poem appears in *Ōkagami* (KT, *Rekishi,* 947). There is a pun on *iru,* meaning "to set (of the sun or moon)" and "to shoot."
4. An *ōuchigi,* a robe whose sleeve length and skirt length were made especially long. It was worn under the *nōshi,* an outer robe used by courtiers for daily wear.
5. This poem appears in *Ōkagami* (KT, *Rekishi,* 948), with the fourth line reading *Fukite kinurashi. Amatsu kaze* ("the heavenly wind") is an *engo* for *shirakumo* ("the white clouds") and refers to the emperor's patronage. There are puns on the words *kata,* meaning both "shoulder" and "direction"; *oriiru* ("to descend") and *ori* ("to weave"); and *kitsurashi,* meaning "to come" and "to wear."

133

1. This poem appears in the *Kintada shū* (ZKT 16414), with the last line reading *Aware narikere.* According to the Shoryōbu text of the *Kintada shū,* this poem was in the form of a *tanrenga,* the Emperor composing the first half of the poem and Kintada completing it. Takahashi Shōji believes that it was in the *tanrenga* form in the earlier versions of *Yamato monogatari.*

134

1. This poem appears as an anonymous poem in the *Shinchokusenshū* (KT 824), with the second line reading *Furebanarikeri.* There is a pun on *akade,* meaning "without having enough of" as well as "without ever tiring of."

135

1. Fujiwara no Kanesuke. See episode 35. He served as the Assistant Director of the Bureau of Palace Storehouses from 903 to 907.
2. This poem appears in the *Shinshūishū* (KT 1232). The woman is fi-

nally admitting that she loves Tsutsumi no Chūnagon after all, for she would rather be with him than have to sleep all alone. The phrase *takimono no* ("incense") is a *jo* for the verb *kuyuru,* meaning "to burn." The verb *kuyuru* also means "to regret." There is a pun on the word *hitori,* which means "a censer" as well as "alone."

136

1. Tsutsumi no Chūnagon.

137

1. Prince Motoyoshi. See episode 90.
2. A road which started from the capital, ran along the foot of Mount Hiei, and led to the province of Ōmi.
3. This poem appears in the *Shinchokusenshū* (KT 301) and in the *Motoyoshi no Miko shū* (ZKT 21266). There are puns on the words *kari,* which means "hunting" as well as "fleeting," and Shigayama, which refers to the mountain at Shiga and suggests *shika* ("deer").

138

1. This poem appears in the *Shinsenzaishū* (KT 1136) as one by Lord Biwa, with the last line reading *Wabishikarikeru.* It also appears in the *Ise shū* (ZKT 18439). The first three lines of the poem are a *jo* for the verb *shirarenu* ("not to know"). There is a pun on the phrase *migakurete,* which means "to be hidden in the water" and also "to be hidden within one's heart."
2. This poem, attributed to Lady Ise, appears in the *Shinsenzaishū* (KT 1137). It also appears in the *Ise shū* (ZKT 18440), with the first line reading *Kakurenu ni.* The short water plant symbolizes the extremely short man. The woman cruelly taunts him about his height, even implying that his love too will undoubtedly be as short-lived as he is short.

139

1. Emperor Daigo.
2. Nothing further is known about this lady-in-waiting.
3. According to the annotation in the NKBT text, the Sokyōden (also pronounced Jōkyōden) no Miyasundokoro was Minamoto no Kazuko, the daughter of Emperor Kōkō and concubine of Emperor Daigo (see episode 65). However, according to the annotation in *Yamato monogatari shōkai,* she was the mother of Emperor Daigo and consort of Emperor Uda.

4. This poem appears in both the *Shūishū* (KT 977) and in the *Motoyoshi no Miko shū* (ZKT 21231), with the last line reading *Mono ni zo arikeru.* There is a pun on Akutagawa, the name of a river in Mishima-gun, Osaka, and the verb *aku,* meaning "to tire of." There is also a pun on Naniwa, the ancient name for Osaka and the phrase *na ni wa,* meaning here "one's reputation." *Tsu no kuni* (the province of Settsu, a part of present-day Hyōgo prefecture) is a *jo* for Naniwa.

5. This poem appears in the *Motoyoshi no Miko shū* (ZKT 21232), with the second line reading *Matsu no e ni furu.* It also appears in the *Gosenshū* (KT 852), with the second line reading *Matsu no e ni furu* and the last line reading *Kuyuru omoi ni.* In the *Kokin rokujō* (ZKT 31601), the last line reads *Kouru omoi ni.* There are puns on the words *matsu,* meaning both "pine tree" and "to wait"; *furu,* meaning "to fall"; and *fu,* meaning "to elapse (of time)"; and *omo(h)i* ("longing"); and *(h)i* ("day").

140

1. Minamoto no Noboru (848–918), the son of Tōru. Noboru attained the position of Major Counsellor, Senior Third Rank.

2. The *hisashi,* a long narrow room between the *moya* ("the central room") and the *sunoko* ("the veranda") in the Heian nobleman's private residence.

3. This poem appears in the *Motoyoshi no Miko shū* (ZKT 21233), with the second line reading *Arishinagara no.* The act of brushing away the dust collected on one's pillow seems to have had some special significance between married couples or lovers. Reference is made to such a custom in a passage in *Kagerō nikki* under the Tenroku 2 (971) section. See NKBT, vol. 20, p. 212. See also Seidensticker, *The Gossamer Years,* p. 95.

4. This poem appears in the *Motoyoshi no Miko shū* (ZKT 21234). It is based on an earlier anonymous poem in the *Kokinshū* (KT 865):

Ureshiki o	With what should I wrap
Nani ni tsutsuman	The boundless joy that I feel?
Karagoromo	Would that
Tamoto yutaka ni	The sleeves of my court robe
Tate to iwamashi o	Had been made wider.

When lovers slept side by side, their sleeves lay one over the other; thus the poet, by saying that he will have his sleeves made larger, is implying that he is preparing to go to her, hinting at his intense joy over the anticipated meeting by alluding to the *Kokinshū* poem. He is also saying, "Please wait until I am successful."

5. This poem appears in the *Motoyoshi no Miko shū* (ZKT 21235).

6. This poem also appears in the *Motoyoshi no Miko shū* (ZKT 21236). Mount Kurikoma is located in what was then the province of Yamashiro, a part of modern Kyoto.

141

1. Probably Tachibana no Yoshie (864–920), according to the annotation in the NKBT text. The office of Imperial Adviser is one belonging to the Great Council of State and ranks after that of Middle Counsellor.

2. Present-day Nara prefecture.

3. Possibly Lady Higaki, for the poems attributed to this woman are included in the *Higaki no Ōna shū.*

4. This poem appears in the *Higaki no Ōna shū* (*Gunsho ruijū,* vol. 15, p. 522), with the second line reading *Tsuki ni miezu wa.* The phrase *mizu wa* can be interpreted as: (1) "If the moon had not seen us" or (2) "If I had not met my lover."

5. This poem appears in the *Fusōshū* text of the *Higaki no Ōna shū* (*Nakajima Hirotari zenshū,* vol. 2, p. 543). The pampas grass is a symbol for the young woman, who insists that, though she is being courted by a man for whom she had no affection, she loves the Secretary only.

6. A letter rolled up in this fashion was called a *musubibumi.* The *tatebumi* was the more formal way of folding a letter: after being rolled up, the letter was either tied with string or slightly twisted at both ends.

7. This poem also appears in the *Higaki no Ōna shū* (*Gunsho ruijū,* vol. 15, p. 522), with the second line reading *Omou kokoro ni.*

8. In present-day Otokuni-gun, a town between Kyoto and Osaka. At this time in history, people boarded the boat at Yamazaki and sailed down the Yodo River.

9. This poem appears in the *Higaki no Ōna shū* (*Gunsho ruijū,* vol. 15, p. 522), with the third line given as *Nami no ue ni* and the fifth line, *Kaerumeru kana.*

142

1. Though some commentators state that she might possibly have been Lady Ise, it is probably best not to attempt to identify her as any particular historical figure.

2. This poem appears in the *Kokinshū* (KT 965) and in the *Ise shū* (the *Nishi Honganji-bon* text), with the last line reading *Omowazu mo gana.* The poem in the *Kokinshū* is attributed to Taira no Sadabumi (Heichū).

3. Spring seems to symbolize her deceased mother and autumn, her step-mother.

143

1. Zaiji-gimi, or Ariwara no Shigeharu, who was the third son of Ariwara no Narihira.

2. Zai Chūjō, or Ariwara no Narihira (825–880), the son of Prince Abo (792–842) and grandson of Emperor Heizei (774–824, r. 806–809). Narihira attained the rank of Middle Captain of the Left Division of the Inner Palace Guards and was called *Zai Chūjō* (*Zai* being another reading for the first character in his family name) in the *Yamato monogatari* text. He was one of the Six Poetic Geniuses of the early Heian period and was known for his elegance and love affairs. *Ise monogatari* is said to be an account of his adventures, amorous or otherwise, and contains a number of poems believed to be his compositions.

The following chart shows Narihira's royal lineage:

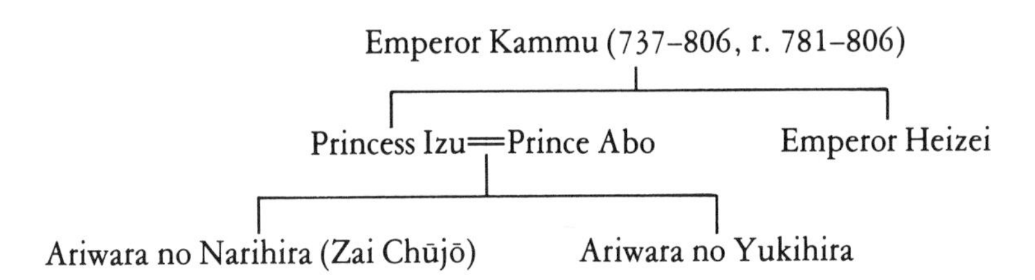

Narihira's children, several of whom are mentioned in this episode, were as follows:

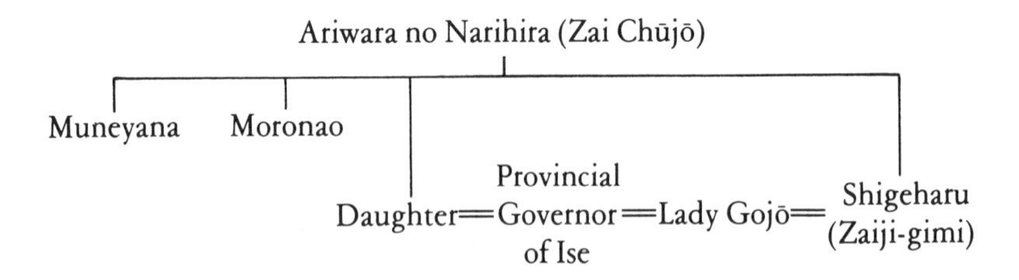

3. Fujiwara no Yamakage (824–888), the son of Takafusa. According to the *Yamato monogatari shōkai* text, Lady Gojō was his daughter.

4. Possibly Fujiwara no Tsugukage.

5. Moronao and Muneyana.

6. Zaiji-gimi is expressing his extreme distress and unhappiness upon discovering that Lady Gojō was also carrying on with other men, among whom were his own brothers. Nevertheless, he is so much in love with her that his present suffering, he declares, is not half as painful as his trying to forget her.

This poem appears in the *Shinchokusenshū* (KT 867). A similar anonymous poem appears in the *Kokinshū* (KT 718):

Wasurenan to	No sooner do I try
Omou kokoro no	To forget you
Tsuku kara ni	Than I vaguely
Arishi yori ke ni	Feel a sadness
Mazu zo kanashiki	Unknown in the past.

Still another similar poem appears in episode 21 of *Ise monogatari* (KT, Monogatari, 56). See McCullough's *Tales of Ise,* p. 86.

144

1. A post-town in what is today Ashigarashimo-gun in Kanagawa prefecture.

2. There are puns on the following words: *namida* ("tears") and *nami* ("waves"); the place name Ofusa (see underlined portion of poem) and *fusa* ("a large quantity"). Moreover, there is an attempt at rhyming in the words *watatsumi* ("the open sea") and *nakitsume* ("to accumulate tears"). The words *nami* and *naki(tsume)* are *engo* of *watatsumi.*

3. In present-day Naka-gun of Kanagawa prefecture.

4. The place name Minowa is mentioned in the fourth line of the poem in the original. A poem on the same theme appears in the *Kokinshū* (KT 189) and in the *Muneyuki shū* (ZKT 16561):

Itsu wa to wa	I always long for you
Toki wa wakanedo	But I feel my longing
Aki no yo zo	Most of all
Mono omou koto no	On a night in autumn.
Kagiri narikeru	

5. Modern Yamanashi prefecture.

6. This poem appears in the *Kokinshū* (KT 862), with the third line reading *Omoikoshi.* Kai, the name of the province, is incorporated in the second line of the poem. Zaiji-gimi is so gravely ill that he knows he is about to die and explicitly says so.

7. Present-day Aichi prefecture. There is some geographical discrepancy here, for Mikawa province was located between Kai province and the capital.

145

1. There were courtesans, referred to as *ukareme,* as far back in history as the Nara period (710–794), for poems attributed to women of this social class have been included in the *Man'yōshū.* Talented in the fine arts and poetry composition, these courtesans continued to contribute poems to the various imperial anthologies and even had their compositions compiled in numerous private collections.

2. This poem appears in *Ōkagami* (KT, *Rekishi,* 944). The plover symbolizes Shiro herself and the cloud-covered mountain, His Majesty's royal throne. *Awa to* means "vacantly" and also "as Awa (province)." The phrase can, moreover, be interpreted as an abbreviated form of the phrase *aware to* ("sadly").

3. This poem, attributed to Shirame, appears in the *Kokinshū* (KT 387). The first three lines are also quoted in *Ōkagami* (NKBT, vol. 21, pp. 280–281). In the *Kokin rokujō* (ZKT 33207), the last line is given as *Kanashikarubeki.* Shiro is saying that if she knew exactly what would happen from one day to the next, perhaps she would not be so unhappy about their having to part. However, since it is the way of the world that one never knows when one will die, she is terribly upset about this leave-taking. In *Ōkagami,* the events of episode 145 and the following episode are recorded in a less detailed manner, and Shiro is called Shirame. See *Ōkagami,* NKBT, vol. 21, pp. 280–281. See also Yamagiwa, *The Ōkagami,* pp. 246–247.

146

1. A detached palace which was located in present-day Mishima-gun, Osaka.

2. Ōe no Tamabuchi, the son of Ōe no Otondo (811–877). Tamabuchi attained the Junior Fourth Rank Lower Grade and was at one time the

Provincial Governor of Tamba, a part of the present-day municipality of Kyoto.

3. This poem appears in *Ōkagami* (KT, *Rekishi,* 945), with the first line reading *Fukamidori* and the third, *Au toki wa.* The place name Torikai appears in the underlined portion of the poem. The phrase *Kasumi naranedo* ("though I am not the mist") also implies the phrase *Kazu naranedo* ("though I am of no importance"). *Tachinoboru* should refer to the rising of the mist, but here refers to the girl appearing before the emperor. The Retired Emperor's palace is also known as "grotto of mist."

4. Probably Minamoto no Kiyohira (877–945), the seventh son of Prince Koretada.

147

1. An ancient province made up of the eastern half of modern Hyōgo prefecture and the northwestern part of modern Osaka. In the original text, this province is called Tsu no Kuni. Poems by Tanabe no Sakimaro (eighth century) and Takahashi no Muraji Mushimaro (eighth century) in the *Man'yōshū* deal with the charming but tragic legend of the Maiden Unai and her two admirers. The poems may be found in the Nippon Gakujutsu Shinkōkai translation of the *Man'yōshū* (Columbia University Press, 1965): Sakimaro's poems (KT 1801–3), pp. 234–235, and Mushimaro's poems (KT 1809–11), pp. 224–225. A Nō play *Motomezuka* is based on this legend.

2. Mubara is a place name for a spot in the vicinity of Ashiya in present-day Hyōgo prefecture.

3. The southern part of present-day Osaka, which in ancient times was called Chinu no Agata.

4. A *hirabari:* a temporary shelter, with canvas stretched straight across the top. It was often contrasted to the *agebari,* another type of temporary shelter, with the center raised and pointed.

5. A river which today flows through Kobe.

6. The *iku* of Ikuta means "to live." By killing herself, the girl will make a mockery of the name of the river.

7. Fujiwara no Onshi, one of Teiji no In's concubines. See episode 61.

8. See episode 1.

9. There is a pun on the word *kai,* meaning "(no) avail" as well as "shell." *Kara* ("remains" or "cast-off shell") is an *engo* for the word *kai*

("shell"). This poem is based on a poem which appears in the *Kokinshū* (KT 528):

Koi sureba	Since I have loved deeply,
Waga mi wa kage to	My body has wasted away
Narinikeri	To a mere shadow—
Sari tote hito ni	Even so, I cannot follow
Sowanu mono yue	My beloved like a shadow.

10. Princess Kinshi (890–910), the eldest daughter of Teiji no In. Her mother was Onshi.

11. This poem alludes to Po Chü-i's famous poem, *Ch'ang hen ko,* in which a Taoist monk is sent in search of the departed spirit of Yang Kuei-fei, the beloved consort of the T'ang emperor Ming Huang (685–762, r. 713–756). The monk succeeds in finding her spirit dwelling in the P'eng-lai Palace, named after a mysterious island located in the Eastern Sea. Paintings on silk screens depicting this highly romanticized story of Yang Kuei-fei were very popular in the Heian court. The writer of *Sarashina nikki* mentions a tale entitled *Chōgonka no monogatari,* which was based on the tragic love story of the Chinese emperor and his beautiful consort but which is no longer extant. See A. S. Ōmori and K. Doi, *Diaries of Court Ladies of Old Japan,* pp. 24–25.

12. The daughter of Fujiwara no Takatsune (d. 893), who became the wife of Tadafusa.

13. She probably intended this poem to express the feelings of one of the men. There is a pun on the phrase *Tsuka no ma* ("a brief interval of time") and *tsuka* ("a grave-mound").

14. Haruzumi Amaneiko, the daughter of Yoshitada (767–870). In the original text, she is called the *Itodokoro no Betō (Bettō).* The *Itodokoro* was a department of the *Nuidonoryō,* the Bureau of the Wardrobe and Court Ladies.

15. The Head of the Sewing Department is expressing the feelings of one of the men. *Kurabu no yama* is an older name for *Kurama no yama.* There is a pun on Kurabu, the name of a mountain, and *kurabu,* meaning "to vie." The last two lines literally mean "though we crossed Mount Kurabu."

16. There are a number of puns in this poem. The word *ōgo,* found in the phrase *au ko(to),* which may be translated "a meeting," means "a shoulder-carrying pole." The word *katami* has three different meanings: "mutually," "to be difficult," and "a bamboo basket." The *kata* of

katami, moreover, means "shoulder." *Nayotake* ("the pliant bamboo") is a *jo* for the verb phrase *tachiwazurau* ("to stand troubled and perplexed").

17. The phrase *Mi o nagete* can be interpreted as either "to cast oneself into the river" or "to throw away one's life." There is a pun on the word *ukimi,* meaning "a wretched body" as well as "a body afloat." In Heian times the subject of an unhappy woman about to drown herself was often depicted in silk-screen paintings. For example, the following poem appears in the *Dōmyō Ajari shū* (*Katsura no Miya-bon sōsho,* vol. 2, p. 315), with the prose introduction stating that it was a poem which might have been written by a young woman on a high river bank contemplating death by drowning:

Tomokaku mo	In any event,
Waga mi hitotsu wa	This body of mine
Nashitsubeshi	Should no longer exist;
Nokoran na koso	I only regret
Ushirometakere	The reputation I leave behind.

18. The rival laments that he had not been chosen. There is a pun on *e ni* ("in the bay") and *en* ("fate").

19. There is a pun on *mi,* meaning "one's body," of the phrase *mi na soko* ("the river's bottom").

20. There are a number of puns in this poem. *E ni* ("in the bay") may also be interpreted as *en* ("fate"); *sumu* means both "to live (together as man and wife)" and "to become clear"; *mi,* meaning "one's body" is inferred in the word *migiwa* ("the river's edge").

148

1. This story is included in *Konjaku monogatari* (NKBT, vol. 26, pp. 224–226). It is also the basis for the Nō play *Ashikari.*

2. There is a pun on *soyo,* which describes a gentle breeze, and *sō ne,* an expression used when someone is in deep thought, meaning "let me see."

3. This ceremony *(harai)* is a part of the indigenous Shintō religion in which individuals offered prayers to the native gods to purify themselves of sin and defilement and to avoid any future calamity. The purification ceremony held at Naniwa is mentioned in *Genji monogatari* (NKBT, vol. 15, p. 121. See also Waley, *The Tale of Genji,* p. 298). It is also mentioned in *Eiga monogatari* (*Nihon koten zensho,* vol. 34, part 4, p. 52).

4. The *shitasudare,* or silk curtains, hung along the lower half of the inner side of the rattan blinds in an ox-drawn carriage.

5. This poem appears in the *Shūishū* (KT 540). In the *Kokin rokujō* (ZKT 32731), the third line is given as *Omou ni wa.* It also appears in *Konjaku monogatari* (KT, *Monogatari,* 1867), with the third line also reading *Omou ni wa.* There is a pun on the phrase *Ashikarikeri* ("to meet with bad times") and *ashi kari* ("to cut rushes").

6. According to the annotators of the NKBT text, this poem is believed to have been added as a note by an early copyist; however, throughout the centuries, it has become a part of the main text. This poem appears in the *Shūishū* (KT 541), with the second, third, and last lines given as *Yokaran tote zo/ Wakareken* and *Ura wa sumiuki.* The poem also appears in *Konjaku monogatari* (KT, *Monogatari,* 1866) in a slightly different version: Ashikaraji/ To omoite koso wa/ Wakareshika/ Nadoka Naniwa no/ Ura ni shimo sumu.

In *Konjaku monogatari,* the order of the poems is reversed: the woman is said to have composed the poem beginning with the line *Ashikaraji* and the man the return poem beginning with the line *Kimi nakute.*

149

1. The western part of Yamato province, now made up of Minami-Katsuragi-gun and Kita-Katsuragi-gun in modern Nara prefecture. Different versions of this story appear in the *Kokinshū* (see the prose section following KT 944) and in episode 23 of *Ise monogatari* (NKBT, vol. 9, pp. 126–127. See also McCullough, *Tales of Ise,* pp. 87–89).

2. This poem appears in the *Kokinshū* (KT 994) and in *Ise Monogatari* (KT, *Monogatari,* 64). The first two lines Kaze fukeba/ Okitsu shiranami (literally, "When the wind blows, the waves of the open sea . . . ") are a *jo* for the verb *tatsu* ("to rise") of Tatsutayama (Mount Tatsuta). The words *shiranami,* meaning "white crests of waves"; *tatsu,* meaning "to rise"; and *koyu,* meaning "to cross over," are *engo.* Mount Tatsuta is located in Ikoma-gun, Nara prefecture. The word *shiranami* also means "bandits," but not in this particular poem. In her heart, the man's first wife is wishing him a safe journey, even though she knows that he is going to see his new wife.

3. This statement seems to be an interpolated comment following the poem.

4. The *Yamato monogatari* version of this story revolves around the poem which is said to have been composed by the first wife who had carefully concealed her jealousy from her husband. According to the annota-

tors of the NKBT text, the description of water boiling when the metal bowl in which it is contained is held against the woman's breast is not merely an exaggeration of her intense jealousy; it is rather a fabrication resulting from the then current *waka* tradition in which fire represented heightened emotions—for example, jealousy and passion—felt in the human heart.

5. A hair-do called the *tsuragushi:* a woman's hair is swept up and held in place at the forehead with a comb. This was a style in which people of humble birth wore their hair.

6. An *ōgimi* in the original, meaning a sovereign's grandson and son of an imperial prince.

150

1. Referred to as an *uneme* in the original text. An *uneme* was a female court attendant who waited on the emperor's table in ancient times. She was usually the daughter of a provincial noble between the ages of sixteen and thirty. During the reign of Emperor Murakami (946–967), the duties of the *uneme* were taken over by those serving in the Palace Attendants Office. This story is the basis of the Nō play *Uneme.*

2. The emperor mentioned in this episode has been variously identified as Emperor Mommu (683–707, r. 697–707), Emperor Shōmu (701–756, r. 724–749), and Emperor Heizei (774–824, r. 806–809). The Nara Emperor mentioned in episode 153 is Emperor Heizei, but this is not necessarily so in this story. Another possibility is that he may have been Emperor Shōmu, the emperor who reigned during the first part of the Nara period. However, taking into account the fact that he is said to have had Kakinomoto no Hitomaro (seventh century) compose a poem in this episode, the emperor was probably Emperor Mommu.

3. A pond near the Kōfuku-ji in Nara.

4. There is a private collection of the poems by this famous *Man'yō* poet entitled the *Kakinomoto shū.*

5. This poem appears in the *Shūishū* (KT 1289) and in the *Kakinomoto shū* (ZKT 15289), with the first line given as *Wagimo ko ga* (an affectionate term for someone with whom one is intimate). This poem is also included in a twelfth-century work entitled *Shichi daiji junrei shiki* (vol. 4 of *Ikaruga kokyō sōsho*). According to this passage, Emperor Heizei composed this poem in his grief over the suicide by drowning of his consort (Ise Tsuguko), who had lost his affection to a young servant.

6. This poem appears in the *Kokin rokujō* (ZKT 32523). It also appears

as an anonymous poem in the *Fubokushō* (*Fuboku wakashō—Hombunhen*—p. 923, poem 760), with the last two lines reading Tama hiku masa wa/ Mizu mo hinaku ni. A poem on a similar theme appears in the *Man'yōshū* (KT 3788):

Miminashi no	How I resent Miminashi Pond! *
Ike shi urameshi	I wish its waters
Wagimo ko ga	Had gone down
Kitsutsu kazukaba	When my beloved
Mizu wa asenan	Threw herself in that pond.

* A pond at the foot of Mount Miminashi in Shiki-gun, Nara.

151

1. This poem appears in the *Kokinshū* (KT 284); in the *Shūishū* (KT 219); in the *Kokin rokujō* (ZKT 34932); in the *Kakinomoto shū* (ZKT 15246); in the *Shinsen wakashū* (*Gunsho ruijū,* vol. 10, p. 442); and in the *Kingyokushū* (*Gunsho ruijū,* vol. 10, p. 449). Mount Mimuro is at the source of the Tatsuta River. A poem on the same theme appears in the *Man'yōshū* (KT 2210):

Asukagawa	The maple leaves are floating
Momijiba nagaru	Down the Asuka River;
Katsuragi no	Ah, the leaves must be falling
Yama no ko no ha wa	From the trees
Imashi chiru kamo	On Mount Katsuragi.

2. This poem appears as an anonymous poem in the *Kokinshū* (KT 283) and in the *Shinsen wakashū* (*Gunsho ruijū,* vol. 10, p. 442). In the *Kokin rokujō* (ZKT 34373), the second and third lines are given as Momijiba ochite/ Nagarunari.

152

1. In the *Kokin rokujō* (ZKT 33494) is a poem with identical closing lines:

Kokoro ni wa	Deep in one's heart
Shita yuku mizu no	There stirs a silent stream—
Wakikaeri	What one feels but does not express
Iwade omou zo	Is far more intense
Iū ni masareru	Than any word uttered.

There is a pun on Iwate, the place name, and *iwade,* meaning "without saying anything."

153

1. Emperor Heizei (r. 806–809). See episode 150.

2. Emperor Saga (786–882, r. 809–823), the younger brother of Emperor Heizei. Emperor Saga excelled in writing in Chinese and in the art of calligraphy.

3. A similar poem appears in the *Shoku goshūishū* (KT 267): Mina hito no/ Soko ka ni utsuru/ Fujibakama/ Kimi ga tame ni to/ Taoritsuru kana.

The poem appears in the *Kokin rokujō* (ZKT 34567), with the second, third, and last lines reading *Sono ka ni niou/ Kimi no minota o* and *Wataru kyō kana.* It also appears in *Ruijū kokushi* (*Kokushi taikei,* vol. 5, p. 171) under the entry of the twenty-first day of the ninth month of Daidō 2 (807), with the first, fourth, and last lines given as *Miyabito no* and *Kimi no ōmono/ Taoritaru kyō.* The *fujibakama,* translated above as "agrimony," is one of the Seven Herbs of Autumn and was believed to be efficacious in warding off evil.

4. A slightly different version of this poem appears in the *Shoku goshūishū* (KT 268): Minahito no/ Kokoro ni magau/ Fujibakama/ Mube iro fukaku/ Nioikeru kana.

This poem also appears in the *Kokin rokujō* (ZKT 34568) in this version: Oribito no/ Kokoro no mama ni/ Fujibakama/ Ube mo iro koku/ Sakite miekeri.

In *Ruijū kokushi* (*Kokushi taikei,* vol. 5, p. 171), this poem appears under the entry of the twenty-first day of the ninth month of Daidō 2 (807): Oribito no/ Kokoro no manima/ Fujibakama/ Ube iro fukaku/ Nioitarikeri.

154

1. The *aori* was made of leather and was originally attached to the saddle on rainy days to keep the rider's outfit from becoming mud- spattered. It was later used, even on days when the weather was fair, for ornamental purposes.

2. This poem appears in the *Kokinshū* (KT 995). It also appears in the *Sarumaru shū* (ZKT 15833), with the last line given as *Uchitobu kinaku.* In the *Kokin rokujō* (ZKT 32222), the second and last lines are given as *Yūtsukedori zo* and *Tachikaerinaku.* In poem 258, the word *Karagoromo*

("Chinese robe") is a pillow-word for *tatsu,* which means "to cut" and which is also a part of the place name Tatsuta. The words *yū* ("cotton"), *tatsu* ("to cut"), and *ori* ("to weave") are *engo* for *Karagoromo.* In relation to the story told in this episode, the fowl represents the unhappy woman who weeps unceasingly.

3. The first three lines of this poem are a *jo* for the phrase *Yukue mo shiranu* ("without knowing one's future"). The woman, who is uncertain of her future, compares herself to the waters of the river which know not their destination.

155

1. A member of the Bureau of Imperial Attendants, which was under the Ministry of Central Affairs. The members of this particular bureau acted as imperial body guards and also performed a number of other duties. They would often accompany the emperor on his outings.

2. In the ancient province of Iwashiro, now a part of Asaka-gun, Fukushima prefecture.

3. This poem appears in the *Man'yōshū* (KT 3807), with the last two lines given as Asaki kokoro o/ Waga omowanaku ni. In the preface to the *Kokinshū,* it is said that the poem on Mount Asaka was written by a lady attendant for her own amusement (Kubota Utsubo says that this interpretation is incorrect; see *Kokin wakashū hyōshaku,* vol. 1, p. 62). This poem is also included in the *Komachi shū* (ZKT 19671), in the *Kokin rokujō* (ZKT 31861), and in *Konjaku monogatari* (KT, *Monogatari,* 1868). In poem 260, the first three lines are a *jo* for the word *asaku* ("shallow").

4. This tale also appears in *Konjaku monogatari* (NKBT, vol. 26, pp. 223–235).

156

1. Present-day Sarashina-gun of Nagano prefecture, a part of the great Zenkō-ji Plain. This story is also included in *Konjaku monogatari* (NKBT, vol. 26, pp. 236–237). The Nō play *Obasute* is based on this tale.

2. This poem appears in the *Kokinshū* (KT 878) as an anonymous poem, in the *Kokin rokujō* (ZKT 31198), and in the *Shinsen wakashū* (*Gunsho ruijū,* vol. 10, p. 445).

3. The legend of Mount Obasute, including a translation of this episode, is discussed by Professor Keene in his study "Bashō's Journey to Sa-

rashina" (*Landscapes and Portraits,* pp. 109–130). *Obasute* literally means "abandoning one's aunt." Mount Obasute is often alluded to when one is especially grief-stricken and inconsolable. The following poems, based on poem 261, either mention or allude to Mount Obasute. The first of these, attributed to Fujiwara no Norinaga, appears in the *Goshūishū* (KT 849):

Tsuki mite wa	Though one does not find himself
Tare mo kokoro zo	At the foot of Mount Obasute,
Nagusamanu	He feels inconsolable
Obasuteyama no	As he gazes at the moon.
Fumoto naranedo	

The second poem, attributed to Ōshikōchi no Mitsune, appears in the *Shinkokinshū* (KT 1259):

Sarashina no	Even when the moon shines
Yama yori hoka ni	On a mountain
Teru tsuki mo	Other than that in Sarashina,
Nagusamekanetsu	It cannot console my heart
Konogoro no tsuki	In this time of sorrow.

157

1. Modern Tochigi prefecture. This story is also found in *Konjaku monogatari* (NKBT, vol. 26, pp. 237–238).

2. This poem appears in *Konjaku monogatari* (KT, *Monogatari,* 1870), with the first two lines reading Fune mo koji/ Makaji mo kojina. There is a pun on Makaji, the name of the young servant, and *kaji* ("rudder"). There is yet another pun on *fune,* which refers to the *mabune* ("trough") and also means "boat." *Kaji,* moreover, is an *engo* for the word *fune.*

158

1. This tale is also told in *Konjaku monogatari* (NKBT, vol. 26, pp. 240–241); however, it states that the setting of the story was the province of Tamba, a part of present-day Osaka.

2. This poem appears in the *Shinkokinshū* (KT 1372). It also appears in *Konjaku monogatari* (KT, *Monogatari,* 1872) in this version: Ware mo shika/ Nakite zo kimi ni/ Koirareshi/ Ima koso koe o/ Yoso ni nomi kike.

There is a pun on the word *shika,* meaning both "deer" and "in that way."

159

1. Somedono no Naishi. According to various commentators, she was either the daughter of Fujiwara no Yoshisuke, the Minister of the Right, or the daughter of Fujiwara no Yoruka, the Secretary of the Palace Attendants Office.

2. Minamoto no Yoshiari (845–897), the son of Emperor Montoku. Yoshiari served as the Minister of the Right.

3. This poem appears in the *Shoku goshūishū* (KT 877), with the second line given as *Aya no iro me mo.* In the word *aya* ("design") is implied the phrase *ayame mo wakanu* ("to be unable to distinguish"). Yoshiari declares that his unhappiness has rendered him incapable of distinguishing one color from another.

160

1. This poem appears in the *Kokin rokujō* (ZKT 31286) and in the *Gosenshū* (KT 223) as an anonymous poem. There is a pun on the word *aki,* which means both "autumn" and "to surfeit." She is accusing Zai Chūjō of having grown tired of her.

2. A slightly different version of the poem appears in the *Narihira shū* (ZKT 16138): Aki hagi o/ Irodoru kaze wa/ Hayaku tomo/ Kokoro wa fukaji/ Kusaba naranedo.

In the *Nishi Honganji-bonshū,* this poem is said to have been an answering poem to the preceding one by Narihira.

The poem also appears in the *Kokin rokujō* (ZKT 31294), with the first and third lines reading *Aki hagi o* and *Hayaku tomo.* There is a pun on *aki,* meaning both "autumn" and "to tire of." There is, moreover, a pun on *kareji* ("not to wither") and *sakareji* ("to grow distant").

3. The *ōnusa* is a sacred wand made of strips of cloth attached to the *sakaki,* or sacred Shintō tree, and pulled by participants in the purification ceremony to rid themselves of their sins and impurities. These offering strips are then set afloat down a nearby stream. In this poem, the *ōnusa* represents Narihira, the famous lover, who was pursued by countless women. *Yoru se* literally means "the shallows in which the strips of cloth may be caught," thus referring to a faithful wife. There is also a pun on *shika,* meaning "deer" as well as "only."

4. This poem appears in the *Narihira shū* (*Katsura no Miya-bon sōsho,* vol. 1, p. 98), with the second line given as *Nani to ka shiran.* The poem may also be interpreted: Though you speak harshly to me now, you once sought my affection; is that not why you say I resemble a sacred wand pulled by countless women?

A similar exchange of poems may be found in the *Kokinshū* (KT 706–707). The above poems also appear in episode 47 of *Ise monogatari.* See McCullough, *Tales of Ise,* p. 102.

161

1. Fujiwara no Takaiko (842–910), the daughter of the Prime Minister Nagayoshi and consort of Emperor Seiwa. She is believed to have entered the palace in 860.

2. This poem appears in episode 3 of *Ise monogatari* (KT, *Monogatari,* 19). There is a pun on *hijiki,* a variety of seaweed, and *shiki* ("to spread out").

3. Takaiko became an imperial concubine with the name Harunomiya no Nyōgo in 866.

4. The Ōhara Shrine at the foot of Mount Oshio in modern Otokuni-gun, Kyoto, is a branch of the Kasuga Shrine, which was built in honor of Amenokoyane-no Mikoto, the clan deity of the Fujiwara family.

5. This poem appears in episode 76 of *Ise monogatari* (KT, *Monogatari,* 154). It also appears in the *Kokinshū* (KT 871) and in the *Narihira shū* (ZKT 16158), with the fourth line reading *Kamiyo no koto mo.* In the *Kokin rokujō* (ZKT 31793), the third and fourth lines are given as Kyō shi koso/ Kamiyo no koto mo. Finally, it is alluded to in *Ōkagami* (NKBT, vol. 21, p. 44; see also Yamagiwa, *The Ōkagami,* p. 22). Narihira is reminding her of the enchanted years during which they were lovers.

162

1. This poem appears in episode 100 of *Ise monogatari* (KT, *Monogatari,* 191) and in the *Narihira shū* (*Katsura no Miya-bon sōsho,* vol. 1, p. 97). In the *Shoku kokinshū* (KT 1270), the third line is given as *Naruramedo.* There is a pun on *shinobu* ("to remember") and *shinobugusa* (literally "herb of remembrance"). In this poem, Narihira is saying that he has not forgotten her and hopes for future meetings with her.

2. Actually, the herb of remembrance *(shinobugusa)* is a variety of fern and the grass of oblivion *(wasuregusa)* is the day lily, but the writer has mistaken them to mean the same plant.

163

1. This poem appears in the *Kokinshū* (KT 268), in episode 51 of *Ise monogatari* (KT, *Monogatari,* 112), in the *Narihira shū* (*Nishi Honganji-bon sanjūrokunin shū,* p. 209, poem 6), and in the *Kokin rokujō* (ZKT 34575).

164

1. *Kazarichimaki,* or rice cakes usually wrapped in bamboo leaves (though here they seem to have been iris leaves) and tied attractively with string of variegated hues. They were made especially for the *Tango no Sekku,* a festival celebrated on the fifth day of the fifth month.

2. This poem appears in episode 52 of *Ise monogatari* (KT, *Monogatari,* 113) and in the *Narihira shū* (*Katsura no Miya-bon sōsho,* vol. 1, p. 95). The *ayame,* or iris, is associated with this festival, also known as *Ayame no Sekku.* The *kari* of *ayamegari* means "to cut" and *karu,* "to hunt." The poem implies that they had both gone through great hardships to obtain the gifts that they presented to each other.

165

1. Emperor Seiwa is called Mizu-no-o no Mikado in this episode; he is also mentioned in episode 38.

2. The office of the Major Controller of the Left is a rank below that of Imperial Adviser in the Great Council of State. This Major Counsellor is not identified.

3. This poem appears in the *Narihira shū* (*Katsura no Miya-bon sōsho,* vol. 1, p. 97), with the second line given as *Itodo kokochi no.*

4. This poem is included in the *Kokinshū* (KT 861). In episode 125 of *Ise monogatari* (KT, *Monogatari,* 224), the second line is given as *Michi to wa aete.* It also appears in the *Narihira shū* (ZKT 16178). The road mentioned in this poem symbolizes death.

166

1. This poem appears in the *Kokinshū* (KT 476) and in episode 99 of *Ise monogatari* (KT, *Monogatari,* 189). In the *Narihira shū* (ZKT 16140), the third line is given as *Koishiku wa.*

167

1. The words for pheasant *(kiji),* wild goose *(kari),* and wild duck *(kamo)* appear in the underlined portions of this poem.

168

1. Emperor Nimmyō (810–850, r. 833–850) is referred to as Fukakusa no Mikado in the original text, for his tomb is located in a place called Fukakusa.

2. Yoshimine no Munesada (815–890), who is called Rō Shōshō in the

original text. He became a Minor Captain of the Left Division of the Inner Palace Guards in 846 and First Secretary of the Sovereign's Private Office in 849. Upon Emperor Nimmyō's demise, Yoshimine took the tonsure and was henceforth known as Sōjō Henjō. He is one of the Six Poetic Geniuses.

3. The original text gives the phrase *Ushi mitsu* for the time. In one of the ancient systems used to tell time, the "twelve branches" (the twelve signs of the zodiac) marked the various watches. A day was divided into twelve equal parts and each part *(hitotoki),* which was approximately two hours long, again into four equal parts. Between midnight (*Ne,* or the Hour of the Rat) and approximately 2 A.M. (*Ushi,* or the Hour of the Ox) were the following points in time: *Ne hitotsu, Ne futatsu, Ne mitsu,* and *Ne yotsu* (what might correspond to *Ne itsutsu* would be *Ushi,* and so on). The phrase *Ushi mitsu,* therefore, roughly corresponds to three in the morning.

4. This *tanrenga,* or short linked-verse, appears in the *Shūishū* (KT 1184) and in the *Henjō shū* (ZKT 18873). The phrase *Ushi mitsu* means "to realize how cruel you are," as well as the third quarter of the Hour of the Ox (3 A.M.). There is a pun on *ne,* meaning "the Hour of the Rat (midnight)" and "to sleep."

5. Hatsuse-dera, or Hase-dera, which is located in Shiki-gun, Nara prefecture.

6. This sentence is omitted in the *Yamato monogatari shōkai* text.

7. The period of mourning following the demise of an emperor lasted for an entire year. Emperor Nimmyō died on the thirty-first day of the third month of the year 850.

8. It was customary for loyal subjects to purify themselves in the river when they changed from their robes of mourning.

9. This poem appears in the *Kokinshū* (KT 847) and in the *Henjō shū* (ZKT 18880). Mourning for the deceased Emperor, he had wetted his sleeve with his tears.

10. Fujiwara no Junshi (809–871), the daughter of Fuyutsugu and consort of the deceased Emperor Nimmyō.

11. This poem appears in the *Kokinshū* (KT 367), with the last line given as *Okurazan ya wa,* and in the *Henjō shū* (ZKT 18883), with the third and last lines given as *Narinu tomo* and *Okurazarame ya.*

12. Ono no Komachi (late ninth century). She was one of the Six Poetic Geniuses, and a collection of her poems is entitled the *Komachi shū.*

13. Located in modern Higashiyama-ku, Kyoto.

14. *Darani,* a mystic Buddhist formula, recited in Sanskrit and believed to be efficacious in curing all ills.

15. This poem appears in the *Gosenshū* (KT 1196), in the *Henjō shū* (ZKT 18881), and in the *Komachi shū* (ZKT 19602). In the *Kokin rokujō* (ZKT 33270), the fourth and fifth lines are given as Koke no mikoromo/ Shibaraku kasane yo. Poems 282 and 283 appear in the story "Amatsu otome" in *Harusame monogatari* by Ueda Akinari (NKBT, vol. 56, p. 161). See also *Tales of the Spring Rain,* translated by Barry Jackman, pp. 41–43. The version of poem 282 appearing in Ueda Akinari's work goes: Ishi no ue ni/ Tabine wa sureba/ Hada samushi/ Koke no koromo o/ Ware ni kasanan.

16. This poem appears in the *Gosenshū* (KT 1197), with the fourth line reading *Kasaneba tsurashi;* and in the *Henjō shū* (ZKT 18882), with the first and fourth lines given as *Yamabushi no* and *Kasaneba utoshi.* In *Harusame monogatari* (NKBT, vol. 56, p. 161), this version is given: Yo o suteshi/ Koke no koromo wa/ Tada hitoe/ Kasanete usushi/ Iza futari nen.

17. Located in Higashiyama-ku, Kyoto. It is also known as the Gangyō-ji.

18. Rō Shōshō or Sōjō Henjō had two sons—Yusei (841–914) and Harutoshi (dates unknown), better known as Sosei Hōshi. It is uncertain as to which of the two brothers was the older. However, since Sosei Hōshi once did serve as a Lieutenant of the Inner Palace Guards, he is probably the son referred to in this passage. Sosei Hōshi is one of the Thirty-six Poetic Geniuses of the period.

19. This poem appears in the *Gosenshū* (KT 123) and in the *Henjō shū* (ZKT 18867). The Three Worlds represent the Past, the Present, and the Future.

20. There is a pun on *mine,* meaning "without seeing" and "mountain peak." *Okurenuru* may be interpreted as "you (the young woman) did not come together with (your brothers)" and "I lead a meaningless life."

169

1. Actually the Ōmiwa Shrine in Shiki-gun, Nara prefecture.

2. The episode ends abruptly at this point. Abe Toshiko (*Kōhon Yamato monogatari to sono kenkyū,* pp. 26, 193–194) cites two poems given in different texts of *Yamato monogatari* which may be found in the Kyoto University collection. One text contains this poem:

Tokikaeshi	We exchanged as souvenirs
Ide no shitaobi	Our obi at Ide;
Yukimeguri	Oh, waters of the Tama River,
Au yo ureshiki	How happy our reunion will be,
Tamagawa no mizu	Even though he goes a-roving.

In the *Gyokuyōshū* (KT 1429), the second and fourth lines read *Ide no shitakusa* and *Ōse ureshiki.*

Another text contains the above poem along with a second poem:

Yamashiro no	Though I drink the water
Ide no tamamizu	I have scooped up
Te ni musubi	From the Tama River at Ide
Tanomishi kai mo	In the province of Yamashiro,
Naki yo narikeri	It was all in vain
	For me to trust in you.*

**Tanomishi* can be interpreted as either "to trust in" or "to drink out of one's hands."

This is an anonymous poem which appears in the *Shinkokinshū* (KT 1367), with the third line given as *Te ni kumite.* It also appears in episode 122 of *Ise monogatari* (KT, *Monogatari,* 220).

170

1. Fujiwara no Korehira (876–938), the son of Toshiyuki. He was appointed Provisional Middle Captain of the Inner Palace Guards in 924 and Counsellor in 934.

2. Prince Atsuyoshi. See episode 17.

3. Probably the daughter of Fujiwara no Kaneshige. See episode 56. She is called Hyōe no Myōbu in this episode.

4. In the prose section preceding the poem, there appears a phrase *yama(h)i mo,* meaning "such an illness as (referring to his cold)." This phrase contains the word *himo,* meaning "string," and the words *ito* ("thread") and *yoru* ("to twist") are *engo* for *himo.* There is, moreover, a pun on *yoru,* meaning "to twist" and "to visit." *Kaze,* furthermore, means both "wind" and "a cold"; therefore, when the poet speaks of bending before the wind, he is saying that he has come down with a cold.

5. Lady Hyōe is trying to cheer Korehira, telling him not to be undone by a mere cold.

171

1. Fujiwara no Saneyori. See episode 96. He served as the Minor Captain of the Inner Palace Guards between 919 and 928.

2. This poem appears in the *Shoku gosenshū* (KT 850). There is a pun on *kuyuri* ("to burn") and *kuyu* ("to regret").

3. This poem appears in the *Shoku gosenshū* (KT 851), with the second line reading *Taenu keburi mo. Kuyuru* here is interpreted to mean "to regret." There is a play on words on *omo(h)i,* meaning "to love," and *hi,* meaning "fire."

4. Minamoto no Moroakira (903–955). He was the son of Prince Tokiyo (886–927), Emperor Uda's son. Moroakira served as a Gentleman-in-Waiting from 925 to 929. The office of Gentleman-in-Waiting came under the Ministry of Central Affairs.

5. The text ends abruptly at this point. The sentence and poem which follow are the notes inserted by a later copyist.

6. This poem appears in the *Gosenshū* (KT 789).

172

1. A temple of the Shingon sect of Buddhism in Ōtsu City, Shiga prefecture, which was founded by the Priest Ryōben.

2. Of Ōmi (present-day Shiga prefecture) where the Ishiyama Temple is located.

3. Ōtomo no Kuronushi, a great-grandchild of Emperor Kōbun (648–672, r. 671–672). He is one of the Six Poetic Genuises. This story is also related in the *Ishiyama-dera engi* (*Zoku gunsho ruijū,* vol. 28, pt. 1, pp. 918–919) and is said to have taken place sometime after the twentieth day of the ninth month of 917.

4. This poem appears in the *Shinsenzaishū* (KT 1655), with the second, third, and fifth lines given as *Hima naku kishi o/ Arau nari* and *Kite mo miyo to ya. Sazaranami,* like *sazanami,* was a pillow-word for Ōmi, the site of the poem. By means of this poem, Kuronushi attempts to convince His Majesty that the Provincial Governor is a loyal subject.

173

1. An *uguisu,* which is usually translated "nightingale" but more resembles the bush warbler since it does not sing at night.

2. An anonymous poem on a similar theme in the *Kokinshū* (KT 1011) reads:

Ume no hana	A stranger draws near
Mi ni koso kitsure	Merely to view the plum blossoms,
Uguisu no	But the nightingale,
Hitoku hitoku to	Resentful of the intruder,
Itoi shimo aru	Cries, "Someone approaches."

In both poems there is a pun on *hitoku,* which, on one hand, imitates the sound of the nightingale's song, and, on the other hand, means "someone approaches."

3. There is a play on words on *uguisu* ("the nightingale") and *uku* ("to be grieved").

4. This poem appears in the *Shoku gosenshū* (KT 24), with the fourth line given as *Nozawa ni idete.* A *Kokinshū* poem on a similar theme (KT 21) goes:

Kimi ga tame	For you,
Haru no no ni idete	I went out into the spring fields
Wakana tsumu	To gather the young greens
Waga koromode ni	While snow fell gently
Yuki wa furitsutsu	Upon my sleeves.

5. Emperor Nimmyō.

6. There are numerous puns in this poem: *furuya* ("old hut") and *furu* ("to fall"); *utsubushi* ("to lie prone") and *utsubushi(zome),* which is a method of dyeing cloth a light black using the dye extracted from the nuts of the sumac; *asa,* meaning both "hemp" and "morning"; and *kesa,* meaning "a priest's robe" and "this morning."

There are three different versions of this poem. One of them, an anonymous poem in the *Kokinshū* (KT 1068), reads:

Yo o itoi	This is the black robe of hemp
Ko no motogoto ni	Of one who,
Tachiyorite	Having abandoned the world,
Utsubushizome no	Lies down to rest
Asa no kinu nari	At the foot of every tree
	He comes to.

A version similar to the above appears in the *Henjō shū* (ZKT 18900), with the fifth line given as *Asa no kesa nari.* The third version, attributed to Sosei Hōshi, appears in the *Kokin rokujō* (ZKT 32308), with the last line reading *Koke no koromo zo.*

In the *Yamato monogatari shōkai,* this episode is followed by episode 174, which corresponds to the long episode designated I which follows.

I

1. I and II correspond to various episodes in *Heichū monogatari.* According to Hagitani Boku, the first suitor was Fujiwara no Tokihira and the second, Taira no Sadabumi (Heichū). The young woman courted by the two men was probably Lady Ise before she went into the service of Teiji no In. I was added to several of the Nijō texts of *Yamato monogatari* some time after the Muromachi period (1336–1573).

2. The following chart shows the relationship between the Emperor's mother, Princess Hanshi, and the second suitor, Heichū:

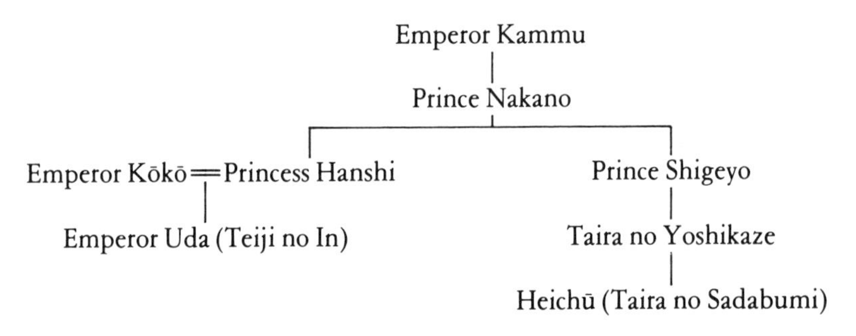

3. Hagitani Boku believes that at this time Heichū was serving as a Provisional Junior Secretary of the Right Division of the Bureau of Horses.

4. This poem appears in the *Kokinshū* (KT 964), in the *Kokin rokujō* (ZKT 32228), and in the *Shūishū* (KT 481). In all the above anthologies, the fourth line of this poem is given as *Nadoka waga mi no.* In episode 1 of *Heichū monogatari* (NKBT, vol. 77, p. 51), the fourth line reads *Nazo mo waga mi no.*

5. This poem, said to have been composed by the man and not the woman, appears in episode 1 of *Heichū monogatari* (NKBT, vol. 77, p. 52), with the first two lines reading Uki na nomi/ Tatsuta no kawa no. The place name Tatsuta contains the word *tsuta,* meaning "ivy." *Ukitatsu* also suggests the spreading of rumors about one's private affairs. Moreover, the red maple leaves are compared to the sleeve reddened by the tears of blood the poet claims she has shed over the ugly rumors that are rampant.

The following poems are based on a similar theme. The first appears in the *Gosenshū* (KT 332):

Kiekaeri	The autumn robe
Mono omou aki no	That I wear
Koromo koso	While longing for you
Namida no kawa no	Is like the maple leaves
Momiji narikere	On a river of tears.

The second poem appears in the *Ise shū* (*Gunsho ruijū,* vol. 15, p. 549):

Momijiba ni	I cannot distinguish
Iro miewakade	The color of the maple leaves;
Chiru mono wa	That which now falls
Mono omou aki no	Are the tears I shed
Namida narikeri	As in autumn I long for you.

6. This poem appears in episode 1 of *Heichū monogatari* (NKBT, vol. 77, p. 52), with the first and second lines given as Mi no umi no/ Omoinaguma wa. There are numerous puns in the poem: *umi* ("sea") and *ushi* ("sorrowful"); *nagisa* ("shore") and *nagusamu* ("to console"); *ura,* meaning both "a bay" and "one's heart." *Umi, nagisa,* and *ura* ("a bay") are *engo* as are *ushi, nagusamu,* and *ura* ("one's heart").

7. This poem appears in episode 1 of *Heichū monogatari* (NKBT, vol. 77, p. 52), with the second line reading *Sora naru tsuki o.* "The Heavenly River" refers to the Milky Way.

8. Ōshikōchi no Mitsune and Ki no Tomonori.

9. This story is based on episode 37 of *Heichū monogatari.*

10. The poem, as it appears in *Heichū monogatari* (NKBT, vol. 77, p. 103) goes:

Numa mizu ni	Though you do not grow
Kimi wa oinedo	In the waters of the marsh,
Karu komo no	Like the water-oats that I harvest,
Me ni misumisu mo	You grow more lovely
Oimasaru kana	Each time I gaze at you.

In the *Yamato monogatari* poem, there is a pun on *miruma,* meaning "as I look on," and *miru,* a variety of seaweed.

11. This poem, as it appears in episode 37 of *Heichū monogatari* (NKBT, vol. 77, p. 103), is slightly modified:

Karu komo no	As I gaze at you,
Me ni miru miru zo	I dislike you more and more,
Utomaruru	For you seem to be a man
Kokoro no asaka no	Whose heart is as shallow
Numa ni miyureba	As the waters in the marsh.

The woman is saying that, since he has such a shallow heart, he must grow increasingly weary of her each time he sees her.

12. Poems 7, 8, and 9 appear in episode 34 of *Heichū monogatari.* In the *Heichū monogatari* version of poem 7 (NKBT, vol. 77, p. 96), the fourth line is given as *Kakete chikae yo.* This poem also appears in the *Shinkokinshū* (KT 1220), with the fourth line reading *Kaketsutsu chikae.* Tadasu-no-Mori is the name of the woods in which the shrine called Shimokamo Jinja stands. It is a part of present-day Sakyō-ku, Kyoto. The verb *tadasu* means "to investigate or verify."

13. The fourth and fifth lines of this poem, as they appear in *Heichū monogatari* (NKBT, vol. 77, p. 96), read Haru o kagiri to/ Chiru wa mietsutsu. The man is saying that he knows very well she no longer loves him —it is as clear to him as the scattering of cherry blossoms which signals the end of spring.

14. In the version of this poem which appears in *Heichū monogatari* (NKBT, vol. 77, p. 97), the fourth line is given as *Kaze shi fukazu wa.* The woman is saying that, like the wind that causes the blossoms to scatter, he has been responsible for the way she feels about him.

15. Walls erected in this fashion: pillars were set up; wooden boards are placed between them; the space between the boards is then filled in with mud which was allowed to dry; finally, the wall is topped with a tile roof. This story is based on episode 36 of *Heichū monogatari.*

16. At one time, the western part of the capital along Rokujō Avenue was a desolate spot.

17. Poems 10 through 16 appear in episode 36 of *Heichū monogatari.* In poem 10 (NKBT, vol. 77, p. 99), there is a pun on *aki,* which has the dual meaning of "autumn" and "to weary of."

18. In this poem (NKBT, vol. 77, p. 99), the young man is seeking permission to call on her, promising that he will come so often the grass will not have a chance to grow thickly over the pathway.

19. This poem appears in *Heichū monogatari* (NKBT, vol. 77, p. 99), with the fourth and fifth lines given as Koyu bakari ni shi/ Araba kite toe. Mount Otoko, or Otokoyama, is a mountain located in Yawate-chō in Tsuzuki-gun, Kyoto. The Iwashimizu Hachiman-gū is also located here.

20. In the vicinity of Gankōji-chō, Nara prefecture.

21. Actually a sloping road which led to Nara.

22. In *Heichū monogatari,* it is the woman who says that she has not forgotten him. The man then wonders whether she had been brought to this place by another man (NKBT, vol. 77, p. 101). The *Yamato monogatari* version of this anecdote has been so drastically shortened that the details are not clear.

23. This poem appears in *Heichū monogatari* (NKBT, vol.77, p. 101), with the first, second, and third lines reading Kuyashiku zo/ Nara e to dani mo/ Tsugetekeru. *Tamaboko (no)* is a pillow-word for road; it can also be interpreted as *tamasaka* ("occasionally").

24. Poem 10 in this section.

25. This poem appears in *Heichū monogatari* (NKBT, vol. 77, p. 101), with the second and fourth lines reading *Nara ni kado to wa* and *Na ni ya ou to zo.* The woman had earlier told him that her home was in Nara; *nara* is also the name for the Japanese oak.

26. This poem appears in *Heichū monogatari* (NKBT, vol. 77, p. 101), with the third, fourth, and fifth lines reading Watareru mo/ Waga tame ni to ya/ Kimi wa kakotan. There is a pun on *se,* meaning both "occasion" and "rapids." *Se* is also an *engo* for *kawa* ("river").

27. This poem appears in *Heichū monogatari* (NKBT, vol. 77, p. 102), with the fourth line reading *Kaeru mamonaku.*

II

1. In the *Mikanagi* and *Suzuka* texts of *Yamato monogatari,* this particular section is inserted between episodes 172 and 173 of the main text. Though mainly based on episodes 19 through 27 of *Heichū monogatari,* it differs greatly in certain passages.

2. Minamoto no Muneyuki (see episode 30), whose name was erroneously written in by a later copyist. Since the anecdotes in this section are based on those appearing in *Heichū monogatari,* "the man" in II is probably Heichū, not Muneyuki.

3. One of the Seven Herbs of Autumn. In summer and autumn, this plant bears tiny flowers of a pale yellow hue.

4. This poem, as given below, appears in episode 19 of *Heichū monogatari* (NKBT, vol. 77, p. 74):

Yukigate ni	People have gathered here,
Mube shimo hito wa	Finding it difficult
Sudakikeri	To pass right by:
Hana wa hana naru	How lovely the flowers are
Yado ni zo arikeru	At this stately mansion!

5. This poem appears in episode 19 of *Heichū monogatari* (NKBT, vol. 77, p. 74), with the fourth and fifth lines reading Mamoru hito nami/ Hito to nasu nite. He is requesting that they do not walk about the garden, heedless as to whether or not they are ruining its loveliness.

6. Emperor Uda (Teiji no In).

7. The Ninna-ji, a Shingon temple in Hanazono-chō, Ukyō-ku, Kyoto. It was built by Emperor Uda and was his residence after he took the tonsure.

8. This poem appears in episode 20 of *Heichū monogatari* (NKBT, vol. 77, p. 75), with the first and second lines reading Aki o okite/ Toki koso arikere. There is a pun on the verb *utsuru,* which has the dual meaning "to transplant" and "to change color."

9. Fujiwara no Kunitsune. See episode 124.

10. The poem is missing in the *Yamato monogatari* text, but in episode 21 of *Heichū monogatari* (NKBT, vol. 77, p. 75), Kunitsune's poem reads:

Miyo o hete	Having lived for many years,
Furitaru okina	I have grown old;
Tsue tsukite	How I wish I could visit your mansion
Hana no ari ka o	And with my cane,
Miru yoshi mogana	Make my way through the flowers
	Growing all around.

11. There is a pun on *araba,* which has the dual meaning "to be" and "to break off." The *hanagoromo* is a lined robe which is white on the outside and with either a red or purple lining. It could also simply refer to a robe dyed a brilliant color.

A slightly different version of this poem is given in episode 21 of *Heichū monogatari* (NKBT, vol. 77, p. 75): Tamaboko ni/ Kimi shi kiyoraba/ Asajū ni/ Majireru kiku no/ Ka wa masarinan.

12. This poem appears in episode 22 of *Heichū monogatari* (NKBT, vol. 77, p. 77), with the third line given as *Wataruran.* Natorigawa is the

name of a river which flows through Natori-gun in Miyagi prefecture and ultimately into Sendai Bay. It is also an *utamakura,* a place famed in poetry. There is a pun on *Ukina toru* ("to be gossiped about") and Natori, a place name.

13. This poem appears in episode 22 of *Heichū monogatari* (NKBT, vol. 77, p. 77), with the fourth line reading *Tachikakureken.*

14. In *Heichū monogatari,* the man summons the woman to his house. She thereupon goes to him together with an attractive friend of hers and arranges for the man to court her friend. This seems to be more probable than the *Yamato monogatari* version which has the man going to the woman's house and persuading the friend who had accompanied him to stay with the woman.

15. This poem appears in episode 23 of *Heichū monogatari* (NKBT, vol. 77, p. 78), with the fourth and fifth lines given as Koe furiidete/ Naki mo todomeyo. There is a pun on Naniwa-gata (Naniwa Bay) and *nani ka wa* ("how can you do such a thing"); *oki,* meaning "to rise" and "the offing." *Ashitazu* ("the crane among the reeds") is an *engo* for Naniwa-gata and *oki* and refers to the suitor.

16. This poem appears in episode 23 of *Heichū monogatari* (NKBT, vol. 77, p. 78), with the last line reading *Okite yukuran.*

17. With the woman.

18. The woman's father was the Provincial Governor of Ōmi.

19. This poem appears in episode 24 of *Heichū monogatari* (NKBT, vol. 77, p. 79), with the fourth line reading *Na nomi uminaru.* There are numerous puns in this poem: *mirume,* meaning varieties of seaweed and "sight"; *nami,* "waves" and "not to have"; and *ōmichi* ("meeting road") and *ōmiji* ("the road to Ōmi"). *Tachikaeran* ("to flow") and *ura* ("a bay") are *engo* for the above-mentioned sea images.

20. This poem appears in episode 24 of *Heichū monogatari* (NKBT, vol. 77, p. 79), with the second, third, and fifth lines reading *Arashi no kaze no/ Samukereba* and *Nami nomi zo tatsu.* Mount Seki (Sekiyama) refers to both Mount Ōsaka (Ōsakayama), where the famous Meeting Barrier between the ancient provinces of Yamashiro and Ōmi is located, and to her father, who is keeping them apart. Although she is known as the daughter of the Provincial Governor of Ōmi (*ōmi* literally meaning "to meet"), Ōmi to her is just another place name, and she resents bitterly the fact that they cannot meet.

21. This poem appears in episode 25 of *Heichū monogatari* (NKBT, vol. 77, p. 80), with the first and third lines reading *Ōsaka no* and *Sekigawa no.*

22. This poem appears in episode 25 of *Heichū monogatari* (NKBT, vol. 77, p. 80), with the first line given as *Na ni tanomu.* Again, there is a pun on Ōmi, a place name, which also means "to meet."

23. Hoping that in the future they will be able to meet and talk to each other again, he starts out in a direction that is considered to be safe.

24. This poem appears in episode 25 of *Heichū monogatari* (NKBT, vol. 77, p. 81), with the second, fourth, and fifth lines reading *Yukue mo shirazu* and *Michi no sora nite / Madouberanaru.*

25. This poem appears in episode 25 of *Heichū monogatari* (NKBT, vol. 77, p. 81), with the third, fourth, and fifth lines reading Waga tama o / Tague ya semashi / Michi no shirube ni.

26. In Kurita-gun, Shiga prefecture.

27. In *Heichū monogatari,* the woman who is giving an account of her adventure reveals the man's name at this point. His former sweetheart recognizes him and, according to the *Heichū monogatari* version of this episode (NKBT, vol. 77, p. 81), tells them unbelievable stories about the man. According to the *Yamato monogatari* text, however, it is another woman in the group who comments: "He fabricated the most preposterous stories!"

28. This poem appears in episode 25 of *Heichū monogatari* (NKBT, vol. 77, p. 82), with the fourth line reading *Mono omou hito no.*

29. The poem beginning with the line "True to its name—."

30. His own "River of Tears."

31. This poem appears in episode 25 of *Heichū monogatari* (NKBT, vol. 77, p. 83), with the first, third, and fifth lines reading *Mi no uki o, Kitsuredomo* and *Wataru se mo nashi.*

32. This poem appears in episode 25 of *Heichū monogatari* (NKBT, vol. 77, p. 83), with the second, fourth, and fifth lines reading *Wataru se nakuba* and *Nagarete fukaki / Mi o to tanoman.* The word *naraba,* which appears in the first line, is probably a mistake for *nakuba.* There is a pun on *nagarete* ("to flow") and *nakarete* ("to weep").

33. This poem appears in episode 25 of *Heichū monogatari* (NKBT, vol. 77, p. 84) as a short linked-verse, with the woman composing the first half of the poem: Aki no yo no / Yume wa hakanaku / Au to iū o— and the man completing the poem: Haru ni kaerite / Masashikaruran.

34. This poem appears in episode 25 of *Heichū monogatari* (NKBT, vol. 77, p. 84). There is a pun on the verb *akasu,* which means both "to dawn" and "to reveal (her residence)."

35. This poem appears in episode 25 of *Heichū monogatari* (NKBT, vol. 77, p. 84), with the second and fifth lines reading *Fureru namida no*

and *Arawarene to ya.* The poem may also be interpreted: If I show you where my house is, you would soon know all about me.

36. This poem appears in episode 26 of *Heichū monogatari* (NKBT, vol. 77, p. 85), with the first and second lines reading *Yowa ni idete/ Watari zo ka nuru.*

37. This poem appears in episode 26 of *Heichū monogatari* (NKBT, vol. 77, p. 85), with the fourth line reading *Kimi ga watari no.*

38. This poem appears in episode 27 of *Heichū monogatari* (NKBT, vol. 77, p. 86), with the second, third, and fifth lines reading *Kike to shiraburu/ Koto no ne no* and *Koe no suru kana.* There are numerous puns in this poem: *koto,* meaning "a thirteen-string horizontal harp" and "words"; *ai,* meaning "to meet" and "to harmonize"; and *koi,* meaning "to love," and *koe,* meaning "voice."

39. The appended sections end with this incomplete sentence. In the *Mikanagi* text, these sections are followed by episode 173 of the main text.

APPENDIX: EARLY HEIAN LITERATURE

1. Brower and Miner, *Japanese Court Poetry,* p. 11.
2. Ibid.
3. Ibid., p. 163.
4. It should be noted that the *Keikokushū* (827), the third of the imperial anthologies of *kanshi* compiled during the Heian period, includes Chinese poems by women. See Kawaguchi, *Heian-chō Nihon kambungakushi no kenkyū,* p. 19.
5. Hisamatsu, *Nihon bungaku-shi—Chūko-hen,* p. 105.
6. Hagitani, NKBT, vol. 74, pp. 53–66.
7. Abe, *Chūko Nihon bungaku gaisetsu,* p. 113.
8. Hagitani, NKBT, vol. 74, pp. 67–77.
9. Takahashi, *Yamato monogatari,* pp. 162–163.
10. Hagitani, NKBT, vol. 74, pp. 68–104.
11. Brower and Miner, *Japanese Court Poetry,* pp. 195–196.
12. Hagitani, NKBT, vol. 74, pp. 220–243.
13. *Waka bungaku daijiten,* p. 76.
14. Iwatsu, *Utaawase no karon shi kenkyū,* p. 6.
15. Brower and Miner, *Japanese Court Poetry,* p. 239.
16. Tamagami, "Byōbu-e to uta to monogatari to," *Kokugo kokubun* (January 1953):3.

17. Ibid., p. 11.
18. Ibid., p. 9.
19. Ibid., p. 19.
20. Ibid., p. 15.
21. *Waka bungaku daijiten,* p. 848.
22. Hisamatsu, *Nihon bungaku-shi—Chūko-hen,* p. 100.
23. Fujioka, *Heian waka shiron—Sandaishū jidai no kichō,* p. 24.
24. Brower and Miner, *Japanese Court Poetry,* p. 165.
25. Hisamatsu, *Nihon bungaku-shi—Chūko-hen,* p. 228.
26. Ibid., p. 229.
27. Abe, NKBT, vol. 9, p. 211. *Motoyoshi no Miko shū* (16), *Maedakebon Zai Chūjō shū* (11), *Higaki no Ōna shū* (9), *Henjō shū* (7), *Kanesuke shū* (6), *Teiji no In gyoshū* (6), *Ise shū* (6), *Sanjō no Udaijin shū* (5), *Atsutada shū* (5), *Kintada shū* (4), *Saneakira shū* (4), *Kakinomoto shū* (3), *Komachi shū* (2), *Nara gyoshū* (1), *Sarumaru shū* (1), *Muneyuki shū* (1), and *Asatada shū* (1).
28. See E. B. Caedel's article "The Ōi River Poems and Preface," *Asia Major,* n.s., vol. III, part I (1952), pp. 65–106.
29. See E. B. Caedel's "Tadamine's Preface to the Ōi River Poems," *BSOAS,* vol. 18, part 2 (1956), pp. 331–343.
30. Hagitani, NKBT, vol. 74, pp. 67–68.
31. A study and new translation of this work appears in Earl Miner's *Japanese Poetic Diaries* (Stanford University Press, 1969).
32. Ibid., p. 19.
33. Ibid. Temporal progression may be seen in the imperial anthologies. In the *Kokinshū* we see this in the sections on seasonal and love poems. However, this process of association was further developed in the *Shinkokinshū,* the eighth imperial anthology. See Konishi Jin'ichi's article "Association and Progression: Principles of Integration in Anthologies and Sequences of Japanese"; this article has been translated and adapted by Brower and Miner. See *Harvard Journal of Asiatic Studies,* vol. 21 (December 1958):67–127.
34. Ibid., p. 11.
35. See Edward Seidensticker's translation entitled *The Gossamer Years* (Tuttle, 1964).
36. See Donald Keene's translation entitled "The Tale of the Bamboo Cutter," *Monumenta Nipponica* 9 (January 1956):127–153.
37. Sanekata, "Uta monogatari no seiritsu to tenkai," *Nihon bungei kenkyū* 14 (December 1962):5.
38. Chamberlain, *Kojiki,* pp. 90–94.

39. Ibid., pp. 225–227.
40. Sanekata, "Uta monogatari no seiritsu to tenkai," p. 8. See also Chamberlain, *Kojiki,* pp. 249–270.
41. Sanekata, "Uta monogatari no seiritsu to tenkai," p. 7.
42. Nippon Gakujutsu Shinkōkai, *The Manyōshū* (Columbia University Press, 1965), p. 216.
43. Ibid., pp. 216–218.
44. Ibid., pp. 223–224.
45. Ibid., pp. 224–225.
46. Ibid., p. 272.
47. Ibid., pp. 74–76.
48. Sanekata, "Uta monogatari no seiritsu to tenkai," p. 10.
49. A few of these poems are translated on pages 113–115 of *The Manyōshū.* Yakamori was exiled to Echizen after his love affair with Chigami, who served the Priestess of the Ise Shrine. The group of sixty-three poems were exchanged in about the year 738.
50. One of the most popular works was *Yu hsien k'u,* or "The Dwelling of Playful Goddesses" (late seventh century). According to tradition, it was introduced to Japan by the Man'yō poet Yamanoue no Okura (c. 660–c. 733).
51. McCullough, *Tales of Ise,* p. 60.
52. Namba, *Yamato monogatari,* p. 70.
53. Thirty-eight of the episodes contain waka; the thirty-ninth contains a chōka.
54. NKBT, vol. 77, p. 17.
55. Waley, *Tale of Genji,* p. 127.
56. Akiyama, *Kyūtei salon to saijo,* p. 63.
57. Ibid.
58. Hisamatsu, *Heian-chō bungaku shi,* p. 684.
59. This poem is included in the *Kokinshū* (KT 407), with a headnote stating that it was composed when Takamura was exiled to the islands of Oki and that it was sent to someone in the capital (probably a close relation). This poem is also included in the *Hyakunin isshu.*
60. Hisamatsu, *Heian-chō bungaku shi,* pp. 690–691. Although a number of other poems by Takamura appear in the *Kokinshū,* they are not included in *The Tale of Takamura.*
61. NKBT, vol. 77, pp. 10–11.
62. Hisamatsu, *Heian-chō bungaku shi,* p. 345.
63. Ordered by the Retired Emperor Kazan (968–1008, r. 984–986) and compiled by Fujiwara no Kintō (966–1041).

64. Abe Toshiko, *Kōhon Yamato monogatari to sono kenkyū,* pp. 1824; Namba, *Yamato monogatari,* p. 39.

65. The texts of *Tales of Yamato* are discussed in the section that follows entitled "The Texts of *Tales of Yamato.*"

66. Morris, *The Pillow Book of Sei Shōnagon,* p. 19. This incident is also mentioned in *Ōkagami* (see Yamagiwa's *The Ōkagami,* pp. 77–78).

67. Morris, *The Pillow Book of Sei Shōnagon,* p. 19.

68. Ruch, *Otogi Bunko and Short Stories of the Muromachi Period,* p. 62.

69. Sanekata, "Uta monogatari no seiritsu to tenkai," p. 13.

70. Hisamatsu, *Heian-chō bungaku shi,* p. 356.

71. Vos, *A Study of the Ise monogatari,* vol. 1, p. 143.

72. Ibid.

73. This is especially true of the second story in I in which episodes 34 and 37 of *Tales of Heichū* are interwoven to tell a single tale.

74. Matsumura, "Ōkagami to Yamato monogatari no kankei," pp. 1–8.

75. Ibid., p. 8.

76. NKBT, vol. 26, pp. 212–216.

77. *Akutagawa Ryūnosuke zenshū,* vol. 3, pp. 533–558. Akutagawa was greatly influenced by the tales in *Konjaku monogatari, Uji shūi monogatari* (early thirteenth century), and Chinese short stories of the T'ang period. Using them as sources, he adopted a modern psychological approach in depicting the characters and situations. Many of his stories, known as ōchō-mono, are set in the Heian period. A translation of *Kōshoku* entitled "Heichū, the Amorous Genius" is included in Takashi Kojima's *Japanese Short Stories,* pp. 124–144.

78. *Nihon no bungaku,* vol. 23, pp. 363–371, 412–414.

79. Sanari, *Yōkyoku taikan,* vol. 1, pp. 105–121.

80. Kawatake, *Engeki hyakka daijiten,* vol. 2, p. 346.

81. For a translation of this Nō play, see Ueda, *The Old Pine Tree and Other Noh Plays,* pp. 27–36.

82. Ibid., p. 31.

83. Kawatake, *Engeki hyakka daijiten,* vol. 4, p. 530. There is considerable distortion of existing legends about these figures in the dance play. According to tradition, Ono no Komachi (fl. 850) is said to have treated Fukakusa no Shōshō very cruelly, making him come to her home for a hundred nights in succession before allowing him in to see her. The poor man, however, dies on the hundredth night. As for Higaki, she lived dur-

ing the Sumitomo Revolt (939–941). She could not possibly have had anything to do with the Minor Lieutenant if, indeed, there had been such a man.

84. For an English translation of the play, see Donald Keene's *Twenty Plays of the Nō Theatre,* pp. 35–50.

85. *The Manyōshū,* pp. 224–225, 234–235.

86. A translation of this play may be found in *Twenty Plays of the Nō Theatre,* pp. 147–164.

87. Sanari, *Yōkyoku taikan,* pp. 395–410.

88. For a translation of this play, see Keene, *Twenty Plays of the Nō Theatre,* pp. 115–128.

89. According to this legend, there is a stone (believed to be the stone into which the old aunt had been transformed) that weeps at night. See Asakura, *Shinwa densetsu jiten,* p. 455.

90. This travel account has been translated by Donald Keene in *Landscapes and Portraits,* pp. 109–130.

91. Ibid., p. 122.

92. *Tales of the Spring Rain,* pp. 41–43.

93. Ueda Akinari's study of *Tales of Yamato* is entitled *Ueda Akinari kōseihon* based on the Teika text. He may have referred to the *Gosenshū* (KT 1196, 1197) and the *Henjō shū* (ZKT 18881, 18882), which contains the poems Komachi and Henjō are said to have exchanged.

94. *Gendai Nihon bungaku zenshū,* vol. 3, pp. 338–343.

95. *Nihon no bungaku,* vol. 23, pp. 358–464. For a partial translation of this novel by E. G. Seidensticker, see Keene, *Modern Japanese Literature,* pp. 387–397.

96. *Nihon gendai bungaku zenshū,* vol. 102, pp. 85–94. A translation of the story may be found in Inoue, *The Counterfeiter and Other Stories,* pp. 73–96.

97. There are two translations of this work. See (1) Keene, *The Old Woman, the Wife, and the Archer,* pp. 3–50, and (2) Bester, "The Oak Mountain Song" pp. 200–233.

98. *Zoku gunsho ruijū,* vol. 16, p. 783.

99. NKBT, vol. 9, p. 219.

100. Namba, *Yamato monogatari,* p. 55.

101. This textual study is based on one by Namba Hiroshi (see Namba, *Yamato monogatari,* pp. 39–54). The following works have also been consulted: Hisamatsu, *Heian-chō bungaku shi,* pp. 346–351; Takahashi, *Yamato monogatari,* pp. 194–214.

Bibliography

The following abbreviations are used in the bibliography:

BSOAS *Bulletin of the School of Oriental and African Studies*
HJAS *Harvard Journal of Asiatic Studies*
KT *Kokka taikan*
NKBT *Nihon koten bungaku taikei*
TASJ *Transactions of the Asiatic Society of Japan*
ZKT *Zoku kokka taikan*

WORKS IN WESTERN LANGUAGES

Aston, W. G. *A History of Japanese Literature.* New York: D. Appleton and Co., 1899.

Bester, John (trans.). "The Oak Mountain Song." *Japan Quarterly* 4 (2): 200–232.

Brower, Robert, and Miner, Earl. *Japanese Court Poetry.* Stanford: Stanford University Press, 1961.

Caedel, E. B. "The Ōi River Poems and Preface." *Asia Major,* n.s., vol. 3, pt. 1 (1952):65–106.

———. "Tadamine's Preface to the Ōi River Poems." BSOAS, 18 (2): 331–343.

Casal, U. A. "The Lore of the Japanese Fan." *Monumenta Nipponica* 16 (1960):53–117.

Chamberlain, Basil Hall. *Kojiki,* 2nd ed. Kobe: J. L. Thompson and Co., 1932.

———. "The Maiden of Unahi." TASJ 6, 1st series (1878):103–117.

Ch'en Shou-yi. *Chinese Literature—A Historical Introduction.* New York: The Ronald Press Co., 1961.

Florenz, Karl. *Geschichte der japanischen Litteratur.* Leipzig: Amelang Verlag, 1906.

Frank, Bernard. *Kata-imi et katatagai; étude sur les interdits de direction à l'époque Heian.* Tokyo: Maison Franco-Japonaise, 1958.

Gundert, Wilhelm. *Die Japanische Literatur.* Potsdam: Akademische Verlagsgesellschaft Athenaion, 1929.

Inoue Yasushi. *The Counterfeiter and Other Stories.* Trans. by Leon Picon. Tokyo: Charles E. Tuttle Press, 1965.

Hightower, James Robert. *Topics in Chinese Literature.* Cambridge: Harvard University Press, 1965.

Kokusai Bunka Shinkōkai (ed.). *Introduction to Classic Japanese Literature.* Tokyo: Kokusai Bunka Shinkōkai, 1948.

Keene, Donald (ed.). *Anthology of Japanese Literature.* New York: Grove Press, 1955.

______. *Japanese Literature.* New York: Grove Press, 1955.

______. *Landscapes and Portraits.* Tokyo and Palo Alto: Kōdansha International, 1971.

______. *Modern Japanese Literature.* New York: Grove Press, 1956.

______ (trans.). *The Old Woman, the Wife, and the Archer.* New York: Viking Press, 1961.

______ (trans.). "The Tale of the Bamboo Cutter." *Monumenta Nipponica* 9 (4):127–153.

______ (ed.) *Twenty Plays of the Nō Theatre.* New York: Columbia University Press, 1970.

Konishi Jin'ichi (trans. and adapted by Robert H. Brower and Earl Miner). "Association and Progression: Principles of Integration in Anthologies and Sequences of Japanese Court Poetry, A.D. 900–1350." HJAS, 21 (December 1958):67–127.

Levy, Howard S. (trans.). *The Dwelling of Playful Goddesses.* Tokyo: Dai Nippon Insatsu, 1965.

McCullough, Helen Craig. *Tales of Ise.* Stanford: Stanford University Press, 1968.

Miner, Earl. *An Introduction to Japanese Court Poetry.* Stanford: Stanford University Press, 1968.

______. *Japanese Poetic Diaries.* Berkeley: University of California Press, 1969.

Morris, Ivan. *The Pillow Book of Sei Shōnagon.* 2 vols. New York: Columbia University Press, 1967.

______. "Marriage in the World of Genji." *Asia* 11 (Spring 1968): 54–77.

Nippon Gakujutsu Shinkōkai (trans.). *Japanese Nō Drama.* Vols. 1, 2. Tokyo: Nippon Gakujutsu Shinkōkai, 1959.

———. *The Manyōshū.* New York: Columbia University Press, 1965.

Omori, Anne Shepley and Doi, Kochi. *Diaries of Court Ladies of Old Japan.* Boston and New York: Houghton Mifflin Co., 1920.

Reischauer, R. K. *Early Japanese History.* 2 vols. Princeton: Princeton University Press, 1937.

Revon, Michel. *Anthologie de la littérature japonaise dès origines au XXe siècle.* Paris: Delagrave, 1923.

Roggendorf, Joseph. *Heian Literature with Special Reference to the Uta Monogatari.* Unpublished master's essay, University of London, 1940.

Ruch, Barbara Ann. *Otogi Bunko and Short Stories of the Muromachi Period.* Unpublished doctoral dissertation, Columbia University, 1965.

Sansom, G. B. *A History of Japan to 1334.* Stanford: Stanford University Press, 1958.

———. *A Short Cultural History of Japan.* New York: Appleton-Century Crofts, 1962.

Seidensticker, Edward G. *The Gossamer Years.* Tokyo: Charles E. Tuttle Company, 1964.

———. *The Tale of Genji.* New York: Knopf, 1976.

Tsunoda, Ryūsaku; de Bary, Theodore; and Keene, Donald (eds.). *Sources of Japanese Tradition.* New York: Columbia University Press, 1958.

Ueda, Makoto. *Literary and Art Theories in Japan.* Cleveland: The Press of Western Reserve University, 1967.

———. *The Old Pine Tree and Other Noh Plays.* Lincoln: University of Nebraska Press, 1962.

Vos, Frits. *A Study of the Ise Monogatari.* 2 vols. The Hague: Mouton and Co., 1957.

Waley, Arthur (trans.). *The Pillow-Book of Sei Shōnagon.* New York: Grove Press, 1960.

———. *The Tale of Genji.* New York: Random House, 1960.

Yamagiwa, Joseph K. (trans.). *The Ōkagami.* London: George Allen and Unwin, 1967.

WORKS IN JAPANESE

Abe Akio. *Chūko Nihon bungaku gaisetsu.* Tokyo: Shūei Shuppan, 1961.

______. *Nihon bungaku shi—Chūko-hen.* Tokyo: Hanawa Shobō, 1966.

Abe Toshiko. *Kōhon Yamato monogatari to sono kenkyū.* Tokyo: Sanseidō, 1954.

Abe Toshiko and Imai Gen'e (ed.). *Yamato monogatari.* NKBT, vol. 9. Tokyo: Iwanami Shoten, 1957.

Akiyama Ken and Yamanaka Yutaka. *Kyūtei salon to saijo. Nihon bungaku no rekishi,* vol. 3. Tokyo: Kadokawa Shoten, 1967.

Akutagawa Ryūnosuke zenshū. Vol. 3. Tokyo: Iwanami Shoten, 1934.

Asakura Haruhiko (ed.). *Shinwa densetsu jiten.* Tokyo: Tokyo-dō, 1963.

Endō Yoshimoto and Matsuo Satoshi (ed.). *Hamamatsu Chūnagon monogatari.* NKBT, vol. 77. Tokyo: Iwanami Shoten, 1964.

______. *Heichū monogatari.* NKBT, vol. 77. Tokyo: Iwanami Shoten, 1964.

______. *Takamura monogatari.* NKBT, vol. 77. Tokyo: Iwanami Shoten, 1964.

Fujioka Sakutarō. *Kokubungaku zenshi—Heianchō-hen.* Tokyo: Kaiseikan, 1905.

Fujioka Tadaharu. *Heian waka shiron—Sandaishū jidai no kichō.* Tokyo: Ofūsha, 1966.

Hagitani Boku. *Heianchō utaawase taisei* (vol. 1). Tokyo: published by the author, 1957.

Hagitani Boku and Taniyama Shigeru (ed.). *Utaawase shū.* NKBT, vol. 74. Tokyo: Iwanami Shoten, 1965.

Hanawa Hokinoichi (ed.). *Gunsho ruijū.* Vols. 10, 15. Tokyo: Zoku Gunsho Ruijū Kanseikai, 1928–1934.

______. *Zoku gunsho ruijū.* Vols. 16, 17, 18, 28. Tokyo: Zoku Gunsho Ruijū Kanseikai: 1928–1934.

Hirohashi Kazuo. "Yamato monogatari seiritsu kō." *Kokugo kokubun.* 5 (7): 1–30.

Hisamatsu Sen'ichi. *Heianchō bungaku shi.* Tokyo: Meiji Shoin, 1965.

______. *Nihon bungaku shi—Chūko-hen.* Tokyo: Shibundō, 1955.

______. *Shinwa densetsu setsuwa bungaku. Nihon bungaku kyōyō kōza,* vol. 5. Tokyo: Shibundō, 1957.

Igarashi Chikara. *Heianchō bungaku shi.* Vol. 3. Tokyo: Tokyo-dō, 1937.

Ikeda Kikan. "Ise monogatari to Yamato monogatari to no seiritsu ni kansuru kōsatsu." *Kokugo to kokubungaku* 10 (10): 39–66.

______. "Nihon bungaku shomoku kaisetsu (II)—Heian jidai (I)" *Iwanami kōza Nihon bungaku,* vol. 1. Tokyo: Iwanami Shoten, 1931–1933.

Imai Gen'e. "Hikaru Genji." *Nihon bungaku* 5 (9):1–10.
Inoue Yasushi and Tamiya Torahiko. Gendai Nihon bungaku zenshū, vol. 102. Tokyo: Kōdansha, 1961.
Iwatsu Motoo. *Utaawase no karonshi kenkyū.* Tokyo: Waseda Daigaku Shuppan-bu, 1963.
Kaneko Takeo. *Ogura hyakunin isshu no kōgi.* Tokyo: Taishūkan Shoten, 1961.
Katsura no Miya-bon sōsho. Vols. 1, 2, 20. Tokyo: Yōtokusha, 1949–
Kawaguchi Hisao. *Heian-chō Nihon kambungakushi no kenkyū.* 2nd rev. ed. Tokyo: Meiji Shoin, 1964.
_____ (ed.). *Kagerō nikki.* NKBT, vol. 20. Tokyo: Iwanami Shoten, 1958.
Kawatake Shigetoshi (ed.). *Engeki hyakka daijiten.* 6 vols. Tokyo: Heibonsha, 1960–1963.
Kōno Tama (ed.). *Utsubo monogatari.* NKBT, vol. 10. Tokyo: Iwanami Shoten, 1959.
Kubota Utsubo et al. (ed.). *Waka bungaku daijiten.* Tokyo: Meiji Shoin, 1962.
Kuroita Katsumi (ed.). *Kokushi taikei.* Vol. 3. Tokyo: Kokushi Taikei Kankō-kai, 1934.
Kyūsojin Hitaku (ed.). *Nishi Honganji-bon Sanjūrokuninshū seisei.* Tokyo: Kazama Shobō, 1966.
Kyūsojin Hitaku and Yamamoto Sueko (ed.). *Yamato monogatari to sono kenkyū* Nagoya: Mikan Kokubun Shiryō, 1957.
Matsumura Hiroji (ed.). *Eiga monogatari. Nihon koten zensho,* vol. 34, pt. 4. Tokyo: Asahi Shimbunsha, 1956–1959.
_____. *Ōkagami.* NKBT, vol. 21. Tokyo: Iwanami Shoten, 1960.
_____. "Ōkagami to Yamato monogatari no kankei." *Kinjō kokubun* 9 (1):1–8.
Matsuo Satoshi. *Heian jidai monogatari no kenkyū.* Vol. 1. Tokyo: Musashino Shoin, 1955.
Matsushita Daizaburō and Watanabe Fumio (comp.). *Kokka taikan.* 2 vols. Tokyo: Chūbunkan Shoten, 1931.
_____. *Zoku kokka taikan.* 2 vols. Tokyo: Chūbunkan Shoten, 1931.
Mori Ōgai. Gendai Nihon bungaku zenshū, vol. 3. Tokyo: Kaizōsha, 1928.
Motoori Toyokai et al. (ed.). *Kokubun chūshaku zensho.* Vols. 3, 17. Tokyo: Kokugakuin Daigaku Shuppan-bu, 1907–1910.

Nakamura Yukihiko (ed.). *Ueda Akinari* (NKBT, vol. 56). Tokyo: Iwanami Shoten, 1959.

Namba Hiroshi (ed.). *Yamato monogatari (Nihon koten zensho)*. Tokyo: Asahi Shimbunsha, 1961.

Oka Kazuo and Matsuo Satoshi. *Ōchō no bungaku* (*Nihon no bungaku,* vol. 2). Tokyo: Shibundō, 1966.

Origuchi Shinobu. *Nihon bungakushi nōto II*. Tokyo: Chūō Kōron, 1957.

Ōsone Shōsuke. "Ōchō kambungaku no shomondai." *Kokubungaku kaishaku to kanshō* 28 (1):19–27.

Ōtsu Yūichi and Tsukishima Hiroshi (eds.). *Ise monogatari* (NKBT, vol. 9). Tokyo: Iwanami Shoten, 1957.

Ozaki Masayoshi (comp.) and Irita Seizō (ed.). *Gunsho ichiran*. Tokyo: Nichiyō Shobō, 1931.

Ozawa Masao. *Kokinshū no sekai*. Tokyo: Hanawa Shobō, 1961.

Sanari Kentarō (comp.). *Yōkyoku taikan* (vol. 1). Tokyo: Meiji Shoin, 1930.

Sanekata Kiyoshi. "Uta monogatari no seiritsu to tenkai." *Nihon bungei kenkyū* 14 (4):1–13.

Sasaki Nobutsuna (comp.). *Nihon kagaku taikei*. 20 vols. Tokyo: Kazama Shobō, 1956–

Takahashi Shōji. *Yamato monogatari*. Tokyo: Hanawa Shobō, 1962.

Takeda Yūkichi and Mizuno Komao. *Yamato monogatari shōkai*. Tokyo: Yukawa Kōbundō, 1936.

Tamagami Takuya. "Byōbu-e to uta to monogatari to." *Kokugo kokubun* (January 1953):1–20.

______. *Monogatari bungaku*. Tokyo: Hanawa Shobō, 1960.

Tanizaki Jun'ichirō (*Nihon no bungaku,* vol. 23). Tokyo: Chūō Kōron, 1964.

Yamada Yoshio (ed.). *Konjaku monogatari* (NKBT, vol. 26). Tokyo: Iwanami Shoten, 1963.

Yamagishi Tokuhei (ed.). *Genji monogatari* (NKBT, vols. 14–18). Tokyo: Iwanami Shoten, 1958–1964.

Yatomi Hamao and Yokoyama Shigeru. *Nakajima Hirotari zenshū*. 2 vols. Tokyo: Ōkayama Shoten, 1933.

Finding List for Japanese Poems

The poems discussed in this study are arranged according to the sources from which they are taken. Whenever available, *Kokka taikan* (KT), *Zoku kokka taikan* (ZKT), and *Yamato monogatari* (YM) numbers are given. The page numbers on which the poem is mentioned or quoted, followed by the episode and note numbers, are also provided.

Index of First Lines

The numbers within parentheses correspond to poem numbers used throughout *Tales of Yamato;* the italic numbers designate those poems in appended sections I and II.

General Index

Tales of Yamato is abbreviated as TY. Note citations include episode and note numbers.

Index prepared by Daniel R. Zoll, Department of East Asian Literature; Graduate School of Library Studies, University of Hawaii.

Production Notes

This book was designed by Roger Eggers and typeset on the Unified Composing System by the design and production staff of The University Press of Hawaii.

The text typeface is Garamond and the display typeface is Tiffany Demi.

Offset presswork and binding were done by Halliday Lithograph. Text paper is Glatfelter P & S Offset, basis 55.